# IN THE MIDNIGHT HOUR

A wealthy woman befriends a handsome teenage busker, hoping he may be her son who vanished from a Norfolk beach twelve years previously. The boy offers convincing proof but her husband, Polar explorer Jack Cable, remains sceptical. Laura Principal is called in to investigate whether Liam is really the lost child or an interloper. What does he want from the Cables – and what is his connection with the violence that begins with his arrival and ends, almost inevitably, with murder? In her search for answers, Laura comes face to face with a loss that threatens to turn her own world upside down...

# In The Midnight Hour

*by*

Michelle Spring

**Magna Large Print Books**
Long Preston, North Yorkshire,
BD23 4ND, England.

British Library Cataloguing in Publication Data.

Spring, Michelle
  In the midnight hour.

  A catalogue record of this book is
  available from the British Library

  ISBN  0-7505-1821-9

First published in Great Britain 2001 by Orion
an imprint of the Orion Publishing Group Ltd.

Published in Large Print 2002 by arrangement with
Orion Publishing Group

Magna Large Print is an imprint of Library Magna Books Ltd.

Printed and bound in Great Britain by
T.J. (International) Ltd., Cornwall, PL28 8RW

*For Pat and Lynelle with love.*
*And for my editor, Yvette Goulden.*

# ACKNOWLEDGEMENTS

While researching *In the Midnight Hour*, I benefited greatly from the information provided by the National Missing Persons Helpline, and in particular by Di Cullington, forensic artist, and head of the Identification and Reconstruction Unit. Any readers who wish to contact the National Missing Persons Helpline can do so by writing to PO BOX 28908, London SW14 7ZU, or by ringing 020-8392-4545, or freephone 0500-700700.

The process of writing was made easier and more enjoyable by help and advice from friends and colleagues. I should like especially to thank Inspector Chris Bainbridge, Dr Liz Cruwys of the Scott Polar Research Institute, Nora Kelly, Janet Rifkin, Jane Selley and Dr Alison Weissberg of Petersfield Medical Practice, along with Terri Apter, Dirk Bister, Montserrat Guibernau, Mary Hamer, Joshua Held, Rosa Held, Dr Richard Higginson of Ridley Hall, John Lant, Marilyn Meadows, Sue Pope, Dr Russell A. Potter of Rhode Island Linguistics College, Ian

Purkiss of Hockey's, Janet Reibstein, Lynne Voce, and Jill Paton Walsh. I won't list in detail the acts of kindness for which I am indebted, but, like the dreaded anonymous caller, I know who you are and I know what you did. Many thanks.

Thanks especially for Yvette Goulden's enthusiasm for the project from its inception and for her spot-on plot suggestions, for Joe Blades' unflagging support, for Michele Topham's careful reading, and for David Held's constructive and insightful comments.

I am indebted to the following authors and books: L.P. Kirwan, *The White Road: Polar Exploration from the Vikings to Fuchs*, Hollis & Carter, 1959; Kim Kluger-Bell, *Unspeakable Losses*, Penguin, 1998; Ursula Le Guin, *Steering the Craft*, The Eighth Mountain Press, Portland, Oregon, 1998; Genevieve Jurgensen, *The Disappearance*, Flamingo, 1999. The reference to Phyllis McGinley in Chapter 13 is to her 'Lament for a wavering viewpoint' in *Short Walk from the Station*, Viking Press, New York, 1951.

## AUTHOR'S NOTE

*In the Midnight Hour* tells a story set in two times, and in two places – Grantchester, separated from Cambridge by water meadows, Cleybourne in north Norfolk. Grantchester refers to the village captured by Rupert Brooke in the poem of that name. Although it is much as described in my novel, there is, as far as I know, no Grantchester Farm, nor will you find Cleybourne on any map of Norfolk except the one in my head. Cleybourne has been formed by merging Cley next the Sea with Weybourne; the four or so miles of coastline that separate the two villages have been magically compressed. My apologies go to the people of Salthouse, who have been swept away in the process.

# Prologue

On the southern side of the Wash, where the North Sea worries away at the exposed coast, there is a shoreline that has been carved into a perfect crescent. The eastern half of the crescent is overhung by a ridge of heathland that stretches many miles towards Sheringham. Towering cliffs loom like castle walls above the beach below. For hundreds of years, these stalwart cliffs have been locked in battle with the waves. In spite of their best efforts, the North Sea buffets and wheedles its way steadily inland.

At the point where the cliffs subside, midway along the crescent beach, and parallel with it, a broad path rises to the cliff top. Its curve is swift and sure, like a brushstroke. From a distance, it makes a rust-coloured slash against the clipped clear green of the heath.

A storm has been edging nearer throughout the morning, shouldering the blue sky out of its way. The beach has gradually emptied until, at the foot of the path, two solitary figures remain. The man is tall and lean with a weather-browned complexion. His back and his hair are arrow-straight.

The child's hair is finer than his father's, and fair instead of brown. Many times before he has scampered up the path, but on this blustery day the climb is beyond him. The man hesitates for only an instant. Then he scoops his son up and transports him with resolute strides to the top of the ridge.

They stop just short of the point where the cliff edge axes away to the shingle below. There a crude cement structure is embedded in the hillside. It is a pillbox. Sentinels stood watch here during the Second World War, and in conflicts all the way back to the Armada, lookouts patrolled this spot, alert against invasion. It affords a commanding view of the crescent; from here you can see west all the way to where Blakeney Point unfurls like a frond of fern into the sweep of the sea.

Jack Cable sets his son Timmy on the cement ledge. Suddenly he goes down on one knee and enfolds the boy in a hug. A shudder shakes them; perhaps it's the wind gusting off the sea. Jack removes his own jacket and gathers the boy into its warmth.

'Better?' he asks.

The sky is thick with charcoal clots of cloud. A shaft of sunlight breaks through and sets Timmy's hair ablaze with sudden light.

Timothy Cable has always been passionate about this stretch of beach, though, being only four years of age, he would not have put it quite like that. He has spent the morning in eager exploration. He puzzled over a rugby sock camouflaged amidst the kelp. He constructed a miniature fort, hauling rocks of a desirable size and shape from one side of the spit to the other. Most absorbing of all, he locked grave glances with a seal.

These adventures behind him now, Timmy appears content to shelter in the lee of his father's body. There have been times before on this cliff edge when the child has felt fiercely insecure, but not now; his father's robust presence, his father's strong arm around his waist, is proof against a fall.

Jack clutches the damp little fellow close; the heat from the man's body should warm them both, but Timmy shivers still. Or maybe the tremor comes from Jack; it is impossible to tell.

And at last, Jack begins to whisper. He turns his son's face gently, oh so gently, seawards. He kisses the crown of Timmy's head, where the hair parts of its own accord. He tells Timmy for the umpteenth time the story of the sea.

'That's where Daddy goes, Tim. There, to the Faraway.' Jack Cable points into the bleak distance. 'And that's where the sea goes too. Day after day after day, it rumbles back on to the beach, weary from its travels, and protests loudly about the never-ending journey. The clamour and clash of the waves – you hear? – that's the sea in a fit of temper. But once it has shouted its anger to the cliffs, do you know what the sea does then? Well, of course you do.'

Jack smiles and for the briefest of instants touches his cheek to Timmy's. 'The sea does what you do when you are very, very tired, my Tim. It curls up to sleep on the sand.'

Timmy has heard this story before, but he doesn't interrupt. His face is utterly impassive, as if emptied of thought. If there is a crease of anxiety between his brows, a frown of reproach, it is slight and swiftly gone. The child's eyes never waver from the distant horizon – the Faraway – where a narrow band of Norfolk purple separates a silver-grey sea from a coal-grey sky.

*Cambridge*

# Chapter 1

There's a time in England, towards the end of January – when the sociability of the Christmas season has long faded and summer is far too far away – when it can sometimes seem as if the world has been drained of colour. When the afternoon sky is so leaden and low that it presses down on people's spirits. When dawn doesn't stumble in until half past seven. When greyness overhangs the morning like a shroud.

In the countryside surrounding Cambridge, the January scenery is unsparing. Any perspective on the landscape is like an X-ray: it pierces straight to the bone. It lays bare the rural skeleton – the angles of a field, the line of a dyke, the perimeter of a wood. Farmhouses, crouching in barren fields, look lonely and vulnerable. On the horizon stand the eerie silhouettes of oak trees, their melancholy branches stark against an aluminium sky.

There is rain everywhere. Moisture glimmers on the hedgerows; it trembles on the trees. The fields are spongy, the paddocks pooled with water. The ponies stand in mud and bow their heads before the downpour.

And always in the background are the desolate sounds of winter. The hollow rustle of reeds along the riverbed. The tap-tap-tap as the seed pods of poppies on their stilt-like stems knock together in the wind. The drip-drip-drip of water: gushing in the ditches, running through the roots of the field elms, falling from the gutters. The kaah-kaah-kaah of carrion crows.

The city of Cambridge, too, huddles against the damp and chill. Long gone are the May Balls, the leafy walks, the picnics by the river. Rows of punts lie chained up together by Magdalene Bridge with water puddling in the bottom; the river is dark and deserted except for the odd indifferent duck. Rain makes greasy streaks down the front of fine old buildings. The branches of wisteria that clump on college walls are matted and dry like a hag's hair. The trees along the Backs reach skeletal arms to a sunless sky.

And on the northern edge of the city, on a short street lined with nineteenth-century terraces, people trudge down the hill to-wards the River Cam, towards town, with their hoods raised, their heads down. I turn aside from the fire for a moment and watch them through my rain-streaked bay window. Then I dive once again into my daydream.

I imagine a wardrobe, blissfully empty except for seven perfect outfits.

There's a silk dress, for starters, of surpassing simplicity, and an exquisite wool suit; there's a handsomely tailored casual outfit, straight out of a Katharine Hepburn film. Every piece of clothing is impeccable – no missing buttons; no strained seams; no coffee stains. There's a silk sweater or a fine shirt to complement each outfit, and footwear of Italian leather.

None of the shoes would pinch my feet.

All would be perfectly polished.

I add a mackintosh here, a mini-skirt there, and consider the effect. Nothing hangs on my decision. This is merely a fantasy – an amusing speculation, as the dictionary puts it. A whimsy. A caprice.

In my twenties, when I was less sure of who I was, I was tempted once or twice to use these imaginary costumes as a standard of judgement. Against those seven perfect outfits my own come-as-you-are wardrobe seemed distinctly wanting, and, by implication, so did I.

Not any more. One of the most satisfactory things for me about growing up is learning to live with the choices I've made. To accept that, rather than scouring the shops, I've chosen on countless occasions to do other things: to hang out with my friend Helen, or cuddle with Sonny; to take to the river in a rainstorm; to throw myself into work. These choices haven't provided a perfect wardrobe. They haven't left me with a home with picture-perfect paintwork.

But they have left me with a life.

I comforted myself with this thought as I pulled away from the fire and peered into the awkwardly shaped space under the stairs. Even the feeble light from a forty-watt bulb couldn't disguise the fact that my cupboard was in chaos. It was a sure-fire, eighteen-carat, only-one-per-customer mess.

In all other respects, my house in Clare Street is the answer to a maiden's prayer. It's snug and bright, it's within walking distance of the centre of Cambridge, and though it isn't big, it's big enough for me. I can run the Cambridge branch of Aardvark Investigations from a room upstairs. When my partner, Sonny Mendlowitz, spends the night, we're cosy rather than crowded.

So far so good.

But storage space, or rather the lack of it, is the fly in the ointment. The cupboard under the stairs serves as pantry, cellar and lumber room combined. Inside, there's a chair waiting to be re-caned and bottles to be recycled. There are board games and picture frames and camping gear. There's a whole case of baked beans marked '20% Off' that I purchased in a rare fit of frugality. And away at the back, at the most inaccessible point, there's an electricity meter. I suspect that the person who installed it in that position was a card-carrying sadist. And now a fellow sadist, posing as an agent from the electricity board, has demanded that I take note of the numbers on the dial.

That's why I was to be found on a January morning leaning against the doorframe of the understairs cupboard with a mug of coffee in my hand and working up the courage for a clearout.

I was waiting for a client. I looked at my watch. Half an hour to go. Time to make a start.

I began with the bulkiest items – sports equipment, rolls of wallpaper, tubs of paint – which went immediately into the kitchen, where the door could be shut on them if the need arose. Most things had to be dragged out. It was dusty work and heavy, but not without its rewards. I found a forgotten gift and a box full to the brim of family photos. I found a fine bottle of burgundy.

When only a stack of crockery and some in-line skates remained between me and the meter, I called time out. I picked my way between boxes to the coffee percolator in the kitchen and refilled my mug, returned to the living room, settled on to a floor cushion and looked around.

My home may not be perfect, but I've been dripping away at it for several years, and it is more or less the way I want it. On the ground floor, two tiny parlours and a narrow hallway have now been melded together into a substantial living room with large windows at each end. The fireplace has a pine surround with vine leaves carved into the wood; there are alcoves on either side for my books and stereo equipment. The old floorboards have been sanded and sealed so that in the light from the fire they take on a golden glow.

Helen, my number one girlfriend, never tires of saying that a woman can flourish with a room of her own, and I'm beginning to think she's right. For me, this room is a place where peace comes dropping slow. Where I've lately noticed – somewhat to my surprise – a core of happiness curled up in my chest, waiting for some small circumstance to set it free.

I sipped my coffee and sat very still while this light-heartedness swept over me again. Was this – this sense that something wonderful might be just around the corner – what other people meant by happiness? I wondered. It wasn't a wholly positive sensation; it left me, an essentially cautious person, feeling a touch too exposed. But it was, like a once-in-a-lifetime adventure, irresistible all the same.

The first time was three or four months ago. I'd been working my socks off on a long-drawn-out divorce case. A man had been shouting in court about his wife's infidelities; her solicitor wanted me to establish whether he had peccadilloes of his own. The issue turned out to be not *if* but *how many*. Long hours of surveillance numbed my brain and my butt, and the way the case ended left a nasty taste. I did my job, and I did it well, but when I came away, it didn't feel like a job well done.

To compensate, Sonny and I took a rare day off together. We drove to Norfolk, to the weekend retreat which I own with two friends, fully expecting to have our fingers nipped by the October winds. Instead, the day took on a golden glow. By the afternoon, we were well into a touch of Indian summer. We headed for Holkham Bay, where we trekked out through the pine woods and across the mud flats and ate sandwiches by the sea. We rolled up our chinos and paddled in thc waves. As the sun went down, we raced each other back across the dunes. Sonny slipped on the side of a muddy channel and lay laughing in inches of water like a stranded seal, and had to be persuaded to strip off his trousers and sweatshirt and sneak back to the car park wrapped only in a rug.

Then, when we pulled up in front of Wildfell Cottage, the electricity had failed. No hot bath, no comfort food. We couldn't find the matches, the village shop was shut and the neighbours were away. We considered ditching the day and driving back to Cambridge. But just at that moment, a cloud shifted in the evening sky. The moon emerged directly above the meadow and suddenly, without speaking, we knew exactly what to do. We went back inside. And there, in perfect silence, I removed the rug from Sonny's shoulders and warmed his body in the old-fashioned way. We shook a duvet out beneath the French doors that gave on to the garden. We forgot about lighting a fire. We dispensed with candles and music. We didn't use condoms or wine or any of the other usual paraphernalia. We looked at each other naked, with the moonlight glinting off our eyes, and made perfect love; we didn't say a word.

It was an evening out of the ordinary. I didn't expect it to be repeated, and it hasn't been. But what has recurred since at odd moments is this feeling of sweet anticipation.

Even the clamour of a voice as I answered the telephone didn't dampen its effect.

'Laura?' Speak of the devil, it was Sonny himself, with a chuckle in his voice. 'Listen, you lucky creature! I think I've got the Baxter contract almost wrapped up, so I can come to Cambridge tomorrow. Where shall we meet?'

'Congratulations, Sonny. That's great

news, on both counts.' As usual, I couldn't find the appointments page in my new palm-top organiser, so I went by memory instead. 'How about Hobbs Pavilion, half-past twelve tomorrow?'

'That'll do. What've you got on today?'

'Baby-doll pyjamas and a great big smile.'

'The clients might like it, but don't you think a trouser suit would be a more professional look? Seriously, Laura – what are you working on?'

'Besides sorting out the understairs cupboard? And scattering the contents all over the house? Well, I'm glad you asked, Sonny, because in less than ten minutes I've got a meeting with the client of the year.'

'Who's that?'

'He rang me last night. Someone local,' I said.

'Only a hundred and twenty thousand Cambridge people to choose from. That really narrows it down. Come on, give me a clue.'

'You'll have to wait till tomorrow. Anyway,' I said, 'it may all come to nothing.'

'Speaking of nothing' – Sonny likes to take liberties with the language – 'where are you hiding the junk that comes out of the cupboard? A nice impression this client will get if it's strewn all over the floor.'

'He'll get me, Sonny. What more could any client want?'

The doorbell rang. I hung up the phone on Sonny's reply, kicked a pair of wellies back into the cupboard, straightened my collar and dashed to the door. I was minus the baby-dolls, but I did take care to clothe myself in my most enchanting smile.

# Chapter 2

My clients – there turned out to be two of them – sat close together on the sofa in my living room, facing the fire. They looked uneasy, like underage lovers called to account by a disapproving parent. But I was neither a parent nor disapproving, and Jack and Olivia Cable were a long way from young.

Jack gripped his wife's hand. From time to time he kneaded her knuckles with his thumb. Olivia looked straight ahead, her eyes fixed on my face. Her torso was angled away from her husband, as if she were fearful of what he might say.

Jack spoke first. His question was nothing if not direct.

'Have you ever lost a child?' he asked.

It wasn't what I'd expected. I considered before I replied.

I've suffered the usual run of losses – no more, and probably no less, than most people of my age in this part of the world. I lost (as they say) my virginity. I lost (more accurately, I abandoned) an academic career. I lost a kitten named Simone; she was found under the wheels of a neighbour's Ford Sierra, which left me down in the dumps for days.

I lost my father.

They're irrevocable losses, all of them; but in the big scheme of things, there's only one that really matters.

'No, never. I've never lost a child.'

Someone had to break the ice, so I spoke his name. 'You mean Timmy?'

Until that point Olivia Cable had been silent, which had given me a chance to observe her remarkable face. Mrs Cable wasn't a beauty – the apple cheeks were more Jilly Cooper than Claudia Schiffer – but the word striking could have been invented to account for her colouring. Her complexion glowed like that of a toddler who has just woken up from a nap. Her eyes, like the sky in a child's poster painting, were an intense shade of blue. Her shining hair brushed her shoulders in a thick bob and, quite unexpectedly, every strand of it was white. That combination of blue eyes and white hair reminded me of ads for holidays on the island of Crete.

And while Jack stroked her knuckles, Olivia stared at me with an avid yet wary interest.

'You know about Timmy?' she asked, leaning forward.

'Only a little,' I said. 'Tell me more.'

Olivia and Jack exchanged glances. An unspoken question passed between them; it was settled in seconds. In a voice that was eerily casual, given the subject matter, Olivia began.

'Our son Timothy Andrew Cable had just turned four,' she said, 'when he disappeared. We were staying near Cleybourne, on the north Norfolk coast. Do you know the area?'

'I share a cottage with friends at Burnham St Stephen's.'

'Ah.' A first flash of acceptance. 'Almost neighbours,' she said. 'But of course, we don't go there any more.'

Jack Cable took up the telling. His words came out so fluently that I suspected he'd rehearsed them many times before. He seemed to have worn smooth the rough edges of emotion.

'The details don't matter for present purposes, Miss Principal, but it was me. I was the one who took Timmy down to the beach. I lost sight of him, for a minute or so, and he vanished. Olivia and I looked everywhere. The police and coastguard were on alert for weeks. It was the biggest search operation ever mounted in Norfolk, did you know that?'

I shook my head. No.

Jack turned his hands palms-up. *Well, there you are*, the gesture said.

'Forgive me for asking, Mr Cable. They've never found a body?'

29

'Not a trace. It's as if Timmy vanished off the face of the earth.'

'And this was what – ten years ago?'

'Twelve.'

From what I knew of Jack Cable (which was only what everybody knew) I reckoned that he was probably forty-five, forty-six years of age. He looked older. He was vigorous; you'd expect that of the polar explorer whose televised adventures had gripped the nation's attention in the pre-Christmas schedules. His body was strong, his jaw-line firm. But the folds that ran from nose to chin had a crevasse-like quality, and there were lines that went deeper than weather wrinkles around his eyes.

'Twelve years, four months.' Olivia glanced at her watch. 'And six days.' She didn't mention minutes. It was a testimony, an act of defiance. It wasn't just that she remembered the day of Timmy's disappearance. Most emphatically, Olivia Cable refused to forget.

They were waiting. I cleared my throat. 'Over the years, Mr Cable, there must have been leads. Sightings that looked promising, say?'

'Certainly.' Jack was matter-of-fact. 'In the first few months, Miss Principal, the Norfolk police heard from eleven hundred people–'

'Closer to twelve hundred,' Olivia insisted.

30

Jack accepted the amendment without comment. 'Twelve hundred callers who said they'd seen Timmy. He was spotted by a railway worker wandering in the woods. Someone noticed him sitting high up in the cab of a truck, with his face pressed against the window. A pensioner claimed to have seen him playing by a pool in Majorca.' Jack scratched absent-mindedly at his beard. The rasping sound went well, I thought, with the discomfort in the room.

'You can't fault the police,' Jack continued. 'They were thorough. They followed up leads, interviewed passers-by, tracked people through immigration. Where there were persistent reports, they even mounted house-to-house enquiries.' He hesitated.

'Nothing?'

Olivia caught my eye. 'He was everywhere and nowhere,' she said, in a voice barely above a whisper. 'It was as if he were a little ghost. Each time we thought we might get close, he vanished again. We tried to steel ourselves against raised expectations; tried to be realistic about the odds. But when it's your child...'

I was suddenly pierced with a small, sharp sense of what it must have been like. 'Each time it would be like losing him all over again.'

Olivia smiled at me. For the first time she looked almost at ease. I thought she would

31

speak, but Jack got in first.

'The closer we got, the harder it was.'

'Derbyshire? Didn't something happen there?'

Jack lowered his eyes. The seconds ticked conspicuously away.

'Mr Cable?'

When he spoke, his voice was redolent of long periods in the Arctic wilderness. I heard a blizzard blowing through the bleakness of his tone.

'Timmy had been gone a year. The police got wind of some newcomers in a Derbyshire village – people with dark wavy hair who'd turned up out of the blue with a fair-haired five-year-old boy. Discreet enquiries were made. The set-up was strange; the police thought there was a chance that it was Timmy.' He paused.

'But it wasn't?'

'The police didn't want us to follow, but we couldn't help ourselves. We stayed in a hotel room. The superintendent and the social worker went in first. Forty minutes we waited.'

He spoke the words as if forty minutes were forty hours. There leapt to my mind an image of Olivia and Jack sitting stiffly side by side on the edge of a hotel bed, the telephone within reach. Sipping complimentary coffee that neither wanted; adding powdered creamer that neither liked. Tuning the television to game shows, unable to tear themselves away from the compulsive dramas of good fortune and bad fortune, loss and recovery. I imagined them not looking at each other. Neither would want to face up to the fierce hope shining in the other's eyes.

Jack paused in his recounting. Olivia had tugged her fingers free of his grasp. She clenched her hands as if to restrain them. Her fingers were strong and stubby. Her nails were bitten to the quick. When we'd shaken hands, I'd noticed a callus where a pen would rest on the middle finger of her left hand.

'The similarity was superficial,' Jack said. 'The child was blond and slightly built, but apart from that, he wasn't like Timmy at all.'

How many five-year-old boys, thin, fair-haired little lads, lived in England at the time of that desperate journey to Derbyshire? Thousands, perhaps. And only one who belonged to Olivia and Jack. Only one if they were lucky, that is. A year after the disappearance, it was unlikely that Timothy Cable was alive at all.

'And the leads have continued?' They would still trickle in, I thought. So many people want to believe in the possibility of reunion, even after a decade or more.

Jack nodded. 'At Christmas – was it two years ago?'

'Three,' Olivia said.

'A woman came to our door. She'd discovered Timmy hiding in a shed, she said, and brought him up as her own. If we reimbursed her for the cost of his upbringing, we could have him back.'

'And was there a boy?'

'Her teenaged son. He had to be taken into care. The poor woman was deranged.'

'I wish we could have done more for the child,' Olivia said.

'And only a couple of months ago,' Jack continued, 'a French social worker found a teenager with a trace of an English accent sleeping in a warehouse on the outskirts of Paris. The boy claimed that he'd been snatched off a beach by paedophiles when he was a baby.'

I puzzled over this. 'But surely a child wouldn't retain an accent for so many years?'

Olivia waved my question aside. 'The French officials quickly put paid to the story,' she said. 'This boy, Ferdinand something, had psychiatric problems. It was all in his mind.' She made a gesture with her shoulders, as though she was shaking something off. 'It's been explained to us. Accounts of missing persons attract those whose own identity is fragile.'

'That's why,' Jack added, speaking with greater urgency now, 'there have been so many letters from children's homes. So many boys pleading to be fetched home. They tell us that–'

'Enough,' Olivia said. Tenderly, she kissed his hand. She placed it in her lap.

It was time to bring things to a close. I fancied the idea of the Cables as clients, but they'd suffered enough disappointments. I wasn't going to make another entry in their catalogue of pain.

'Mr Cable? Mrs Cable? You've come to see me, I suppose, because you want me to reactivate the search for your son.' I waited for them to confirm.

But Olivia looked at me as if she'd forgotten my presence. She shook her head – her hair swung back and forth across her shoulders – but she didn't speak. I kept to my resolve and carried on.

'You want me to succeed where the police have failed. I have to be blunt with you. It's impossible. I cannot find your son.'

'No,' Olivia said. 'Don't worry, Miss Principal. It's all right.'

'My colleagues and I have worked on dozens of mispers.' I knew I wouldn't have to explain to the Cables, of all people, that 'mispers' was police-speak for 'missing persons'. 'This is experience speaking, Mrs Cable, it's not worry. After twelve years, there's nothing that can be done. The trail will be colder than an iceberg.'

'You don't understand,' Olivia protested. 'It's over, you see.'

She tossed me a smile that would have illuminated the Christmas lights on Oxford Street. It was my turn to be surprised.

'Over?' I couldn't think what she meant. To find Timmy's body might be a relief of sorts, but hardly a cause for smiles. Olivia came to my rescue.

'He's returned,' she said. 'My son Timothy. He's alive and well in Cambridge.'

Within seconds of announcing that Timmy had been found, Olivia Cable was transformed. It was as if saying it somehow made it true. She disentangled her hand from Jack's. She assumed centre stage. She evinced a certainty that I would have sworn in the early minutes of our meeting had no part in her make-up.

'I'm almost certain I've found my son, Miss Principal.' She shone with a joy that was almost painful to watch.

'Laura,' I said. Formality didn't fit with that intensity of feeling. 'Please, call me Laura.' I watched her face as she spoke, unsettled by the force of her conviction. You'd have thought that the dashed hopes of the past twelve years would have dulled her capacity for belief. Not a bit of it. Olivia Cable blazed with triumph. Her optimism was unclouded.

'We'll have to tread carefully,' she said, 'so as not to alarm him.' She stood up and took a few steps towards the window. Then, calmly at first, she began pacing from one end of my sitting room to the other. Her steps were slow and deliberate, punctuation marks to her thoughts. Each time she reached a window, she spun around on the ball of her foot, and then tossed another comment at Jack and at me.

'Can you imagine what Timmy's been through?' She paced again, and spun again. Her hair swung like a bell. 'He could have been anywhere. London, Edinburgh – you name it. Even abroad.'

Jack nodded, but didn't speak. He and I followed Olivia's progress across the room, our heads turning from one side to the other like spectators at a tennis match. Olivia was magnificent in her delusion. We were appalled.

'He has a whole other identity. Another name,' Olivia was saying. 'Ah, that's a point, Miss Principal.'

'Laura,' I repeated.

'We mustn't call him Timmy. He calls himself Liam now; that's what he told me.' She paused for a few seconds, considering. 'Liam – it's not bad.' The pacing started up again. 'Liam it is until he's ready to return to the name he was born with.' She glanced at me quickly, to see that I concurred, and stumbled into a floor cushion. I reached over and shifted it out of her way.

'A whole other identity,' Olivia murmured. 'That means – doesn't it? – a different birthday. The bastards who took him' – she said 'bastards' as casually as someone might say 'salad fork' or 'Labrador' – 'wouldn't have known his proper birthday. They probably made one up. He may want to celebrate on the date they gave him, the date he's used to, for the time being.'

Jack spoke for the first time in minutes, picking up the refrain. 'A whole other identity, Livi. You know that includes–'

He paused, while Olivia tried to assume a look of nonchalance. 'Another father, another mother. I know that, Jack. Almost certainly.' She smiled to show she could handle it, revealing perfect white teeth that matched, more or less, the perfect white hair. Then she continued her short and complicated route across my sitting room and back. She was like a wind-up toy, turning ideas over and over in her mind: how it would be when she told him the truth, what she would say, how he might feel.

What problems they'd encounter.

How the problems would be solved.

It seemed to me that Olivia was sorting through difficulties the way people sort through bric-a-brac for a jumble sale. She

38

was labelling the problems. She was bagging them, one by one by one, ready for disposal.

She displayed no caution. It didn't cross her mind that these difficulties might overwhelm them. That these problems might have no solutions. No solutions, at least, that a mother could live with.

She didn't want to consider the likelihood that the boy she'd found had not been and never would be Timmy Cable. Or the possibility that, if he had been Timmy, he might be inextricably settled in his new existence. He might be a Timmy (or a Liam or a Charles or an Ed) who wouldn't care to call the Cable household home.

Olivia prattled on, afire with fantasy. Her husband never took his eyes off her. There was anguish on his face. Jack Cable had caution enough for the two of them.

'You see how it is, Miss Principal? She first spotted this boy – a beggar, he is – only three days ago, and already she's made up her mind.'

Olivia didn't back down. 'He's not a beggar, Jack. He's a musician. He plays the guitar. He plays well.'

Jack demurred. 'Looking for handouts,' he said, but gently. Then, pleading: 'Olivia, you know nothing about him. You've spoken to him – what, twice? He's told you nothing.'

'He's told me all I need to know.' Her blue eyes blazed with conviction under the thick white fringe. 'Jack, his face. It's like Timmy's face.'

'After twelve years, Olivia, how do you know what Timmy looks like? He's grown, he's changed, he's–'

Olivia interrupted. 'His voice is just like Timmy's. Oh, of course it's a young man's voice, but the timbre is the same. Do you think I wouldn't recognise the voice of my son?'

'Olivia–'

She took three steps across the room until she was standing in front of her husband. She held both his hands in hers. 'For God's sake, Jack' – she closed her eyes and drew in a long, long breath – 'this boy – this youth – he even smells like Timmy.' She held her breath for one second, two seconds, three, as if she had taken into her lungs once again the skin-scent of a baby, as if she had held it inside her all these years. When at last Olivia exhaled, her tears began to flow.

Jack hesitated. I had him pegged as the embodiment of the English middle-class male, buttoned up, trained to channel emotions into only the most intimate of moments. Trained to maintain a private stance, to preserve a private face. But now his training slipped. Jack's countenance became as transparent as a crystal. I could see determination and resistance, concern and circumspection play across his features.

I could see it all collapse. His face softened with pity. He shrugged and pulled Olivia to him. Pulled her on to the sofa and enveloped her in his arms.

Her head curled into his shoulder. Jack looked at me over that ivory hair with an expression that seemed to me at the time to be pure helplessness. I only realised later, when I thought about it in the middle of the night, that it was far from pure; that it was helplessness laced, almost certainly, with despair.

'I'll call you,' he said. Even though he was here, in my home, it rang as a dismissal.

# Chapter 3

I watched from the window as Jack and Olivia drove off in a Lexus. It had the blackest, shiniest paint job I'd seen in ages. Someone washed that car regularly. Someone waxed it. I was willing to bet the scratch on the side of my Saab that it wasn't either of them.

I resolved to put the Cables out of mind until I'd decided what to do with the understairs cupboard. If I crammed the boxes and bags back in, then the next time I needed an air mattress or electrical tape I'd be forced to repeat the whole painful process. If, on the other hand, I did the job properly – even without re-caning the chair or consuming the baked beans – I'd be at it for the rest of the day.

Speaking of baked beans, a decision like this required nourishment.

It was too early to start on the bottle of wine, so I went for freshly brewed coffee instead. I extracted some back bacon from the fridge and set a few slices to sizzle. Warmed the oven and inserted a soft white roll; put the mustard and ketchup on standby. And I thought, as I always do when

I'm struck by the smell of bacon, of my father. Whenever he was at home, my mother would make a full English breakfast. It was the only meal she liked to cook, and she went the whole hog, with bacon and eggs, fried bread, mushrooms and tomatoes; sometimes she'd fry up the mash from the night before with onion and butter. Eating for England, we called it.

Paul Principal was a long-distance lorry driver. He plied the route between the West Country and the Continent in the days before Eurotunnel; the uncertainties of the Channel crossing meant that we never knew exactly when he'd get in. Some evenings I'd fall asleep waiting and miss his homecoming. But the following morning, sparked awake by the sweet smell of bacon, I'd rush for the kitchen and Dad would sweep me up into his lap. The disappointment of the evening before would be forgotten.

Maybe it was the memory of breakfasts with my father that made me bring the box of photos to the table too, along with the bacon roll and the orange juice and coffee. I hadn't looked at these for years – at all the members of my family, in the muted colours and bordered edges of cheap snapshots from the sixties and seventies.

My father appears in characteristic pose. He's propped up in a Laz-Z-Boy, poring over a *National Geographic* magazine. It would have delighted him to visit exotic places – places out of the way and unfamiliar, not the routine and frugal travels required by his job. But he never had the time or the money; the *National Geographic* was as close as he ever got.

And there's my brother Hugh, in his first year of secondary school, playing midfield for the local football team. His expression combined bravado and resolution, and I recognised the cocky face he affected when his team was being trounced. He wore a similar expression last year when he went through a really bad patch with the business. It's one of those traits that has been consistent from the child to the man; my brother is firm under fire.

And there's me, on my way to the park. I'm wearing a coat in that hideous dark pink that's reserved for little girls and I'm pushing a pram. I can't be more than six or seven years of age. Seeing the strain on my face in the photo brought back vividly how heavy the pram was and how difficult to steer. I was fearful of pedestrian crossings in case I should somehow cause my baby cousin to tumble into the path of the oncoming traffic. In fact, there was little danger; Aunt Marjorie and Mum were always close behind me, always watchful. They talked a mile a minute but their gaze was on me and their tender gossip swept over me in a warm, inclusive glow.

We visited the local park every Sunday, and I would pretend that the baby was mine. Sometimes I made it all the way to the playground before I tired of the game. But at the first glimpse of the tall metal slide, with its silvery surface scored by hundreds of small bottoms and heels and hands, I'd surrender the pram and rush off to join the queue at the bottom of the steep steps.

I remember something else: my mother used to watch me on the slide as if her gaze was my guardian. Each time I prepared to take the giddy plunge over the top, I'd shoot a glance in her direction; each time she'd be staring at me with furious intent. Her heart was always in her mouth at that moment, she told me; she never ceased to think of me as the toddler who had to be coddled up the slide. She never relaxed until I had swooshed into her arms at the bottom.

*Have you ever lost a child?* That was what Jack had asked. The question invoked the range of fears that parents confront. There are the accidents – on the roads, in fires, from drugs, from sport. There is estrangement – the wrong crowd, the runaways, the no turning back. There are suicides, unable to cope with the temporary turmoil of adolescent lives. There is the finality of death.

I returned the photos to their box, one by

one, and set the lid back on top. I'd been trying to avoid thinking of the Cables' tragedy, but I couldn't put it off any longer. How did they bear it? They'd had four years of caring for Timmy, twenty-four hours a day. Nights spent singing him to sleep or dealing with his wakefulness. Days spent struggling to understand his quirks and idiosyncrasies, the things he liked and didn't like, his hesitations and his passions and his fears. Interpreting his babble, facilitating his friendships, coping with his tantrums. Above all else: keeping him safe.

And then, in a matter of moments, their child was gone.

The assignment arrived the next morning. The central heating was blasting away when I came downstairs; the kitchen was stuffy and dry. I opened the back door to let in a gust of fresh air, and as I did so, the telephone rang. Jack Cable didn't waste any time on small talk.

'Look,' he said, 'maybe Olivia's right. The boy might be Timmy. There's a chance.'

Although I questioned Jack – *A chance, but astronomically small?* – I wasn't surprised that he'd given in. What if I were in his position? If I couldn't summon belief any more? If I could no longer ignore the cold voice of reason proclaiming Timmy's death? Would I want to be the one to grind a heel in the face of his mother's hope?

Jack continued. 'We've been through this too many times before. Had too many disappointments. But Olivia – as long as we don't have a body, she says, we have to assume that he's alive. We saw a grief counsellor who advised us to accept his passing. Olivia says that would be like abandoning our baby.'

'So where do I come in?'

Jack cleared his throat. 'I'll pay for protection.'

'Beg your pardon?'

'I want you to stick close to her. Her sense is that he's Timmy; she needs time to put her gut feeling to the test. Can you be present at their meetings? Make sure he doesn't harm her?'

'You believe he could be dangerous, Mr Cable?'

'Olivia insists he's just a kid. But I looked at him. I drove past where he was sitting, and I looked at him.' A sigh drifted down the telephone wires. 'All I can say is he's a big kid. And we don't know anything about him. He might be scamming her; he might see Olivia as an easy touch. He might even be–'

'Crazy?'

'He wouldn't be the first. And if he's only sixteen, there's got to be some reason why he's hanging out on the corner instead of going to school.'

Chaperone-cum-bodyguard. I rolled it over in my mind. It didn't sound impossible. Not improbable even. Except for one thing.

'Your wife, Mr Cable. How will she feel about me dogging her footsteps?'

'It's already sorted. You see, Laura, Olivia likes you.'

'You're surprised.' He hadn't tried to hide it.

'Well, some of the agents we've worked with in the past – let's just say they weren't her cup of tea. But she trusts you. She didn't even object to the second assignment.'

So chaperone-cum-bodyguard was just the taster. With a sinking feeling I waited for Jack to explain.

'Check out this kid's background for me, will you? Find out where he grew up. Have a look at his school record, that sort of thing. But don't spook him.'

'Meaning?'

'Olivia is adamant. Don't heavy the boy, don't do anything that might make him back off.'

'And how do you expect me to find out about him if I'm not allowed to push a little?'

'God damn it, you're the PI. Either you can do it or you can't.' Jack Cable's cross-ness crackled down the line.

'Mr Cable, this will cut our chances of establishing the kid's identity. Whereas a forceful interview...'

'Don't even think about it. I'm not paying you to break Livi's heart.'

'You're the boss.'

All PIs use this form of agreement from time to time. Clients like it; they find it reassuring. But of course, *You're the boss* is only half the story. The other half is: *And what the boss doesn't know won't hurt him.*

'When should I start?'

I glanced towards the kitchen floor, where the debris from the cupboard was still scattered. I pictured my desk, littered with loose ends that needed tying up, most of them by yesterday. Fingers crossed that Jack Cable wasn't in a hurry.

He mentioned a church at the corner of St Barnabas Road and Mill Road where Olivia had first come across Liam. She'd gone there today, he said, hoping to find him.

'So you want me to–?'

'Go now.' There was no room for negotiation in Jack Cable's tone. In all relationships except his marriage, he was accustomed to command.

# Chapter 4

It was an hour later that I came across Liam for the first time.

He looked seventeen, maybe eighteen, that was my initial impression. He was dressed for the cold in a standard-issue roll-neck sweater. He wore a long sheepskin coat, straight out of the seventies, and the kind of hat that's synonymous with street cred. Like many a busker before him, he played an acoustic guitar.

So far, so commonplace.

But then he turned his head, and the difference became clear. The kid had a bruise that was one in a million. Streaks of puce and liver and chartreuse crept from his hairline to his brow. A scattering of scabs across his temple marked the track of a recent wound.

He sat on a low brick wall outside St Barnabas Church, in the uncertain shelter of a cherry tree. He faced the road; the antique shop on the opposite pavement was only three car-widths' away. But I'd swear he hadn't noticed the nostalgic display of polished chests and fireguards, so absorbed was he in his music. One of his ankles crooked across the other knee to cradle the guitar. His body curved tenderly towards it, his ear hovered inches from its neck. It was as if he were whispering sweet nothings; as if the sleek wooden instrument was the object of an obsessive love.

The door of the church porch suddenly opened behind him. A woman with eyes the colour of cornflowers stepped out into the murky morning light. The young man didn't seem to register Olivia's presence.

She put her hand out and checked the weather. A soft rain had begun to fall. She was opening her umbrella when her glance fell upon him. Like a child in a game of Musical Statues, she froze, holding the umbrella at a forty-five-degree angle to the ground.

I was sheltering twenty metres away in the doorway of a bank, peering through the haze of moisture, studying Olivia's face. Her sudden stop took me aback. I was uneasy as I observed her watchfulness and saw the steadiness of her stare. She conveyed an impression of perfect composure, her blue eyes focused on his back. There was no hint of surprise in her manner, no tincture of alarm. She was not excited or joyful. If expression was anything to go by, she was not even curious.

What was it then?

Maybe hunger: in the way she fixed on the

boy, there was something of the fox staring at the rabbit – a rigidity, a longing, an instinct to devour.

Maybe concern. She could have been a naturalist, encountering for the first time the rarest of butterflies. She might have believed that a breath, a step, a swish of skirt would cause the creature to vanish once and for all.

The drizzle stopped as I left my cover. I moved quietly towards the church, keeping them both in view. That was why I didn't see the accident coming. I was halfway across the road when there was a screech of brakes and a slap of rubber. I put up my arm to ward off the collision. A cycle clattered to the ground at my feet. The cyclist was up again in an instant. She had the stick-girl shape of a pre-adolescent, but her stream of reproach was anything but child-like. It combined the force of adult rage with the vocabulary of a marine.

'You fucking stepped in front of me,' she railed for starters, furiously inspecting her elbows and knees for damage.

I held up my hands in apology. Ignored the prickle of blood on my wrist where the bike had scraped me as it fell. I was relieved she wasn't injured.

'Should've checked the road,' I agreed.

The kid from the corner was headed in our direction now, his face a study of concern. Olivia fell into step behind him. At their approach, the cyclist ceased her shrill complaint. She swung the bicycle upright, adjusted her hood and retreated back the way she'd come as fast as her spindly legs could pedal.

'Guess she didn't want our help,' Olivia said, drily.

'Cambridge,' I replied, and laughed. They both knew what I meant. The streets are narrow and the bicycles abundant. The city is full of foreign students whose inexperience on the roads is matched only by their exuberant indifference to pedestrians. In the summer, collisions are two a penny. But January is not a favourite season for visitors, and on this occasion the fault was mine.

Now that Liam was on his feet, I could see that he was tall and broad at the shoulder. But even in the bulky coat he was skinny – the way runners are skinny, all sinew and endurance. Or, maybe, skinny in the way of a teenager who hadn't yet matured into adult strength. The cyclist was retreating into the distance. He glanced at her, and then back at me.

'You all right?' he asked.

A few isolated drops of rain fell again, flat and cold, as if they might turn into snow. I brushed at the imprint of the cycle tyre on my trouser leg.

'Maybe a little shaken,' I said. I accepted a

tissue and mopped the droplets of blood from my wrist. And, as if the idea had just occurred to me, 'Do you think we could go somewhere and have a drink? Get out of this rain for a while?'

A wild hope flared in the cornflower eyes. Had I moved too fast?

The kid was reluctant. His guitar was slung across his back. He shifted it awkwardly and stared at the wet pavement as he spoke. 'A drink? I don't know, I–'

Mrs Cable remembered her umbrella at last. She opened it with a flourish, and, reaching as high as she could, held it above the boy's head. 'I'll pay,' she said.

'In that case,' he countered, resting back into the shelter of the umbrella, 'let's go somewhere and have two.'

So Liam agreed to join us for a drink. He might have been driven by thirst; he said he hadn't had anything since breakfast. Perhaps it was an act of kindness, after my run-in with the cycle. And perhaps he had another reason for accepting – something more sinister, or at any rate, more strategic.

Olivia pointed the way to a nearby pub. 'Over there,' she said, gesturing towards the Black Swan. It wasn't quite what I'd expected; she looked like the kind of lady (using the word 'lady' quite deliberately) who wouldn't know her saloon bar from her snug. But she led the way through the shadowy interior of the Swan like an old hand.

Olivia opted initially for a tonic water, but at the last minute asked for a splash of vodka. It was eleven o'clock in the morning. I didn't know her well enough to decide whether this was a sign of nerves or of a creeping addiction.

Liam all but licked his lips at the thought of a pint.

'You old enough to drink?'

'They don't normally ask,' he said.

I by-passed a pint, not without regret, in favour of tomato juice. I was the only one on duty. But I looked again at how skinny Liam was and added cashews to my order.

Liam went off to the loo. He and I returned to the table at the same moment; Olivia rose nervously to greet him. Though her fingers fidgeted, her appearance was cool and collected. She wore a long charcoal-coloured coat dress in loosely woven wool and a matching pair of trousers. The outfit had hardly any shape beyond what her figure provided. It looked so plain and unpretentious that any woman would know it cost a packet. But Olivia seemed no more aware of her own appearance than she did of our surroundings. All her attention was focused, once again, on the boy.

We had taken up position at a rectangular

table. I settled myself alongside Olivia and made a ceremony of distributing the drinks. On the opposite side, Liam was having difficulty finding a comfortable position. He attempted to straighten his legs, but the table had a cross-piece that got in the way. He sat upright, feet planted firmly on the rug, his knees pressed against the underside of the table.

I sympathised. 'It's like camping,' I said. 'Everywhere you spread your sleeping bag, there's a problem. Here, a stone that digs into your back; there, a dip.'

Liam shot me a crooked smile that made me aware for the first time how good-looking he was. It was not only the bruise that would make him stand out in a crowd. He finally found a comfortable position. Olivia sighed. Her mouth gave a twitch of relief.

Introductions came late in the proceedings. 'By the way, I'm Laura. Thank you for coming to my aid back there. It's not much fun having a run-in with a kamikaze cyclist.'

The young man seemed to be amused by my description. His laugh was just a shade too hearty. My witticisms rarely get a reaction that goes beyond a chuckle.

He wiped his palms on the hips of his black jeans and offered to shake with me. 'I'm Liam–' The voice rose as if to add a surname, and then fell back. 'Liam,' he repeated. 'And thanks for the drink.'

'And this is Olivia,' I said.

Liam turned to Olivia, apparently unfazed by the way she strained towards him across the table. She was like an enthusiastic family dog, the kind that only needs the slightest encouragement to lick a visitor's face. He didn't quite pat her on the head, but nor did he do anything to push her away.

'How's my best customer today?' Liam's accent was vaguely southern. He followed his words with a crooked grin and his whole face lifted, except where the scabs had immobilised the skin on his forehead.

'Customer?' I asked.

Mrs Cable's blush made her complexion even rosier. 'He performed "The Skye Boat Song" for me, from beginning to end. That's how we met. I put some money in his hat.'

'Some money?' he said. 'It was a fortune.'

I pointed to his temple. 'What happened there?'

Liam took a long swig from his beer before telling me how he'd been busking near the Chinese supermarket when two men had demanded money with menaces. How he had told them to fuck off. ('Excuse me, Olivia.') How they'd come back later, when the street was empty, and given him a thrashing.

Olivia reached tentatively in his direction, as if she was going to stroke the spot where the scabs grew. Liam looked at her out of the corner of his eye, and she withdrew.

I shrugged it off. 'An everyday story of city folk,' I said.

'Story' was the operative word. I'd bet my tomato juice that none of it was true.

'This happened when, Liam?'

'Weekend before last,' he said. 'Friday night.'

'You reported it?'

I'd earned some points by buying drinks, but now I'd forfeited them again. A dollop of sullenness darkened Liam's tone.

'What?'

'This assault. You reported it to the police?'

I sensed Olivia stiffen. I was careful to avoid her eye.

'It was, like, Friday night. Anyway, the cops–' He hesitated.

'I know. They're not always sympathetic to street people. But you're not a rough sleeper, Liam, are you?' That much was obvious. His black jeans fitted with scarcely a wrinkle. His Folk Festival T-shirt wasn't Persil fresh, but it wasn't filthy either. And he had no bedding. 'You live in Cambridge? In this area?'

He drained the last of the beer and rose to his feet. Olivia followed suit. Liam swung his guitar over his shoulder.

'Got to go now,' he said. 'I appreciate the drink.'

Olivia looked stricken.

'You'll have another?' I asked, trying to buy her some time.

But Olivia wanted more than that.

'Liam.' Olivia tugged nervously at her scarf. 'Liam, I live quite near here, in Grantchester.' She sounded short of breath. 'Maybe you'd like to come for lunch. Maybe tomorrow?'

She'd gone too far too fast. Liam's good humour gave way. When he spoke, his voice was cranky with unease, like that of a younger, less confident child.

'Look, I'm not sure what's going on here. What do you want with me? Why are you doing all this? I'm just a kid – a nobody.'

'What do I want with you?' Olivia was overcome with confusion.

I mounted a rescue operation. 'Liam, please sit down. Let me explain.'

He plonked himself on the edge of a bench. No smiles now.

'Mrs Cable had a son. He'd be your age now, or thereabouts. You're – what, sixteen? Seventeen?'

He hesitated, embarrassed now. 'I'm sixteen.'

'Her son disappeared when he was four. Olivia would like your company, that's all.' I thought back to Jack Cable's opening words. 'Can you imagine what it's like for a mother to lose a child?'

59

The young man looked at Olivia out of the corner of his eye, as if a straight-on glance might be too much of a commitment. As he watched her, her mouth trembled into a brave little smile.

Seconds later, Liam swung his guitar into position and fingered the strings. The version of 'The Skye Boat Song' that emerged was as precise and delicate as swan's down. 'Carry the child that is born to be king...' He sang the entire refrain before he made up his mind.

'All right,' he said, smiling a small sad smile back at her. 'All right, Olivia, maybe tomorrow.'

# Chapter 5

From inside the Black Swan public house I had been aware of the rising of the wind. It had huffed and puffed at the door. It had probed with friendly fingers at the edges of the windowpanes. But by the time I'd said goodbye to Liam and then to Olivia, and made my way down Mill Road, the wind had become aggressive. It blundered towards me, forcing me to button up my suede jacket and secure my scarf. It was not nudging now, but shoving, and, like a vandal, it had left its mark all along the street.

The newsagent's board lay flat on the side of the road, the imprint from someone's muddy boot right across the shoutline. The awning on the front of Barney's Discount Store had been torn. The wooden sign above the Locomotive flapped furiously with a hollow rocking sound and rubbish was scattered up and down the pavement near the internet café.

If the wind wanted attention, it got it. Students seemed exhilarated as they scurried by with their long coats clasped around them. Children spread their arms and waited to be nudged by the wind. An elderly man, emerging from the mosque, looked impressed as his cap was flipped across the street.

As I neared Parker's Piece, my eyes lifted to the sky. Above the green, a rainbow of a kite, a bold parabola, vibrated madly. Its colours were cerise and mauve and indigo, hues far removed from the subtle bluey-greens and browns that are the glory of the English countryside. And yet it looked entirely as if it belonged. It hovered to the east of the University Arms Hotel; it swooped towards the fire station, rallied and rose again.

My eye travelled down. The kite was worked by a man whose flop of fair hair was lifted by the wind, whose movements were as familiar to me as toast. I threw back the hood of my jacket and watched, engrossed, as Sonny tugged on the reins of the kite to bring it to heel.

He didn't see me coming. Nor did he seem aware of the two boys who emerged from the public lavatories in the distance and began to jog in his direction. He had eyes only for the sky. He stood some distance from the cycle path, with his overcoat buttoned up to his chin, leaning back at an angle as the kite billowed and shook. His eyes were almost shut. They scanned the winter sky, taking in every strain and flutter of the kite. His wrists moved incessantly, anticipating its motion. When I was close enough I heard the way he whispered encouragement to the kite in its battle with the wind.

There are many circumstances, especially at work, when Sonny displays the poise that a young man, if he's smart and lucky, can bring away from public school. He knows how to keep cool in the face of provocation. How to deflect anger. How to disguise what he really wants so that the lack of it will never lead to ridicule.

But I far prefer the instances, like now, when poise takes a back seat and Sonny's face screws up with concentration. When there's no cool, ironic talk. His involvement can be so intense that it seems as if he's after the secret of existence.

I circled around behind him. The grass, still soft from the rain, cushioned my steps, and their sound was further obscured by another sound, like the wind slapping the sails of a tall-masted ship, that came from the kite itself.

I crept close. My intention was to place my hands over Sonny's eyes, nothing more than that, and to announce myself with a *Guess who?* But as I got within reach, the wind did an abrupt about-turn. The kite hesitated and twisted and then plunged towards the ground. Sonny, without so much as a glance over his shoulder, began to race backwards with staccato steps, struggling all the while to keep the kite aloft. I managed to match his pace for only half a dozen steps before I crashed, arms flung out behind me to break my fall. Sonny stumbled over me and landed on the grass; his long legs sprawled across mine. But the kite still rode high on the wind, the reins were still tight in his grip and his face glowed with triumph.

The boys from the loo dashed up. Sonny stood and carefully transferred the reins into their keeping. It took both of them to bring the kite back under control. Sonny waved their thanks aside.

'My pleasure,' he said, and there was no doubt whatsoever that he meant it.

When the boys moved away, pulled by the pressure of the kite, Sonny hunkered down next to me on the grass. He looked me up and down. He ran a finger along the hem of my jacket.

'Grass stains,' he said.

I checked. Sure enough, grass stains. There went my best bargain from the midwinter sales.

'And here,' he said, pointing to my trousers, 'mud.'

'It'll blend nicely with the tyre tracks on the other side.' I told him about my encounter with the bicycle.

'Two accidents in one day begins to look like something more than coincidence, Laura. Maybe you're getting clumsy.'

'And maybe you're watching too many episodes of *The X-Files.*' Something more than coincidence, indeed. 'You'll be going on about alien invasions next.' I jumped to my feet in one fluent movement, hoping he'd noticed. 'Anyway, I can outmanoeuvre you any day.'

And with that, I took off across the grass. I was running with the wind now, not against it, and making great time. But of course Sonny, who gave chase immediately, was running with the wind too, and he wasn't far behind me. I wheeled round and swung sharply to the left, then headed back the way I'd come. The ploy would have succeeded except that Sonny cheated. He hurled himself through the air and grabbed me around the knees. My legs buckled and we rolled on the ground like a pair of mud-wrestlers.

'Let me go, Sonny. That's not fair!'

I felt more indignant than the situation demanded. Granted, the ground was sloppy; granted, it was a cavalier tackle and it came completely out of the blue. But it wasn't the first time I'd been thrown to the ground and he hadn't actually hurt me. What stung was the charge of clumsiness.

'Can I be held responsible if a cyclist is

hell-bent on hitting me? Or if you start running backwards without a by-your-leave?' I was reminded of another grievance. 'Anyway, what are you doing hanging around here?'

'Take a look at your watch.'

I rotated my arm until I could see my wristwatch around the obstacle formed by Sonny's shoulder. Almost one o'clock.

'You're late,' Sonny growled. 'You said half-past twelve, remember?' He leaned forward and gave me a soft, cool winter's kiss, to show there were no hard feelings.

'Weren't you supposed to meet me at—'

Before I could say 'Hobbs Pavilion', Sonny had bounced to his feet and loped off towards the edge of the green. He had the head start this time. I righted myself, seconds behind, and narrowed the distance between us. I wove between a clutch of Korean tourists who had stopped to read their map, raced up the wide cement steps of the former cricket pavilion, and just as Sonny dashed through the door, I caught the belt of his greatcoat in my fingers.

I entered in triumph – jacket streaked with grass stains, hair tousled by the wind, clutching Sonny's coat – and found myself face to face with a man who was poised to leave.

It was my client, Jack Cable. His eyes slid over Sonny and away again.

'Miss Principal,' he said solemnly.

I felt like a kid caught flicking spitballs in class when she should have been doing sums.

'Mr Cable, this is my partner, Sonny Mendlowitz. We've just–'

He did that man thing, a quick sizing-up, and then offered Sonny his hand. 'Jack Cable,' he said. Sonny managed a hand-shake. I could tell that he was well and truly impressed.

Cable signalled *Wait* to a short, power-ful-looking man who'd been standing beside him as we entered. Then he drew me into a corner.

'Well?' His eyes searched mine for signs of a verdict.

'Mr Cable–'

'Jack. Call me Jack while you're on the payroll.' He lowered his voice. 'Have you met him? What do you think?'

'I think I need to remind you that there's no such thing as instant results. Not in a case like this.'

'You mean – it's too early to tell?'

'That's exactly what I mean. This Liam – I only met him today. But your wife has invited him to Grantchester. And of course, if he comes–'

'To our home? When is this supposed to happen?' He didn't raise his voice, but agitation sharpened the edges.

'Tomorrow lunch time.'

'So soon,' he murmured. He gave a quick glance in the direction of the far wall, where Sonny stood alongside Cable's companion in apparent silence. 'You'll be there?'

'I'm not one hundred per cent certain the boy will show. But if he does, I'll drive him; that's the deal. Don't worry, Mr – Jack. I'll make sure your wife is not in any danger.'

We moved towards the other side of the room. The stocky man rejoined Jack immediately; he paid me no attention beyond a fleeting and not too friendly glance. He reached for the door and held it open. Jack Cable dipped his head under the man's arm and stepped through. Just like that, they were gone.

As soon as they turned away, Sonny commandeered a table in a quiet corner. He was keen to draw me out about the case.

As my business partner, of course, he was entitled to know. At Aardvark Investigations we offer clients the devoted attention of one agent and, when it's needed, the brains of two. All part of the service. Besides that, it's good business practice. Explaining to someone who isn't a yes-man what you're doing and why is the best way of ferreting out disasters in the making.

The not-a-yes-man doesn't have to be a man, of course. It doesn't have to be Sonny. Stevie, our longest-serving and trustiest employee, can expose gaps in strategy at the drop of a hat. But on this occasion, she wouldn't fit the bill. I needed information that only Sonny could provide.

Sonny, I should explain, is the kind of guy who can swing both ways. I don't mean sexually. I mean that while he's comfortable with women, he can also bloke with the blokes: he can talk football or cricket or cars; he can do that punch-on-the-arm thing; he can make light of heavy feelings. But generally, he has the same view as Shania Twain about action men; they don't impress him much. My client, Jack Cable, is an exception.

Cable's was the first polar expedition to take place in the glare of televised attention. Sonny, a stripling at the time, was entranced. He tuned in faithfully to every news broadcast. He studied potted biographies of Cable and his colleagues. He kept a map on his bedroom wall and plotted their progress. In short, when it comes to Jack Cable, Sonny Mendlowitz is a follower; a fan.

'Sit down,' he said, pointing me to a padded bench, 'and tell me all about it.'

'First I've got questions for you.' We ordered just enough food to make up for the fact that I'd missed lunch. The soup came in a blink. While it cooled, I quizzed Sonny about Jack Cable.

I knew the basics, as would anyone with

access to the media. The image of Cable – tall, lean and slightly stooped, his close-cropped beard and long straight nose barely visible behind the hood of his parka – is as familiar to the British public as a motorway sign. It is inseparable from a vision of the Arctic. In the popular imagination, Jack Cable stands forever in acres of snow.

But he stands also for British virtues that have otherwise been buried in rhetoric – for resoluteness and determination, for resilience and courage, for tough-mindedness and daring. I summed it up. 'Jack Cable is as close as Britain comes to a national hero. He's Sir Edmund Hillary, Douglas Bader, Alex Ferguson and Michael Owen rolled into one. Yes?'

'Why not put it on a world stage?' suggested Sonny. 'Then you could throw in Marco Polo, Charles Lindbergh, Nelson Mandela and Muhammad Ali for good measure.'

I didn't argue. Enthusiasts are allowed to overstate.

'But how did he get to be a hero? What exactly did he do?'

Sonny rested his spoon carefully on his soup plate. He leaned forward and gave me a searching look. 'You're not kidding me?' he said. 'You really don't know?'

'Give me a break, Sonny. Jack Cable is a celebrity, but he's hardly Santa Claus.

Anyway, I had better things to do in my younger years than to follow the exploits of an adrenaline junkie.'

'Uh-huh, Laura. Like crawling on your knees on the Dyfed coast, looking for ancient bits of tooth?'

I considered this a low blow. In my teens, thanks to a fifth-form history teacher who'd wowed me with a real Roman button, I'd developed a passion for ancient remains. I'd spent an entire half-term as a volunteer scraping away at the hard earth that covered a burial ground. I wouldn't do it now. But that didn't stop me resenting the scoff in Sonny's tone.

'Hands off my midden,' I warned.

He raised one dark eyebrow.

'Midden,' I explained. 'An ancient rubbish heap. One of the best sources of archaeological materials. I'm amazed you didn't know that.' The salad arrived; I picked up my fork and buried the hatchet. 'Let's call a truce, Sonny. An end to cracks about your taste in heroes, promise. But I still want the background on Cable.'

He poured us each a glass of iced water. 'Okay, Laura, since you've waved the white flag so prettily, I'll tell you what I know. Eighteen forty-five. That's when it started.'

'Amazing. Cable doesn't look a day over fifty.'

'Laura, this is serious.' Sonny waited until

I was safely tucked into my salad and then told me the whole story. How in the nineteenth century, during a wave of popular enthusiasm for polar exploration, the Admiralty had mounted a major expedition, led by Sir John Franklin, to the Arctic archipelago.

'The purpose?' It was a rhetorical question. Sonny was in full flood. 'To test out new screw propellers that made it possible to sail under steam and deliver broadsides at the same time; they beefed up British fighting capacity. To do scientific studies – magnetic observations and the like. To beat the Americans and the Russians in Arctic exploration. And – here's the clincher – to find a navigable northern route from the Atlantic to the Pacific. The legendary Northwest Passage.'

Sonny must have been waiting a long while for someone to ask him that question. It wasn't an answer, it was a lecture.

'And what happened?' Enough preamble, I thought. Let's cut to the chase.

He refused to be rushed. 'They set sail from Woolwich in May. The crew was thrumming with excitement. They were sure of success.'

'Why so confident?' If you can't beat 'em, join 'em.

'There had been attempts before, but this time everything was right. Franklin was an old hand at Arctic exploration; this was his fourth trip. Both his ships, HMS *Erebus* and HMS *Terror*, were veterans of Antarctic voyages. And, of course, they were equipped as no expedition before.'

'Of course,' I said.

Sonny gave me a warning glance, but carried on. 'Their bows were overlaid with iron to withstand the ice. They had a new hot-water system to warm the cabins, and reserve engines that could push them along at four miles an hour. They even had an ingenious device for raising the screw propellers clear of the ice.' He pushed his plate aside. 'And when it came to the stores, Laura, it was no expense spared. The ward-rooms were fitted out with cut glass and china and Victorian silver. Each ship had a library of twelve hundred volumes, and slates and arithmetic books so that classes could be held, and a hand-organ that would play fifty different tunes.'

'A life on the ocean wave, eh, Sonny? How long did the voyage take?'

'It took forever,' Sonny said.

For a second or two, I didn't understand.

The waitress handed him a dessert menu. He passed it on to me without a glance. 'You see, Laura, they never returned. The two ships simply disappeared.' He shook his head. 'Franklin and his crew – one hundred and thirty officers and men – had hand-organs and heavy silver, but they didn't have whatever it took to survive the Arctic winter.'

He looked at the waitress, who was piling dishes up her arm and pretending not to listen. 'I'll have my usual,' he said. 'The crêpe with chocolate sauce, marshmallow and whipped cream.'

'Sonny!' I laughed. I couldn't decide whether I was aghast or impressed.

'It comes from thinking about all that cold and snow,' he said.

'One hundred and thirty deaths would give anyone the shivers.'

The waitress paused and looked at me. Her expression said, *Been here before.*

'You guessed it,' I said. 'Make it two.' I took mental stock. 'Look, Sonny, the Franklin expedition sounds like a boys'-own adventure. But how does Jack Cable fit in? He wasn't around in – what was it? – eighteen forty-five.'

'Be patient and all will be revealed. Forty expeditions searched for traces of Franklin and his party in the immediate decades after their disappearance. They never found either ship. The search continued on and off for almost a hundred and forty years, without success. Then Jack Cable came along. Twelve years ago, he set out with a party of twenty and scoured the area near O'Reilly Island. They found pieces of copper sheeting, bronze nails, iron bolts. They found the weathered skulls of two Caucasians and a dog. And finally, using sonar equipment and divers, they found the wreck of the *Erebus*. She'd lain there undiscovered, in only thirty metres of water, for a century and a half.'

'Were there bodies inside?'

'A couple of skeletons. And a sealed container with a document that told the full story of the original expedition.'

Two steaming crêpes were slid on to the table. Sonny tucked in like there was no tomorrow. I asked my question.

'So Jack Cable is famous for locating the remains of an old sailing ship?' I couldn't keep the disappointment out of my voice. 'I had thought there was more than that. Something more – well, heroic.'

'If it's a hero you want, you can't go wrong with Cable,' Sonny declared, loyal to the last. 'He's a great explorer. He knows everything there is to know about navigation and tides and landforms and currents. He has intuition and vision and–' He checked himself. 'And besides that, he found something that had eluded all the others. Your crêpe, Laura. Don't let it go cold.'

'I guess my eyes are bigger than my stomach, Sonny.' Up close and personal, the crêpe had lost its glamour. It had taken on a sickly edge.

He reached across and speared a morsel.

'Now you tell me, Laura – I've been the picture of patience – what exactly are you doing for Jack Cable?'

Jack Cable. A man, Sonny said, who could find things.

'How much do you know about Cable's personal life?'

Sonny considered. 'Extraordinary-looking wife, yes? They married young. After the tragedy, Olivia Cable wrote an account of the disappearance. Became famous in her own right.'

I sat up. 'What did you say?'

'You didn't know about the tragedy? Their child died a long time ago. Drowned–'

I interrupted. 'It's because of the child that they've hired me. But what's this about Olivia Cable? She wrote an account of the disappearance?'

'That's all I know. Do you mind?' Sonny pulled my plate towards him.

'Not at all.' I was glad to see the back of the crêpe; the sight of oozing marshmallow was making me queasy.

I looked away. It was still blowing outside. Clots of dark cloud were scudding across the sky.

Sonny polished off my crêpe as if it were an after-dinner mint. I guess it's true what they say. It's an ill wind that blows nobody any good.

# Chapter 6

The outskirts of Cambridge have changed over the past twenty years. On the southern approaches to the city, under the pressure of population growth, there's been a slide towards suburban sprawl. In Trumpington, for example, a semicircular parade of shops coils on to an open patch of lawn on the High Street as a reminder of a time when things were smaller in scale; but even so, you can see the stretch marks: the small close packed with modern housing, the pub pressed back into service after years of disuse, the estate agent's office crowding the corner by the war memorial. And then, of course, there's the traffic.

But once you make the turning into Church Lane – once you pass the Unicorn, on your way to Grantchester – you are out of the suburban rut and into a rural landscape. It's an imposing sort of rural, to be sure. Not a rutted lane between turnip fields, but the cool sanctuary of a stand of chestnut trees. Not the bleak bus shelters of a fenland village, but Trumpington Hall in seclusion behind a plantation of pines. Not tumbledown sheds, but fine farm buildings of timber and stone, and equipment that's more BMW than pickup truck.

Grade II-listed rural, you could call it.

I drove slowly, glancing at Liam from time to time out of the corner of my eye; wondering how to crack that adolescent shell of indifference.

I hadn't known until the last minute whether or not he'd come. Before we'd separated at the Black Swan, I'd arranged to pick him up on Mill Road the next day at twelve o'clock sharp. I was there at eleven. I took up position on a bench near the telephone kiosks with an excellent view of the junction. Yesterday's copy of the *Cambridge Evening News* obscured my face. I wanted to watch Liam arrive, in hopes of an answer to three simple questions: the direction he came from, how he travelled, and with whom.

After a few minutes I was joined by a tall man with a big black beard. His suit was brown. His feet were bare. He stared at his fingers and muttered to himself.

I skimmed a news article about school arson in Swavesey. I flipped through mini-accounts of world events. There was still no sign of Liam.

The man with the beard had bent forward to examine his feet. His toes, like his chin, were covered in hair.

'Gonna be here long?' he mumbled.

78

Was this question aimed at me? I wondered. I looked directly at him.

He turned away. He inspected his feet with greater intensity. Then he mumbled again: 'Gonna be here long?' From the direction of his gaze, I half expected the toes to respond, but they didn't. They just lay there, silent and hairy.

No sense beating around the bush. 'Are you talking to me?'

He acknowledged my question by lifting the little finger of the hand nearest me. He wedged his fists tightly in his lap. His gaze remained fixed on his feet.

'Only I'm expecting some people,' he said.

Oh, so that was it. He was entertaining. He wanted me gone.

'Don't worry, I'll be off soon. I'm waiting for a young fellow who often sits on the wall over there and plays the guitar. Do you know him?'

I must have waved a hand too near the bearded man. He strained in the other direction, like a boat with a list. He began to shake his head from side to side. It moved slowly at first – a recognisable *no* – and then faster and faster, as if it had acquired a life of its own.

He wouldn't accept money from me, though he looked as if he needed it. I had to do something. I picked my way through the traffic, crossed the street to Lally's newsagent's. I checked the area in front of the church – no sign of Liam. I dashed to the fridge at the back of the shop, picked up a bottle of juice, dropped some coins on the counter and made my way outside again. I'd been a minute, max.

When I reached the street, the bearded man was gone. Liam was sitting under the naked branches of the cherry tree, watching the traffic.

Liam and I made the short journey to the Cables' home in Grantchester in an uneasy silence. He shrugged off my attempts at conversation. He wasn't rude, just disengaged. I asked whether he'd grown up around here. He gave me a back-off kind of smile, but said nothing. I asked him when he'd first tried busking; he couldn't recall. I asked him what he knew about Olivia Cable. Not much, he said. She seems like a nice lady.

I tried to pinpoint Liam's mood. Compared with the day before, he seemed dispirited, I thought, or distracted – like somebody mulling over a problem. He had less warmth than he'd had during our meeting in the pub. He seemed not much interested in anything. Until, that is, we crossed the river.

'We're in Grantchester now,' I told him. I must have sounded like a tour guide who was counting the minutes to home.

He sat forward in the car, and focused on the landscape for the first time. He twisted around and peered at the Brasley Bridge as it faded behind us into the distance.

I felt I was getting somewhere at last. 'Perhaps you know Grantchester? Rupert Brooke, the war poet, lived here. You may have heard that famous line – the one about honey for tea.'

If Liam had heard it, he wasn't telling. But he stared at the scenery now with frank curiosity. He craned his neck to look at the millpool as we passed, at the Old Mill, at the sign that marked the entrance to Cantelupe Farm. He stared as if one of these landmarks held a secret. Finally he spoke.

'Where's Grantchester Meadows?'

'In that direction, over there.' I waved an arm. 'Would you like me to take you down? We've got time. They're not expecting us at the Dower House for another half an hour.'

His 'no' was emphatic, as if the prospect of a stroll in the meadows by the river was faintly alarming. He added a perfunctory 'thanks'. It didn't make us mates, but it suggested that I had Liam's attention at last.

'This is the River Cam?' he asked.

'If you're a stickler, all of the river upstream of Laundress Green becomes the Granta. But to hell with sticklers. Call it the Cam if you like.'

81

He leaned back in the car and relaxed.

'Cool,' he said.

I felt proud of myself. *Cool* was a clear sign of progress.

I drove slowly from then on. The road zigzagged upwards between walls over-shaded by stately trees, with bare branches studded with rooks' nests. Sometimes the homes behind the walls were visible, like the Old Vicarage, and sometimes not. We passed a pair of sober wooden signs that marked the entrance to the Orchard Tea Room. We passed the massive roofs of Riversdale. There was one more sharp corner where a chestnut tree stood sentinel, and then the scene opened and we emerged from the dappled gloom of the Mill Way into the ivory brightness of a winter's afternoon.

Here the Mill Way ran along the lower reaches of a hillside, with a thick hedgerow on the right. It nudged the hedge for a distance and then curved up towards the breast of the hill, becoming The High Street, Grantchester, as it climbed. The Church of St Andrew and St Mary stood proud three-quarters of the way to the top. The road passed within its shadow. Then it turned right and disappeared into the spiky tops of the trees on its way into the centre of the village.

'That's where we're going, there,' I said. 'That's where the Cables live.' I pointed from the one spot on the Mill Way where you could catch a glimpse. Liam was fiddling with the radio, he missed his chance.

The Cables' home had been positioned in some earlier century as if for maximum privacy. In the top right-hand corner of the hillside, the bulk and the blunt tower of the church and the tall trees that unfurled above it commanded the eye. Lower down on the left, just inside the brick wall that separated the Cables' farmland from the road, was an imposing series of stone outbuildings. The Dower House was nudged up into trees on the high horizon. Discreetly positioned between the outbuildings and the church, it could easily pass unnoticed.

We followed the curve of the wall and swung left, immediately before the church, between a sturdy pair of posts. The house sat to the right of the long drive, in a pocket formed by the meeting of two stands of trees. On one side, enormous pines shielded it from the fields beyond; on the other, a stand of broad-leaves was thick enough even in winter to obscure the view of St Andrew and St Mary's.

The house itself was shaped like a letter E. Three wings projected towards the drive, each with its own distinctive design –the leading wall fronted by a massive set of chimneys in one case, by a windowed porch in another. Part of the house had been surfaced in dull brick that was mottled with age. The rest, like the paintwork around the casement windows, was rendered in white. The roofline was higgledy-piggledy, the outline informal. The effect was impressive and yet homely, an elegant expression of money at ease with itself.

The house – indeed, Grantchester Farm as a whole – had an empty noonday feel. But as I swung my legs out of the car, there were footsteps on the drive behind me. I turned and saw Olivia. Presumably she'd been standing alongside the drive, among the trees, watching for us. We must have passed her on our way in. I stood by the car and waited to greet her. She scarcely noticed me. Her attention was locked on the passenger door, from which Liam would alight.

But he didn't.

After a few seconds of silence, I glanced in. Liam was slouched in the seat, arms behind his head, elbows akimbo, as if he might have dozed off, but his eyes were open wide. He was peering through the windscreen with wonder on his face. Taking it all in – the house, the chimneys, the casement windows. The bright slash of winter jasmine by the front door. The border collies that burst around the house in a spurt of energy, and came banging their black tails against the side of the car.

I crouched down so that my eyes were on a level with his. 'Not bad?' I asked.

He seemed about to smile. The candid brown eyes looked at me with a gleam almost conspiratorial. Then the enthusiasm drained away as swiftly as it had come, and he shrugged. His expression disclaimed the interest that had sparked there seconds before.

'Mrs Cable is waiting.'

She stood behind the car, perfectly still.

Liam unfolded himself slowly from the Saab. He tossed me an uneasy glance over the roof of the car, and then addressed himself to Olivia. He cleared his throat. 'Hi,' he said. 'Nice house.'

I'll say this for Liam; he made no attempt to turn my client's head with the gift of the gab. But to look at Olivia, you might have thought he'd announced that she'd won the lottery. She burst into smiles, skipped across the driveway like a child and, taking his reluctant hand in hers, pulled him into the house.

I looked around for somewhere to park. The outbuildings I'd seen from the road provided the nearest shelter. In the past they might have housed horses or farm machinery; now they were faced with scaffolding. Renovations were under way. I decided not to park amongst the rubble; didn't want to risk a chisel through the roof.

I moved a few yards further down the drive, put the car into reverse and eased it underneath the massive branch of an ancient yew tree. It was cool and still there, and dark, like a cave. I sat for a moment, gazing out.

The farm was not nearly as empty as it had seemed at first glance. To a city girl like me, accustomed to crowds, rural spaces can easily appear barren because you don't know where to look or how to read the signs. You have to take a moment to focus. You have to allow yourself to be still.

And as I sat still, as my eyes adjusted to the gloom under the tree and the relative brightness beyond, things began to appear. In the old stable, something flashed in the shadows. And again. I realised finally that there was a workman seated on a pile of rubble, reading a tabloid newspaper. The movement as he turned the page was caught by a ray of light that sliced through a window in the stone wall.

Then off to my right, at the far end of an open field, a Land Rover jounced along close to a line of poplars. As I watched, the vehicle stopped. Two men clambered out and headed up the hill, striding in sequence side by side, until they were beyond my line of vision. One of them carried a shotgun under his arm. Jack Cable, I thought, and someone else – not the stocky man I'd seen with him at Hobbs Pavilion, but a man who more closely resembled Jack in build and carriage. Did the Cables have another son besides Timmy? They hadn't said so at our first meeting.

But then, I thought – kicking myself – I hadn't asked.

One final, telling sign of activity. Above the top of the wall that shielded Grantchester Farm from the road, a head appeared, followed by a small torso. Someone had lifted a child above the wall so she could get a decent view. Even sturdy Cambridgeshire brick, it seemed, didn't prevent Jack Cable from paying a price for celebrity.

I picked up my palm-top and attempted, belatedly, to enter today's appointment, When I next looked up, Liam was standing in the driveway, hands shoved into the pockets of his black jeans. He wore a disengaged air that could equally be boredom or vexation. He looked every inch a teenager.

Every inch a teenager, perhaps, but miles more good-looking than most. The young have a head start on beauty, of course. But Liam was catwalk material. His wide forehead, the strong planes of his face, his lanky grace – these afforded him a physical charisma that is as rare among sixteen-year-old boys as a clean bedroom. Now that I was used to it, even the bruise on his forehead didn't detract.

He scanned the land in front of the house, searching for something. After a moment he turned and spotted my car tucked away under the yew tree. He gave me a wave. I shoved my palm-top back into the glove compartment.

By the time I reached Liam, Olivia was there. She spoke in a voice so low that I didn't catch the words, only the tone of entreaty. She waved her arm towards some point behind the house.

Liam gave a shrug of compliance. 'If you want,' he said, 'I don't mind.' It would be hard to imagine a more noncommittal *yes*.

'Laura, there you are.' Pinker than usual with the effort of persuasion, Olivia explained, 'There's a car around the back that used to be Jack's pride and joy. An E-type Jag. Hasn't been used in years. Liam and I are going to have a look.' She cast him a shy glance as if checking that he hadn't withdrawn his consent. Then, with less enthusiasm, she offered to include me. 'Would you like to come?'

Over Olivia's shoulder, the blunt nose of the Land Rover edged into view. It stopped at a fence. The passenger sprang out to open the gate.

'I'll join you later.'

Olivia took it as tact. She scampered off, the panels of her flared skirt flipping around her ankles. She touched Liam lightly to steer him in the right direction. He fell into step with apparent good grace, but moved a few inches to the side. Mrs Cable's hand slipped from his shoulder.

On the boundary between the driveway and the grove of trees there was a small granite post. I took a step up and balanced on the top of it to make room for the vehicle. The Land Rover bounced along the rutted drive and braked a few feet away.

The men who stepped from the vehicle were alike in more ways than one. Each of them was tall and spare. Though one was bearded and the other not, they had kindred expressions. Both their faces were stamped with determination and strength; both were unleavened by humour.

Jack Cable was the elder by twenty years at least, and his adventures were written on his body: in the rough and reddened skin that showed through the open collar of his shirt, in the slight stoop of his shoulders, in the hint of a limp, in the lines of his face. The other man was in his twenties. There was something about his bearing that conveyed the impression that he'd never really been young.

My client didn't bother to close the door of the vehicle. Hands buried in the pockets of his Barbour, he strode towards me and took up a position only inches away. He would have seemed composed but for the faint persistent jangle of keys.

'Is he here?' Jack asked.

I looked pointedly at the younger man, who had moved quickly in to stand shoulder to shoulder with Jack. As I did so, I picked up the trace of a sound from behind me, a slither, as if someone had brushed the branches of the huge old tree under which I'd sheltered.

The other two didn't seem to notice. Jack hurried through the introductions. 'My nephew, Robin Armstrong,' he said. 'Olivia's brother Max is Robin's father.' He turned to his nephew and added, 'This is the detective I was telling you about.'

At that instant I heard a click from behind me. I'd recognise it anywhere. It was the door on the driver side of my Saab.

I tried to concentrate on the nephew. Robin offered me a smile of elaborate formality, as if he'd seen one illustrated in an etiquette book and was trying it out. He needed more practice; it wouldn't pass as the genuine article. 'You've got quite a job ahead of you, Miss–'

'Principal,' I said. 'Laura Principal. You don't envy me my task, Mr Armstrong?'

Jack Cable glanced impatiently towards the house. Robin answered anyway. 'My Aunt Livi's a wonderful woman. But on the subject of her missing son, she loses objectivity, as any mother would.' He turned abruptly back towards his uncle. 'The foreman's in the old barn. Shouldn't we have a word about those braces?'

Jack Cable hesitated. He glanced towards the stone building, and then at me again, as if he'd forgotten what he'd asked me. I helped him out.

'Liam's around the back with Mrs Cable,' I said. 'Inspecting a car.'

'And why aren't you with them?'

The soles of my feet were beginning to feel tender from the pressure of the post, but I wasn't climbing down just yet.

'I'll join them soon. Liam isn't going to harm your wife now, Jack, not with all of us within shouting distance. Anyway, she needs the odd moment alone with him.'

Jack considered this and nodded. He and Robin clambered back into the Land Rover, but before driving off he leaned out of the window with a final instruction.

'The odd moment,' he said.

When they'd disappeared through a stone arch into the barn, I headed for the tree. Through the gloom I could make out someone sitting behind the wheel of my car. She was looking straight out at me.

I crouched down next to the window. 'You are—?'

'Catherine,' she said, staring me in the eye. There was something bold in the tilt of her chin. 'Catherine Cable. Daughter, eldest child – only surviving child, probably – of Olivia Cable, writer, and Jack Cable – well–'

'Well?'

'Everyone knows Jack Cable,' she said. 'And who are you?'

'Laura Principal, private investigator. I've been hired to stick close to a young man whom your mother believes might be Timmy. And you, Catherine Cable, eldest child, are sitting in my car.'

'Oh,' she said. Not about the car, but about my occupation. Suddenly her breathing was audible.

'You didn't know?'

'No one tells me anything.' A hint of petulance. Or was it panic? Then backtracking. 'Oh, I knew about the boy, of course. Another one of Mother's hopefuls.'

'Do you always climb into strange cars?'

Catherine's breathing became more ragged. Her eyes, almost as vividly coloured as her mother's, darkened and her forehead creased in a frown. 'I saw my father coming in from the fields,' she said. 'I've just recovered from a bout of flu. I was going to ask him if he would drive me back to Birmingham at the weekend – back to university.'

Her wheeze was getting sharper. She scrabbled in the pocket of her fleece, pulled out an inhaler and took two sharp puffs.

'There.' She inhaled, shallowly at first, and

then more deeply, and forced a grin. 'Only asthma,' she announced. 'It plays havoc with my cool image.' In one swift movement she swung open the car door and stepped out on to the carpet of needles under the tree.

'You didn't speak to your father?'

'No. Didn't you notice? That *things-to-do, people-to-see* expression on his face? *Not now, Catherine,* he'd have said. That's why I took the liberty of clambering into your car. I was hiding.' She shrugged, as if it didn't matter. 'Do you know where my mother is?'

'She's taken Liam to see the E-type.'

'Oh God!' Catherine knocked her wrist against her forehead in a show of exasperation. 'They'll be hours. It's that bonnet; boys always see it as a penis extension. Cousin Robin's been angling to take possession ever since puberty.'

'Don't you like it?'

'Me, I wouldn't have it if you filled it to the brim with David Beckhams.' She returned the inhaler to her pocket and looked at me as if she were trying to decide whether I could be trusted or not. Something must have clicked. 'Come on,' she said, putting out her hand to grasp mine as a little girl might. 'You want to see the house?'

The Cables' home was larger inside than it had seemed from the outside. Much of the ground floor was taken up by a massive sitting room. It had two levels: a stone fireplace with a wrought-iron log-basket in the upper portion, and in the lower chamber a chic arrangement of sofas with French doors that looked out on to a garden. A trio of stairs linked the two areas; those, and the floors throughout, were of pale polished oak. While I took it all in, Catherine Cable kept up a running commentary on the rooms and the people who lived in them.

'That's Dad's chair, over there,' she said. 'If ever you need to find him, that's the first place to look.' She wasn't pointing to either of the pale yellow sofas, with their plump cushions, but to an antique wooden chair that was as upright and angular as a piece of Shaker furniture, as lovely to look at, as unyielding. Jack Cable's idea of comfort bordered on the masochistic. I guess that's an adventurer for you.

Directly opposite Jack's chair there was a wall of shelving. It housed a music system and a substantial collection of albums and discs. These were arranged in an orderly fashion, carefully lined up, without photographs or trinkets to disrupt the uniform display. No *objets* – except for one. Off to one side, against the background of a whitewashed alcove, stood a sculpture of a head in terracotta. The features included the short nose, pointed chin and large grave eyes of a small child.

I examined Catherine's round cheeks and her pronounced chin. I couldn't tell if it was her. I don't have the kind of imagination that can see the child in the woman.

'Is this you, Catherine? Or your little brother?'

'Neither,' she said. 'It's certainly not me, but I would say it's not really Timmy either. An artist put it together from photos, after the disappearance. It's supposed to show what Timmy might have looked like a couple of years on from his disappearance. But it's not at all the way I remember him.'

I sat down on the sofa and left room for Catherine to join me. She remained standing, staring at the sculpture.

'What can you tell me about Timmy, Catherine? How do you remember him?'

'I was only seven, for God's sake!' This outburst was delivered in a peppery tone that said, *You should know better.* 'It was twelve years ago! What do you expect from me?'

'I'm sorry. I wasn't looking for a photofit. I just wondered what kind of an image your brother left behind.'

'The truth is, Miss Principal–' She walked slowly towards me.

'Laura.'

'The truth is, Laura, I don't know what I remember. I have an image, but how much of it is my imagination? Or cobbled together from what the others tell me? Or taken from dreams?'

'But this image, however hazy...'

'Oh, it's not hazy at all.' Catherine slipped out of her loafers and settled herself on the arm of the sofa. Her bare feet nestled on the empty seat. 'It's very precise. If you really want to know...?'

I nodded.

'When I think of Timmy, I think of someone small and fast and fierce, like quicksilver. Someone with swift little steps, who only comes up to here on me–' Catherine raised her hand toward her chest, and then giggled and retracted it, caught out by the irrelevance of comparing the size he was twelve years ago with the size she was now. 'Someone who looks at me as if he is committing every line of my face to memory. Who is tiny and thin and apparently frail, but who always knows precisely what he wants.' She glanced back at the bust of her brother and gave a vehement shake of her head. 'Nothing like *that*,' she said, 'with those dull eyes.'

I had to agree: the eyes were the least successful aspect of the piece. The pupils had been gouged out so that there was a variation in tone and shadow, but they still looked blank and unfocused. They looked – let's face it – inhuman.

'I'm sorry,' Catherine said. She said it as if

the inability to see her brother in the terracotta image was a failure on her part. As if she hadn't looked closely enough or with sufficient care.

'The artist was trying to reproduce the bone structure, Catherine. He–'

'She.'

'She looked for the shape of the eye and the curve of the skull. You looked for the person inside. The two images were bound to be different.'

Catherine had had enough. She stood up, abruptly, and slid her feet into her shoes, then slapped her hands briskly together. 'Well,' she said, 'here we are again, as ever, talking about Timmy. I suggest we move on. You want to see the pool, Laura?'

When she said *as ever, talking about Timmy*, she obviously meant some 'we' that didn't include me. I let it go.

'You have a swimming pool?' A warm pool in the line of duty is the kind of occupational perk that I dream about.

'You could call it that,' she said, as if it were a joke, and led the way.

The conservatory was built in the Victorian style, with glass panels suspended in a delicate framework of wood. It was remarkable for its fine proportions and for the fluent curves of the pool in the centre.

Even more remarkable was the fact that the pool was as dry as a bone. There was no turquoise shimmer, no gurgle from the pump. The sides of the pool were studded with tiny tiles in silver and blue.

'Your parents keep it empty?'

Catherine nodded.

'Even in the summer? That must be a disappointment to you and your friends.'

'I detest swimming,' Catherine declared. She jumped down on to the floor of the pool. 'Besides, it has other uses.' Sure enough, lying at the shallow end, where the bottom levelled out, was a collection of heavy silver-coloured balls.

I climbed down the chrome ladder into the deep end. Catherine made the first move. She rolled a ball up the slope with a confident underarm. I slipped into bowling position as if it weren't ten years since I'd played pétanque, but my throw had too little force behind it. The silver ball mounted a slight incline in the direction it ought to go, and then rolled back and landed at my feet. Its rough weight bumping across the tiled floor made a noise like far-off thunder.

'A crap shot,' Catherine said. It was a dispassionate assessment rather than a calculated insult.

I admitted it. 'Will you show me the rest of the house? I can do the walking thing better than the bowling thing.'

'I hope you can, because it's upstairs and downstairs the whole way.'

She was right. We went up to the dining room, and down to the kitchen, where there was an aroma of roasting chicken. We ended up in a large cluttered bedroom under the eaves.

'My studio,' Catherine announced, with obvious pride. She crossed the room in a series of pirouettes and bounced on to the bed.

The term 'studio' couldn't have been less appropriate. Catherine's studio looked like a little girl's room, right down to the kidney-shaped dressing table draped in chintz. Everything in it – from the teddy bear and the pile of pillows on the bed to the faded copy of *The Water Babies* to the pink-painted wicker chair – everything seemed to be old, seemed to be well-worn, seemed to be dated. It was as if Catherine had slid from early childhood to late teens without the growing-up process making any impact at all on the room in which she lived. As if her room, and the life she lived there, remained locked in childhood.

As if – it was a horrible thought – it had been her, and not Timmy, who had disappeared.

I lowered myself gingerly into the wicker armchair. It seemed very small and very frail. 'Tell me,' I said, 'about your cousin Robin.'

'I'll tell you about them all. What do you want to know?' And with that, Catherine spilled the beans. She turned her family's history into a fairy tale.

'It's really very simple,' she said. 'Olivia Armstrong and her little brother Max grew up in Norfolk, in a crumbling country home' – Catherine rolled the *r* in *crumbling* – 'with a crumbling country father who didn't care much for children once he was widowed, even his own. Jack Cable was Olivia's escape. He came on to the scene, all dash and daring, and swept her away to Cambridge. For a time they were poor but happy. Then the crumbling father died, leaving money, and Olivia and Max and Jack had a bright idea for a business.'

'Which was?'

'Is,' Catherine corrected me. 'You've not heard of Cable Explorations?'

'Is it successful?'

'You mean does it make money? Oh yes, indeed. Pots and pots of it, by arranging corporate sponsorship for people with their hearts set on far-flung parts. Ever since Dad found Franklin's ship – you know about that? – the consultancy has boomed.'

'Your cousin Robin – is he part of the business too?' And I added, as an after-thought, 'Does he live here?'

'Good heavens, no. On both counts. Robin is studying economics at Cambridge

100

University. Got a First in his Part One; I could only manage an Upper Second. Robin, unlike yours truly, has ambition.'

Somehow that didn't surprise me. That young man had looked not merely lean, but lean and hungry.

'Robin's mother ran off years ago. Robin and Uncle Max live near Cleybourne,' Catherine continued, 'in a property left by my grandfather. My mother and father have a house there too, but that's where Timmy disappeared, so we haven't been for years. Oh, and Max runs the business, by the way. Calls himself the CEO.' She looked puzzled. 'What made you think that Robin might live here?'

'Oh, just that he seemed to be very familiar with the farm.'

'He loves to play lord of the manor, Robin does. To be fair, he and Dad spend a lot of time together. They're – well, they have a lot in common. You know, men's things. Hunting, sports.'

'Cars?'

'That sort of thing.' She shrugged to show her indifference. 'Whereas I'm more like my Uncle Max. A bit clumsy, a bit of a clown. You wouldn't describe either of us as impressive. That's an adjective people save for Daddy and Robin.'

She tried to take the sting out of this statement by punctuating it with a merry smile. It didn't work.

'You're not clumsy, Catherine. From what I've seen, I'd say you're a nice little mover.'

Catherine's thick hair was tree-bark brown, and scraped back into an artless ponytail. She tugged off the band and shook her hair free. 'That's just my dance classes. When it comes to sports, I'm a disaster. Last to be chosen, that's me. But that doesn't matter – what I meant to say about Max is that, underneath his bluster and his funny way of speaking, he is very kind and very loyal.'

'Loyal – to your father?' Jack Cable was the kind of man, I guessed, to whom people would commit.

'To the whole family. Like when I had a run-in with a teacher at St Mary's because I had one flipping cigarette. It was blatantly unfair and my parents were away. But Max was a tiger. He made that teacher back down and I didn't get disciplined. My father never even knew about it.'

'How would your father have felt if he had found out?'

'My father,' said Catherine – and this time there was no smile – 'is an old-fashioned sort of man. People might think he's a flashy sort, like other celebrities, but they'd be dead wrong. My father is a man who always does what's right.' Catherine said this solemnly. She demonstrated 'upright' for a moment with her posture. Then she went on.

'Like even after T-Day – oh, sorry. That's shorthand for the day that Timmy disappeared. It sounds flippant, I know. I don't mean it to. It's just that...'

'*The day that Timmy disappeared* is kind of a mouthful. You were saying about your father?'

'Just that a few months later, he went away to the Arctic. My mother was really wiped out by what had happened, she didn't want him to go. But the expedition was planned, they had sponsorship, and my father didn't feel he could back down. He had promised to try to find the remains of the Franklin expedition, and he was bloody well going to do it. It wasn't easy for either of them.'

'Not easy for them. How was it for you, Catherine?'

Catherine stepped to the window. It was a dormer, with frilly curtains tied back by bows. Hanging near the window was a pair of binoculars. Catherine lifted them off the hook. She shooed away a pigeon and leaned her elbows on the ledge, looking through the lenses at the scene below.

I tried again. 'What I mean is this. For months there'd been great unhappiness in your family. Your little brother was gone. And now your father was leaving you. It could easily have seemed to a child – you were what, seven? – as if everything was falling apart.'

*And you could feel abandoned.*

Catherine gave a squeal like a six-year-old fan in the front row of a Spice Girls concert. She backed away from the window and pressed the binoculars into my hand. 'Etta and Joe are back. Look. Down by the barn.'

'Etta and Joe?' I took up position by the window and fiddled with the lenses. Sure enough, I saw a man and woman in animated conversation.

'Etta sort of runs things here. She's our housekeeper. And Joe does everything from repairs to occasional driving.'

It was odd being perched in the window, high up in the Dower House, looking down towards the barn. I had as clear a view of the couple as if I were standing next to them with my feet planted, like theirs, firmly on the rubble-strewn ground. Etta was in her mid-thirties, though her long pleated skirt and old-fashioned cardigan looked as if they belonged on a much older woman. She was wide-hipped and solidly built. She had a big, flat, round face on a long narrow neck, like a lollipop. Joe was considerably older and no beauty either. His hair had retreated leaving only a narrow grey band across the back of his head from ear to ear. He had pudgy lips and a suet complexion. Etta might be described as plain; Joe was almost comic-looking.

And then, as Etta backed away, pulling one end of a steel tape measure while Joe held the other, she surprised me. She stopped. 'Here,' she said, digging her heel into the ground, and smiled at Joe, and with that her face became for an instant bright and clear. She was almost pretty.

Catherine bubbled away behind me. 'You should meet them, they're way nice. Joe's cool. He's great with kids. He used to let me work with him around the farm. Don't be offended, though, if he doesn't speak to you. He really only talks to me, and of course to Etta. I think he's ashamed of his English or something. Come on,' she said, tugging at my hand, 'I'll take you to meet them.'

Her enthusiasm for Etta and Joe seemed genuine. More than just a pretext for avoiding my question about her father.

She bounced down the stairs and I followed after. 'And Etta?' I asked. 'Is she cool, too?'

Catherine stopped so suddenly that I almost ran into her. She turned to face me. 'Etta's probably the kindest person I know,' she said. 'On the day that it happened' – by now I didn't need to be told what *it* was – 'while Mother and Dad were tied up with the search, Etta looked after me. She shooed the police away, and she put me to sleep in her own bed. I love her,' Catherine said. She said it solemnly, and defiantly too, as if she imagined she might be challenged.

'I'm glad,' was all I said.

'Catherine!' someone called. 'Are you there?'

Catherine put her finger to her lips. 'It's my mother. And that boy. Please don't tell her where I am.' And with that, she bounded back up the stairs towards her eyrie in the roof.

Liam's meeting with Etta and Joe could have been difficult but wasn't. Joe set aside his digging as soon as we approached, wiped his palms down his overalls and shook hands all round. As Catherine had predicted, he said virtually nothing; but he followed the conversation closely, and from time to time beamed at Liam like a beacon.

Etta, for her part, talked a mile a minute, filling in each and every gap that arose in the course of the conversation. She seemed nervous as well as intrigued, but by guiding us to mundane topics, she took much of the awkwardness out of the encounter.

Joe and Etta spoke about their break in Leicester, visiting odds and ends of family. 'Too many cups of tea, too many slices of cake,' Etta chuckled, patting her roly-poly hips.

She praised the progress the workmen were making on the barn.

Most of all, she turned the conversation to the car. Liam's enthusiasm for the E-type made him more talkative than usual, and far more articulate.

'It's incredibly cool,' he said, catching my eye. 'Leather seats inside, and tortoiseshell dashboard. And the engine looks just like new. The whole car even smells new,' he added. He seemed overcome by the marvel of it.

I recalled what Olivia had said to her husband about Liam: *he even smells like Timmy.* It's true, I guess; how smell works at some level that is so distant from language that the memory isn't whittled away by time. How a whiff of an odour can take you back to a garden, to a stay in hospital. Even to breakfasts with your father.

'Timmy used to love riding in that car,' Olivia blurted out. The implicit comparison – Timmy, Liam – hung in the air like a holograph image, until Etta stepped in.

She spoke in a warm Midlands accent. 'I shall never forget,' she said, hugging her cardigan closer around her bosom with remembered delight, 'I shall never forget how he looked. One summer's day – hot, it was – I came across him and Mr Cable in the Jaguar. Timmy had nothing on but his nappy, and his skin was all pink and moist from the heat. He was standing up on the seat, holding on to the wheel. Holding on

107

with his little fists, and yanking it ferociously from side to side. "What are you doing, my little love?" I asked him. "Driving, driving, driving." That's what he said.'

Olivia broke in. 'And remember how he looked, Etta, when he was three or four, and Jack would take him out for a spin? They'd put the top down and turn the radio up to full volume. Timmy moved his arms in time to the music. As they drove off, all you could see of him were his little wrists, his little hands in the air, swinging from side to side.'

Olivia and Etta, taking pleasure in their memories, exchanged smiles. Then Olivia turned to Liam.

'Perhaps you'd like to drive it sometime, Liam. When you get your licence. When you're seventeen.'

A shadow passed across Liam's eager face.

His momentary uncertainty triggered something in Olivia.

'Where's Catherine?' She shaded her eyes against the winter sun and looked up towards the dormer window. There'd been a flicker of movement at the window; it quickly disappeared. 'I told her to be down early,' she said. She was clearly annoyed. 'She has to meet Liam.'

'I'll chase her up now. Do you want me to check the chicken while I'm in there?'

'Yes, Etta, thanks.'

When Etta opened the door, the black and

white collies bounded out and tore across the yard to join us. Liam crouched to receive them. He patted their backs and stroked them under the chin. He laughed as the larger of the two licked his face in greeting. 'All dogs should have big open spaces to run in,' he said. 'My dog would love it here.'

'You have a dog?' Olivia looked delighted. 'What kind?'

Liam described a lurcher by the name of Wonder. Short for Stevie Wonder, not the Wonder Dog, he said. Staying at the moment with a friend.

'Why don't you bring Wonder here? Give him a taste of the country? There's plenty of room.'

Liam looked as if he found this proposition interesting.

All of a sudden I felt a stab of unease. We'd only been here a few hours.

First the car.

Now the dog.

Things were moving fast.

# Chapter 7

## TWELVE YEARS EARLIER

*I won't sleep yet. I won't. Not for ten hours at least. Not for ten days.*

*Not until my daddy gets home.*

*I pressed the button and phoned him all by myself. I phoned him but he didn't answer. I left a message for him. 'I'm waiting for you, Daddy,' I said.*

*Mummy told me he'd be here after supper. But it's been after supper for ages now. It was after supper when I called Blackie in from the marsh. It was after supper when I had my bath. It was a way long time after supper when Mummy read me a story about the water babies and gave me a kiss and a cuddle and told me to sleep. 'But I want to see Daddy,' I said. 'Daddy is coming very, very soon. He must be coming. He said he would.'*

*Mummy said something funny then. What did she say? Mickey, what did Mummy say?*

*Mickey's eyes don't shine at night-time. They are dark and sort of flat like stones. But I can still see them.*

*I remember what Mummy said. 'Don't count on it, Timmy.' That's what she said. 'Don't count on it.'*

She looked funny when she said it. Like maybe she was cross. But then she smiled. 'Don't worry, baby,' she said. She tickled her fingers along my arm. 'Daddy's coming. When you wake up, for sure, your daddy will be here.'

'Will he take me to the beach?'

'I'll see to it,' she said.

# Chapter 8

Can you check out someone's background without heavying them?

That's what I'd asked Jack Cable when he'd given me this assignment. And that was the problem I pondered again as I chauffeured Liam back to the centre of Cambridge.

At lunch with the Cables Liam had been an amiable presence, but quiet. He'd eaten with gusto, taking second helpings of potatoes and thirds of pud; but he'd volunteered virtually nothing. His manner didn't encourage questions, and no one seemed prepared to push. Most of the time, one Cable or another held the floor in the desultory way that marks family meals; and the only real conversation in which Liam took part was when he and I swapped gossip about music. He busked with British folk tunes, but blues, especially Delta blues, was what he really loved.

I discovered that he knew things. Knew what a diddley bow was, and a bottleneck slider; knew the difference between a gospel and a field holler. Self-taught, he said; Liam might not be the quickest boy in class, but when something took his fancy, he could learn.

Jack Cable, I noticed, sat in bemused silence during this exchange. According to his CD collection, he was strictly a chamber music man. The expression on his face suggested that a twelve-bar blues might be music from another planet.

As we drove back down the Trumpington Road, Liam became talkative once more. His imagination was fired again by the thought of Jack Cable's convertible.

'Do you think she'd really let me drive it?'

'Olivia? I imagine so. But like the lady said – you'd need a licence. Ever had any driving lessons?'

'Sure. I used to take my sister's car up and down the driveway; I can even do a three-point turn.'

'Being able to drive is one thing. Being licensed is another.'

He looked at me blankly.

'You have to be seventeen,' I said. 'You need to have a birth certificate. You need to have a surname.'

There was a long pause. We stopped at the pedestrian crossing outside St Faith's school while a girl – she couldn't have been much more than Liam's age – struggled across with a double pushchair. Then we swung into Brooklands Avenue. I was concentrating on the road when Liam grabbed my wrist.

'I'm not going back,' he said.

'Back where?'

'Back home.'

His grip was too rough for comfort. Maybe, given that I was driving, too rough for safety. I shook it off.

'Tell me why you left, Liam. Did they give you a hard time?'

Liam twisted around in his seat so he was facing me. I didn't like the way he fingered the gear shift, but in the circumstances, I let it pass.

'When people see a kid who's left home, they always think the worst. Like, you know, maybe he's been–' He couldn't bring himself to say it.

'Abused?'

A vigorous nod. Liam was glad I'd said it and not him. 'That's exactly what they think. But I've never been – you know, abused. I had everything a boy could want – a BMX bike for my tenth birthday, computer games, guitar lessons. It's just that I felt stifled. I needed more space.' He gave me a defiant glance. 'So I left.'

'So you left.' I thought about it for a minute. Soon – too soon – we would reach the spot where Liam had asked to be dropped off. I decided to go the long way round, down Cherry Hinton Road and along the ring road, and then to come at Mill Road from the south. Liam didn't blink. That told me one thing: he didn't know this part of Cambridge.

'Does your mum know where you are?'

'She was probably glad to see the back of me. She never had much time for me anyway.' His voice wasn't angry, just resigned.

'What about the BMX bike?'

'That's for kids,' he said. There was a touch of indignation in his tone. 'I've outgrown it.'

'No, I mean, if your mother didn't care much for you, then why would she buy you expensive presents?'

'The bike was a gift from my sister. Gemma looks out for me, sends me money. She's kind of like a mother to me.'

'And your father?'

Liam rolled down the window. He leaned out and spat, then relaxed back again. Luckily, there was no one on the pavement.

'What father,' he said. It was a statement, not a question.

'You never knew him?'

'His name was Albert. It was just a passing thing between Mum and him. He was gone by the time I was born.'

'What was he like? Have you seen pictures?' Was there really an Albert? was what I meant, but Liam took my questions at face value.

'My mother said she destroyed them all.

Didn't want to be reminded of him.' He shivered and rolled the window up. 'I sometimes think she wishes I'd never been born.'

Liam was getting restless. I'd have to draw my questions to a close; we were only half a mile from the dropping-off point.

'Liam, if you don't want to talk about your family, that's all right. But tell me just one thing, OK?' The road narrowed and we almost scraped bumpers with a Robert Sayle delivery van. I braked in the nick of time.

Liam laughed at me. 'Who needs driving lessons now?' It was the first joke he'd made in my hearing. One more thing clear, I thought: Liam wasn't cut out for a career in comedy.

But that really set me thinking. How someone asks a simple question – *What's he like, then?* – and off we go, summing up an individual, tossing off a thumbnail sketch like a pavement artist. But making these judgements is a lot harder than it's cracked up to be. Harder because the person who is shy and uncertain with strangers may be the life and soul of the party when he's with friends. Because personality and attitude alter with circumstance and time.

And Liam? As far as I could judge from my brief acquaintance, the dominant note in his temperament was passive good humour. He took few initiatives. His reactions to things going on around him seemed easy to read, transparent and fairly predictable, as if his emotions were tidily arranged along the surface.

I'd seen him bored and distracted. I'd seen him wary, when confronted with something new. And after the tour of the Jaguar, I'd seen him excited, even covetous. But what I saw in Liam most of the time was a willingness to oblige, as long as it wasn't too much trouble. A bland amiability.

Was there more?

Just before the railway bridge, I threw another question. Snuck another look.

'Tell me, Liam, did anyone in your family – your sister Gemma or your mum, perhaps – ever mention a child who disappeared off a beach in East Anglia? Maybe using it, as lots of parents do, to warn you not to speak to strangers?'

Liam was slumped in his seat, chewing his bottom lip, deep in thought. His eyes were narrowed. My question had provoked a reaction I hadn't seen before and, like his other reactions, its meaning was hard to mistake.

At that moment Liam wasn't amiable; he wasn't good-humoured; he wasn't excited. At that very moment, asked about a child on a beach, something calculating had pierced the bland demeanour.

Liam looked, in a word, shifty.

'I don't remember,' he muttered. Then he

glanced at me and brightened. 'But I'll tell you something, Laura. It's funny ... when I was a child, I had these two frightening dreams – nightmares, I guess. One of them takes place in a dusty yard on a hot day. I'm surrounded by these weird-looking birds, monster birds they are, way taller than me, and their eyes are black and piercing. They talk, in horrible garbled voices, and they're trying to tell me something but I can't understand what it is.'

Liam's leg was moving in an agitated way. It was clear he found the nightmare upsetting.

'And the other?'

'About a beach. About a man. About being dragged into a car.'

I waited for the traffic to clear and then turned into Guest Road, on the lookout for a parking space. I found it hard to concentrate. I found it hard to breathe.

'This man. What was he like?'

'Medium build, black hair. Sort of ordinary.' He anticipated my next question. 'Not like anyone I know.'

'Can you recall anything else from this dream? About the beach? The car?'

'I can remember colours. The beach was sandy, a kind of pale golden brown. The water and the sky were very blue. There was a pier nearby. That's it. That's all I can remember.'

I pulled the car up alongside a single yellow line and turned off the engine. 'Do you still have this nightmare, Liam?'

'No.' He shrugged and reached in the back for his guitar. 'It was all a long, long time ago.'

That evening I cocooned myself in bed. For some reason I felt as if I'd been used as a trampoline by a sumo wrestler. My back ached; the ache was right down in the base of the spine where you can't do a thing to bring relief. My head throbbed. I tried to drown the discomfort with two fingers of single malt whisky, but only succeeded in adding queasiness to my other complaints.

At seven thirty, the doorbell rang. It was Nicole. Judging by her outfit and her slicked-back hair, she'd just had a work-out, and she was even more bright-eyed and bushy-tailed than usual. I resisted an impulse to shut the door firmly in her face.

Nicole stepped inside without waiting to be asked. 'Are you ill, Laura?' she said when she saw my pyjamas. 'Or merely entertaining?'

'Neither, Nicole. I'm worn out, so I've gone into hibernation. Any signs of spring yet?'

'Not unless you count the rain. It's pissing it down.' Her trainers left mud tracks on my floor. 'And how have you reached this state of exhaustion? Serving summonses? Tracking down missing cats?'

'Hah bloody hah.'

Nicole Pelletier, former student of mine at Eastern University, and hot-shot detective inspector with the Cambridgeshire force, is tireless – she never tires of trying to provoke me. She likes to imagine that my job consists of kids'-stuff inquiries that leave hands clean and spirits high; she likes to pretend that being a private detective is nowhere near as challenging as police work. When it comes to the uniformed branch, she has a point; I'd be the first to concede that there's nothing in private work that's quite as dispiriting as pulling bodies out of a motorway pileup. But if I hadn't been too weary to argue the toss, I would have reminded her that private investigators have their fair share of hard graft and heartache.

'I'm not in the mood, Nicole.' I folded myself up on a floor cushion and took up a pose as pathetic as I felt. 'I feel dreadful.'

Nicole was next to me in seconds. She reached out and laid her palm on my forehead. Her hands were much like the woman herself – warm, blunt and capable to the core. 'You've not got a temperature,' she said.

'I told you, it's exhaustion.' Or something. 'Maybe food would help. You want to stay, Nicole? I could ring for Indian takeaway.'

She jumped at the chance. 'I've just been shopping. I'll deposit my ice cream in your freezer and rustle us up a stir-fry.'

'What flavour?'

'Well, aren't we the fussy one? How does pork, sweet peppers, five spice, that sort of thing, sound to you?'

'No, I meant the ice cream.'

Nicole laughed. 'Toffee crunch.'

The image of toffee crunch ice cream lifted my spirits. I plonked myself down at the kitchen table. While Nicole sautéed the pork, I helped myself to an ice cream hors d'oeuvre and plied her with questions. When the main course was ready, she took a big helping and I took a small one. It was an eccentric meal, but I began to feel better.

Nicole had been glowing when she arrived. The mention of my new clients, the Cables, brightened her up even further.

'Jack Cable? You mean that fit bloke who located the remains of the Franklin expedition?'

I nodded. Did everyone know Jack Cable's biography but me?

'Why's he hired you?' she asked. 'If it's not too confidential.'

Client confidentiality is important, of course. But I could hardly expect Detective Inspector Pelletier to help me out with information, as she often did, if I clammed up at a simple question.

'Never too confidential for you, Nicole,' I said.

Nicole has eyebrows so expressive they practically speak. I must have laid the anything-you-want-ma'am on a bit thick. She arched one now, and its message was poised between a question and a warning.

I rounded off my meal with another scoop of ice cream and launched into an account of the case.

For seven out of the nine terms of Nicole Pelletier's undergraduate years, she put more effort into perfecting her netball and her party technique than she did into her work. But when she joined the CID, that changed. She works hard and long. She analyses information like a junior minister with an eye on his senior's post. She excels, above all, at that most underrated of investigative skills – she listens.

She listened now with impeccable concentration as I related the story of the teenager who'd turned up on Mill Road. She knew little more than I did about Timmy's disappearance; twelve years is a long time, she pointed out, and it was the Norfolk Constabulary, not Cambridgeshire, who'd handled the case. But she volunteered to try to find someone in Norfolk who could tell me more.

Nicole refused to let me clear the table. 'No, you sit still. I've got bags of energy,' she said when we'd finished the meal. She hung her fleecy cardigan on the back of the chair and went to work, rinsing the dishes and quizzing me about the case. 'I know it's early days, Laura, but what's your gut feeling about this Liam?'

I popped up and put what little was left of the ice cream back in the freezer. Noticed the bottle of burgundy standing on the work surface; I must have been feeling spectacularly bad to have overlooked that.

'The intriguing thing about Liam,' I said, sitting down again, and wrestling with the corkscrew, 'the thing that makes him different from the others, is that he didn't come looking for the Cables. They've been approached plenty of times before by impostors. But in this case, Olivia Cable made the running. She saw Liam on Mill Road and gradually came to believe that he might be her missing child. I got the impression that she's never stopped noticing boys of the right age.

'As you would,' Nicole interjected. She ran a damp cloth over the table.

'Indeed. But this is the first time she's felt certain enough to follow it up.'

Nicole sat down again and accepted a glass of wine. She sipped, then picked up the bottle and inspected the label. 'Not bad,' she said.

'I found it in the cupboard.'

'Lucky you. What if he's working a scam, Laura? Maybe Liam knew she'd be on Mill Road. Maybe he deliberately attracted her attention. After all, being Jack Cable's heir would have its advantages.'

'I've been watching him closely to see how he's playing it. He doesn't give the impression of being out for what he can get.'

'Meaning?' Nicole looked sceptical. Police work doesn't develop the trusting side of your nature.

I gave her the instance in the pub; Olivia was hustling Liam to come to Grantchester but he gave every sign of wanting her to back off. That didn't fit with the idea of someone who was eager to be accepted as the prodigal son. Nor did Liam's diffidence on our drive to Grantchester. He hadn't seemed to relish the visit at all.

'If this is a boy dead set on deception – on convincing the Cables that he is their son – he isn't going about it with particular zeal.' I was thinking aloud now. 'If I had to make a bet, it would be that Liam hasn't the cunning to set up a scam like this. Hasn't the guile, on the whole.'

Except, perhaps, for that one moment in the car. When I'd asked him whether he'd known about Timmy Cable's disappearance. When he'd looked shifty.

'And the Cables. How do they relate to Liam?'

'Very differently,' I said. 'Olivia is not one hundred per cent certain that Liam's her son, but she's so open to the boy, it's as if she has raw wounds all over her body. She's desperate to please him. Like she has to make up for losing him all those years ago.'

'Terrified she'll lose him again?'

'That's why I have to go softly, softly,' I said. 'Liam could bolt. I don't want to be the one to scare him off.'

'And our intrepid explorer?'

'A different story. Jack's deeply concerned about Olivia, but he's holding his emotions rigidly under control; he's keeping a distance. It's as if he can't bear the prospect, for himself or for her, that it might all come to nothing.'

'Any other children?'

'The daughter, Catherine, put off meeting Liam for as long as she possibly could. She's scared of something; I'm not sure what.'

I saw in my mind's eye how, prodded by Etta, Catherine had finally emerged from the farmhouse. She'd paused for half a minute or more inside the porch, gathering her courage. And then she had flounced out into the sunlight, her sneakers squeaking as she crossed the yard. She had come to a halt a few feet away from our group, uncertain what to say. Liam, unusually, had made the first move. 'You must be Catherine,' he'd said, and made room so she could squeeze in between him and Olivia. When we'd returned to the house, they'd retreated upstairs, and shortly afterwards I'd heard the sound of 'Greensleeves' being played by two instruments, a guitar and a flute.

'I asked Liam what he thought of her when we were on the way home. He's a kid of few words, but in this case the words were warm. 'She's sort of gentle," was what he said. And then came the cruncher: "People aren't always gentle."'

Nicole did that thing with her eyebrow again.

'You should see the bruise. He looks like he fell head-first out of an upstairs window.'

'And Catherine? What did she think of him?'

I'd searched out Catherine before I left. Found her sitting by the pool, alone, looking thoughtful. 'He's kind of cute,' that was what she said. The tone was grudging, as if she'd expected a gargoyle and was disappointed to find someone quite acceptable instead.

Nicole looked at her watch and then at me again. 'Look, I've got to go soon. But before I do, I want to hear something more concrete about this case. Like what evidence do you have about Liam's origins? And what's your plan of action?' Suddenly I could see her in the station-house, talking to a sergeant in just those terms.

'You want evidence? There's not much, Nicole. He's more or less the right age. More or less the right build. And he has fair hair, like Timmy.'

'For what that's worth,' said Nicole dismissively. 'Many kids are fair at four and mousy by their teens. Anything else?'

'He's spoken to me of a mother who's short on maternal devotion. Of a sister called Gemma. And of a father named Albert who buggered off before he was born.' I poured her another glass of wine. 'To the cook,' I said.

'Very convenient,' Nicole replied, clinking her glass against mine.

'My sentiments exactly. Albert could easily be a figment of the mother's imagination.'

'He could even be the kidnapper,' Nicole said. 'He might have passed the child on to the woman who poses as his mother.'

She thought for a moment while she collected her things.

'Here's what you do. You've got to speak to Liam's extended family and his neighbours and so on. If you can show that baby Liam was with the uncaring mum any time before the age of four, then, whoever he is, he can't be Timothy Cable. A child can't be in two places at once. It's as simple as that.'

'But how simple is it to find family and neighbours when you don't have any personal details, not even an address or a surname?'

Nicole's nothing if not open-minded.

'Sounds impossible,' she said.

Nicole ascertained my plans for the next day – Grantchester again; Liam wanted to walk his dog there, so I was meeting him at the house – and started off down the steps. I called her back. My organiser was still in the car, I explained, handing her the keys. 'Be a love, will you?'

The car was parked directly in front of the house. I stood half in, half out of the doorway, shivering in my pyjamas, while Nicole looked everywhere but where I'd told her to.

'The glove compartment,' I shouted. I had a moment of angst, thinking of all the addresses and phone numbers that I'd managed to feed into my palm-top, and the appointments that I hadn't. That brought me bounding down the steps.

'Hey,' Nicole said. 'Laura, you're still in your pyjamas.'

'Pretend it's a leisure suit,' I said, leaning into the door of the car. I flipped on the map light, threw the glove compartment open and reached inside. To an empty space.

I looked back at Nicole, startled. 'It's–'

'Gone,' she said.

## Chapter 9

The road was slick with rain as I made my way towards Grantchester. I was early. I wanted to have a chat with Catherine Cable about other people's property, and particularly about palm-tops, before Liam and the wonder dog arrived.

But Max Armstrong, Olivia's brother, headed me off. He opened the door and ushered me inside with a studied look of welcome on his face.

He was built powerfully and low to the ground, as if he'd been designed to withstand a storm. His face matched: it was solid and square, with a thick brow and heavy jaw. His voice was warm and deep and safe.

He extended his hand. 'Wonderful to meet you,' he said. Max's eyes were a thin blue, a pale imitation of Olivia's. I was certain that they didn't say *wonderful* as well.

'Olivia's popped out to the High Street. She asked me to look after you. Splendid, say I; a chance to get acquainted.'

Max escorted me down a stretch of corridor and into a room with lead-paned windows looking out over the lawn at the side of the house.

'The office,' he said. It was done up in a quietly masculine style – an old oak desk, a brass paperweight, a ship's clock. There was the usual equipment – telephone, computer, scanner and fax machine. There were yellow chrysanthemums in a vase on the filing cabinet, and a compelling series of framed photographs on the wall.

'Were those taken in Norfolk?' I asked. One image, of a low headland with a church spire poking up above the trees, reminded me of Blakeney.

Blakeney, Max confirmed, and other points nearby on the north Norfolk coast. Taken from his boat, he said, and promptly launched into a stream of nautical reminiscence. I was less than fascinated; in spite of growing up within spitting distance of the Bristol Channel, I've never been attracted to a life on the ocean wave. Rowing on the Cam is one thing; the smell of diesel is quite another.

So I paid only enough attention to keep the conversation bobbing along on the surface. To steer us back towards the Cables. I didn't have to use a heavy hand. The Cables – and particularly Jack – constituted Max's favourite topic of conversation.

'I've got a question.' It had been sitting in my pocket, unanswered, ever since my lunch with Sonny in Hobbs Pavilion.

130

'Jolly good,' said Max. 'Fire away.'

No one says 'Jolly good' nowadays, except army officers or diplomats in novels written by foreigners. I'd guess that he had watched too many Battle of Britain films.

'You may laugh, Max – it's a simple question – but here goes.' How to phrase it? 'What is it exactly that makes Jack Cable a hero? Locating the remains of HMS *Erebus* is pretty impressive, I'll grant you. Is there anything else?'

Running Cable Explorations involved Max in using Jack's reputation to promote sponsorship deals. From his answer to my question, he was in the right job. The words poured out. There was not one thing that made Cable a hero, there were many. To begin with, his single-mindedness when they were debating where to site the search; Jack had spent a full three months poring over old charts, I was told, reconstructing currents and studying ice formations, so he could pinpoint the spot where the *Erebus* might have sunk.

'He worked nonstop, night and day, until he had narrowed it down to two sites. He scarcely slept. The family were in Norfolk; he didn't see them for days on end,' Max said. 'D'you know, if Olivia hadn't insisted that he join them in Cleybourne the evening before Timmy disappeared, Jack might never even have had those last few hours

131

with his son.'

I could see it like a movie playing in my mind's eye: the darkened room, the smoke-wreathed air, the men bending over charts, unshaven, unwashed, unaware of anything except the problem in hand. It was a familiar kind of heroism. And, I reminded myself, it was a heroism that depended, utterly, on the efforts of others who saw to the daily grind; who ensured that children were secure and bellies filled and houses repaired and illnesses tended.

'So, he's single-minded,' I repeated. 'Dedicated.'

'And fearless,' Max said. 'Here, have a seat.' He waved me into an armchair. 'My brother-in-law is the most courageous man I've ever known. You're aware, of course, of his injuries? No?' Max's voice suggested that my ignorance was not easily overlooked.

'Tell me,' I urged.

Max seated himself. He planted his legs firmly in the well of the desk. He leaned towards me and lowered his voice. 'It happened on a tiny island just at the western end of Lancaster Sound. Jack and three other crewmen were searching for signs of a landing when a sudden storm blew up. Do you know what an Arctic gale is like, Laura? No?'

Max crossed his arms as if for warmth. 'The wind can turn you to ice in minutes if you don't find shelter. And when the snow is swirling all around, it's like being in a tunnel. You see nothing. Nothing at all.'

He used his voice to advantage, like an actor, and involuntarily, I shivered.

Max continued. 'They had to get off the island fast and back to the safety of the ship. But one of the party got separated. A geologist, in his early twenties; Moorhouse was his name. The helicopter came to pick them up. It couldn't hang around; had to return to the landing pad and be strapped down before the wind reached its peak. Do you have any idea what Jack did?'

'Not the faintest.'

'Jack ordered the other two men on their way. He refused to come with them. When the storm died down hours later, and the party returned, they found Jack and young Moorhouse, safe. Unable to see the ground beneath his feet, Jack had searched on hands and knees until he'd found the geologist; then he'd dragged him to a hollow where there was some shelter from the wind and wrapped himself around the boy. Without Jack's extraordinary efforts, Moorhouse would have died.'

'I'm impressed,' I said, and meant it. This was the real thing. No-holds-barred heroism. Maybe Sonny was right about the guy.

'That's not all,' said Max. He leaned back and looked at me as if waiting for me to fill in the blanks. When I didn't respond, he told me the rest. The story might be pure Hollywood, but it didn't have the triumphant ending that the studios prefer. 'Jack lost a leg, poor chap. He got wet somehow and there was frostbite and that was that. He must have lain there for hours, holding the young man, knowing that he was in trouble himself. He had to cut back his adventures after that. A prosthetic leg is not the best equipment for mountain-climbing.'

Somehow this story made me think of being ten years old. By the time people become adults, most of them have lost that childhood preoccupation with heroics; they've settled into a just-get-by mentality. But it's different for children; children are under pressure all the time to confront shorter, sharper tests. To explore whether they are smart enough, fast enough and, yes, brave enough to withstand life's trials. At ten years old, my friends and I used to play a heroism game. We'd set questions and struggle to answer them with absolute honesty. *If a baby was trapped in a burning building, would you rescue her? If you saw a gang of thugs setting upon someone, would you go to their aid? If you saw a drunk man asleep on the railway line, and heard the train coming, would you try to roll him off?* Much of the time the answer was a shame-faced, regretful *no*. But there was comfort in the unanimity of our answers.

'That kind of courage, Max. That self-sacrifice. Are some people just born with it? Was Jack?'

'Not me,' said Max, 'that's for sure. But in Jack's case...'

A door slammed some distance away. There was a commotion and the cadence of raised voices. Heavy footsteps coming our way. Max paid them no attention. I'd set a train of thought in motion and he was riding it still.

'Miss Principal, you know what some people say about his heroism? They say that Jack jolly well couldn't help himself.'

I didn't understand. But before I could tell Max so, the door burst open and Joe, the handyman, staggered into the office. Blood ran down his right forearm, which was cradled across his chest. Blood lay like a broad band of scarlet on his workshirt. His eyes were wild.

Max stood rooted to the spot, staring with horror. He watched as the blood spilled over on to the rug. 'Oh my God,' he said. 'What's happened to your wrist, Joe? Oh my God.'

I guided Joe to the armchair and sat him down. Tore off my jacket and jumper and cotton shirt. Wrapped the shirt around Joe's wrist and lifted his arm into the air above his head.

'Joe,' I asked, 'how did you cut yourself?'

What I thought he said – his words were faint – was *Door. The door of the gatehouse.* He was breathing shallowly. His face was paler than putty and slick with sweat.

Olivia's brother was still standing like a waxwork dummy near the desk. I had to shout to get his attention. 'Max! Listen to me. Ring 999. Get an ambulance here, fast.'

Max blinked, finally, and picked up the phone. At that moment, Jack Cable strode into the room.

Jack could have been forgiven if he had baulked at the scene that confronted him: Max clutching the telephone receiver and staring at Joe in alarm; me naked from the waist up except for a bra, holding Joe's arm aloft by the wrist as if I were the referee and he the winner in a heavyweight bout; and Joe himself slumped in a chair, just this side of consciousness.

But Jack didn't hesitate. He stepped past me and went down on one knee. He looked into the handyman's face. 'Joe. Joe.'

Joe turned towards him and muttered something in a language I didn't recognise. His eyes were barely focused. Jack placed his fingers on the older man's throat and began counting.

Olivia came running in with a first-aid kit.

'The butterfly clips,' Jack said. 'And some blankets, my dear. Quickly. I think his temperature is dropping.'

136

Max spoke at last. 'The ambulance is on its way.'

Jack nodded and relieved me of Joe's injured arm. He attached a tourniquet and tightened it by gripping one end in his teeth. He unwrapped my shirt, which was wet with blood, from Joe's arm and tossed it to me. Working methodically and quickly, he applied a series of clips, pressing the edges of the gaping wound together. He passed me things to hold. I would have liked to pause to cover myself, but this was clearly a crisis, so I aimed for nonchalance instead.

We heard a siren. When Olivia came back in with blankets, the paramedics were hard on her heels. They strapped Joe on to a stretcher and edged him out through the narrow doorway. Etta came running up, unearthed by the sound of the ambulance from wherever she'd been; Olivia and Jack gathered round her and they all trailed out to the ambulance behind the stretcher like mourners at a funeral. Suddenly the office seemed shockingly quiet.

I found my jumper and slipped it on. I looked at Max. He was sitting at the desk again, his head in his hands.

'You all right now?'

Max nodded. 'Bad in a crisis. Never pretended otherwise,' he said. Both statements were true. 'Whereas Jack – well, he equipped himself for expeditions. He knows first aid, and – as you can see – he's not afraid to use it.' Max looked thoroughly depressed. The heartiness had drained out of him.

'About what you said, Max.'

There was incomprehension in his pale eyes. He didn't remember our earlier conversation.

'About Moorhouse,' I reminded him. 'You said Jack couldn't help himself. What did you mean?'

Max slowly regained his composure. He made the effort to focus on me.

'Couldn't help himself. Yes, indeed. The expedition, you see, took place only months after Timmy went missing. Jack was still in a kind of mourning. He risked his life for Moorhouse because he couldn't – that's what Olivia says – couldn't let another boy in his care just slip away.'

# Chapter 10

It was a while before things calmed down again at the Dower House – before the ambulance had flashed away and the tension had subsided. I used the time to check out the E-type for myself, trying to figure out what all the fuss was about.

Yep, sure enough, it was a car.

When I came back to the house, the boisterous noise of a small motor led me to the kitchen, where Olivia was standing at the worktop, controlling the spin on the bowl of an electric mixer. Her hands were shaky. There was a glass of red wine nearby.

She didn't hear me the first time I spoke.

'Mrs Cable,' I said again.

She whirled. She had a plastic spatula in her right hand and a dusting of icing sugar down the front of her blouse. She was wearing leather shoes with mud around the soles. 'Laura,' she said, and offered me the spatula. 'Taste this. Does it need another drop of vanilla, would you say?'

I transferred a fingerful of icing on to my tongue.

'Perfect,' I declared.

'For Liam,' Olivia explained. She lifted the

beaters clear of the bowl, and put a mound of icing on the top of an enormous sponge cake. 'Part of me wants to scrawl *Welcome Home* in big bold letters across the top. To begin to celebrate in the grand style.'

Olivia made the top of the cake as smooth as marble, and then began spreading icing along the sides. I picked up a kitchen knife and went to work opposite her. My style, a mixture of hope and inexperience, left a great deal to be desired.

'Why don't you do just that?'

'Because the other part wants evidence. You know? Wants to be sure.' Olivia suddenly leaned her back against the counter, faced me and folded her arms. The spatula, still gripped in her fist, pointed into the air. 'You don't have children, Laura, do you?'

'Uh-uh.'

Is it my imagination? Every time someone asks that question (and it happens increasingly often these days) I sense a pressure to tack an explanation on the end. To justify the still-not-quite-respectable state of childlessness... *I haven't met the right man... I'm not sure I'd make a good mother... Later; I'm building a career right now...* These are the acceptable accounts, the ones that invoke sympathy and encouragement.

But there are also the less acceptable. The accounts that are just whispered in the darkness... *I'm afraid of getting fat... I'm too busy enjoying life... Children are like little vampires who suck your creativity...*

Some things can be said and some things can't.

Maybe one morning I'll be gripped by a desire so fierce that I'll muster the dedication to mother. The truth is, it hasn't happened yet; I simply don't feel the need. And without that hunger, how can anyone take on a child? Searches in the Arctic require dedication; but when you go on expedition, you expect to come back again. You expect it to end.

Being a mother never ends. Ask Olivia Cable.

'Laura?'

'No,' I said. 'No children.'

'Then I don't know whether you can understand.' Olivia drained her glass of wine. She collected her thoughts before laying them out for me to examine. 'For the past twelve years, apart from the agony about what Timmy might be enduring, I've had to live with two terrible fears. I fear that Timmy will return.'

I looked up, startled.

Olivia signalled with her hand – *Just wait* – and carried on. 'He'll trudge up the drive with a rucksack on his back and I'll not recognise him. After all the false hopes, I'll be fearful of opening my heart, and I'll send him away. My own son.'

She looked up at me sharply. Her blue eyes were as hard as jewels. It was as if she were challenging me to try to comfort her. To try and, inevitably, to fail.

'Your second fear?'

'That Timmy will struggle across half the world to get to us. He'll walk quietly up to the window and he'll watch us for a while, wanting to see what kind of people we are before barging in. He'll be a sensitive boy, you see.'

Olivia smiled, letting me know that she was perfectly aware that this scenario, however powerfully imagined, was merely fantasy. I smiled back. Fantasy or not, I was gripped.

'He's full of anticipation,' Olivia continued. 'Envisaging the welcome he'll get. And then' – she caught my eye – 'then he sees something that destroys him forever.'

'There's no one here? Is that it? You've moved? The house is empty?'

She shook her head: no. I hadn't got it at all.

I tried again. 'The family's broken up? Dispersed? Dead?'

'No.' Olivia couldn't hide her disappointment. She had obviously hoped I would understand her dread. 'No, it's much, much worse than that, Laura. We're here, all right, and well, and happy – but so, you see, is Timmy.'

I was flummoxed. What did she mean? I studied her face. Was Mrs Cable completely off her little blue-eyed rocker?

She read my mind. 'No, I'm not crazy, Laura. My son struggles home only to discover that someone else, an impostor, has been allowed to take his place. He slinks away. He's lost forever. Do you see?'

Enough that it filled me with pity.

'You must be terrified,' I said. Talk about Sophie's choice. Disaster either way: too quick to acknowledge someone who's an impostor, or too quick to deny.

She whispered, as if she were chanting a little prayer, *I'd know you anywhere*. Isn't that what we say to our children? But what in God's name will happen if I get it wrong?'

She reached into a cupboard and pulled down a tiny bottle. Slowly, thoughtfully, she added a few drops of colouring to what was left of the icing. And when it had turned a leafy green, she packed it into a piping bag. Suddenly she whirled again to face me.

'You tell me,' she exclaimed, brandishing the instrument. 'I don't dare to write *Welcome Home*, though I might want to. What shall I write on this cake?'

Slowly, aware of my inadequacy, I reached out and took the bag from her hands. Holding it at an angle, as I'd seen my mother do many times before, I made a border for the cake, folding the pale green icing forward and back on itself, like a wave. When the border was complete, I wrote three words in the centre, and turned the cake around so Olivia could read them. She looked and, to my relief, her frown fell away.

*For my children*, it said.

In spite of Olivia's fears of an impostor, I never doubted for a minute that she longed for the uncertainty to end. We talked long and hard about what it was like to be the mother of a missing child. To have a child and not to know the detail – where he was or how he was or what he was doing – was a daily agony, she said.

'Every time I see a boy who is Timmy's age, I find myself wondering about him. Making up stories. Was this boy at Timmy's school? I think. Did they play football together? Did Timmy run eagerly up behind him, tackle too roughly, give away a penalty? Have they been wary of each other ever since?'

'Or,' she said, 'I bump into a girl, a pretty girl with her belly button showing below a cropped top, the way girls dress now; and I think: perhaps she was his first date. He might have gone with her to the cinema to see a film and put his arm around her in the dark. He might have met her at a club and danced with her and come home with his face shining because there was a girl there and she liked him and he liked her.'

And when I asked her whether other mothers understood, I heard for the first time a note of bitterness in her voice. Still, I supposed, she was entitled.

'Do you know, Laura, mothers of teen-agers have spoken to me of their children. *Oh, he's so secretive now. He never tells me anything. They* know nothing? *They* feel shut out? It's been twelve years since I last set eyes on my child, twelve years since I touched him. I've been forced to construct a life for him out of thin air. If Liam hadn't come along – well, I don't think I could have lived much longer with *I don't know.*'

Olivia pulled herself together then. You could see her back straighten and her face lift. She changed the subject abruptly.

'Max,' Olivia said. 'My brother. What did you think of him?' She began to make coffee.

A dangerous question. Private investigators aren't paid to think – at least not about the intimates of the people who hire them.

'We only spoke for a few minutes. A lot of it was about sailing.'

'Max is obsessed,' she said. 'Talks as if he invented the sport. And all his money goes into that damned boat. We tease him that perhaps he has a woman tucked away somewhere, to account for why he's always broke.' Her chuckle suggested that Max wasn't much of a man for the ladies. 'Are you a sailor too?'

'Not in the least. For me, sailing is on the same level of attraction as bull-fighting or bridge. Which is to say, no attraction at all.'

'You'll have to forgive him, Laura. He's not a fool, you know.'

'I didn't imagine he was.' In spite of his peculiar turns of phrase, there was something quite alert about Max Armstrong.

'Some people see Max's manner and they don't take him seriously. That's a mistake. He's a decent man, with a good head for business. If he hadn't kept things going after Timmy disappeared, Cable Explorations would have collapsed altogether. We owe much of our current prosperity to Max.' She added, quietly, 'And the survival of our marriage, too.'

She brought mugs of coffee to the table. She brought milk and sugar and a plate of home-made shortbread. We sat down. I fortified myself with the flavour of French coffee and two fingers of shortbread. It was clear from Olivia's manner that some confidence was on the way.

'You see, Laura, in the months after our tragedy,' Olivia said, 'I went badly astray. It was Max who persuaded me to stay with Jack.'

'You wouldn't have been the first couple to part under the strain of losing a child.'

Olivia picked up a finger of shortbread, looked at it pensively and put it down again. 'I didn't want to blame Jack for Timmy's disappearance, but when he went looking for the Franklin ship, only six months afterwards, I was angry – angry that he'd run off to the Arctic instead of staying here, with me, to watch for Timmy. He was always buttoned up, always hard to talk to; but this was like a betrayal. The first few weeks he was away, I ... I hated him for it.'

In the distance, through a window which was cracked open, we heard a dog barking. Olivia glanced at the corner of the room, where the two collies were curled around one another, fast asleep. One lifted its head and listened. 'It's all right, Bess,' Olivia whispered. The dog settled down again.

'It was Max who saved our marriage. I'd always known he admired Jack – hero-worshipped him even – but I hadn't realised till then how well he understood him.'

There was a movement in the doorway. Olivia, intent on her memory, appeared not to notice. Over Olivia's shoulder, I saw Catherine standing on one leg, poised like a stork, waiting for the right moment to interrupt. When our eyes met, she raised a finger to her lips.

Olivia continued. 'Max made me see how badly Jack had suffered. How impotent he felt in the face of Timmy's disappearance.

How devastating it was for the great Jack Cable, the master of control, when he found himself unable to control the thing he cared most about in the world.'

*The thing he cared most about...* I wasn't certain – there were deep shadows in the doorway – but it seemed to me that Catherine's eyes darkened.

Then she was gone.

As Catherine's soft footsteps moved away along the corridor, I fully expected Olivia to fall silent, to ask who'd been there, to turn around. But she seemed completely unaware. She carried on speaking as if Catherine had been a ghost.

'Searching for the Franklin expedition was Jack's substitute for finding Timmy,' Olivia said. 'Max explained it all to me. Thanks to Max, I could see Jack's pain, and not only my own. And when he came back, after the loss of his leg–'

'You dedicated yourself to him.'

She looked at me calmly. 'By then it was easy,' she said.

Olivia glanced at her watch. Her smile faded. The time set for Liam's arrival had long gone, and he was nowhere to be seen.

'You're sure he's coming?'

I offered a raft of reassurances, but Olivia still seemed uneasy, so I agreed to check.

I borrowed a wool scarf from a hook near

the front door and set off the short distance towards Grantchester Meadows. I crossed the High Street. The footpath was damp and deserted. Terracotta pots in the gardens alongside were filled with sludge. Dead hollyhocks stood stiffly against a fence, as if they'd contracted rigor mortis. Even the barren branches that overhung the path were bowed down by rain.

Not a day for walking. When I scanned the meadows, the only signs of life were two dogs and their dutiful owners, anoraked and wellied and gloved against the weather. Neither of the owners was Liam.

On the way back, I tried to take a more positive view of the season. The gardens might have been cheerless, but the houses near the footpath gave promise of warmth. Lights shone in their windows; smoke drifted up from their chimneys; in downstairs rooms you could see the flicker of a fire.

But back on Cable property, just inside the boundary of Grantchester Farm, the effect ended abruptly. Joe and Etta's gatehouse was dismal and deserted. And leading away from the front door was a dark brown trail of blood.

*My door.* Was that what Joe had said? *The door of the gatehouse?* I must have misheard. How could someone acquire such a nasty cut, virtually a slit wrist, from a door? The front door of my own house was one hundred and twenty years old, but it had never given me so much as a splinter.

The gatehouse perched on raised ground to the side of the driveway. It was small and rather cutesy, as gatehouses often are, like the image of English homes in a Disney film. The walls were of red brick. The windows had tiny panes inside a pointed neo-Gothic shape, as if the gatekeeper was meant to defend the driveway with bow and arrow. The house was unlit.

Two strides brought me to the front door. It was made of heavy planks with wrought-iron fittings, and had a shallow porch with a pointed roof that left it wreathed in shadow. It was only when I peered closely that I saw what had done the damage.

The razor blade was strapped in place with an ingenious arrangement of electrical tape and wire. It was positioned so that any-one reaching out to open the door, anyone taking a firm, swift grip on the latch would lower their wrist directly on to it. The surer and more swift the grip, the deeper would be the cut.

Joe's accident was no accident. Someone had intended harm.

I reported to Olivia what I'd found at the gatehouse. Reassured her that I had re-moved the blade and made the door safe. I didn't tell her that I had photographed it first, using the camera I kept in the car; that I had worn gloves; that I had carefully wrapped all the components of the booby trap in plastic and placed them in a box, ready for the police. She refused to ring the police. 'That's not the way we do things at Grantchester Farm,' she said.

She was adamant, too, that she knew of no one who would wish harm to Etta or Joe.

'Absolutely not. They're a lovely couple. Etta's been with us since she was eighteen. There was some kind of trouble at home, so she looked for a live-in job. I don't know much more than that,' Olivia said, sensing my unspoken question. 'Etta's a very private person.'

'Joe came later?'

'It was a whirlwind romance, a complete surprise. Thirteen years ago, Etta Humm – as she was then – took a coach tour to Yugoslavia and returned with a fine engagement ring. Shortly afterwards they were married.'

I thought of Etta's reserve – *she's a very private person* – and of Joe's shyness. This wasn't just a whirlwind romance, this was a miracle.

There was a pause, while Olivia nibbled at a finger of shortbread, like a caged bird with a piece of cuttlebone.

I seized the opportunity.

'Tell me something, Olivia. That terracotta

bust in the sitting room – is it a good likeness of Timmy? What was the name of the sculptor?'

Olivia seemed flustered. Maybe she guessed my intent.

'The eyes are wrong,' she said at last. 'Timmy didn't have those big round baby eyes, like the infants in Pampers ads. He had long, thoughtful-looking eyes. And long lashes.'

'Like Liam,' I said.

'I'll show you.' She pulled out a side drawer in the scrubbed pine table and scattered a handful of papers. Underneath were some photos. She removed one, studied it for a moment and passed it to me.

I stared for the first time into the face of Timothy Andrew Cable. I saw a narrow face, pale hair, pale brows. Almond-shaped eyes, squinting into the sun. The photo had been taken in front of the farmhouse. It was summer, if the flowers in the border were anything to go by. The child was alone. He wore yellow dungaree shorts and a white cotton shirt with pale yellow stripes. He was squatting. His knees were streaked with dirt. His hand was held straight out towards the camera, and there was something small and dark nestled in his palm.

'A caterpillar,' Olivia said. 'Timmy liked their fur coats.'

'What else did Timmy like?'

Olivia's lips turned up in a grin. 'Bathtime – Jack used to whip up the bubbles until Timmy was almost covered in foam. Windmills – there's a wonderful one in Cleybourne. Oh, and he liked Milupa hot cereal.' Her nose wrinkled. 'I found a box of it tucked far away at the back of a cupboard, years after he'd gone. I wanted to make myself a bowl, just to have that aroma of apple and cinnamon, just to remind myself of Tim, but when I opened it' – she shuddered – 'the box was full of maggots.'

Just then a peal of laughter drifted in from another room. There was a clatter in the corridor, and an ungainly dog loped through the doorway, paws slipping, nails clicking on the quarry tiles. Olivia started and stood up abruptly. Her chair toppled over.

Liam burst into the kitchen a second later, still laughing, with Catherine on his heels.

'Wonder!' The dog made straight for the corner where the border collies slept. They leapt up, their ears alert, braced for trouble. 'Wonder!' Liam called again.

The lurcher was as goofy-looking as they come. Its narrow head projected from the end of an elongated neck, and strands of wiry hair hung down like straggles of Spanish moss. It returned, half in obedience and half in fear, to stand at Liam's heel. The collies were mollified. They sniffed around

153

Wonder with a good-natured interest.

Liam apologised for being late. The walk had taken longer than he'd expected, he said; and he'd bumped into Catherine on the way in and she'd been showing him around.

It was Catherine, not Liam, who received Olivia's reproof. 'Didn't you know we were waiting?' she asked.

Catherine ignored the criticism. 'Etta rang,' she said. 'They've put eleven stitches in Joe's wrist. If they can find a bed, they'll keep him in overnight for observation.'

Within minutes sandwiches were produced, and a pot of tea, since Liam said he preferred tea to coffee, and the cake was ceremoniously cut. Catherine looked uneasy when she saw the inscription. Liam pretended not to notice.

Jack came in from the fields. He cleaned his shoes on a scraper near the back door, hung his jacket on a hook and sat at the head of the table. Max popped his head in; he collected a cup of tea and a slice of cake and took them back to the office. He had one or two things to finish off, he said, before departing.

Tea passed without event – until the final moments. After we had eaten, and exhausted the obvious items of small talk, there was a moment of awkward silence. Liam lifted his rucksack, balanced it on the edge of the table and began rummaging through. He cleared his throat.

'Olivia,' he said, placing on the table a battered notebook, a soft toy and a tin of tobacco, 'is it all right to smoke in the kitchen? Or would you rather I went outside?'

Olivia's mouth fell open. On her face was a look of utter astonishment. She stared at the clutter, blue eyes widened, as if Liam had exposed a sackful of rubies.

Gradually the attention of everyone around the table came to focus on her face. Then she reached an arm across and grasped the soft toy. She pulled it towards her. It was a pale and shabby creature. It had long legs and arms, black button eyes and a worried face.

Liam spoke. 'I'm really sorry,' he said, stretching out towards the toy, trying to take it back. 'I have no idea where that monkey came from. It's not mine.' It was as if he had committed a serious breach of etiquette; he seemed desperately concerned to redeem himself.

But Olivia, for once, denied him. She kept her grip on the creature, a grip both tender and intrigued. She held it by its fake leather hands, as if she might dance with it, and then, still dangling it in the air, she angled it so that that the blunt nose and button eyes were directly in her husband's line of vision.

'You see, Jack?' She pressed the pale creature to her breast, and whispered, in a voice soft and sweet and oh, so satisfied, 'It's Mickey Monkey.'

Liam's face – the puzzled brow, the baffled eyes, the astonished mouth – was a study in bewilderment. He picked up the tobacco tin, located the lighter in his rucksack and made a bid to escape. He looked awkwardly from Olivia to Jack and to Olivia again. For that moment, neither of them acknowledged him.

'I'll just go outside and have a smoke,' he said.

Jack didn't say a word. His attention was focused on Olivia.

'I'll come with you.' Catherine stood up and scooped Liam's things back into the rucksack.

Suddenly Olivia flared into life. She pressed the soft toy into her husband's reluctant hands and stepped around the table until she stood inches away from Liam, looking up at him. He stiffened. She flung her arms around him.

There was something close to panic in his eyes.

When, after ten seconds or longer, Olivia released the young man, she took one of his hands in her own and held it firmly. 'Come on, Liam. This time, while we're on the farm, you'll do the driving.'

I got to my feet. 'I'll come too.' I had an idea what was going on and I wasn't sure I liked it.

'There's not room for three,' Olivia shot back. 'You stay here and listen for the phone.' She led Liam to the door. Wonder trotted after them, his tail swinging with excitement.

Jack drained his cup of tea and stood up.

Catherine studied his face, as if something she needed might be found there.

'Daddy!' she exclaimed. Her voice was higher than before, like the voice of a much younger child.

Jack didn't look at her. His face was dark and strained. He started towards the back door, calling the collies to him.

'Daddy, what's happening?'

Jack flung open the door to let the dogs out, and followed after them.

Catherine sat down heavily. All the merriment was gone from her features. It was as if some underpinning had collapsed; her face was flat and lifeless. She excused herself, and a moment later I heard the front door shut softly behind her.

It didn't seem the time to ask her about my missing palm-top.

# Chapter 11

## TWELVE YEARS EARLIER

*Mummy says I have ears like a fox. She doesn't mean they're pointed. She means that I can hear well. And I can. I'm listening out for Daddy. This time I'll see him first. I have something important to show him, something he'll like.*

*Daddy laughed when I told him I was going to watch for birds while we're in Cleybourne. Etta will take me, I told him. She's bought me an album, with pictures. If I can spot ten birds she said, one for every day of our holiday, it will prove I've learned how to concentrate.*

*Daddy didn't believe me. 'You, Catherine?' he said, and he tickled me behind the ears. 'Concentrate? You can't even stand still. You'll start bouncing and pirouetting and you'll scare all the birds away.'*

*He wouldn't laugh at Timmy. Timmy's practically a baby, he can't even tie his own shoes – but Timmy can concentrate. Daddy says so. 'That kid,' he says, shaking his head. 'That Timmy. I've never seen a child with such a strong sense of focus. He'll do something amazing one day, Livi, you wait and see.'*

*So I'm waiting to show Daddy my album. There are boxes to tick for every bird you see, and I've ticked eleven so far. An oystercatcher and a ringed plover and lots of others. 'Will Daddy be amazed, Mummy?' I asked.*

*'He'll be amazed, darling,' she said. And she gave a great big sigh.*

*So I'm listening, with my ears like a fox. And I can hear him now. There's a car coming down Beach Lane. Yes, it's slowing, It's crunching on the gravel. The engine's off, oh! – the music was loud. Now he's turned it off. Clunk, click. A car door – open, close. Now the front door. Mummy's voice, Daddy's voice. Mummy sounds a bit cross. I tiptoe out of bed and crack open the door.*

*'...children,' I hear him say. He starts up the stairs. My room is right at the top. It's the first one you come to. Good thing I'm fast.*

*I race back to bed and leap up and dive under the bedclothes. I place the bird album on my chest and pull the covers up high, so that when Daddy pulls them back he'll see it right away. I can imagine the look on his face – all amazed. 'Catherine!' he'll say. 'Did you do this? All by yourself? You are getting to be a grown-up girl. Perhaps you're ready to come on one of my adventures with me.'*

*I am so excited lying there in the dark that I don't notice the time go by, but it does. I'm getting very hot under here. My cheeks are starting to burn.*

159

*I listen hard. Maybe Daddy's already in the room. Maybe he's standing next to the bed, looking at me, wondering where I am. Or maybe he's got a present for me; perhaps he is wrapping it, perhaps that's what's taking so long.*

*Slowly I roll back the covers. I see the glow-stars on my ceiling. I see the bed with its lumpy pink counterpane, all the way to the end. I see the wooden floor and the old rugs and the rocking chair. But no Daddy.*

*Where can he be?*

*I get up again and tiptoe to the door. I'm still clutching my album. I listen. Sure enough, I hear Daddy's voice. Crooning quietly. I tiptoe down the hallway and push open another door. He is kneeling on the rug beside Timmy's bed. Timmy is fast asleep. He is holding Timmy's hand, and singing. 'Bye baby bunting, Daddy's gone a-hunting.' He doesn't hear me or see me.*

*I creep back to bed and put my album away on the shelf and go to sleep.*

# Chapter 12

It was strange being alone in the big old kitchen of the Dower House. The room was quiet without being peaceful. The appliances were turned off and the conversation silenced, but the atmosphere retained an edge-of-the-seat quality. Some of the tension of the afternoon hung in the air like woodsmoke.

Whatever that monkey meant to Olivia, it had clearly triggered a change of heart. When she'd stood face to face with Liam at the last, she'd been exultant. There was no desperation; perhaps for the first time since Timmy's vanishing, no ambivalence. Only absolute certainty. Olivia had her son again.

But not everyone around that table had shared the mood of triumph. Liam had initially seemed puzzled by the appearance of the monkey. And then he'd been bewildered and embarrassed; as Olivia threw her arms around him, his eyes were shaded, his body stiff. Had there even been a hint of revulsion in his posture at the moment that Olivia had claimed him?

Jack had been stunned. He'd recognised Mickey Monkey, I was sure of that, but there was something resembling fear in his demeanour. Was he frightened about what Timmy's return might mean for the family? Or frightened about what might happen if, even in spite of this positive sign, Liam was an impostor?

And then there was Catherine, the other child. Who had seemed baffled. Bereft. Even angry.

I sighed and stood up slowly from the table. The remnants of our tea lay scattered about where the family had left them: the used cutlery and plates, the cups with their pale residue, the crumpled napkins and a few small sandwiches curling at the corners. The curious monkey with its dangly arms slouched on the chair where Jack had abandoned it.

The remains of the cake occupied the centre of the table. The rectangle of pale green sponge had been reduced to a ragged L. The last three letters of the inscription I'd done for Olivia had been shaved away, instead of *For my children,* the dedication now read, *For my child.*

I shivered and set to work; there was nothing else to do. I scrambled through the cabinets until I found some aluminium foil. I covered the cake and placed it on top of the refrigerator, out of the reach of the dogs. I cleared the table, rinsed the plates, loaded the dishwasher. Finally I poured myself a drink of water, leaned against the sink and glanced idly around.

My eye followed a thin shaft of afternoon light that shone through the pane of glass in the back door. It illuminated an ebony stain near the end of the old pine table. Probably, I thought, an ancient burn mark. At some point in the past hundred and fifty years, a candle had been felled by the wind. The flame had smouldered its way into the wood before anyone noticed.

I stared at the scarred pine, thinking of the Cables. Thinking of the enduring effects of a single careless moment.

But as I gazed, the sunlight was extinguished at a stroke, as if someone had snuffed out a candle. The table was plunged into shadow. The stain disappeared.

*...Here comes a candle to light you to bed. Here comes a chopper to chop off your head...*

I whirled. Through the glazing in the door I could see the trees. They were near and dark and deep, and the sun drifted between their tall tops, pale and unobscured. The clouds hadn't quite reached that corner of the sky. There was only one explanation for the failing of the light: someone had placed themselves in the slanting path of the sun.

Catherine? I wondered.

I stood quite still, watching and waiting. I didn't want to frighten her away.

Finally, after a minute, I pushed open the

door and stepped out on to the patch of lawn that carpeted the way to the woods. Softly I called, 'Catherine?'

There was no reply. I thought I might have heard a shuffling sound in the woods beyond, thought there might have been a shift in the density of shadow underneath the trees, but I couldn't be certain.

I returned and closed the door. She'd come in when she was ready.

I took one last look around the kitchen. It was large and cluttered and comfortable, the way kitchens are in many country houses, modestly furnished and welcoming. Everything about it was homey – the fireplace with its cheering heat; the old pine dresser, lined with blue and white plates with cracks in their glazing; the deep colours of the quarry-tiled floors; even the coil of dog blankets in the corner. Only one thing seemed out of place. I picked the pale monkey up off the chair and found it a prominent place between a soup tureen and a milk jug on the dresser. Its legs dangled over the edge of the shelf.

Then I opened wide the drawer in the side of the kitchen table. I ran my hand underneath a scattering of papers and pencils and keys and coins and came up with a clutch of photos.

I slid two of the photographs into my pocket. Just then there was a noise at the side of the house. I thrust the rest of the photos back in place, pushed the drawer closed and dashed out of the kitchen. Behind me, on its great old set of hinges, the door banged to and fro.

I stopped in the corridor to listen. No sound from Max's office. No echoes from the conservatory. And no movement from the split-level sitting room. If my ears were to be believed, I was the only person in this wing of the house,

I wasn't sure where I should go, and what I should do. But it isn't good for the reputation to be found creeping around an empty house, so I made myself conspicuously comfortable. I plumped the cushions, and curled myself up on one of the pale yellow sofas in the sitting room, then took the photos from my pocket and examined them.

The first showed Jack Cable. The adventurer stood high up on a headland – north Norfolk, I thought; probably Cleybourne – with a small boy. Their bodies were turned outwards, towards the scudding clouds, and the wind tugged at their hair. In the distance there was a thin line of indigo-coloured ocean. I didn't doubt that this was Timmy. He wore a red duffle coat and a striped scarf, one end of which flapped behind his shoulder. His face and his father's were turned towards the camera. Jack smiled confidently, as if he might have been on the edge of laughter. Timmy's eyes were partially closed against the brilliance of the sea-sky, but his back was straight. Little as he was, he refused, like his father, to flinch from the force of the wind.

The other photo showed Timmy on his own. It was taken in extreme close-up, slightly out of focus, as if the photographer had been tracing a moving target. Timmy had been swimming. There were rubber armbands above his elbows. His hair was pushed back from his forehead in an exuberant quiff; it dripped, and there were droplets of water suspended from the lobes of his ears like jewels. His bare shoulders were hunched forward with the cold; his hands clasped the edges of a towel that was wrapped like a sarong around his chest. Timmy the swimmer looked full face at the camera, and his look, this time, was of pure glee. He grinned; his eyes danced; his baby teeth gleamed.

I propped the photos on the back of the sofa. I studied them for a moment more, and then closed my eyes. Two things about the images stayed with me.

First, Timmy: how even in delight he had a thoughtful look. Perhaps it was his delicate features, perhaps his long lashes. Whatever the reason, this little four-year-old had looked both anxious and wise. But what would he look like now, I wondered, if he were still alive? Would time and the trajectory of normal development have smoothed out the frown between his brows and replaced his worried look with a happy-go-lucky air? Or would his experiences – growing up who knows where – have hardened the anxiety into terror and the wisdom into hopelessness? Would he be different now?

And then there was Jack. What struck me most about Jack was how he'd changed. Now, Jack Cable had a slight stoop, but in the photo, which must have been taken at least twelve years ago, his bearing was arrow-straight. His eyes had a warmth and vigour about them that I had never seen, and the face radiated confidence. You'd still call Jack Cable good-looking today, but his current look was colder and bleaker. Only twelve years had gone by since Timmy's disappearance, but he'd aged twenty-five.

These photos carried me away from the present. Perhaps that was why it took me a while to register the sounds.

On the glass of the French doors, the tip-tap of rain could be heard, the prickly warning of a storm. Wind whistled down the chimney.

But that wasn't all. From the kitchen there were footsteps. Quiet, careful footsteps. Padding to and fro.

I rose to my feet and headed for the corridor. As I did so, the noises became amplified. Someone had suddenly cranked up the volume. I headed more quickly. There was an agonised muttering and a crash, and then a loud metallic clatter as if something had been flung to the floor.

It was only then that I remembered the photos. I turned back to the sitting room, scooped them off the sofa and shoved them deep into my pocket. And at that very second, the noise from the kitchen reached a climax. Running footsteps. A subdued crash. A drawer jerked open. A long-drawn-out metallic echo. The sound of something shattering, again and again.

As I approached the kitchen door, there was a thud and a twang and then silence.

'Catherine?' I called, as I burst in.

The Cables' comfortable kitchen was in chaos. A chair lay sprawled on its side across the quarry tiles. A paste like mud, with pale green slashes and shards of crockery mixed in, was splattered over the floor and the nearby cabinets. It took me a second to recognise this as the remains of Olivia's cake. *For my child* was gone forever.

Sharp fragments of china were scattered about like shrapnel. Every dish had been swept off the dresser on to the floor. All that blue and white crockery that had survived the hubbub of family life for thirty, forty, fifty years – smashed in a moment.

In the centre of the room, a drawerful of kitchen knives had been up-ended on to the floor. They lay in an untidy heap like a deadly game of pick-up sticks.

All this was unsettling. But what captured my attention, what really chilled me, were the sorrowful eyes that stared out at me from the opposite wall.

Mickey Monkey hung five and a half feet in the air. His wrists were impaled on hooks. His arms extended sideways in a bizarre parody of crucifixion. His head lolled forward. And in the centre of his pale body, right where his heart would be (if he only had a heart), there protruded the handle of a long, broad-bladed knife.

Someone had taken a knife from the floor and skewered Mickey Monkey to the wall.

I took a deep breath. Suddenly there were footsteps coming from all directions. Thudding down the stairs. Along the corridor.

The door burst open. Jack Cable took a stride into the room and ground to a halt. Catherine came running up behind him.

'What's going on?' Jack demanded. His gaze swivelled to the furry creature that hung on the wall opposite. 'What's happened here?'

I didn't take the time to answer. I did what I should have done immediately. I opened the back door and stepped out into the rain.

I checked the side of the house. There was a semi-circle of stone paving there, a container garden, a round wrought-iron table, chairs bent forward to allow the rain to run off. No sign of an intruder.

I set out for the trees behind the house. Clouds had bunched up overhead; the rain was pelting down. It blew fiercely into my face and obscured my vision, until, that is, I reached the shelter of the woods. In a mini-environment that allowed only for a mist of rain rather than a downpour, I stood still and scanned for movement. Waiting for a human form or colour or shape to distinguish itself from the palette and the textures of the wood.

Waiting in vain. I stood there for some time. Rain gathered in the upper branches and dripped slowly down. A shower of droplets splashed on to the back of my neck and trickled like a sliver of ice between my shoulder blades. There was a scratching behind a stump; when I stepped forward, a grey squirrel with a twig in her precise little paws scrambled off along a narrow path that led through the trees towards the east. Nothing else moved.

Jack Cable's voice rumbled out from the back door. 'Laura, what's going on?' He sounded rattled.

Eventually I gave up and returned to the house.

The kitchen looked more or less as it had when I'd left it – as if someone with a grudge had lashed out in impotent fury at the Cables' celebration cake and at the pathetic little monkey.

More or less as I'd left it, but not exactly so. Jack and Catherine had wandered off. And on top of the pyramid of knives was a pair of cashmere gloves.

I found Jack Cable in the sitting room. He lay on the yellow sofa, with one long leg stretched out along the seat and his other foot on the floor. Catherine was curled like a baby on top of him, her head tucked into his shoulder. Jack stroked her hair. From the colour of her face and the shine on her cheeks, she'd been crying.

Jack withdrew his gaze from his daughter and looked up at me. 'What were you doing in the woods?'

'Searching for the person who trashed your kitchen. But either he had hot-footed it away before I got there, or–Where does that path go to, Jack, by the way?'

'It comes out above the church. On the High Street, nearer the village.' He cleared his throat. 'Or?'

'Or he, stroke she, was never in the woods at all.' I smiled. 'Where were you two when all that crashing and smashing began?'

'Down at the barn,' Jack said. He eased Catherine to a sitting position, took a handkerchief from his pocket and gently dabbed her face. She sniffed and stood up. Jack carried on. 'I heard the commotion the minute I came in. My first thought was that the dogs might have got at the left-overs.' He snorted. 'If only.'

Catherine walked over to the music system in her stockinged feet and began scanning the shelves of CDs.

'Who else was out front, besides you?'

He cast me a sharp glance. But he answered. According to Jack, Olivia and Liam had returned in the E-type a few minutes before. Olivia then popped out to visit a neighbour; Liam hung around in the garage, he thought, fiddling with the car.

'Anyone else? Your brother-in-law, Max? His son, Robin?'

Catherine selected a disc, slid it into the drawer, clicked a button on the remote control. The room was filled with a bright Latin American rhythm.

'Robin's gone for a run, I believe. Grantchester Meadows. And Max, if he's not in the office, is probably on his way back to Norfolk. He only came in today because of an appointment.'

A shadow of annoyance passed over Jack's face. He scowled at Catherine. 'Can't you turn it down?' he asked.

Catherine seemed not to hear him.

Jack gave up. He left the sitting room.

Catherine didn't say goodbye. She danced round the room in an improvised salsa. Her movements were stylish, provocative, witty. And her distress about what had happened in the kitchen seemed to have passed.

I waited until the track finished, enjoying the show, and then stepped over to the CD player and turned it off. Catherine looked at me in surprise.

'Catherine, a question. Where were you when all this happened?' I waved my hand in the direction of the kitchen, though I needn't have bothered. She knew what I meant.

'Upstairs, of course. In my bedroom. Packing.' She leaned against the alcove; the upper part of her body obscured the terracotta head. 'I came running down when I heard the noise.'

'Carrying your gloves?'

'Pardon?'

I took the black gloves out of my pocket and showed them to her. 'These are yours?' I noticed for the first time that Catherine had dark circles under her eyes.

She nodded. 'Oh, yes. I must have been about to pack them. I really don't remember. It's all been such a shock.'

Catherine put her hands to her cheeks. 'I suppose I look a mess,' she said. And with that, she excused herself and bounded away up the stairs.

173

I found Jack Cable ten minutes later, lying in the dark at the bottom of the pool. Though it was late afternoon, he hadn't turned the conservatory lights on. He lay on the tiled surface, flat on his back, staring up at the glass panels in the ceiling.

By now the sky had turned a gun-metal grey. The cloud cover hovered like a fog above our heads and the rain beat down fiercely on the glass panels, like hundreds of small fingers tapping for attention. It set my teeth on edge.

But Jack was exhilarated.

'To be here,' he said – I jumped at the sound of his voice, which was deep enough and loud enough to carry over the din – 'to be all safe and sound, while the storm rages outside. Don't you find that comforting, Laura? That nothing can touch us?'

Nothing? What if those misted glass panels shattered under the force of the storm? What if the spears of glass hurtled through the air? He'd be directly in their path.

I flipped a switch. Not the spotlights but the wall lights. They created an intimate glow.

Jack gestured with one hand to the lip of the pool. I lowered myself down and let my legs dangle over the side. Now the panels were directly above me, too.

'She used to swim like a fish, you know.

174

Catherine, I mean.' Jack smiled to himself. 'Olivia and I used to call her our water baby. When she was a little thing, still in nappies, I'd call her and she'd throw herself in the pool and plunge down under the water. She always trusted that I'd be there to lift her out. And when I plucked her from the water and tossed her up in the air, the sound of her giggles filled the whole room.'

I cut across his thoughts. 'Until Timmy disappeared,' I said.

Jack's eyes had, just for a moment, some of the energy I'd seen in that photograph. He gave me a piercing look. 'How did you know that?'

But he didn't wait for my reply. He averted his gaze from mine.

'Yes,' he said. 'Catherine developed asthma about that time. The sight of the water seemed to bring on an attack. We finally had the pool drained.'

'Have you ever suggested that it might be used again?'

'A couple of times. I've had it serviced.' Jack ran his hand over his bristly beard. 'Catherine became rather upset. It seemed better to leave it.'

The rain was easing now, pattering steadily and softly, instead of lashing, against the glass. The temperature in the conservatory had risen slightly.

Jack spoke again.

'You know about Mickey Monkey, too, I suppose? Timmy's favourite toy? That he disappeared with Timmy?'

'I'd guessed. It seemed the only thing that could account for your wife's elation. She's sure now? That Liam is your son?'

There was a pause before Jack spoke. 'You saw her,' he said. 'Not a shred of doubt. As far as Olivia's concerned, she's got her baby back.'

'And you, Jack? What about where you're concerned?'

At that moment there was a flash of lightning so incandescent that I could see everything, inside and outside; could see Wonder sniffing around near the trees; could see a beetle trundling along the edge of the pool; could see the glint of Jack's eyes. I began a slow count in my head... One, two, three...

But he shot back his answer. 'I'm not certain of anything any more.'

Coming from Jack Cable, I guessed, this was a major admission.

The thunder rumbled in from the west.

Jack stood up from the bottom of the pool. He dusted off his trousers and came and stood beside me.

'Can I ask you something, Laura?'

There was only a few feet between us. I could smell Imperial Leather.

'Ask away.'

'What do you think would happen to a child who was snatched from his family at four years of age? Who was raised by strangers? Held captive for over a decade?'

'I'm a private investigator, Jack, not a forensic psychiatrist.'

He didn't let me off the hook. Just kept standing there, an inch too close, as if he were in need of comfort.

I gave in. 'I suppose it depends on how he was treated. On how stable the new environment was. On what story he was told about his family. If it was handled right, if all the conditions were favourable, then I'd guess that in spite of the traumatic beginnings, he might eventually become a healthy adult. But in Liam's case – well, we don't know anything at all about the circumstances. About how he might have been treated; where he might have been.'

I filled Jack in on what little I'd learned so far from Liam himself. Jack listened intently. When I'd finished, he picked up one of the boules. He hefted it up and down, as if testing its weight. He spoke again, and this time, he was looking at the ball, not at me.

'What if he's a danger?'

'Beg your pardon?'

'All Livi can think about is the fact that he's here. She won't want to think about what might have happened to him, not yet anyway. She'll just want to revel in his return. But what if he's been abused, Laura? What if – oh, I don't know – what if he's been locked up, like those children in Belgium? Would that be inclined to make him, do you think, just a little bit crazy? To make him violent perhaps?'

'You're talking about what happened back there, in the kitchen? And about Joe?' I told him about the razor blade tied to the door handle. 'You think that could have been Liam?' I asked.

Jack dropped the silver ball from one hand to the other. And again. And again, in a steady back-and-forth motion. The thump-thump-thump of the heavy ball provided a background rhythm to his words. 'There was talk – way back then, at the time of the disappearance – of–' He hesitated before voicing the word. 'Of paedophiles. Perverts, I think they called them then.' He gave a deep sigh. 'Timmy wasn't the only child to vanish, did you know that?'

'From the same stretch of beach?'

He nodded. 'Years before. A young girl, just into her teens. There one minute, gone the next, like Timmy. And like Timmy, they never found her.'

'Not like Timmy now,' I pointed out. It was a question.

I had time to watch a droplet of rain teeter on the edge of the gutter and then slowly

178

slide down a pane of glass before Jack slammed the ball into his palm for the last time.

'Not like Timmy now,' he agreed.

We couldn't go on like this. I'd worked on cases where I'd been asked to do the impossible. I'd worked on cases where everyone was lying to me – some to hide their own guilt, some to implicate an enemy, and some just for the hell of it. I'd worked on cases where my instructions were metres short of legal and a mile short of ethical.

But I'd never worked on a case before where my own responsibilities were so damned unclear.

'Look, Jack, what is it you want me to do?'

'Now that Timmy's back, you mean? I want you to help us, Laura. Find out where the boy's been, what he's been through. Find out if he was responsible for what happened to the kitchen. For what happened to Joe.'

I interrupted. 'We've got malicious damage here. In Joe's case assault – maybe even attempted murder. We need to notify the police.'

'No!' Jack's shout echoed through the conservatory. It seemed to make the panes of glass in the windows shiver and shake. It came close to making me jump.

'I'm sorry.' His apology was quick and heartfelt. 'We can't involve the police. It would scare the boy away long before we knew whether or not he's in any way to blame. No, we have to sort it out ourselves. And if he's capable of that kind of thing, he'll have to have help.' He read my hesitation. 'Please,' he said.

It was more compelling than all his barks of instruction.

'Still no interrogation, I suppose?'

'Please,' he said again. He held the silver ball towards me. 'Laura, you know how people talk about going to the ends of the earth? I've actually been there. I've been to the North Pole and the Antarctic and other places even harder to get to and even more exotic. But everything that really matters to me is here, in this house. My home. My daughter. My wife. And – maybe – once again, my son.'

Jack placed the ball in the palm of my hand and wrapped my fingers around it. 'Help me to take care of my family.'

I've always been partial to a family man. But I'm not completely stupid.

'I've got to go, Jack. I've got a meeting this evening. I'll let you know my decision in the morning.'

He heaved a sigh of relief. Before he could interrupt I continued. 'But if I take this on, are you prepared for whatever I might find?'

'I don't understand. What do you mean?'

'Meaning that the person who trashed the

kitchen may not have been Liam at all. It could have been someone else. Someone, perhaps, from your own household.'

'That's ridiculous, for Christ's sake.' Jack's voice was close to a shout. 'Don't even go there.' Again, the panes of glass seemed to rattle.

I got quickly to my feet. I spun on my heel and headed towards the sitting room. I have a firm rule that says never spit in the face of employers, and walking away seemed the best way to ensure that I'd stick to it.

'Laura!'

I heard the vibrations as Jack climbed the chrome ladder out of the pool. I didn't turn around. I set the boule on a side table as I passed, and carried on walking.

'Laura!'

He caught up with me and put his hand on my shoulder. 'Please stop,' he said.

Yet another *please*. I had to stop. And once I'd stopped, I didn't move.

He let his hand fall from my shoulder and walked around to face me.

'I understand,' he said. 'You've got a job to do.'

'And if I do decide to continue on the case – to find out who vandalised that room, who knifed the monkey, who injured Joe–'

'All right. Agreed. You'll take it wherever it goes.'

# Chapter 13

We had a clear arrangement: six o'clock in the Red Lion public house in Grantchester, Helen, Stevie and me. But as far as I could see, only one of us was there.

I checked the nooks and crannies. Scanned the bar, where a number of men in what one might politely call late middle age slouched on stools, chewing over local events. Peeped at the illicit lovers who were positioned behind pillars. Cast an eye over an alcove where hats and streamers had been strewn round the tables in preparation for a party.

I even looked in the Ladies. All it offered was a quotation mounted under glass on the wall: *Parents are the last people who ought to have children.* Thank you, Samuel Butler; just what women need as they touch up their lipstick. I wondered whether the Gents had been similarly blessed.

But I saw no sign of my friends.

That Stevie was late didn't surprise me in the least. She'd been tailing a man for the past two days who was fond of all-night clubbing; she was singularly short of sleep, she'd pointed out, a little sourly, when I'd

182

asked her to meet me here.

That Helen was late was more un-expected. Helen Cochrane is my dearest friend, and in terms of timing she's as dependable as a turkey at Christmas. In the old days, Helen was the only student I knew who kept to the letter as well as the spirit of social arrangements. We'll meet in the Eagle, we'd say, at seven thirty. Helen would be sitting in the courtyard of the pub from 7.29 precisely, with her dark blonde hair tucked behind her ears. With that sense of precision, it's not surprising that she went on to become a librarian.

I amended that in my own mind. Librarian isn't a grand enough term for the woman who is now in charge of library services on three campuses of Eastern University. But librarian or not, Helen wasn't in the Red Lion.

The round table in the bay window emptied as I strolled past, so I took possession. I ignored the frowns of a couple who raced me for it and missed; they obviously thought that one person at such a table was one person too few. I settled back with a pint of Greene King to experience a moment of calm in what had been a decidedly untranquil day.

I had until tomorrow morning to come to a decision about whether or not to continue with the Cables. I had no need to extend the case. At Aardvaark we'd done our balancing job well that month; we'd kept back the committed and delayable and tackled the urgent or uncertain, with the result that we had a comfortable backlog of work. What I did next was entirely up to me. I could design a security program to keep animal rights activists out of a nearby laboratory that did unspeakable things to small animals for (so they told me) the purest of motives. I could provide the back-up for Stevie's surveillance. I could make one last effort to crack my longest-running case – to track down Mrs Henley's childhood sweetheart. In short, I was a girl with options; the Cable case was far from being the only game in town.

On the other hand, none of these prospects fired me up. Restraining rabbits under lock and key; sitting alone in a nightclub nursing a Coke; searching for an old man who'd abandoned Susan Henley decades before – these weren't the kind of cases to set the pulse racing.

Whereas working with the Cables offered an intriguing set of questions with no easy answers – and *Could I do it?* was the biggest question of all.

Could I find out where Liam had been in his growing-up years, and how long he'd been there, and – crazy question – who he really was? And if Olivia was right – if it turned out that Liam was indeed Timmy Cable – then could I get to the bottom of what had happened to the boy? The thought of what abuse Timmy might have suffered since his disappearance haunted Jack Cable. Without pressing Liam, had I any chance of finding out? And was it even fair to do so? What damage could I cause by raking it all up again?

Compared to that, there were the 'easy' questions. Could I establish who had strapped that razor blade to the door handle, like a landmine on a forest path, in the clear and certain expectation that, eventually, someone would fall prey?

Could I discover who had crept into the Cables' kitchen and whirled out again, like a tornado, leaving destruction in their wake? Could it be someone with a grievance against the Cables – a workman who'd been dismissed, perhaps, or a contractor who felt cheated? The grudge motive had an obvious flaw. Why would a stranger with a grievance take their fury out on a furry toy? Why attack poor little Mickey Monkey, unless you knew that his restoration might change the Cable family forever?

That suggested someone in the household. We could rule out Joe, the handyman, stuck in a bed in a corridor in Addenbrooke's. We could rule out Etta, his wife, who was sitting by his side. Olivia had been to see a neighbour, she'd said, and there was no reason to doubt her. But what about Max? He hadn't been in the kitchen when Liam pulled the monkey out of his rucksack; but he might have entered later and seen the soft toy sitting on a shelf and understood exactly what it meant. No one had actually seen Max leave; and even if he had driven off before the damage was done to the kitchen, what was to stop him parking on the High Street three minutes' walk away and creeping back along the path in the woods?

That left Jack or Catherine or Liam himself. Any one of them could have come around the side of the house to the kitchen door and left again without a witness. The obvious person was Catherine – who was supposedly upstairs packing when the room was trashed, but who'd dropped her gloves in the kitchen, as if she'd come in from outside. Catherine, who had climbed into my car uninvited, round about the time my palm-top disappeared. Catherine, who had the strongest motive: that the return of the long-lost son, of *the one her father cared most about,* might knock her out of place.

The case presented a challenge all right, I thought, finishing off my pint. Too much of a challenge? A PI who wants to stay in business has to be mindful of her track record. Nothing succeeds like success, they say. But if that's true, then nothing flops like failure.

I looked at my watch. It was almost half past six and the Red Lion was filling up fast. The No Smoking section was overflowing with a family party; they ran the gamut of ages from two years to eighty-two. A couple in their seventies – she creased with giggles, he beaming – sat squashed together at one end of a long table. Three pre-schoolers led the company in a chorus of 'Wannabe'. A young woman on the margins of the group put a tiny wrinkly-faced infant to the breast and gave a sigh of relief when it settled into a rhythmic suck. I smiled and amended my estimate; from two weeks to eighty-two years.

And still no sign of my pals.

I couldn't ring them. I was prevented by prejudice. Out of a raging dislike for overcoat pockets that play 'Amazing Grace' or handbags that bleep, I'd left my mobile in the car. And if I trotted over to the car park to fetch my phone, I'd have to surrender the table and be forced into that dreary corner by the fruit machine.

I considered. Looked around my alcove. Took in for the first time the decor. The wood panelling below the banquette, scarred by scraping heels and spilled drinks. The dull red patterned carpet. The design of the upholstery, in shades of cream and green and rose. The curtains at the windows, with their weave of orange and blue. Gathered up my raincoat and made my way out.

And there, blocking my exit, scraping the mud off her boots, was Stevie.

'We've been trying to ring you,' she said. 'Don't you ever check your messages?'

'No phone.' I spread my arms to prove it.

'Helen and I are across the street in the Green Man.'

The Green Man was blissfully quiet. Customers were murmuring rather than singing. No fruit machines, no family parties – and, apart from some quietly faded curtains, only original beams and floors of bare planks and walls of old wood. Not a pattern in sight.

Helen sat at a table near the wood-burning stove. She wore jeans and a rollneck sweater under a denim jacket. Her dark blonde hair was so wet it looked almost black. Her skin was free of make-up.

'Don't mind me,' she said, 'I was caught in a rainstorm.' She waved towards her raincoat. It was draped over a chair near the fire, giving off a gentle mist.

'You look as fresh as a daisy.' We exchanged a kiss and she helped me arrange my coat next to hers. Stevie was at the bar fetching drinks. 'What are you two doing

188

here? I thought we were going to meet at the other pub?'

Helen leaned forward. She lowered her voice. 'Stevie was put off by all the children,' she said.

Stevie sauntered up. She carried three pints of Adnams as if to barwork born. 'OK with you?' she asked, setting the glass down in front of me. 'They serve decent New World wines if you'd rather.'

'This will do me nicely. Cheers.' We clinked glasses. 'So what was your beef with the Red Lion, Stevie? I thought you liked children.'

Stevie's one of my few child-free friends who can carry on a conversation with Sonny's boys, Dominic and Daniel, as if they're human. Which, of course, they are. She's shown herself in the past to be attentive to their welfare in ways that make me blush, because I don't come off well in the comparison.

Stevie leaned over and eased off her boots. She stretched out her legs. She propped her feet on the edge of the hearth and wiggled her toes in contentment. Only then did I get an answer.

'No more and no less than I like adults,' she said.

Blame it on the beer, which had begun to relax my brain. I didn't get it.

'I don't get it,' I said.

'Laura, even when you're as thick as two short planks' – Stevie smiled to show it was a run-of-the-mill tease rather than an attack – 'I count you among my friends. And you,' she said, exchanging extravagant air kisses with Helen. 'And,' she added almost shyly, 'I'm rather fond of Geoff.'

Helen and I bandied sly glances. Rather fond? After months of steamy togetherness, Stevie still looked at Geoff as if he were the hottest thing since the eruption of Vesuvius.

Wisely, Stevie ignored us. 'And there are plenty of adults – Doreen Lawrence, for starters, Joseph Fiennes, for looks, and Daley Thompson and Emma Goldman and Rosa Parks – who make it on to my personal honours list. But that doesn't give carte blanche to adults in general. It doesn't mean for a minute that I'd welcome Ian Brady or Margaret Thatcher to dinner.'

I figured it out at last, what Stevie meant. That they're all different. That you can't have a view of children, or adults, en masse.

'So why did you run away from the Red Lion?'

Stevie's answer shot back. 'Why don't you try hanging out in the Ministry of Sound night after night? Reel from the flashing lights. Cringe before the drunken choruses. Feel the bass in your breastbone. Then see if you don't cross the street for a bit of peace and quiet.'

Fair point. I wondered whether, as Stevie's employer, I should have issued her with ear protectors. It didn't seem very Philip Marlowe – but then neither did respecting women or loving men or enjoying life, and I was into all of those.

Helen wasn't satisfied with Stevie's answer. 'Seriously, Stevie,' she said – in the kind of tone that struggles to be light – 'what do you think of children?' A faint blush floated up above the top of her rollneck and flowed over her jawline and on to her cheeks. 'I mean, it's strange, isn't it? There've been weeks – before Geoff, I mean – when we practically lived in each other's pockets. And I still don't know. Can you imagine yourself with kids?'

It was a startling question coming just like that, out of the blue. Parents ask that kind of question; so do nosy in-laws, and people from the old neighbourhood who really ought to know better. But among friends, usually, issues of motherhood are left until they just float to the surface. Until one friend says, in passing: *Thank God I've got other things to do with my life*. Or: *I've always wanted to have a daughter named Alicia*. Then you'd take other information about that person – the serious relationship that ended abruptly, the ovarian cyst, the career shift – and you'd put it all together and know as much as you needed to know. Asking outright would be too inquisitive. It would border on the aggressive, and especially so when the person doing the asking already had a child. Helen didn't have to account for herself; her daughter Ginny, thirteen and thriving, told us all we needed to know.

So I was startled; and Helen, I suspect, had surprised even herself when she dropped that little bombshell. It wasn't just the blush that gave her away. It was that uncharacteristic hesitancy; she knew the ice was thin.

But still, I could see where she was coming from. We had spent a lot of time together, the three of us, mostly in Norfolk, at Wildfell Cottage. Another friend, Claire, sold it to Helen and me for a song, determined to distance herself from the place where her father took his life. And when we found, after the roof needed mending and the shutters re-hanging, that we couldn't keep it up out of our own incomes, Stevie emerged as the perfect third. She brought a steady good humour that overrode Helen's occasional nerviness, a practical bent that was good for the fabric of the house, and a new gusto to our conversations, which lasted after her arrival even later into the night.

And that was why it seemed odd that Helen didn't know, that I didn't know, such a fundamental thing – whether Stevie wanted children.

So Helen's question exploded into the room. Stevie had been wiggling her toes in the warmth of the fire. She stopped. She withdrew one leg from the hearth. I felt a stab of sympathy. The woman was worn out; she'd hurried up here from London at my insistence, only to be confronted by a question that she didn't want. But when Stevie spoke, there was no trace of indignation in her tone. Nothing more than a studied distance.

'Helen,' she said, 'I'm very fond of you. I admire your generosity and value your advice. I even have a sneaking regard for the way you cheat at poker.'

This was intended as a joke, but none of us smiled. The rose in Helen's cheeks became more intense. She and I were waiting for the *but*.

'So I won't tell you to fuck off. I won't even say it's none of your business, though that would be true. I'll tell you what you want to know. I was sterilised when I was twenty-one,' she said, 'by a private surgeon in Harley Street. I worked all summer at a boatyard in Wales, and saved my money, and paid for the operation myself. I'd tried to get it done earlier, you see. I'd pestered my mother, who was appalled. I'd pestered my GP; I'd finally spoken to a gynaecologist. Uniformly, they said no. I was too young, they said. I'd regret it.'

There was a few seconds' pause. Stevie studied the course of a raindrop as it skidded down the window pane.

'But I wasn't,' she said, 'and I didn't. Ever since my cousin Hedy gave birth just before her sixteenth birthday, I'd known that there was no way I'd ever have a child.'

The expression on Stevie's face was half pride, half pain. Like she was sure of what she'd done, and sure also that she'd be despised for it.

We sat for a moment in dead silence. I was stunned. To know your own mind at such a young age seemed astonishing to me. When it came to children, I'd been stumbling for decades towards a decision.

'So now you know,' she said.

A little voice nagged at me. Once, in my late teens, I'd renounced all animal products. It lasted less than a year. Would Stevie come to regret it, still?

Helen saw it differently. 'My God,' she said. She reached across and lifted Stevie's hand off the table. She laid it palm to palm with her own. She examined it, finger by finger, as if she were about to give a manicure.

'My God,' she repeated. 'Just like me.'

Helen? Sterilised at twenty-one? Not as far as I knew. When Helen was twenty-one, she and I lived on the same hallway in Newnham College, Cambridge. We ate together and studied together and cycled around the city together. Sometimes we even slept together, in a purely platonic way. We shared everything. Helen would never have contemplated such a radical move without talking it over with me. She couldn't have nipped off to Harley Street for a snip – or whatever you call the female equivalent – without me registering her absence, noticing her pain. Could she?

More to the point, Helen was Ginny's mother and Ginny was a wanted child. How could Helen say she and Stevie were the same?

Helen was still holding Stevie's hand.

Stevie searched her face. 'Just like you, Helen?'

'So certain,' Helen said. 'As if there was never a decision to be made. I can't remember a time when I didn't look at babies in the street and feel a longing. When I didn't imagine a future that included children. Several children, I used to think.' She laughed, and released Stevie's hand at last. 'Put that bit down to inexperience. Once I'd learned what an assault on the self there is in looking after a child, the idea of half a dozen of the little darlings lost its charm.'

Helen raised her pint glass to her lips, and then stopped. As if to punctuate her statement, she added, 'I vacillated about whether to have a second, but never about whether to be a mother in the first place. I was always certain. Like you.'

The relief was palpable. Helen had done it again. Here was a difference so sharp-edged it could slice through the firmest of friendships. Could leave two women of otherwise compatible age, interests, temperaments on opposite sides, bristling at the intolerance of one and the smugness of the other. But Helen had plucked this difference and opened it up and found agreement inside. The woman who couldn't imagine a life without children, and the woman who found motherhood abhorrent: *just like me.*

And Stevie? I knew precisely why Stevie had never told us before. In spite of the fact that motherhood is supposed to unite women, that it is supposed in some accounts to be what we have in common – actually, probably because of those accounts – positions on motherhood divide women more ferociously than anything else. Stevie had held back because she'd feared being the outsider again; if she told the truth about herself, she'd feared she'd be left beyond the boundary looking in.

Helen had taken a piece of chalk and redrawn the circle so that Stevie stood inside, with her.

Stevie was all smiles now.

And where did that leave me?

'The blackboard, girls,' Stevie proclaimed, pointing us towards a menu scribbled in chalk. 'Who's for a burrito?'

'Laura,' Helen said, and she wasn't referring to the choices on the menu, 'you're more ambivalent, aren't you?'

Suddenly, involuntarily, I thought of Olivia Cable. Had she been sure about motherhood? Had she been untroubled by doubts, confident about the future? First Catherine and then Timmy: were these babies always expected, always longed for?

Or did Olivia, as sometimes happens, surprise herself – was she a reluctant mother, an irresolute mother, struggling to reconcile herself to pregnancy? Was she then suddenly won over by the beauty of her child?

And when Timmy disappeared – when the moments stretched into hours, and the hours into days – did Olivia ever, even for a moment, regret his birth?

I had tried to imagine what it would be like. How much pain you could fit into – how long had she said? – twelve years, four months and six days?

How many times would you think of your child during that span?

How often would you turn a corner and be pierced with disappointment when he wasn't there?

How often would you hear a call of

'Mummy!' and spin around, an answer leaping to your lips?

The heretic thought crept into my mind again... Surely it is better never to have had a child than to have had a child and lost it.

'Laura?'

'Sorry, Helen. It's this case.'

We ordered burritos and salads and a big bowl of chips to share, and I unburdened myself about the Cables.

'Can I tell you something – strictly in confidence? Something Olivia Cable told me?'

It took me a while to get started. Stevie and Helen waited, patiently, sipping their beer, until at last I felt able to begin.

'Olivia tried to explain to me what it's like to lose a child. She told me a story. It went like this...

'"Sometimes a little girl who lives nearby comes to visit. She's been told about Timmy. She's fascinated. She's less inhibited than her parents. She asks questions. 'Your little boy, the one who disappeared,' she says. 'He's younger than me, yes? Does he go to school?' How do I answer? Timmy is older than her, now – much older. He was just about to enter reception class the year he went away, but now he'd be sitting GCSE exams. I imagine him, his papers spread all over the kitchen table, hurrying to complete his coursework, selecting the subjects he'll study at A level, struggling with maths, romping through DT."

'And now, Olivia told me, her son is here. And she has to try to grasp the reality of this young man and make it match up with the son who lives in her imagination. "It's like they are two blurry images," she said. "When I superimpose them, the outlines don't quite coincide."'

Stevie remembered something too. She recalled a memoir written by a Frenchwoman about the death of her daughters in a road accident.

'Olivia must have been through something like that,' she said.

'No. Not like that.' I was emphatic. 'We talked about that book – *The Disappearance*. Olivia complained about the title. "It's not about disappearance, it's about death," she declared, "and that makes all the difference." I had to ask her what she meant. She referred me to the opening lines of one chapter, where Jurgensen, the Frenchwoman, wrote, "Well, it is twelve years now. On Sunday we went to the grave." When Olivia read that, she said, she was overwhelmed with envy. She was desolate at the thought that she would never be able to visit a grave. Never weep for Timmy in that way. Never let him rest.'

'The poor woman!' Stevie said. You don't

have to be a mother to identify with despair.

By unspoken agreement, we moved on to lighter things. To food. Stevie chased up our order. I noticed her calm assurance as she moved to the bar. When I turned back, Helen was watching me.

'You didn't answer, Laura.'

'Hmm?'

'I asked you a question about motherhood. About ambivalence.'

And again, an image leapt unbidden into my mind. This time it was a woman, tall and strong and bursting with news. And a man, thrilled by what she had to tell him. And the woman was me. The image was so vivid that for a moment I could feel my abdomen swelling, sense the excitement of something growing inside. I could feel the weight and the warmth as the man placed his possessive hand on my proud belly.

'Laura?'

Am I ambivalent? Helen wants to know. Helen cares enough to push.

'What was it Phyllis McGinley said, Helen? About indecision? Shivering naked in the draught from an open mind – that's me.'

# Chapter 14

I rose early and reluctantly, after a restless night spent listening to the drumming of the rain and considering the Cables. A current of cold air cut through me as I struggled out from under the duvet. I yanked the sash window shut, picked up my rowing clothes from the hook on the back of the bedroom door and raced for the bathroom.

I ran the shower on hot. The temperature of the room lifted. I adjusted the setting down a notch and stepped through the steam into the full force of the spray. My muscles are happier to strut their stuff on a winter's morning if I treat them first to something resembling a tropical waterfall.

Leggings and a sweatshirt, socks and trainers, a bowl of porridge and a mug of coffee, and I was on my way.

It was six thirty a.m. The city was dark. The pavements, still slicked with water from the last downpour, had a burnished glow in the light from the streetlamps. Someone might have walked this way minutes before, scattering a trail of gold.

Two or three cars crept by me with sleepy drivers at the wheel. A cyclist whizzed out of

Carlyle Road, scarcely bothering to look for traffic, and pedalled off towards the Backs. Her tyres made a slick sound on the wet surface of the road. I strode on towards the boathouse.

It took time to undo the locks and roll open the massive doors and manoeuvre my scull into the water, but it was worth the wait. Worth it, as always, for that deliciously familiar sensation, the excitement rising in me as I lowered myself into the boat – steady, steady – as I fixed the seat, strapped my feet in and positioned the oars and set off. As I became – slowly, slowly – one with the river.

A few lights glimmered in the windows on Banhams Close, but apart from the people who lived in those houses and a grumpy duck, its black eye open and unseeing, I might have been the only living being in the world. The surface of the river looked as dark and shiny and solid as obsidian.

I rowed with a long, steady stroke past Midsummer Common. It took an effort to bring the movement of legs and arms and wrists into harmony, to maintain a straight back, to open my chest, to feel the muscles move under the skin. By the time I swept silently under the willows opposite Riverside, I was beginning to find my stroke – to feel the rush of confidence as my breathing found a level in rhythm with the oars. I knew I'd turned the corner when the initial ache in my shoulders gave way to an awareness of strength and my legs began to pump of their own accord.

No uncertainty now. Just that extraordinary feeling, as if I could go on for ever and ever.

I glided past Stourbridge Common, where a pair of bedraggled ponies were huddled near a hedge. Skimmed by the deeper green of Ditton Meadows. Flew by Chesterton Fen and under the motorway and all the way to Bait's Bite Lock.

My cheeks blazed with exertion on the return journey. The night was losing its grip. It no longer sat like a shroud of black velvet on the tops of the trees. It was reduced to a colourless curtain of gauze, bleaching as the timid light of winter dawn began slowly to bring objects into view. I could see clearly the clouds of breath that hung behind me like a jet trail. The arc of Elizabeth Way Bridge. The trickle of pedestrians trudging across Midsummer Common. And in the distance I could make out the ghostly silhouette of the chestnut trees that marched across Jesus Green.

By the time I put the boat away, the morning air was pearly grey, the branches on the trees stood out sharp and clear and I'd made up my mind.

When I wound my way up the Mill Way and pulled, eventually, into the driveway of Grantchester Farm, it was just short of noon. The farm was far from isolated this time. On the roof of the outbuildings, men in orange safety vests and helmets were stripping slates. They moved across the pitched roof with a wary grace. In the distant field, where the first of the spring barley spread its vivid green dust among the clods, a tractor manoeuvred at the edge of the ditch.

And near the house, a car that I knew to be Olivia's was parked in the middle of the driveway. The Renault Clio's doors stood open. I brought the Saab to a halt. Catherine Cable appeared, backside first, from the door on the driver's side. She was brandishing a car vacuum. She straightened up and waved to me as Liam appeared with a hosepipe in tow. It didn't reach as far as the driveway. He set the nozzle down near the corner of the house.

Catherine hailed me.

'Laura, you're just in time to help. We're going to pick Joe up from Addenbrooke's. They've discharged him. We thought,' she added, with a smile of complicity for Liam, 'that Etta and the injured man deserved a vehicle that was shining and shipshape.' She turned off the vacuum and called to Liam. 'There are buckets and brushes and cloths in the garage.'

A little bossy-boots was Catherine. But Liam didn't seem to mind.

'I know.' He loped off towards the garage without waiting to be told.

'Look.'

She pointed to the dashboard of the Renault. Mickey Monkey was hunched there, a large trouser patch in denim covering the hole in his chest where the knife had gone in.

'He needs a crutch,' I laughed. 'He looks like an old war veteran.'

It took less than a quarter of an hour to clean the car. Record time, it seemed to me, but then I hadn't done it often enough to know. Liam, being the tallest, soaped and rinsed the roof and the bonnet; there was a splodge of suds down the front of his jumper. Catherine scrubbed the underside and the wheels with a stiff brush until they gleamed and then doused the paintwork with buckets of icy water. She shouted, 'Heave ho!' before she threw each bucket, and Liam leapt out of her way.

I dried my hands on a scrap of towel and quickly reached for my camera. Catherine was advancing on Liam with a full bucket. He backed away in mock terror, laughing and stumbling. Then he noticed me as I stood, camera poised. His mood altered in an instant.

'I hate photographs,' he said.

In one strong movement he made a grab for Catherine, tore the bucket from her hand and threw it to the ground. He spun her around so that she stood directly in front of him, and ducked behind her shoulder. She was startled, but only until she noticed me. Then, with a breathless giggle, she reached for Mickey Monkey and held him out at arm's length towards me, dancing him up and down in a wild rhythm.

'Say cheese,' I said, and hit the shutter.

Only when I'd walked back to the Saab and traded my camera for a bulky shoulder bag with a gaudy silver clasp did Liam relax. Something had worried him, but it wasn't my poor taste in accessories. He and Catherine gave the car a final wipe and climbed in. Catherine took the wheel.

Liam retrieved his cigarette lighter and tobacco tin from the dashboard as he sat down. His rucksack was nowhere to be seen.

I was standing on Liam's side a few feet distant from the car. His face was angled away from me. He had that sixteen-year-old sullenness again. I called his name.

I called his name again.

When he turned towards me, I spoke very, very quietly. He was forced to look up at my lips.

'Liam,' I said, in a voice just above a

whisper, 'I'm sorry about the photo.'

He was a good-natured kid. He shrugged and gave me a wary smile. I smiled back.

He didn't notice that I depressed the clasp of the handbag. Didn't hear the tiny click. And another. And another. And another.

My parting words were for Catherine. 'We need to talk, you know.'

She appeared to be blithely unconcerned. 'No problem,' she said. 'We'll be back in an hour. By the way, Dad's waiting for you, in the sitting room.'

And with that she slammed her neat little foot down hard on the accelerator and they roared off down the drive.

Jack Cable was in the sitting room all right. His hard-backed chair had been turned so that it faced the alcove in the opposite wall. He sat well forward, legs planted far apart, elbows on knees. His chin rested in his hands.

He was staring at the terracotta image of Timmy. He might have been in conversation with it, so close was his attention. His eyes flicked from one feature to another, hungrily. His expression was quizzical, as if he were interrogating the sculpture, looking for some kind of answer.

His concentration was so intense that he didn't hear me come into the room.

'Mr Cable?' Something about the situation made me want to revert to formal terms.

He didn't acknowledge me. His focus never wavered.

The sitting room was oppressively hot. The wrought-iron basket in the stone fireplace had been piled high with chunks of log. The fire flared and crackled. All the lights in the room – the table lamps, the downlighters in the ceiling, the spotlights in the alcoves – had been turned on. The room was ablaze with light.

Was this the single-mindedness Max had boasted about? Was it this dogged focus, this capacity for unwavering attention, that had enabled Jack to take a party of men and women into the inhospitable northern regions and come back with the prize that they'd sought?

I shuffled my feet. Jack Cable might have been cocooned in a cone of silence for all the notice he took of me.

Finally I had no choice but to step close to him, so close that we could have touched, and speak again. He gave a slight shake of the head, as if emerging from a trance, and looked up at me.

'Laura,' he said. 'Forgive me.'

He gestured towards one of the pale yellow sofas.

I sat down, wondering what he thought he should be forgiven for. I unlooped my scarf and placed it on the seat next to me. I kept my jacket on, in spite of the heat. That's winter for you, I thought. Either too hot or too cold.

'You'll continue with the case?'

He'd been expecting my decision. He wasn't being smug about it – wasn't assuming that what Jack Cable wanted, Jack Cable got. His tone was, for the first time, quite humble. It was simply, I thought, that he understood how I felt.

I told him what little – how little – I'd learned so far. He listened quietly.

I warned that it would take time to come up with anything concrete about Liam's background, or Joe's accident, or the incident in the kitchen.

He didn't find that off-putting.

He didn't want the details of how I intended to proceed. He said he was interested in results, not in my methods.

'But there's one thing.'

'I know,' I said.

He raised an eyebrow.

'Don't heavy the boy.'

Jack smiled. The smile was bleak.

It was even bleaker when I told him that he and his family might be in danger. That it couldn't be an accident that Joe's injury and the attack on the kitchen had occurred so soon after Liam's arrival.

'You mean–'

Maybe Jack was right, was what I meant. Maybe his son Timmy, the baby with the thoughtful eyes and the wise, anxious face, had been reincarnated as a damaged young man. Someone determined to make others suffer for the suffering he'd been through.

'I mean be careful.'

It sounded trite, even to me. How could Jack and Olivia Cable take steps to ease the distance and hurt that had accumulated over the years – to compensate their son for the life he had lost – and at the same time take care? How? By keeping him at a distance, holding him at arm's length, distrusting him, avoiding intimacy? That their long-lost son should return and then be treated this way was unthinkable.

And I knew, by the resigned look on Jack's face, by the slump of his shoulders, that he knew it too.

Jack's gaze was fixed again on the sculpture.

'Was that done by a local artist, Jack?'

'No, no. She's not an artist, exactly, she's a forensic specialist. Barbara Dobson. We came across her through a missing persons charity. The resemblance to Timmy is really quite good, you know, but I – I find the thing difficult to look at. It's the eyes. They're so lifeless.'

The terracotta head seemed to me to be slightly larger than life-size. The features were carefully sculpted; the shape of the brow, the line of the mouth, the curve of the cheek looked authentic. Looked, that is, as if they might be reproduced, just so, on a living, breathing human being.

But the terracotta eyes were something else. There was no sense of looking outward. They made the sculpture look like a shell of a person whose self was somewhere else.

Jack stood and walked slowly over to the alcove. I noticed an asymmetry in his stride – the result, I supposed, of the artificial leg. He stood in front of the shelf. He placed one powerful hand on each side of the terracotta head and lifted it until the eyes were on a level with his own. He remained there, unmoving, unblinking even. A statue holding a statue.

'I partly blame this for my nightmares,' he said.

There was a long pause. I kept completely quiet, willing him to continue. First Liam; now Jack. I seemed to be collecting Cable family nightmares one by one.

'I'm on expedition,' Jack said, 'somewhere on the western edge of Greenland. I come out of my tent into the snow and suddenly I know that my son is missing. There is no sign of him. No footprints, nothing. The sun is shining brightly. It dazzles off the ice. There is only emptiness for miles around. And then, on the high horizon, I see a tiny dot. I watch for minutes, unable to move, as the dot enlarges. As it assumes an elongated shape. As it takes on a little colour. After perhaps an hour I can tell that it's Timmy, coming towards me through a sea of snow, plodding determinedly, his parka the only pigmentation on the landscape. I race out to meet him, stumbling and leaping in my haste. He trudges steadily towards me. He doesn't look up. He doesn't say a word. At last I reach him. The hood of the parka is pulled forward over his face. I throw my arms around him. I rock him to and fro. "Timmy, Timmy. It's Daddy. You're safe!" But he doesn't say a word. He is silent. I push his hood back off his forehead so I can see his face. Timmy's eyelids are swollen and gummy. His eyes are unseeing. He's been blinded by the sun on the snow.'

'Horrible,' I murmured. Not exactly a happy reunion.

There was a flurry of movement as, Olivia came skipping down the stairs. When she saw Jack staring into the blank eyes of the bust, she halted. She didn't need to ask *What are you doing?* The question was there in the way she said her husband's name.

'Jack?'

She moved to within a couple of feet from him, her head tilted at an angle. She tossed me a quick, worried glance, and then turned back to her husband.

'I've been hearing about Jack's nightmare, Olivia.'

'That dreadful one with Timmy snow-blind?' she asked.

I nodded.

She looked relieved.

'Liam has nightmares too, Olivia. About being dragged off a beach. Has he mentioned them to you?'

She shook her head – no – and a worried frown formed between her brows. Her gaze remained on Jack. So did mine. He held the bust at eye-level still, as if in a trance.

'Or the other one?' I continued. 'About the birds? Taller than him, he said they are. They crowd round and speak in a language he doesn't understand. He clearly finds it terrifying.'

My account of Liam's dream had an astonishing effect on Jack Cable. His head swivelled slowly towards me. The colour drained from his face.

'Oh my God,' he said. 'If he knows that... How can he know that?... If he knows that...' At the last, the words were no more than a whisper. He trembled slightly.

I reached out to offer support when, without warning, Olivia burst into impassioned speech.

'Now are you convinced?' Her voice was shrill, just notes away from a scream. 'Did you hear what Laura said? What Liam told her? What more proof do you need?'

Jack was standing as he had been before, facing the alcove, the terracotta bust held high. He'd scarcely moved during my recital. But now, under the force of emotion, his hands began to shake. I stepped to his side and reached for the bust to ease it back on to the shelf, but I was too late.

His hands released their grip. The bust fell the full six feet to the floor. It landed at an angle. There was a sickening crack and then, section by section, it crumbled.

Jack looked once at his hands in astonishment, as if he was surprised to find them empty. Then he turned to Olivia and swept her up in his arms. But though the gesture was his, it was Olivia with her blue, blue eyes who crooned the sing-song words of comfort.

'It's all right, baby. He's come home.'

The only other noise, once the echoes from the crash of the sculpture had died away, was the jagged sound of Jack Cable's sobs.

## Chapter 15

The shattering of the terracotta bust broke some kind of deadlock. Jack accepted – really accepted, I imagined, for the first time – that Liam was the adolescent embodiment of his infant son. Olivia felt secure in his acceptance. They seemed locked in wonder at it together. When they retired upstairs, to their private suite, Jack held her hand like a child and Olivia blazed, once again, with happiness.

But not before I had found out why Liam's nightmare had struck such a chord.

It was Jack's story, really. He had been too overwhelmed to speak, so Olivia did the honours. A long time ago, she'd said, like a kindly grandmother beginning a fairytale, Jack took Timmy out for a drive in the E-type. They drove into Norfolk, towards King's Lynn. They stopped at a farm. Jack had business there. It was a hot day. Timmy had fallen asleep, his cheeks flushed and his thumb in his mouth. Jack made him comfortable and put his bottle of juice next to him and opened the car windows. Then he went into the house, leaving Timmy to wake up in his own time.

As he emerged from the house, Jack heard the child's screams. Timmy had woken up and climbed out of the car in search of his father. He'd attracted the interest of a gaggle of turkeys, a bird he'd never seen before. They had swarmed around him, necks bobbing. They'd loomed over the little boy; they'd squawked and gobbled. Timmy was terrified, and the terror remained with him – well, at least, Olivia had said delicately, until he disappeared.

Monstrous-looking birds, taller than him, gabbling in a foreign language, crowding round, threatening... You could map the child's experience on to Liam's nightmare.

The fit was preternatural, I thought – too close to be coincidence. There were only two possibilities. Either Liam was Timmy. Or Liam knew an uncanny amount about the missing child.

And speaking of missing, now – while Jack and Olivia were ensconced in their room; while Catherine and Liam were off fetching Etta and Joe – might be the perfect opportunity to search. For my missing palm-top and for other things.

I left my ankle boots in the hallway and crept in stockinged feet up the stairs to Catherine's room. The staircase had probably been hammered in place some centuries before; the third step, and then the eighth, gave off spooky-mansion creaks.

The sitting room had been uncomfortably warm under the twin impacts of central heating and an open fire; it had been dazzlingly lit. Catherine's bedroom, at the top of the house, was hot and stuffy and dark. As my eyes adjusted to the gloom, I could sense that something had changed since my last visit. Not the bed, which was still piled with pillows and topped by a teddy bear; not the worn music stand, nor the fragile wicker chair. It was the dormer window. The frilly curtains with their tie-back bows were gone. In their place was a loose length of cotton in a dramatic shade of blue. It wasn't little-girly, it wasn't old and it wasn't worn; it was distinctly at odds with the rest of the room. The curtain suggested that Catherine had suddenly and belatedly begun to grow up.

I didn't want to loop the curtain up; no point in making my presence visible from the yard. Instead, I switched on a lamp on the dressing table. And in its soft light I could see that I wouldn't even have to search. There, on the wicker chair, like a prize on a chintzy pink cushion, was Liam's rucksack.

I emptied the contents out on Catherine's double bed. Disappointment. No address book, no diary, no ID, no credit cards; if Liam had these things at all, he had them, as he did his lighter, on his person. The rest of

the contents were as anonymous as a Big
Mac. There was a pair of gloves, a bottle
opener, a stubby pencil and a few loose
coins. The remains of a bag of Maltesers. I
tested one and carried on. There was a cycle
lamp and a Yale key and a cinema ticket.
Last but not least, there was a postcard. I
pounced on it and took it over to the light.

The card was written all over in blue biro.
The script was careful, neat, naïve – female
handwriting, I would have said, a girl or a
woman, though I may have been influenced
in this assessment by the signature. *Loads of
love, Gemma.* The card had obviously been
enclosed in an envelope; there was no
address, no postmark and no surname for
Dear Liam. But there was an account of
recent events – a birthday party for Jessica,
whoever she might be; a paint-job for the
front of the house; and – Gemma hoped
he'd be pleased – Clifford had won his
argument with Stevenage Borough Council.

Not much to go on, I thought; but better
than a kick in the teeth.

I piled the contents back in the rucksack,
threw the rucksack back on the chair, and
began to poke around. The drawers yielded
nothing beyond clothes and personal items
and an undisguised stash of marijuana. I ran
my hands under the mattress. Nothing
again. I tackled the wardrobe. The bedroom
was neat to the point of prissiness, but the

contents of the wardrobe were sheer chaos. I felt a touch of warmth for Catherine; her cupboard strategy was a lot like mine.

On tiptoe, I felt along the top shelf. I examined boxes and bottles and bags of clothing, but found nothing. Then I went down on hands and knees. I felt along the floor – well, not the floor, exactly. I felt among the heaps of shoes and sweaters and belts and bags that had drifted there like leaves in an autumn wind. I was just rummaging through her partly packed suitcase, which lay on the floor near the end of the bed, when I heard a spooky-mansion sound.

It must have been the eighth step, rather than the third; she was inside the room in seconds. I rose to my feet and waited, trying to look as if I belonged between the kidney-shaped dressing table and the pillow-piled bed.

In this light, Catherine Cable's eyes were the colour of denim. They darted around the room before they came back to settle on me. I tried to read their expression. It wasn't easy, because in the seconds before Catherine finally spoke, the expression shifted several times. She looked more shocked than alarmed at first; and more surprised than angry. Then annoyance entered; she frowned, as if struggling to make sense of something, and at the last, she assumed a knowing look. If this were a cartoon, I'd have seen the light bulb blink on above her head.

The rush up the stairs hadn't winded her at all, but when the light bulb flicked on, her breathing became ragged.

'So it was you,' she said. There was lots of emphasis on the *you* and the emphasis wasn't friendly.

I hadn't expected that at all.

'Me? What was me?'

'Oh, don't give me that.' She moved to the bed in two swift steps and bounced on to it. Fiercely, her irritation showing in her gestures, she rearranged the pillows into a great heap to support her back and punched them into place. She used her inhaler, breathing deeply twice, and then faced me again.

'Yesterday. It was you who went through my case. You threw my stuff on the floor. You broke my hand mirror.'

Now it was my turn to look astonished. 'No way,' I said. 'The only other time I've been in your room, Catherine, was when you brought me here. And today... Today, I'm looking for my palm-top. My electronic organiser. It went missing from my car.'

'What makes you think it might be here?'

'The day it went missing was the day you climbed into my car, uninvited. Remember?'

'Of course I remember climbing into your

car. But I don't know anything about your bloody palm-top.' Suddenly, unexpectedly, the irritation fell from her features and she began to giggle.

I watched her. It didn't seem to be an act.

'What's so funny, Catherine?'

'It's just–' she spluttered, and then began giggling again. 'It's just so tit-for-tat. My suitcase was ransacked. It wasn't you. Your palm-top was stolen. It wasn't me. Touché,' she said, as if that was all there was to say. And she leaned back on her elbows and proceeded to lift her left leg up and down, up and down, as if I had come to her room specifically to watch her exercise.

She was only nineteen, I reminded myself. An emotionally young nineteen at that. I thought about the girl, about her background. An outsider might say that Catherine Cable had a lot going for her. She had an attractive home, her mother's eyes and the kind of poise you'd expect from a girl brought up in this kind of family. She was backed by the Cable money and the Cable reputation. She was clever enough to get an Upper Second in her first-year exams, and even though she disparaged this achievement, it was a good start.

A lot going for her. But was it enough? She'd spent the years from seven until nineteen in a family on whose heads tragedy lay like a toxic cloud. I could only guess at the daily injuries. Had Timmy become, in his absence, the perfect child, the one who could do no wrong? Did Catherine find herself forever being compared? Did she find herself wanting? At Timmy's disappearance, had she lost her right to be a child – to throw back her head and laugh without guilt, to complain and stamp her feet and press for more? Was laughter made to seem, at times, unfeeling? Did any complaint seem selfish when things were (after all) so much worse for Timmy? Should she feel grateful to be the one not missing? Guilty even? Survivor guilt?

And besides all this, there was the simple pain the sister might feel at the loss of a brother.

And the period immediately after the disappearance? *I don't mean to be flippant,* she'd protested, referring to that moment as T-Day. Her brother gone. The family in turmoil. Her mother in mourning. And, soon, her father absent. Catherine clearly loved her father; I remembered her curled up on his chest like a baby. When Jack went off to the Arctic, had Catherine felt it as a kind of punishment? Had it seemed that now his baby boy was gone – *the thing he cared most about in the world* – he was rejecting her too?

'Catherine?'

Catherine had finished fifty or sixty leg

raises – I wasn't counting – with the left leg and then the right. She flattened her shoulders and back on to the bed and, in one sinuous movement, lifted her hips high into the air. She began to bicycle.

I stepped around to the side of the bed so I could see her face. I make it a rule never to speak to a backside.

'Catherine, your mother and father seem to be convinced that Timmy has returned. That Liam is your missing brother.'

'Uh-huh,' she said. It was noncommittal. She pedalled even faster, counting rapidly under her breath.

'What do you think?'

'Twenty-two, twenty-three... About what?'

'About Liam. You're not ancient, like the rest of us; you and he talk the same language. And you've hung out with him. Has he told you anything about himself?'

Catherine stopped pedalling suddenly. She stayed stock still, hips in the air, one leg bent, the other straight. She gave the impression of thinking really hard.

'Sure,' she said. 'He told me he likes Eminem, and Manic Street Preachers, as well as all that old blues stuff. He told me that he isn't very bright. *Other people always get there so much faster than me*, was how he put it. Oh,' she said, suddenly remembering, 'he also told me his birth sign. He's a Leo.'

'You don't remember Timmy's birth sign, do you?'

'Timmy was born on March the fifteenth. I should know,' she said, with a twist to her mouth. 'We've celebrated without him every March for the past twelve years. Or maybe *celebrated* isn't quite the right word... Do you know, the very first time I ever played a flute solo on stage, at the music festival, my mother didn't show up. She said she was ill, but I knew that wasn't it. My performance fell on March the fifteenth. My mother was in bed, in tears.'

'March the fifteenth. That would make him—'

'Pisces,' she said. She looked at me challengingly as if daring me to compare – Liam was a Leo, Timmy was a Pisces.

'What do you think, Catherine? What's your gut feeling, deep down, about Liam? Is he your brother?'

She stared at me for a moment. Then, with a flip of her leg, she started pedalling again. Round and round and round. And as she pedalled, she tossed off an answer.

'He doesn't say so,' she said.

# Chapter 16

Things moved quickly after that.

Catherine led me down the stairs, and up the stairs, and to a wing of the house that I hadn't been in before. She tapped with her knuckles once on the door and entered. It was her parents' bedroom.

I hung back in the corridor, feeling distinctly out of place. But through the doorway I could see everything. Could see an enormous room with a beamed ceiling and a thick white carpet and a four-poster bed. Could see white curtains that billowed softly at the windows. Jack Cable sat in bed, wearing – as far as I could tell – only a pair of reading glasses. The covers were pulled up to his waist and his chest was bare. Papers spilled out of a briefcase on to the bed. When the door burst open, he glanced up over the top of his spectacles and then returned his attention to the document in his hand.

Olivia perched on an upholstered chair in front of the dressing table, brushing a shine into her ivory hair. She turned at the sound of Catherine's footsteps and greeted her with a happy smile.

'Darling, do come in,' she said. 'The most wonderful news!' She didn't mention Liam; perhaps the newfound certainties were so overwhelming she assumed that, as if by osmosis, everyone would already know. 'We're going to spend the summer in Cleybourne. We're going to open up the cottage by the sea. Your father has just gone over it all with Max.'

She waved vaguely towards the telephone, as if to indicate how little she cared for details; we'll humour the men, her gesture seemed to say.

'Before we can move in, Max says, we have to do some checks—'

Jack's voice interrupted. 'It's been locked up for twelve years, Livi. The fabric might have rotted away.' He was defending his concern with detail.

'Yes. So. Max will arrange for a structural engineer or whatever you call it to do a survey and we'll get the builders in as soon as we can. Think of it! All of us together again. Summer by the sea.'

Olivia held out her arms to her daughter. Catherine stepped forward slowly and pressed her cheek to her mother's, but not before she cast her father a worried glance.

'Think of it,' she said. Her face looked pinched.

After a moment, Olivia sent her daughter off to find Liam, and, as Catherine exited,

226

noticed me in the corridor. She set her brush down on the dressing table.

'Laura! What are you standing out there for?' Standing there awkwardly, she might have said, but didn't. 'Do come in. We want a word.'

This invitation didn't put me at ease. There are unspoken rules of engagement for private investigators; many of these are designed not to blur the boundaries between professional duties and private dalliances. They hold especially true for women. You never take a drink, alone, with a client of the opposite sex. No one should get the wrong idea; it's a meeting, not a date. And unless your client happens to be an invalid – a qualification which didn't apply to either of the Cables – bedroom consultations are typically taboo.

Still, as my mother Dorothy says, rules are made to be broken. It's a philosophy that makes her a creative hairstylist. It also makes her an appalling driver.

I made my way to the middle of the room. 'Mrs Cable?'

I half expected her to bring our contract to an end. To say, with her white, white smile and her blue, blue eyes: *Thank you, dear little detective; all our problems are sorted now and you can be on your way.*

But she didn't.

Instead Olivia explained – with Jack's

assistance; he removed his glasses and tossed in the odd comment – that she and her husband had been thinking. They'd been pondering what to do now that Timmy was back.

'We're hoping you can carry on working for us,' she said.

She used the word *hoping*, but the smile she gave me was bright with confidence; it didn't seem to cross her mind that I might choose to cut myself free. Nor that Jack and I might already have discussed Liam's upbringing. To Olivia, this idea appeared to be blindingly new.

'We think, Jack and I, that it would be a good idea if you looked into Liam's background. After he disappeared, I mean. After Cleybourne. To find out as much about the past twelve years as you can.' Olivia took a solemn turn. 'You see, Laura,' she said, 'our son has had a trauma, being wrenched from his family at such a tender age. He may not be able to speak about his experiences for a long, long time. That's what often happens with people who go missing. But if Jack and I know something of the circumstances, we can be prepared to help him with whatever emerges. You see?'

'I see.' And since I knew what was coming next, and didn't want to hear it again, I headed her off. 'And you don't want me to ply Liam with questions, right, Mrs Cable?'

Olivia clapped her hands together and her rosy skin flushed with pleasure. 'Oh, Laura,' she said, 'you're so empathic. I just knew you'd understand.'

Joe Laskovic struck me as one of life's workers, one of those intriguing, exhausting people whose greatest contentment comes when they're absorbed in a project. Back from hospital for less than an hour, already he was hard at it. He was making a new home for the wood stack, away from the old barn.

And maybe Liam was one of those people who like to be busy, too. I'd never seen him more at ease than he looked now, working alongside Joe. They had marked out the area for the wood stack at the side of the garage. They had cleared and levelled the ground. Now they were erecting a roof to protect the logs from the rain.

A pair of sawhorses stood on the patchy grass; when I showed up, Liam was holding a piece of timber with his knee and sawing with fierce concentration. He had removed his sheepskin coat in spite of the cold, and a sweat stood out on his forehead. Mounds of bright sawdust were scattered on the muddy ground. Wonder put his chin on his paws and studied the movement of the saw intently, as if it might be his next meal.

Joe braced the end of the timber. His bald

head was covered by a woolly hat. His face was as pasty as ever.

I reached over and moved the sleeve of Joe's donkey jacket away from his wrist. The wound was covered with a bandage. The bandage was snowy white and streaked with dirt.

'How does it feel?' I asked.

Joe looked at me for a moment, as if weighing something up; then he turned the corners of his pudgy lips up in a smile and gave a slight, ironic, shrug of the shoulders. The meaning was clear. *Well as can be expected*, the gesture said. And I noticed for the first time that the smile was cherubic. He might be comic-looking, but his face had a peculiar charm.

Liam glanced over his shoulder. He nodded when he saw me, but he didn't miss a stroke. The rasping of the handsaw made conversation difficult.

At that moment Catherine staggered around the corner of the garage. Her arms were piled high with sections of log. She was overloaded; she teetered slightly. Liam and Joe released the plank and rushed to relieve her of her burden, just as Catherine's cousin, Robin Armstrong, stepped into view.

'What do you think you're doing?' he barked.

Joe, Catherine and Liam exchanged quick

glances, as if to say: *Who, me?* Catherine began brushing cobwebs off the front of her jacket. Joe went back to his position at the end of the plank.

'Who, me?' Liam said.

Robin continued with his complaint, and this time there was no doubt that it was aimed at Liam. 'If you want to help, that's one thing. But don't involve Catherine. Look at her.' We all did precisely that. 'Covered in dust. She could have hurt herself.'

'For heaven's sake, Robin, they're logs, not hand grenades. I'm perfectly all right, and besides, I want to help.'

'You'd be better off finishing your packing, Catherine. I'll drive you back to Birmingham this evening.'

'Robin, there's plenty of time.' From Catherine's tone, it was clear that the thought of going back to university – or was it the thought of being driven there by Robin? – held little charm.

The episode was brief but it soured the atmosphere. Liam continued sawing, though perhaps more furiously than before, and he looked as if the thoughts he was thinking were far from friendly. Catherine seemed downcast. Only Joe, the handyman, was his imperturbable self.

When the roof was finished, Joe signalled that they'd stop. Catherine perked up again.

'Come on, Liam,' she said. She handed him his sheepskin coat. 'Let's do something.'

It was at that moment that Olivia and Jack came round the corner of the garage. They were here, they said, to admire the new construction.

'What's wrong with Robin?' Jack asked. 'We just passed him. He was in a furious state.' The question was aimed at Catherine. There was something accusing about the way he said it.

Catherine ignored her father's question. 'Come on, Liam,' she pleaded, tugging at his sleeve. 'Let's play pétanque. I challenge you to a match. Anyone else for boules?'

Liam didn't say anything for a moment. There was something bitter in his look, as if the encounter with Robin might have left him off-beam. He took a moment to examine the faces around him: Olivia, confident and cheerful; Jack, whose calm stance seemed to cover a grumpy mood; Joe, the only relaxed one in the group; Catherine, impatient and fretful. The delay while Liam looked around had an effect. Whether he'd intended it or not, it brought everyone's attention to bear on him.

Finally, with a kind of flex of his shoulder muscles, he turned back to Catherine. He detached her fingers from his sleeve. He said, in a voice loud enough for all of us to hear, 'Pétanque is boring.'

There was a pause.

'I'm hot,' he said. 'I want to swim.'

In the shocked silence that followed, I thought – perhaps we all did – of the gently curved pool that had been empty for twelve long years. Of the asthma attacks. Of the little girl who'd been a water baby until her brother disappeared.

It was a power play, and everyone knew it. Liam looked triumphant. *There, I've said it!* was what his expression conveyed.

Joe looked sad. He knew exactly what Liam's demand signified.

Catherine looked incredulous. As if she'd been betrayed.

Olivia looked stricken. Years of dealing with only one child had dulled her capacity for diplomacy.

Only Jack looked much as he'd looked before – irritated. His expression said all those things that people say when they don't want to deal with a problem: *Do we have to? Let's get on with things. Enough of this nonsense.*

And then, rather suddenly and unexpectedly, Jack spoke. He gestured to Joe to follow him. He announced a decision.

'The pool's been empty long enough. Let's fill it, Joe,' he said.

I'll never forget that evening. I stayed with

the Cables at the Dower House until after ten p.m. Jack said he wanted to talk about my plan of action, when he'd finished with the pool. He wasn't in a mood for disagreement.

And Catherine begged me to stay.

'Don't go yet,' she said. 'Please. I feel frightened.'

She wouldn't tell me why.

So I stayed.

We had a tense and cheerless supper in the kitchen, while the sun slipped down behind the woods. Afterwards, Jack and Joe went to work on the pool. They hoovered the surface and wiped the tiles down. They inspected the hoses and the inlets. They opened the ducts and discovered, with mild surprise, that everything was in working order.

By nine o'clock there was six inches of water in the pool and the level was slowly but steadily rising.

Outside, the cloud cover had lifted. The tops of the trees made a jagged line against the sky, which was as sharp and black as coal. The panes at the side of the conservatory were misted with condensation, but through the glass in the roof above I could see the first bold scattering of stars.

The scene in the conservatory was surreal. Spotlights blazed, cutting rippling swaths of light across the shallow surface of the water. Joe stood watch. Jack paced impatiently.

Etta was in another part of the house making up a bedroom for Liam. They'd provided him with spare clothes from Jack's wardrobe, with a new toothbrush, with toiletries. He was planning to stay.

Olivia and Catherine moved anxiously back and forth between the sitting room, where they read a bit and fidgeted and talked in a desultory way, and the conservatory. Catherine had declined her cousin Robin's offer of a lift; she'd decided to wait another day or so before going back to Birmingham. Robin Armstrong had left the house after supper, in a black mood.

When the water rose to the level of the bottom step, Liam rolled up his jeans and dipped his foot in. It was cold, he complained.

Jack said that it could take two or three days to reach a suitable temperature for swimming.

Catherine shivered.

And in spite of the heating in the conservatory, which was boosted by two large vents that blew warm air into the room, I shivered too. I'd begun to feel cold in my bones, as if I'd caught a chill.

I walked to the windows and used the sleeve of my sweater to rub the last traces of condensation off one of the panes. Above the woods, I traced the line of the Little Dipper, the only constellation I'm able to recognise. The moon cast a beam of light like a laser across the lawn from the woods to the house. It highlighted a cluster of snowdrops shivering in the grass. It echoed, in a thinner and colder form, the shimmering path of the spotlights on the surface of the pool.

Inside the conservatory, there was frenetic activity. Outside, it was still. Nothing was stirring. *Not even a mouse,* I thought, but then deleted that notion when I saw Wonder, his tail swinging from side to side, sniffing at the base of the trees. He raised his head for a moment to the moon, and then, with a quick bark, dashed off into the undergrowth. I waited for a few seconds, but he didn't re-emerge.

I tried to imagine myself moving up and up, out of the conservatory, into the woods, like someone in an out-of-body experience. Tried to imagine the scene around the pool as it would appear from the outside. The way the conservatory would look, sheathed in glass, so brightly lit. The condensation was easing; from outside, I thought – from the edge of the woods, say, staring in – a person could see everything. Could see precisely what was going on inside. Could watch the Cables going about their business. It would be like viewing a domestic drama on telly, with the sound turned off.

Only Catherine noticed as I crossed the

sitting room and headed for the corridor. She glanced up from her magazine and tried to catch my eye.

'Back in a minute,' I promised.

It was dark in the kitchen. I left it like that. In the light from the moon, I picked my way to the back door. I stood for a moment, peering out. There was still no sign of Wonder. But at the edge of the lawn, just where the woods began, I fancied I saw a movement, a little twist of darkness, a shifting of the shadows.

I gripped the handle of the back door and was about to go outside when the thought of Mickey Monkey popped into my head. I saw him suspended from the wall, with his head lolling at an unnatural angle, and his little black eyes looking unnaturally sad.

I turned back into the kitchen.

I chose a small knife with a thin blade and a good grip, slipped it neatly into my pocket and stepped out on to the lawn.

Outside, there was the beginnings of a frost. The grass was stiff and slippery underfoot. Avoiding the centre of the lawn, where the moon had laid its path, crouching, moving stealthily, I made my way towards the woods. I was playing on the possibility that I wouldn't be noticed against the dark backdrop of the kitchen wing. That if anyone was watching from the woods, their attention would be fixed on the bright

237

spectacle in the conservatory.

But my approach was not as silent as I'd intended. The lawn was cut at the edges with a curve like the blade of a sickle. Near this border, I heard the snuffle of a hedgehog. I turned sharply aside and stepped with a sharp crack on to something hard and unyielding. It felt like a paving stone, flat and rectangular in shape. Whatever it was, I'd broken it. The snap-crack echoed in the frosty air.

And within the woods, footsteps started up, small and hard and swift, racing away. I gave chase. The woods were dark and deep. I couldn't see a thing. I charged past the two massive fir trees that stood sentinel at the edge of the woods and found my way on to the path. There were fewer obstructions here, but the needle-strewn surface was soft and slippery from rain. It slowed me down.

I dodged protruding branches and circled around the trunk of an ancient elm.

Suddenly there was a noise to my left. I stopped, peering off the path among the trees. I slid my hand into my pocket and gripped the handle of the boning knife.

Two eyes gleamed at me from the dark.

'Wonder!' I breathed, with a mixture of relief and irritation.

I sped off down the path again. Then, in an instant, it happened.

Suddenly, out of nowhere, I felt faint. As if

the blood had rushed from my head. My heel hit something slimy – a patch of wet leaves or the remains of a bird – and I fell. My bottom plummeted downwards; if I hadn't been wearing trousers, I would have flashed more private parts than Sharon Stone. But as I tried to pick myself up, I was less concerned with the visual thrills I might have provided than with the strange sensations in my lower body.

I struggled to my feet. To my relief, they still went step-step-step on command. But I could hear, receding in the distance, the thud of someone else's running feet.

And that was when it began in earnest.

The cramp originated from somewhere below my navel. It grew in intensity – first like menstrual cramps; then more powerful and more widespread, like the churning before a violent sickness. Finally it cut down towards my groin like a knife. The spasm came with such force that I forgot to breathe. All the systems in my body gave way before the onslaught.

I turned back towards the house. I had to grit my teeth to prevent myself from doubling over. As another spasm ripped through me, I had an image of a horse lying in the straw on the floor of a stable, writhing in pain. Colic, someone had told me; horses often die of it. Their guts twist and contract and the pain is so intense that their heart gives way.

You're not a horse, Laura Principal, I reprimanded myself. Human beings don't die of colic.

But no human being felt like this without something being dreadfully wrong.

I got as far as the lawn, and halfway across, shaking with alarm, before the pain stopped me. One arm clutched my abdomen. I staggered. I hardly noticed when someone flipped a switch and the lawn was filled with light. But I looked up, and saw a woman inside the conservatory, her face pressed against the glass. It was Catherine, a look of horror on her face, her mouth a big red O. I almost twisted around to see what she was staring at. Then, with horror, I realised it was me. She was pointing at my legs.

Slowly I looked down. I saw the lawn, glittering with frost. I stood amongst the cluster of snowdrops. Their delicate white petals were suspended from slender stalks, shining in the light.

And I saw that the petals were speckled – no, streaked – with bright red blood.

That was what Catherine had seen. Gushing from between my legs, as if my insides were falling out, were great scarlet splashes of blood.

*Norfolk*

# Chapter 17

## TWELVE YEARS EARLIER

*They are out there, all of them, on the cliffs. On the beach. On the marsh. With torches and walkie-talkies, shouting his name. There are dozens of them. Hundreds of them. They'll find him.*

*I know they will, they'll find him.*

*I couldn't stay. I had to bring Jack back here to the cottage. He is shivering violently. He must be ill. I should take his temperature, but I can't move from the window. I have to be watching when they bring Timmy back from the beach.*

*I've asked the policewoman to look in the bathroom for the thermometer. She's very obliging. Perhaps she's pleased to have something practical to do. This is not the nicest of duties for her, poor thing; the panic in this room, the sense of helplessness, is horrible, even for me.*

*I hear her rummaging about in the medicine cabinet. She comes back in, holding the thermometer in front of her. She offers it to Jack.*

*Jack is sitting in a wing chair with a blanket around his shoulders. He is dry now, anyway. I made him change out of his wet trousers while we waited for the police. He kept stumbling in and out of the surf, reaching blindly through the black waves, as if he supposed he might just put an arm down and clutch Timmy's hand and lift him up and out of the sea.*

*Jack is dry now, but he's ill. He's slumped over with his head in his hands. The policewoman is trying to persuade him to put the thermometer in his mouth. I look away.*

*There's a quick tap on the door. It is Etta, bringing Catherine. Oh my poor darling. I've not forgotten you, I want to say, but right now I have to focus on Timmy. I have to bring him home.*

*I manage to speak her name. 'Catherine.' I take a step towards her, but she has gone immediately to Jack. The policewoman moves to the side, out of the way.*

*Catherine stands in front of Jack. She waits for him to notice her. At last he raises his head and looks up, bleary-eyed.*

*'Daddy,' she says. 'Daddy! Where is Timmy?'*

*Jack looks at his daughter blankly as if he doesn't know who she is. Then recognition flicks in. His voice, when he speaks, is dull and slow, as if he's under the water. Or as if it's a struggle to remember the meaning of words.*

*'We don't know, Catherine.'*

*He fumbles for her hand and holds it gently, clumsily, but he fixes his eyes on her face. He repeats the words, just as slowly. Just as quietly. They're intended only for Catherine's ears. But I hear them, and the words batter the insides of my skull.*

*They sound as loud to me as the echoes of a gong.*

*As a klaxon.*

*As a death-knell.*

*'We don't know where Timmy is,' he says.*

*I have a premonition that these words will never go away.*

## Chapter 18

The operation took place the next morning,
after an ultrasound scan. By late afternoon
I'd been discharged. Sonny collected my car
and picked me up from hospital. He drove
me to Clare Street. He packed a box of
groceries and put it in the back. All I had to
do was select a few items of clothing, stuff
some odds and ends in my briefcase and we
were off.

'You're certain, Laura? You want to go to
Norfolk, tonight?'

'That's the only place I want to be right
now, Sonny. Wildfell Cottage.' I flashed him
a brief smile intended to convey the kind of
confidence I would have liked to feel.

'You'll see. As I told Jack Cable, after a few
days' rest I'll be right as rain. Back on the
job in a week.'

Sonny didn't comment. He adjusted the
passenger seat of the Saab to the reclining
position. I curled up as best I could, protect-
ing my tummy, which still felt fragile. He
tucked a blanket over me.

'You're sure you're all right?'

'Just cold,' I said.

The anaesthetic was still in my system; I

slept. When I awoke, I struggled into a sitting position. The car was speeding through the dark. Through open countryside. There were no houses, not a single light in view. Only a narrow road with low hedgerows either side, and scatterings of isolated trees. The trees were hunched and gnarled, as if the winds from the coast had aged them before their time.

'We're almost there?' I asked.

'Ten miles or so,' Sonny said. 'There's a pub just further on. Do you want to stop for a coffee?'

I shook my head. I didn't want to stop at all. I wanted to get to Wildfell. I tried to visualise the inside of the cottage – the fire, my favourite sofa, the neighbour's cat, the old oak dresser. It didn't work. All I could see was the accident and emergency department at Addenbrooke's Hospital, where I'd been driven last night in the Cables' shiny clean Lexus, with a pile of towels underneath me to soak up the blood and another between my legs.

In A & E I was seen almost immediately. I was helped on to a bed in a bay shielded by curtains. A nurse took my pulse and my temperature and helped me to remove my clothes. A doctor came; very young she looked, and very tired. She inserted things gently into my pelvis and prodded my abdomen. Then she laid her instruments down and took my hand.

'How many weeks pregnant are you?' she asked.

There'd been such a lot of bright red blood. It kept coming and coming. There'd been pain. The cramps had felt at one point as if someone had thrust a fist up my vagina, as if he'd twisted his fingers around my guts and pulled. There were streaks of darker bloody matter, frightening to look at, more frightening to name.

But in spite of the blood and the pain, the scan had showed some foetal matter remaining in the womb. 'Retained products of conception,' the doctor called them. They had to be 'evacuated'.

My body was like a public building with a bomb hidden deep inside.

We were almost there. I saw splashes of light outside the window – Burnham St Stephens – and felt the car slow down to take the turning, and I braced myself as the car jolted along the rutted lane. We stopped. Sonny climbed out and shifted the wooden gate and got in again, and finally we pulled up outside the darkened cottage.

Sonny left me on the sofa, warmed by a duvet from the bed upstairs, while he arranged everything. While he switched on the lamps. While he piled the logs high in the fireplace and crumpled balls of news-paper and stacked the kindling. While he touched a match to the paper and blew to help the kindling catch fire. While he moved the sofa near enough to the fire that its warmth could fall around me. While he made a pot of tea, and a plate of scones with butter and cheese.

Normally, I take pleasure in the appearance of the cottage, with its high-beamed ceiling and masses of light. Not this time. I just burrowed down into the sofa and ate my scones and drank my tea and fell asleep.

The first two days in Wildfell passed quietly.

I listened to the radio. To Radio Norfolk. The music wasn't my music, but the talk was comforting. It was of local things, concrete things: answers to questions about compost; a protest against the housing of released paedophiles on a disused airbase; an account of the erosion of cliffs on the Norfolk coast.

Sonny lent me his laptop; I sat at the old oak table in the dining area and did something I rarely bothered with at home – I surfed the internet. I took the free tours on adult sex sites and looked at the alien life forms there. I inspected statistics on globalisation. I visited the website for Cable Explorations and stared at the images of Jack Cable, bearded and erect, tramping through the snow. Hour after hour went by like this. I scarcely noticed.

And I read. The bookcase contained guidebooks and old novels, many of them left there by Ginny, Helen's daughter, for holiday relief. I read *Peter Pan*. I'd only seen the film before. I re-read *Lord of the Flies*. I read *Street Child*, by Berlie Docherty. All of them, for some reason, were about lost children. Lost boys.

'Talk to me,' Sonny said, more than once. He would sit down next to me at the table, or he would kneel on the floor by the sofa and take my hand.

He asked questions he didn't need to ask.

*When did it happen?*

There was only one possible time; he knew that. Here, at Wildfell, three and a half months ago.

He asked questions I didn't want to answer.

*Didn't you realise? Didn't you have any idea?*

How would I know, Sonny? Yes, my breasts have been tender; yes, I've sometimes felt a little strange; yes, I've had moments of queasiness. But how would I know this meant I was carrying a child? I bled, six weeks after conceiving. And I've never been pregnant before. This was my first pregnancy, Sonny. My only one.

*Laura. Did you want it?*

I stared at him when he asked that. Studied him as if I'd never seen him before. The thick fair hair falling over his forehead.

The unruly eyebrows. The lean wrists.

Did *you?* I thought. But I couldn't bring myself to ask. He seemed, like the bloated figures on the sex sites, to represent an alien form of life.

'I'll go,' Sonny said, 'if you're sure you're all right. I'll leave you the laptop.' He looked defeated. 'I'll be back on Thursday.'

'As you like,' I said, and went to sleep.

I didn't stay indoors all the time. I had the car; I dropped Sonny off at King's Lynn and he took the train back to London. When it stopped raining, I drove to Holkham Bay and trekked along the dunes.

But it wasn't easy to relax, because nothing was straightforward any more. My foot touched a slippery patch and I remembered when Sonny had lain laughing on a muddy bank, like a stranded seal, and how he'd tramped back to the car wrapped only in a rug.

I went back to Wildfell. A sliver of moonlight crept underneath the curtains and I remembered Sonny, naked on the floor, with the left side of his face plunged in darkness and the right side dusted with silver. I remembered how cool the skin on his back had felt, and how it had warmed under my touch. That was when it must have happened.

I picked up the memoir, Olivia's memoir.

Sonny had located a second-hand copy in Camden Market. I found it in my briefcase after he'd left.

I opened it up at a more or less random point, where Olivia seemed to be recounting the events of the evening before Timmy's disappearance.

With a sigh, I buried myself in someone else's past.

Olivia wrote:

*That evening, waiting for Jack, Timmy couldn't sleep. He was fretful and impatient. Every time he heard a car in the lane, his foot fluttered. Timmy's foot always tapped when he was excited. Blackie would start barking, say, or we'd hear the ice cream van, and the rat-a-tat-tat would begin; it would continue, often, until someone or something soothed it away.*

*I sat beside the bed and sang to him.*

*Keep your foot still, darling, I whispered. And amazingly, he did. Two seconds later he was fast asleep, in that way that children have, passing from wakefulness to unconsciousness in the blink of an eye. As if for them, the barrier between consciousness and sleep, between life and death, is permeable. As adults, every night, we trudge our way with difficulty over the peak of our daytime cares and into the ravine of sleep. Children like Timmy fly across on gossamer wings.*

I did my best to focus. Olivia hadn't written a true crime book, a whodunnit and how; that was clear. Her memoir had an out-of-time quality, as if she had jotted things down according to some internal schema that had little to do with the clock or the calendar. It wasn't a memoir of incident, it was a memoir of emotion. Of what Timmy was like. Of what it was like to lose him.

But as I read, threading forward and back through the pages, fitting together this remembrance with that, I began to get for the first time a clear picture of the circumstances of Timmy's going.

Olivia wrote:

*He was boisterous that day, unusually so; he got into trouble for heaping jam on his plate. Not long after breakfast, after Catherine had trotted off to meet Robin, Jack took Timmy to Cleybourne Hoop. A storm was forecast for the afternoon. They wanted to hit the beach before the weather broke. I'm going to catch a seal, Timmy said. I'll bring it home with me.*

*It was ten a.m. when they left the cottage. There were darker clouds on the distant horizon, but the sun was golden and the air was still warm. I wore a cotton dress with thin straps and blue flowers across the bodice. I remember every detail of those last moments with my son. How I knelt down and buckled his sandals. How he held himself rigid while I rubbed suncream over his face and neck and ears. How I packed a rucksack with biscuits and carrot sticks and juice and a towel and prepared him for his disappearance.*

I flicked ahead in the memoir. Found the place where Olivia described the moment when she'd learned that Timmy was missing. It was nearing midday. She'd done some errands in the village. She decided to walk towards the beach along the raised path over the salt marsh to meet her husband and her son.

*I walked towards the beach so innocently, so free of premonition, so ignorant of disaster. Wanting to hurry them home for lunch, wanting to remind Timmy to bring his rucksack and his towel. Wanting to ask whether he and Jack preferred cauliflower cheese for supper or fried chicken. Expecting to take their hands and walk, swinging our arms, all three, Timmy in the middle, until the path became too narrow for three, when I would step ahead and lead the way, and Timmy would trot along behind next to his papa.*

*And then, in the distance, I saw Jack stumbling and staggering towards me like a drunk. All my everyday expectations slipped away. A great cold emptiness took their place.*

I set the book down. Outside the cottage, the rain had begun again. It drummed hollowly against the French doors that led to the garden. It gurgled in the gutters.

I made myself a coffee and turned on some more lamps. I sat down again to read. I was back there in an instant on the footpath that ran through the marsh.

*Jack could hardly stand. His clothes were dripping with water. He was alone. But still I hoped; I hoped until we came face to face on the path, and I could no longer escape the implication of the wild fear in his eyes.*

*I knew before he said it. Something's happened to Timmy. Timmy is gone.*

*The news was so momentous that somehow I expected the whole world to know. I needed everyone to know. Needed them to hunt for my baby. Everyone – there was hardly anyone around. But the fishermen were coming in from the sea, riding their boats up on to the shingle, jumping from the bows to the beach, using their rusted tractors to drag the boats up above the high-water mark. They were fresh-faced and muscled and focused on the job at hand. They were unloading crates of crabs and lobsters. I couldn't make sense of it. How could they do this everyday thing when my son had disappeared? How could they work – calmly, vigorously – as if it were just another day, as if the slithering, scuttling crabs were the only things that mattered? And how could the fisheries officer, strolling down on to the shore in his navy jumper, be so nonchalant? I ran towards him, clutching at his sleeve. Help, I said. Help.*

*He turned to me in astonishment, and that was when my knees buckled. I couldn't support myself. I once saw a horse that did that, a thoroughbred; it panicked as it was being loaded into its trailer, and its knees wobbled and its elegant legs bowed and it tried to sink to the floor; then it staggered up, and the process began all over again. Now I was like that horse. I wanted to look for Timmy, but my knees buckled; all the muscles in my legs deserted me; my eyes rolled up in my head.*

*I soon recovered. My legs, at least, returned to normal.*

*As things turned out, it was Jack who was ill.*

Reading Olivia's memoir, alone there in Wildfell Cottage, under a duvet in front of the fire, had the strangest effect on me. For the first time since I went into hospital, I could concentrate. I found myself transported to that time, twelve years ago, in Cleybourne. Found my mind racing to construct a strict chronology from her more fragmented version.

I had to skim back and forth in the volume before I finally worked it out; when Olivia said Jack became ill, she meant it literally.

He had been working too hard and too long, planning the expedition. He had become run down, and the shock and the cold on the beach had pushed him over the edge. He'd contracted pneumonia. He refused to be taken to hospital. He stayed with Olivia, at the cottage, and the local doctor came by twice a day to check on them both.

Olivia recorded her days in minute detail.

Sometimes she stayed in and looked after Jack. Sometimes she visited the adjoining cottage, where Catherine was staying with Etta and Joe, and gathered her daughter in her arms, and they cried together. Olivia recorded that Etta was suffering too; as if Timmy's disappearance wasn't enough, she learned that very week that her father was terminally ill. Maybe Etta found Catherine's presence a comfort, Olivia thought; Olivia hoped.

And as often as she could, as often as they would allow her, Olivia accompanied the searchers, scouring the marshes and the woods. That was how her days went.

At night she took sleeping pills to dull the pain. She welcomed the oblivion; then she woke up dazed the next morning and began to search again. Olivia wrote that she didn't mind how long she searched or where or to what end; what she couldn't abide was the thought of the day – which might soon, surely, come; she knew this as the weeks went by – when the police would say: *It's no use. There is nowhere else to look. There is nothing more we can do.*

From what Olivia wrote, the police were flummoxed. They had little to go on. The account of the disappearance was alarmingly simple. Jack had taken Timmy down to the beach. Timmy wore his sun hat and a pair of yellow plastic sunglasses. He carried a little rucksack on his back. Jack had a tartan blanket slung over one arm; a flask of coffee was tucked away inside his briefcase.

Father and son played together for hours. They climbed the headland to the pillbox and took stock of the distant storm. They played pig-and-wolf, chasing each other along a course they'd marked out, racing for the blocks of kelp that were designated 'Home'. Hours later, searchers could still see the depressions made by their feet, large and small, in the shingle. Timmy arranged mounds of rock to form castles; one or two remained much later, with sticks protruding from their battlements. Finally, Jack took a moment's rest. Timmy, thrilled by the rising wind, was still going strong. Jack sat down out of the wind, his back against an upturned boat; he stopped there for a minute or at most, he said, two, watching the way the oncoming clouds were draining the colour from the fields. When he turned back towards the shingle, when he stood up again and peered over the hump, Timmy was gone. They found his yellow sunglasses, later that week, tossed up on another part of the beach. They never found Olivia's son.

There were only two possibilities; that was what the police reported to Olivia. Olivia recorded them both in her memoir with the matter-of-factness of a mother who hated the fact that a horror concerning her child had now become a commonplace.

Possibility one: Timmy had drowned. The surf was fierce here, far more than most adults could manage, let alone a child; the fact that the child's sunglasses had been in the sea lent weight to that speculation. But if he had drowned, they would have expected the body to come ashore sooner or later. It didn't. No bloated corpse. No tiny skeleton wreathed in weed. No body.

Possibility two: Timmy had been abducted. Someone had approached from the seaward side – from Blakeney Point, or from the stretch of beach below the headland, or down from the cliffs themselves – and snatched him away. But if Timmy had been kidnapped, how had his abductor got away without being spotted?

Perhaps, one theory went, someone had killed Timmy, swiftly and quietly, or knocked him out and hidden him beneath one of the overturned boats that lay between the beach and the car park; when Jack rushed off at last to meet Olivia, this person might have snatched Timmy's body and made an escape. Except – and it was a big except – no one had been seen leaving Beach Lane, with or without a child in tow.

Eventually Olivia supplied the answer. An answer.

*The police begged me to think again, Could you bear to go over it again? they said – as if it was ever ever out of my mind.*

*But I made another attempt at recall. At recapturing that day, as I danced down – I was happy, then – towards the beach to meet up with Timmy and Jack and walk them home for lunch. I made another attempt to conjure the scene, to put myself there, though it greatly distressed me to do so. It worked. I managed to recall the scene from the raised footpath even more vividly than before ... the storm coming, the cascades of rain on the horizon, the fields growing darker. And on the third or fourth recall, I remembered a streak of white along the top of the hedge. It was the flash of a vehicle below me on Beach Lane. It was a white van, I was sure of that. A small white van, the kind that tradesmen so often use.*

And Catherine's cousin Robin Armstrong, waiting for his friends where Beach Lane met the coast road, had seen it too.

# Chapter 19

I'd visited this part of Norfolk over many years and several seasons.

I'd come in late autumn. I'd taken the open ferry along Morston Creek, with its high muddy banks, and out on to the broad, flat, sun-sparkled expanse of Blakeney Channel. I'd scrutinised the dunes at the tip of Blakeney Point – humped, bumped, irregular, like a war-ravaged landscape – and seen the breakers galloping in from the open sea. I'd gazed at the bright beige sand crusted with seals. Seen common seals basking with their pups, and a few dog-faced greys, tiny flippers shooting from their shoulders like thalidomide arms. Seen them balancing on their tummies, tails up. Watched as, at some mysterious signal, they all rushed for the open sea.

I'd driven along the road that follows the contours of the coast in late spring and early summer, when the fields are lush and green or vivid yellow with oilseed rape. I'd stopped to look at newly ploughed fields near Kelling, their brown clods dusted with white stones; in the distance was the bright blue sea and in the foreground the ruined, roofless grandeur of Crankham Barn, its flint and brick walls piled high with rolls of golden hay.

I'd stood on the beach as the fishermen with their yellow aprons and their red woolly hats unloaded crates of crab and lobster. Seen the breakers, two feet high, even on a windless day.

I'd walked the cliff edge from Cleybourne to Sheringham. Looked down from the cliffs to where the waves trace a graceful series of symmetrical curves, like the diagram of a sound wave, on the shingle below. I'd been on those cliffs in April 1999 when the sky was a perfect azure and the sea was calm and fighter planes buzzed overhead like mosquitoes on their way to Italy and then to join the attack on Belgrade.

But I'd never looked so closely at this part of Norfolk – really examined it, I mean – as I did after I'd read Olivia's memoir. I drove slowly, studying the landscape, exploring the byways. I checked what I was seeing against the Ordnance Survey map. At last I had the topography of the area fixed firmly in my mind.

It was, I decided, like this: in north Norfolk, there is a continuous stretch of shingle, beginning in the west near the tip of Blakeney Point and flowing eastward towards Sheringham, that has been honed over centuries by the sweep of the sea into a crescent shape. The shape may account for the name, for it is called Cleybourne Hoop; the last word is given on some maps as Hope.

The coast road dips inland as you approach Cleybourne. You will be intensely aware, from the sound, from the quality of light, that the sea stands off to your left; but it won't be visible. The North Sea has thrown up a high ridge of shingle to protect its privacy at this point, and further on it is hidden behind magnificent cliffs.

The land between the coast road and the sea falls into two broad wedges. In the western wedge, hugging the road, is the village of Cleybourne – a dense cluster of houses, many of them fine stone cottages, plus shops and pubs and a handsome windmill. Behind the village there's a marsh, like a great green sea of whispering reeds, sliced on its western edge by a channel of water that leads to the open sea. Beyond this channel, pushing for miles into the North Sea, is Blakeney Point.

The eastern wedge presents a very different picture. There is a scattering of farmhouses along the coast road, but behind these, in place of marshland, there are open fields that sweep up and up on to the clipped green surface of the heath. It ends abruptly in steep cliffs that tower fifty or sixty feet above the beach.

And in between the two wedges, between Cleybourne village and the cliffs, Beach Lane runs down towards the sea. It is bounded by hedgerows and dotted with signs of habitation. There is a village hall; there is a series of fine houses surfaced in flint that back on to the fields; there is, at the bottom, a car park.

I left the Saab there, nosing in against the bank of shingle that cut the car park off from the sea. Mine was the only car. The *Northern Star* and the *Nathalie Gail*, large open fishing boats, rested on trailers. There was a wooden board with fisheries notices tacked to it and details of tides. There was an emergency telephone that connected to the coastguard. That was all.

An opening in the shingle allowed access to the beach. I stepped through this gap and suddenly, there in front of me, causing me to blink with its brightness, was the silver expanse of the sea.

I stood gazing out towards the far horizon, where a fog gathered. Blakeney Point unrolled for miles to my left and the cliffs rose up on my right. There was not a soul in sight. It felt as if I were completely alone in the world.

I scrunched across a beach formed of mountains of flint pebbles worn sensuously smooth. The shingle resisted my steps; the going was hard.

I planted myself where the force of the wind hit me full in the face, where the waves crashed and pounded at my feet.

*This is where it happened*, I whispered.

*This is where Timothy Cable disappeared.*

It was a good thing that I left for Cleybourne Hoop that day as early as I did; even an hour later and my attempt to come to grips with the landscape would have foundered. While I stood on the beach, thinking about the things in Olivia's memoir, the fog began to roll in from the horizon. It skimmed along the surface of the sea; it climbed up the cliffs; it settled on the marsh. The fog was thin and damp; I could still see at close range, but if I tried to look at anything in the distance, it was obscured by a curtain of cloud.

But fog or no fog, I was determined not to leave until I'd seen what I wanted to see. I hadn't had any strenuous activity since the miscarriage. I braced myself and set off up the path that climbed to the top of the cliffs.

I was halfway up before I realised that I wasn't alone. Someone stood at the top of the path; someone was watching me ascend. A few steps closer and I recognised Max Armstrong, Olivia's brother. For two seconds I was taken aback. I had come to think of Cleybourne as a location unique to the Cables and their children. It had slipped my mind that Max and his son Robin actually lived here.

'Jolly nice to see you again,' Max said, pumping my hand. He behaved as if there were nothing odd about bumping into me here, with the fog curling around us, a long way from Grantchester where we'd last met. 'What are you doing in this neck of the woods?'

I spun a story about needing to get away from town to get some fresh air. It wasn't entirely untrue.

'You certainly chose a day for it,' Max said. 'It's not safe on these cliffs at the best of times, my girl. You never know when a section is going to crumble. But in the fog—'

'Walking in the fog can't be much more dangerous than driving in it,' I objected, and began to move off along the headland.

'I'll come with you,' he said. He tapped my shoulder and pointed down the slope of the fields. I stopped and followed the line of his finger.

'On clear days,' Max said, 'there's an outstanding view from here. That's my house, down there.'

'On Beach Lane?' I asked. I couldn't make it out, but I recalled the fine flint houses I'd passed on my way in.

'Indeed, yes. There's my house, and Jack and Olivia's – the builders started work on it today – and a small guesthouse. You should drop in, have tea with me.'

Maybe some other time, I demurred. I drew his attention to a low L-shaped brick and cement structure dug into the cliff side near the head of the path. At the end of the long arm of the L, a window looked westward towards Blakeney Point.

'And what's this? A pillbox?'

'Second World War.' Max said it with pride in his voice, as if he had personally held off an invasion force from this very site. Then his face took on a more solemn expression. 'Jack and Timmy were fond of this spot,' he said. 'Timmy liked to pretend to stand guard.'

I glanced inside. The pillbox was cramped, more child-size than soldier-size. Away in the corner, something moved. There was a scuttling sound.

I peered closer. It was a child – a boy with a freckled face, aged eight or nine, crouched in a corner, his back against a wall. Fetid water had collected in the bottom of the pillbox. Drinks tins and sweet wrappers bobbed around his ankles.

I smiled. 'Hello. Are you all right in there?'

He looked away from me, out of the window, into the fog. And then, as I stepped back, he made a rush for the exit. He pushed past Max and me and raced away down the path. We could hear his wellies slopping in the distance long after his little frame was swallowed up by the fog.

'A local child,' Max said heartily. 'Nice family, name of Good; quiet, keep themselves to themselves. They live in one of those houses on the coast road. They're referred to as newcomers, but they've actually been here for a decade or more.'

Max seemed to like showing me around his patch. It was a good time for questions. I told him that I'd found the Cable Explorations website; that I'd read one or two interviews posted there in which Jack was invited to reprise his adventures, that I'd noticed Jack avoided questions about the early days of the business. Why was that? I asked.

Max – always pleased to talk about his brother-in-law – confirmed what I'd suspected. That Jack Cable didn't like to be reminded.

'Some people commemorate the beginning of a successful business,' Max explained. 'Recall the triumph. Battles waged and won and all that. Not Jack. He can't help remembering that our take-off coincided with the time that Timmy disappeared.'

'You mentioned before, Max, that it took months for Jack to narrow down the possible sites for the expedition. Narrow them down to two, I believe you said. Just out of interest, who settled on the final destination? Was it you who made the final choice?'

The final brilliant choice, I might have said, but that would be laying it on a bit thick.

Max and I had been walking almost shoulder to shoulder, watching our footing. Max had placed himself on the side nearest the sea; his gallantry required him to take the more risky position. Now, at my question, he halted abruptly. He looked as startled as if I'd suggested that we strip off our clothes and dive from the cliff.

'Good Lord, what an extraordinary idea! I'd never be clever enough to make such a decision, not in a million years. I'm not that sort. I told you – it was Jack who'd studied up on tides and currents and so forth. I was just the catalyst.' He set off again. 'Come on, let's walk. It's cold.'

'Meaning?' It wasn't a question about the weather.

'Catalyst? Oh, well. Just that Jack became very ill on the night my nephew disappeared. Perhaps you knew that?'

I nodded.

'A fever of one hundred and three. I was desperate to help. I reckoned that even if Timmy was found soon, what with Jack's illness and all he'd not be back to work for at least a week. So I went through his briefcase. Checked his diary, cancelled his appointments, finished his correspondence. You know the sort of thing.' He looked sad. 'It was all I could do,' he said. He looked at me in a pleading way. 'It was better than nothing.'

A passage from the memoir came back to me. Olivia writing about the day after the disappearance. Writing about her brother Max:

*He was desperate to help. Poor Max! His nephew missing; and Jack, his hero, incoherent with fever. He wanted so to help. He quizzed me endlessly. How is he now? he asked. Did he sleep? Did he get up in the night? Has he tried to work? Max was so concerned and I was impatient with him. I didn't want his questions. My head was full of Timmy.*

We had been walking for ten minutes or so, with no sound but the surf and the occasional squawk of a gull, when we came to something that was completely un-expected. There, in the middle of nowhere, was a row of four terraced houses. They stood at right angles to the cliff. The one farthest from the sea was painted a bright and buoyant white. As they neared the sea, they became progressively more dilapid-ated; the house with the cliffs at the bottom of its garden was a wreck. The roof was collapsed in places, the upstairs windows were hung with sheets, the yard was overgrown with nettles. The house appeared to be deserted, and no wonder: the bluff had recently broken away; a portion of picket fence dangled by a wire over the edge. I assumed that the recurrent damage from land slippage and the effect on their nerves of living with the prospect of oblivion had overcome its owners' attachment to home sweet home.

But when we stood in front, where wall-flowers grew thickly along the fence, I could see that it wasn't land slippage that had done for the house. Some of the window frames were charred and blackened. The house had been burned out.

'Les and Sally Whitwell,' Max said. 'A double tragedy.'

'Pardon?'

'Their daughter was just into her teens when she disappeared. That was a long time ago, much before Timmy. Twelve years before, I believe. Her body was never found.'

'What do you think happened to her?'

Max shook his head. He didn't want to speculate. 'Some people thought she must have fallen off the cliff. But if so, why didn't they find her body? Lots of people drown on this coast and their bodies are always washed ashore a week or two later. Mary's never was.'

Max sighed. At the mention of the missing girl, he deflated. The heartiness seeped out of him.

He continued. 'As if losing your daughter wasn't tragedy enough, years later their house caught fire.' He nodded at the house in front of us. 'Burned to death, both of them, in the middle of the night. Joined their daughter, you could say.'

It's not my idea of a reunion.

We stood there for a moment, staring at the melancholy sight. Behind the house, in the distance, I was beginning to see patches of pale sky.

'Tell me, Max. What's your view of Liam?'

The fog might have been thinning, but at the question, a cloud settled on Max's face.

'My view?'

He was stalling.

'Your gut feeling, I mean. Is this lad your missing nephew?'

Max's face worked for a moment, his jaw muscles clenching and unclenching, before the words finally burst out. 'My sister doesn't want to hear what I have to say. She refuses to listen. But I know. I know, I tell you! This Liam – he's a scoundrel, out to break Olivia's heart. He's not my nephew Timmy.'

He was breathing quickly now. He certainly seemed agitated. Probably the poor man had high blood pressure. But still...

'How can you be so sure?'

Max extended one stubby finger and tapped it, hard, against the wall of his chest. Against his heart.

'Blood,' he declared. 'A man knows his own flesh and blood. I tell you, that boy isn't an Armstrong. And what's more, there's not an ounce of Cable in him. There's no steel. Why, my son Robin is far more in Jack Cable's mould than Liam is.'

And with that, Max, still observing the formalities in spite of his outburst, excused himself, wheeled on his heel and wandered away into the fog.

I strolled back towards the beach more slowly, thinking it through. Max knew his own flesh and blood, he said. Liam wasn't it.

All very well, that certitude. But Olivia was certain too; certain, in her case, that Liam was her son. So much for flesh and blood. They couldn't both be right.

But the other thing Max had said – that Liam wasn't an Armstrong. That he wasn't a Cable either. That he had no steel. What was I to make of that?

Liam was different, that was for sure. He was good-looking, as all the Cables were, and he was tall. But he didn't have their confidence. Physical confidence, on the one hand; the stuff that made Jack able to venture out into the wilds, and gave even Catherine, whether she knew it or not, an exceptional grace. The Cables, every one of them, leapt and strode and scampered; Liam, slow-talking, slow-thinking, unhurried in his gait, just ambled along.

And he didn't have their social confidence, on the other. This wasn't a matter of genes; it was what my mother used to refer to, with a laugh, as class confidence. The stuff that made some people believe they could do and try and take chances; made them feel entitled. I didn't know how Liam had been raised, but I'd bet my bottom dollar it wasn't in a wealthy household. He hadn't grown up with people to clean for him, with private schools, with travel on demand. The fact that he referred to having had *everything a boy could want – a BMX bike, computer games, guitar lessons* – meant precisely the opposite. Meant that he was fully aware that those things might not have been his. Meant that to him, they didn't seem commonplace.

Most of all, Liam hadn't lived with a hero for a father. Hadn't learned from the television, and from the deference of the people around, that his father was someone very special. Hadn't absorbed the sober message that he'd have to be special himself to be his father's equal. He hadn't been subject to the Cable expectations: hadn't learned, as Catherine had, that if you didn't have ambition, you were nothing.

What effect would this have in the long run? Would Liam's differences be cherished, would his uniqueness be admired? When the Cables talked about Liam among themselves, in a few weeks, in a few months, when the shine of discovery had worn off – would they say, proudly: *He's the only one among us who manages to take things as they come ... who appreciates what he's got ... who really understands the blues?* Or would the theme be something balder, less accepting: *Not like us.*

But it was the comparison with Robin – the contrast, I should say – that interested me most. Max had exclaimed in a moment of high feeling that his son resembled Jack Cable more than Liam did. How much of that was a simple statement of fact? And how much an expression of jealousy? Of competitiveness? Of calculation? For twelve years Robin had been a close companion to his Uncle Jack. They did things together, Catherine had said; men's things. Robin liked playing lord of the manor, she'd said. Was Max counting on Robin being seen as a chip off the old block? Did he feel, perhaps, that this would put his son closer to Jack Cable? Closer, perhaps, in financial terms? If Robin was a chip off the old block – the only chip, so to speak – might he stand to inherit the woodpile? Viewed in this light,

Timmy's return could be downright inconvenient for Max. Infuriating, even.

And if I was thinking of jealousy, of competition, of rivalries, I might eventually have to think about Catherine too.

I didn't want to do that, not just yet. I shook my head and looked around.

The fog had faded now to the point where it was only a pale shadow over the headland. Except for a farmer driving a tractor in one of the fields below me, I hadn't seen a soul since Max left me, and here I was once again at the pillbox.

I looked down the path. A man and woman were climbing up towards me. They were mid-forties perhaps, though it was hard to tell their exact age because the woman in particular had skin that had been crabbed and toughened by the outdoors. She had dark ginger hair pulled back into a single plait. A few unruly strands frizzed around her face.

'Afternoon,' they said, and looked away.

'Excuse me.'

The man stopped. His Alsatian came to heel behind him. More reluctantly, with a glance at the man – as if to say: are you sure? – the woman stopped too.

'Can I help you?' he said. I thought I picked up a Midlands accent.

'I'm trying to get the lie of the land,' I explained. 'I was wondering – do you know

– is Beach Lane the only access to the beach from the coast road?'

'Well, now,' the man said. He reached in his pocket and pulled out a biscuit. He threw it to the dog and then turned back to me. I got the impression that he didn't do a lot of conversation. He was working up to an answer when the woman spoke up.

She sounded local to me, for what it was worth; I often come a cropper on accents.

'There are two routes,' she said, 'apart from Beach Lane. There's a raised path along the dyke that goes from the village to the car park. It begins just behind the windmill. Can you see it?'

That was what I wanted. I peered into the distance, downhill, and sure enough, rising out among the whispering reeds, I thought I could discern a grassy path that crossed diagonally through the marsh. As it approached Beach Lane, it was hidden by a hedgerow.

'Yes, I think I see it. But I can't see where it ends.'

'Just there,' she said. 'It lets you off in a corner of the car park. That's the way most villagers come. And the other route – strictly for the energetic – is over the fields from the coast road and directly up on to the headland. Once you're here, you can follow this path down to the sea.'

I scanned the scene below. 'It's an impressive landscape,' I said. 'Sometimes eerie, always beautiful. It gets under your skin.'

The woman with the plait gave me a curious look. Something was decided. She extended a work-worn hand. 'Mary Good,' she said shyly. 'And this is Donald.'

Donald wiped his hand on a large white handkerchief and extended it to me. The Goods were indeed the parents of the freckle-faced boy who'd fled from the pillbox a short while before.

'You're not afraid for him?' I asked.

'Afraid?' they echoed. They seemed genuinely puzzled.

I felt a little foolish. There was the fog, I pointed out, and the cliffs; Max had persuaded me of the dangers.

Mary pooh-poohed my concerns. She was robust in her rebuff. 'Not when you grow up around here,' she said. 'Brian knows the cliffs like the back of his hand. He's probably in less danger here than he would be in a city from traffic and all.'

'And the disappearances? Timmy Cable? The Whitwell girl? Don't you think there could be a connection? Someone local with an unhealthy liking for children?'

It was Donald who broke in here. 'One of them paedophiles?' he asked. 'That's ridiculous. No one knows what happened to Mary Whitwell. Or to the Cable boy, for that matter. Shouldn't jump to conclusions.' He seemed almost angry. Perhaps the fate of the missing children was a controversial item in the village. 'Anyway, our Brian's perfectly safe. We wouldn't let him play here if we didn't believe that.'

We talked for moments more, amicably. I learned that the newcomers' had spent their honeymoon in Cleybourne the same year Timmy disappeared. In fact, Mary told me in solemn tones, they'd walked along these cliffs on the very day.

'You didn't see him, did you?'

'No,' Donald said. Just like that. 'After our honeymoon we decided to look for jobs around here,' he added. 'We liked it in Cleybourne that much.'

Mary pushed the wispy hairs off her forehead and took up the story. 'We never thought we'd be able to afford a house here,' she said. 'What with people buying them as second homes and all. But Donald was determined, and somehow he managed to come up with the down payment and we got a mortgage and here we are. We always manage somehow,' she said, smiling shyly at Donald.

We parted then, the Goods striding along the cliffs with their dog and me plodding back down the footpath. I felt unaccountably weary. I got in the car and drove slowly down Beach Lane, keeping an eye out for the Cables' compound. Sure enough, there it was: a well-maintained flint wall edged with red brick; two good-sized houses, with shrubs in front, facing each other across a pebbled turning area; and farther back, a smaller cottage. There was a gate that led, presumably, to the fields beyond.

On an impulse, I turned in and parked. I bypassed the house with the skip in front and went straight to the other one. I tapped the anchor-shaped iron knocker on the wooden door. And as I did, in the seconds before footsteps came down the hall towards me and Max opened the front door, I heard a plaintive sound.

A tiny window was open in the wall near the door; probably a cloakroom, I thought. And from that window, low in volume but clear as a bell, I heard a child's voice. It was a very young child. Girl or boy, I couldn't tell.

The voice sounded pleading. Almost desperate. *'I'm waiting for you.'*

The door swung open. It was Max. He looked out of sorts. Impatient. I peered over his shoulder into the hallway beyond. No child.

'Laura, Laura,' he said. 'What a pleasant surprise. You've come for tea.'

His voice was hearty but not happy. I wondered if he'd been crying. It seemed unlikely, but his eyes were suspiciously red.

'No tea, thank you, Max. I was admiring

the house. I came to say goodbye.'

He didn't offer to show me around.

'I heard a child,' I said.

He let out a long sigh. As if my mention of the child had brought him some relief.

'Follow me.'

I followed him along a narrow corridor into a square sitting room that occupied half of the ground floor of the house. It had a luxurious fitted carpet and a fake gas fire burning in the hearth. He led me to the side of the room, where a fitted office, with glass-fronted bookcases and wooden filing cabinets and matching computer desk, had been installed. Through the long windows that looked out on the garden, I could see a cluster of christmas roses nodding on a swatch of grass. They made me think of snowdrops, which made me think of...

I pulled myself back to the here and now and looked around for the child.

There was no one in the room but Max and me.

'Here,' Max said. He stepped over to a bulky piece of equipment, an answering-machine-cum-fax that must have been one of the earliest domestic models. He lifted a beige flap. There was a hissing sound as a tape rewound. He pressed a button, and within seconds a clear, high voice filled the room. The tone was playful at first, then plaintive, then more demanding.

I didn't need to be told who it was. There was background noise, but it didn't obscure the words.

*'Daddy! Daddy! I'm waiting for you, Daddy. I want to go to the beach with you. I want to catch a seal.'*

Max rewound the tape and turned it off.

'I brought it here from Grantchester,' he said, 'all those years ago, when they were searching for Timmy and Jack was ill. I couldn't bear to throw it away. I play it from time to time. It's the last message to Jack Cable from his son. The last we'll hear of little Timmy, ever.'

# Chapter 20

I'd just finished making a plan of action
when Sonny pulled up outside Wildfell
Cottage.

I was pleased to see him. I found myself
talking like an auctioneer on speed about
the Cable case.

'Olivia's memoir opens up the whole issue
of what happened to Timmy when he was
four years old, Sonny,' I concluded. 'No,
wait – listen. I've been to Cleybourne. I've
seen where they lived, and the beach, and
the cliffs above. The shingle on the beach is
humped in the middle; a small child could
easily slip out of sight. I can quite understand how Jack could lose sight of Timmy
for a moment. What's weird is how the child
could disappear completely.'

I gave him all the details.

'Maybe he wandered into the car park,'
Sonny said, 'and was grabbed by the person
who drove that white van. Or maybe – more
likely – his father killed him; Jack Cable was,
as far as we know, the last person to see
Timmy. And just because the man's a
national hero doesn't mean he's above
lashing out at a child in a moment of anger.

Maybe – most likely – Timmy just drowned.'

Sonny spoke wearily, as if what he really wanted was to finish with this discussion.

'May I have a cup of coffee?' he said.

'Sorry, darling. I've been burbling.' I landed a kiss on his unshaven cheek and started to make the coffee. The noise of the grinder drowned out my next few words. I had to repeat myself.

'Guess I've needed someone to share this with.'

Sonny sat down on a kitchen chair and watched me as I decanted water into the percolator and turned on the switch. He looked gloomy, I thought.

The incisive aroma of fresh coffee slowly filled the room.

'Your car park theory seems the most likely,' I said. 'There was huge publicity, and yet the owner of the van never came forward. That suggests that someone had something to hide.'

Sonny was massaging his temples. I stood behind him and took over, running my fingers in small, insistent circles over his skull. But I didn't drop the Cable case. 'And as for the other possibilities – that Jack Cable murdered his own son, or that Timmy drowned – there's the same objection to both.'

'No body,' Sonny said.

'No body,' I agreed. 'Anyway, Sonny, what

I've decided is this. It's time I turned my attention to Liam. To filling in his past.' I ceased the massage and moved to where I could see his face. 'Will you help me?'

Sonny's look was sharp. 'Laura, you promised–'

'I know. I said I'd take it easy, as the doctor suggested, until the end of the week. That's what I'm doing.'

I opened my arms and gestured around the room, pointing to the fire, pointing to my novel – hardly read, but he didn't know that – on the footstool. I stepped over to the dresser and took a small cylinder from my briefcase.

'Can you get these developed?'

'You used the covert camera?' he said, surprised.

'It was the only way. Stevie brought it to Grantchester for me. I got some great pictures – I hope they're great anyway – of Liam. But what I'm interested in most at the moment is a photo of a monkey.'

'Go on. I'm listening.'

'Well, there are two separate pieces of data that eventually convinced the Cables that Liam is their son. One is a dream. Liam dreams, apparently, of being menaced by enormous talking birds; and it turns out that that little Timmy Cable was terrorised by, of all things, a bunch of turkeys. The similarity is uncanny.'

Sonny laughed.

'No,' I objected, 'it's not funny. Have you ever got up close and personal with a turkey? They have these long dangly dark red bits of skin hanging down from their necks,' I said, betraying my city-girl origins, 'and they're loud and they're pushy. To a small child they would look like monsters. Timmy was so frightened, his parents said, that he had nightmares night after night right up until his disappearance. It was one of the things that they gave the police as a way of confirming identification if the boy were ever found alive.'

'And of course,' Sonny said, as if he were trying to hurry me on, 'there's no way that Liam would know about the dream unless he actually is Timmy.'

'Just so.'

'Or unless, somewhere along the line, he'd had a long conversation with Timmy.'

I hadn't thought of that.

I poured out the coffee. Sonny sipped his greedily. He looked as if he needed it. His face was uncharacteristically haggard, and he had circles that resembled bruises under his eyes.

'You look awful,' I said. 'What have you been doing?'

'Grieving.' He said it simply. He wasn't asking for sympathy. He was sharing it with me.

But still, I didn't want to know. Couldn't know. Couldn't hear.

'Leave it, Sonny,' I said quietly. 'Please understand, we just have to get on with life. We have to forget.' I stirred my coffee. I tried to sip. It was too hot to drink; I didn't see how Sonny could stand it. 'Please?'

There was a long pause. Sonny closed his eyes as if he were recalling something from the distant past. Then, eyes still shut, he said, 'And the other thing that convinced the Cables of Liam's identity was a monkey?'

'Well done, Sonny. A furry monkey with a melancholy face. Apparently, baby Timmy was given it as a present and he adored it. It went everywhere with him. Liam, for what it's worth, is carrying the identical toy.'

'And you want me to find out,' Sonny said, 'precisely what it is worth. Fair enough, Laura. I'll be in the West End tomorrow. I'll take the photo to Hamley's.'

As I'd hoped. The staff at Europe's largest toy shop should have an idea, if anyone had, how many of these monkeys happened to be in circulation when Timmy was a child.

'Perfect,' I said, wrapping my arms around him from behind. 'Perfect, Sonny. And now, let's get some sleep.'

We went to bed early. I turned my back to Sonny. He curled up around me.

I had a dream, in the middle of the night, that I heard him crying.

I was beginning to feel besieged. As Sonny left Wildfell for London, one of the Cables rang to report that my electronic organiser was broken. They'd found it, apparently, on the back lawn; it had splintered snap-crack when I'd stepped on it. I couldn't work up any regret. I was glad it was gone.

Then it was Helen. And she had just finished the preliminaries – *Are you warm enough at Wildfell? Shall I take a few days* off *work and join you?* – when Nicole arrived.

'Helen,' I said, 'Nicole's here. I've got to go.'

I leaned over to release the latch on the door. Nicole sauntered in.

'Sure. Will do. Don't worry, Helen, I'll be fine.'

It was clear from her clothes that Detective Inspector Pelletier was off duty. No neat suit today. She wore a big hand-knitted jumper, with bold blocks of colour on the chest. Her bottom half was covered by a tighter-than-duty pair of black jeans. She shed her gloves and scarf and jacket as she came through the door.

'Phew,' she exclaimed. 'Have you been outside, Laura? We're in for some bitter weather.'

I ushered her into the living room and saw her happily ensconced by the fire with her feet propped up on a footstool. 'Better,' she declared, as I returned with mugs of hot chocolate. She had opened her briefcase and taken out some papers. They were spread across the sofa.

'What have you got there?' I asked. 'I thought you were taking a break?'

'Never mind that now,' she said. She cleared off some papers and patted the cushion next to hers. 'How are you?'

I pretended I didn't see the pat, and settled myself in the armchair.

'I'm fine,' I said. 'It was only a little operation. They hoovered out my insides. Spring-cleaning, you might say.'

Nicole didn't laugh. She didn't even smile. 'You know perfectly well what I mean, Laura. How do you feel about the baby?'

'It wasn't a baby.' Even to my own ears the words sounded harsh. 'Sorry, Nicole. All I meant was, it was early days. Fourteen weeks, to be precise. It was a foetus, not a baby; it wouldn't have survived outside my womb.'

'My question was: how do you feel about it, Laura?'

I worked at softening my voice. I gave it a timbre that spoke of reason and a volume that implied control. 'Simple, Nicole. I hadn't known it was there. I didn't choose to be pregnant. And I'm absolutely fine.'

My voice must have done what I'd hoped for. Nicole looked at me steadily for some seconds. Then she dropped her eyes, and dropped the subject.

For the briefest of instants, I felt bereft.

But that feeling of loss passed again as soon as she began to talk about Timothy Cable. Nicole, bless her little truncheon, had done as she had promised. She had chatted up a detective chief inspector who had been intimately involved in the hunt for Timmy twelve years before. Still was intimately involved; the case had never been closed, and was regularly reviewed.

Nicole had been to see Raymond Gaines at headquarters in Norwich. She had downed lager-and-limes with him in the police bar. She had asked questions and assessed answers and even, on several points, persuaded him to check the records. The result was a succinct report that would have won top marks in a speech contest. None of it contradicted what I had already learned from Olivia's memoir.

'Any witnesses?' I asked.

'This is Cleybourne Hoop, not Haringey,' Nicole said, by way of making a point. 'It isn't even a village, it's a lonely stretch of shoreline. If Timmy had vanished three hours before, while the sun was shining, there were at least a dozen people who might have been witnesses. But at twelve thirty, when whatever happened happened, a storm was coming in and the area was virtually deserted. So,' she said, pulling her feet up on to the sofa and wrapping her arms around her knees, 'for witnesses we have only Robin Jackson and Catherine Cable. Catherine was seven at the time; Robin was nine. They'd rambled a mile and a half along the headland, east of Beach Lane, towards Sheringham– You know the area?' she asked.

'I went there yesterday. Once walked, never forgotten.'

'Well, the only people they saw at all during the last hour of their outing were a man and a woman on the beach below. Robin was convinced it was at twelve fifteen; but the sergeant who interviewed him believed that the boy's absolute assurance about the timing was more a matter of style than of substance.'

'Robin saw something else,' I said.

'My, my, you do know your stuff.'

Nicole was pleased, I could tell. Perhaps she'd really feared that I'd be face down on the bed in tears.

'Yes,' she confirmed. 'Robin parted from Catherine at twelve twenty-five – on that they both agree – and raced down across the fields. When he got to the coast road, his pals hadn't arrived. As he sat on the verge waiting for them, a white van turned out of Beach Lane, heading west. The driver was a fat man, that was all he could say. He seemed to be alone. Even a child's eagle eyes, if he's not interested, won't pick up detail.'

'And Olivia saw it too.'

'A few minutes earlier, Mrs Cable had walked over to Cleybourne to pick up a bit of shopping; she decided to come back along the raised path over the marsh and meet up with Jack and Timmy. As she neared the car park, she spotted the white van, or rather she saw its rooftop, moving away. It was very near to her at that point, but largely hidden by the hedge. And other than that,' Nicole said, with a shrug, 'Olivia saw nothing and no one. Until she saw Jack, alone.'

'And Jack?'

'Well, there are problems with Jack's initial account. He was beside himself, not clear at all. And by the time these problems about who saw what became apparent, they couldn't be properly followed up, because he'd fallen ill. Within hours of Timmy going missing, he was virtually delirious with fever.'

'For real?' I asked. The convenience of a delirium at the point of police interview is enough to give any investigator a raised eyebrow.

'Definitely real. I saw the medical reports. A lesser man would have been in hospital. And by the time he recovered enough to be interviewed again, his recall of detail was hazy. He kept making mistakes. Ray – DCI Gaines–'

'*Oooh*,' I said.

'I wouldn't go there if I were you. Detective Chief Inspector Gaines said Jack was in despair; he saw his illness as weakness. He wanted to be out searching with the others.'

'Can we stop for a moment?' No childish teasing about lager-and-lime buddies this time. I needed to be clear. 'What was the problem in Jack Cable's account?'

Nicole leaned over, set her empty cocoa mug on the floor and leafed through her papers until she found the one she'd been looking for. She skimmed it before answering.

'The timing,' she said. 'It never quite gelled. Jack Cable says he noticed Timmy was missing at twelve twenty. He searched for a few minutes. Ran up the footpath to the cliff edge and scanned the beach below. Peered inside the pillbox, where Timmy often played. Then he saw Catherine walking along the cliff edge; Robin had already separated from her by then and headed across the fields. Jack spoke to Catherine: had she seen Timmy? She hadn't. He told her to run across the fields to get help, to ring for the police. She ran off as she'd been bid.'

'So far, so precise,' I said.

Nicole agreed. 'The problems come in the next few minutes. Jack looked down towards the marshes and saw Olivia in the far distance. He ran down the path from the cliff and through the corner of the car park. He set off towards her across the dyke. They met up. They returned to the car park and searched together, briefly. They rang the coastguard. They were joined by the housekeeper's husband, who'd been summoned by Catherine.'

'Joe Laskovic.'

'And minutes later, the police appeared.'

'So,' I said. 'What's strange?'

'Just this. Jack and Olivia's accounts agree; it had to be between twelve forty and twelve forty-five when they met on the dyke. Olivia had seen the white van immediately before their meeting. But Jack, in his initial account to police, didn't mention the van. And after his illness, though he racked his brains, he couldn't remember having seen it. But how is it that he didn't see the van? He checked in the car park during his initial search. And he had to cross the corner of the car park again to mount the dyke, but he doesn't remember the van being there. So where was it during that time?'

'I see what you mean. It's a David Copperfield style of problem. The van had to be there, because Olivia saw it pulling away;

but according to Jack's account, it wasn't. No wonder the investigating officers focused on this. And the vehicle – they never found it?'

'Not a whiff. Interviewed every owner of a small white van in the region, and believe me, we're talking numbers here. There was one man who interested them a great deal. A Barry Jenkins, lived in Hunstanton, had two convictions for indecent assault on children and he grew up in Cleybourne. But he was working that day, helping his brother-in-law lay a patio. They couldn't shift the alibi. Had to let him go.'

'He was the only suspect?'

'The only one who came near to being serious,' she said. 'Of course, there was also the mysterious couple on the beach. You know about them?'

'Olivia's memoir mentioned that a man and woman had walked past Jack while he and Timmy were playing on the beach. And it could have been them that Catherine and Robin spotted from the cliffs a little later on. They were never found, huh?'

'Never found. Robin didn't think they were local, he'd never seen them before. And the calls for these two to come forward even went out on the national news, with no result except for the usual crop of crazies.'

'Suspicious, don't you think?'

Nicole leaned over again, took a brush out

of her bag and began to brush her blue-black hair. She was growing it out. It stood up around her face in great bold clumps.

'I like it longer,' I said.

'You wouldn't if you had to wash it,' she replied. 'And as for the couple who never came forward – well, yes, it was suspicious, but just as likely they were illicit lovers on a dirty weekend as drivers of white vans and stealers of children. No conclusions to jump to there.'

There was a pause.

'Ray mentioned something else. Another child who went missing on Cleybourne Hoop twelve years before Timmy did. A girl. That's what lies behind the depth of feeling among some of the locals about those two paedophiles who have been housed nearby.'

'They aren't a danger, are they?' I asked.

'In the abstract, yes. Both violent, one a child killer. But they served their sentence and, by law, they're free men. The Norfolk police think it's better to keep them in sight rather than let them fade into the community. The nearby residents, especially those with kids, find it hard to agree.'

'Listen, Nicole, about this earlier disappearance. The girl vanished twelve years before Timmy?'

She nodded.

'And Timmy vanished – twelve years ago. Is this a pattern? A child goes missing every twelve years?'

'That's what I asked the chief inspector.'

'And what did he say?'

'Can't you guess, Laura?'

I didn't really want to, but the conclusion was there, unavoidable.

'I expect he said: "Not yet."'

Before she left, off to visit an aunt who had retired to Wells-next-the-Sea, Nicole gave me three more things.

She supplied a copy of the master list of people who had been questioned by the police in connection with Timmy's disappearance. 'Of course, faced with an official inquiry, you'll deny you've ever seen this, Laura, won't you? And there's no way you're going to replicate the police investigation, which involved at its peak hundreds of officers.'

'But I might just like to know, when I speak to someone, that the police did, too. Right?'

Nicole nodded. 'Right.'

She gave me a name I hadn't had before. Jim Prestwick. 'A colleague of yours,' she said. It was a loose usage of the term 'colleague'.

Apparently the Cables had hired Jim Prestwick on two occasions to nose around hostels in London checking out the boys. He was a private investigator who specialised in runaways. 'I know the guy,' Nicole said, 'and I don't think much of him. Let's just say he has a pretty elastic version of ethics.'

Jack Cable had said to me that Olivia hadn't found all the PIs she'd come across to her taste. Maybe he'd meant Jim.

And the third thing Nicole gave me? An offer of further help. As she sat in her car, with the engine idling, she looked up at me, shook her head mournfully and said, 'Laura, you know, if there's anything I can do...'

I took her up on it. Something had been nagging me, I told her. Something about the Cables' housekeeper, Etta Laskovic. Etta Humm, as was.

'Could you look into her background for me, Nicole? I believe she comes from Leicester.'

Nicole sighed, a long-drawn-out, theatrical sort of sigh. 'That's not what I meant by help. But I'll do it,' she said. 'A guy I work with dates a woman on the Leicester force. What do you want to know?'

'What there is to know.'

'And you, Laura? Are you going to take it easy?'

'You can bet on it,' I said.

And I waited until she had driven off down the lane before locking up the cottage and heading back to Cleybourne.

# Chapter 21

It had snowed, lightly, in the night. Bleakness and fog gave way to shimmer. The fields along the coast road were dusted with snow and the sky was the palest of blues.

I pulled into the pebbled driveway of the Cable compound. The door to Jack and Olivia's cottage stood open and a lurid yellow tube like a child's plastic play tunnel dangled from an upstairs window. A man held the end of the tube as barrowloads of rubble thundered down into a skip. He saw me watching and shouted up at the window.

A head appeared briefly and disappeared again. The thundering stopped.

'Help you?' said the shouter. I felt cheated. My neighbours in Cambridge had erected an extension last year, and their builders were never this accommodating.

'I'm working for Jack Cable,' I said. 'Is this his cottage?'

'You've come to the right place,' the man declared.

He was thin and tough as a rake. Over his T-shirt he wore a hunting waistcoat studded with pouches and flaps and zips. He pulled a Benson and Hedges out of one of the pockets and lit up. He also offered me one but, even in the interests of camaraderie I couldn't manage a smoke. He introduced himself – 'I'm Ian Ostler, by the way' – and I introduced myself back.

'You work for Jack Cable,' he said, 'you'll know about the news.'

I waited. What now?

'That kid who disappeared, that Timothy Cable. I hear he's turned up. Is that right?'

'So I understand. What do you know about the disappearance?'

'I was here,' he said. 'Well, not here, exactly, not at this cottage. I was there' – he pointed across the marsh – 'working in Cleybourne. With the crew who restored the windmill. And I met him. Nice boy – not whiny, you know?'

'How did you happen to meet him?'

'His mother, she brought him over; must have been only two days before he disappeared. He couldn't get over the windmill, thought it was bloody marvellous, so we showed him how the vanes moved and how the mechanism worked. We went on and on, as I recall, and he never once got restless.'

He shook his head several times. Looked at his burned-down cigarette. He took one long, final drag, and then flung the butt to the ground and crushed it under the heel of his boot.

'So the kid's turned up again,' he said.

'He's a teenager. Not a child any more. It was twelve years ago.'

'Don't I know it. I used to be a fine figure of a man in those days, and look at me now!'

Ian Ostler was in his late forties. His hair was black and curly, lightened with patches of grey and brick dust. He had the kind of build that you sometimes see on people who have always earned a living with their muscles. Skinny but strong. As if only the sinew remained. When he turned sideways, you could hardly see him.

'Do you remember anything about the day he disappeared?'

'Everything,' he said. 'It was an ordinary working day. Before the police asked us to join in the search, the biggest excitement was when I had to go over to Sheringham to pick up some materials that had been missed off the delivery. The police arrived just after I got back. By then, the storm had hit. We helped to comb the marsh. We had torches and drag poles and the rain was lashing down.'

He shook his head sadly. 'I'll never forget it,' he said. 'Such a nice little kid.'

A pause, then he moved into question mode. 'Listen, what happened to him anyway? D'you know? I always thought it was one of them perverts, you know – paedophiliacs. He's OK now, isn't he? Not –

you know – ruined? Where's he been all these years?'

I had to say that I didn't know. Didn't know where Liam had been all these years.

Didn't know if he'd been ruined.

Max Armstrong had gone off in the car somewhere. It gave me a good excuse to hang around, to wander again along the cliff edge.

I found an extra jumper behind the front seat of the Saab and congratulated myself on my prudence. I put it on over my sweater, underneath my suede jacket. I pulled on sheepskin-lined gloves and a woolly scarf I glanced at myself in the wing mirror and managed a rueful smile. All that was needed now were buttons made of coal and a top hat and anyone might take me for a snowman.

Clouds of vapour issued from my mouth as I climbed the path to the top of the cliffs. I peered into the pillbox; the fetid water was still there, and the litter. There was a new addition: a condom dangled from the lip of a beer bottle. It was probably a good thing that the little freckle-faced boy had found somewhere else to play.

I pulled the scarf up over the bottom half of my face and stared out to sea. The water, dark and rough, flung froth this way and that. The clamour of the waves as they crashed against the shore was harsh and unforgiving.

I began to walk eastwards, keeping a distance from the cliff edge. Max's warnings about danger had been wellfounded. I came to a place where the side of the cliff was newly exposed. I leaned forward until I could see, on the beach below, a massive heap of chalk and rubble. No dishonour in retreat. The damage done by a sixty-foot fall on to flint could last a lot longer, I fancied, than the effects of a mere miscarriage.

I stepped quickly back from the cliff edge straight into the path of a jogger who was moving rapidly towards me. His hands and head and neck were bared to the intense cold. A hard man, I thought; making a statement. And then, as he powered closer, I recognised Robin Armstrong.

When I hailed him, he pulled up, reluctantly, and switched to jogging on the spot. He took a stopwatch and a notepad and pencil from his belt. He consulted the stopwatch and wrote something down.

'You always time yourself?' I asked.

He scowled as if he thought I might be winding him up. 'There's always room for improvement,' he said. 'Uncle Jack was preparing for his first trip to the Arctic by the time he was my age. Ambition is a family trait.'

'Speaking of family, what do you think of

your cousin Liam, then?'

He tucked the notepad away, his face creased in a look of distaste. 'I can't understand what he's up to,' he said. 'Can you?'

'What do you mean?'

'Well, clearly he wants to get his clutches into the Cables. But anyone can see he is not at all their sort of person. I don't know why they give him the time of day.'

Robin looked genuinely perplexed.

I asked for detail.

'Liam's scarcely educated,' Robin said, continuing to jog up and down. 'He can hardly hold a conversation. And he doesn't do anything, as far as I can see, apart from play on that shabby guitar. He's not the sort of person who will fit in with the Cables at all.'

*Catherine appears to like him*, I could have said. But didn't. 'You've been at Grantchester Farm in the past few days?' I asked. 'What's going on there?' And then, in a more joking way, because Robin seemed to have been thrown into gloom by the reminder of Liam, 'What's the gossip?'

'The usual,' Robin said. His tone held just a hint of acid. 'Aunt Olivia is preparing a party for Liam and drinking more than she should; someone with a lot of cheek has pitched a tent near the Meadows; and that bloody lurcher barks incessantly at everyone who comes.'

Robin would regret his forthrightness later, I thought, as I watched him speed off into the distance. But I didn't mind at all that rivalry had loosened his very ambitious tongue.

Ian Ostler and his workmate were nowhere in sight. Apart from a duck squawking nearby, the pebbled turning area inside the Cable compound was quiet. Max's BMW was pulled up now to the side of his house.

I took a moment to check with the office in Camden. Sonny was out; he'd had to pick up his son Dominic from school, Stevie said, and take him to a sports injuries clinic. It was a sprain. Urgent but not serious.

Stevie asked the inevitable question. 'And how are you?'

I was getting tired of it. There are only so many answers to that question; most of them I didn't want to give. *I'm as well as can be expected, Stevie, given that I have been pregnant for the first time in my life, and the baby died before I even knew of its existence, and I may never be pregnant again.*

What I said was: 'Don't worry about me, Stevie dear. I'm right as rain.'

There was a pause. It had the qualities of a sceptical pause. 'You may be right as rain,' she said, 'but Sonny's certainly not. I think you should talk to him, Laura.'

'Will do, Stevie.' Later. 'Any messages?'

Stevie was reluctant to drop the subject of Sonny and me and the miscarriage, I could sense that from her voice; but she has a strong sense of duty, so she put her concerns aside just long enough to relay my messages. Both were from Sonny.

The first was about the photos, they were ready, Sonny reported, and they were good. Especially those of Liam, head-on.

The second was about Mickey Monkey. The soft-toy buyer at Hamley's had placed the toy precisely, clever man, down to the season it was sold. He'd checked the records; Hamley's had sold three hundred and fifty. He'd rung through to the manufacturer and found they'd made ten thousand altogether.

A long way behind Pokémon cards. Popular enough, however, that Timmy mightn't be the only boy who'd fallen in love with a primate.

Stevie returned to the chase. 'And now, Laura, do you want to know what I think?'

'Speak of the devil,' I muttered. 'Got to go, Stevie.'

'What's up?'

'Catherine Cable and Liam—'

'Liam? Remind me who—?'

'The boy-who-would-be-Timmy,' I said. 'He and Jack Cable's daughter, Catherine, have just arrived in Daddy's vintage E-type.'

'Off you go,' Stevie said.

By the time I put the phone away, Catherine was introducing Liam to the intricacies of the compound. Pointing out her Uncle Max's home, and the Cables' holiday house, and the cottage, tucked in behind the other two, that had been used by Etta and Joe. Her cheeks were glowing. She was bouncing up and down, dancing from one foot to the other. Her excitement made sense, I suppose; this had been a childhood haunt, and she hadn't been back for twelve years.

Liam leaned against the car and folded his arms across his chest. He looked slowly around.

'Do you recognise anything?' I asked him.

Liam turned and looked at me, steadily, without a whiff of embarrassment or anxiety. 'Nope,' he said. 'Should I?'

Catherine was the one who seemed put out by the question. The glance she tossed me was barbed, as if I were straying on to territory that I had no right to enter. If her mother were here, I conceded, Olivia might feel the same way.

'The only thing I know for sure,' Liam continued, in his unhurried way, 'is that the sea is–' A pause. He turned back towards Beach Lane. Languidly he raised an arm and pointed. 'Over there.'

Which anyone who has ever seen the sea – seen the way light fractures the air around it

– could be expected to know.

I pointed to the west, across the marshes. A few red-tiled rooftops were visible above the reeds. What really stood out, its roof and vanes gleaming, was the Cleybourne wind-mill. 'And what do you think of that?' I asked.

'It's a windmill,' Liam said contentedly. Without a murmur of interest.

Catherine bounced the car keys in her palm impatiently. 'Let's walk. I want to look at the sea.'

She didn't mind that it was half past three and getting dark. Off we went together along Beach Lane, me in my snowman gear, Liam in his long sheepskin coat with a huge stripy scarf coiled around his neck and Catherine with a hat and a sweater and duffle coat in staggered shades of purple. Catherine was in the middle. At her urging, we linked arms and initiated a side-to-side step as we swung along.

She began a chant as we approached the car park.

'Left, right, left, right, left, right...'

It was only then that I realised she was scared.

We shuffled through the car park and skirted the noticeboard. As we passed the coastguard emergency telephone she began to shake. I could feel the trembling through her duffle coat, through my sweater and my jacket. Liam must have felt it too. He placed his gloved hand over hers.

We stood in silence for a full two minutes, looking out to sea. Looking at the white-caps. Listening to the breakers.

Then Catherine disentangled her arms from ours and turned, slowly. She lifted her gaze up the curving footpath to the cliffs above.

Neither Liam nor I interrupted. Liam looked anxious; I fancied the anxiety was for Catherine's sake.

Finally, he spoke. 'Cathy? Are you all right?'

That question again.

But Catherine was ready to answer, in her own way.

'That's where I found out about Timmy,' she said.

It wasn't for me that she was speaking, I was sure of that. It was for Liam. She wanted him to know what it had been like that day. As she spoke, her voice moved up an octave; it became higher, less clipped, less certain.

'Robin and I often played together on the cliffs. That morning we raced along the headland. We went a long way. We went way beyond the place with the terraced houses. Robin insisted as he always did that soon they would fall into the sea. I was always frightened when he said that.'

Catherine paused. She was remembering – the kind of remembering that isn't in the head but in the senses. The kind of remembering that puts you right back there, in childhood.

'It was exciting, too,' she said, in that strange high voice. 'We could feel the wind rising. We could see the storm as it shouldered its way towards us. But eventually, when it was almost lunchtime, we started back towards home. We got near to the pillbox. Then Robin stopped and pointed.

'"Isn't that your father?" he said.

'I held my hand above my eyes so I had a clearer view. You could always tell my father at a distance because he had the straightest back in England – that's what someone once said – and sure enough, it was him. He was standing alongside the pillbox, looking over the cliff edge. He was staring down at the sea.'

Catherine lapsed into silence. Her eyes were hooded and still. It was as if she remained fixed to that image of her father, cherishing a sight of him that came from a more innocent period of their lives. From the time when Jack Cable had a straight back. The time before she'd learned that Timmy had disappeared.

She cleared her throat before speaking again.

'Robin was meeting friends from the

village. He was eager to be away. He struck out across the fields, down towards the coast road.

'I wasn't supposed to be alone on the headland, so I hurried towards my father. I cupped my hands around my mouth so my voice would carry over the wind. "Daddy! Daddy!"'

Catherine called out in a voice that quivered. The sound was eerie. It bounced back to us from the cliffs... 'Daddy ... Daddy ... addy ... dy...'

She gave a huge sigh when the echo ended.

'At last he heard me,' she said. 'He rushed towards me. He was galloping, as if he were frightened, but that couldn't be, I thought. Everyone knows my father is never afraid.

'"Catherine!" He went down on one knee and peered at me closely. He looked soooo strange. He put his hands on my shoulders, as if he might be thinking of shaking me, but he didn't. He was gentle. "Catherine," he said, "your brother's missing. Timmy's gone. Have you seen him? Did you see anything?"

'Then Daddy started crying. He was sobbing and shaking. I felt very, very scared. I'd never seen Daddy cry before. I didn't know he could cry. But his cheeks were wet and his eyes were red and he was crying, sure enough.

'"Catherine!" He almost shouted at me. "Have you seen anything?"

'I couldn't take my eyes off him. I was so astonished. I thought and thought. I shook my head. No.

'He asked me again.

'"Nothing?"

'"Nothing at all, Daddy." My heart was pounding. I looked away. I couldn't bear to watch him any more. "Nothing."

'Daddy let me go. I didn't want to leave but he said I had to. I had to run, quickly, quickly, down across the fields, the way Robin had gone. I had to get help. I should stay with Etta, Daddy said.

'I ran as fast as I could down across the fields. I didn't look behind me. I didn't want to see Daddy crying any more.

'And as I ran, I was crying too. It felt as if I'd never, ever stop.'

I've seen something similar happen to other people before. The experience of being on the beach again, of seeing the cliffs, had destroyed Catherine's defences. Had made her want to share – certainly with Liam. Maybe even with me.

'Did you know that Mother had an affair?' she asked as we were walking back from the beach. It had happened mere months after T-Day, she said, while Jack was away with the Franklin expedition. Catherine had heard her mother talking about it with her Uncle Max. She knew it had happened; she didn't know with whom.

'Poor Daddy!' she exclaimed. I wondered whether she might have blamed her mother for her father's absence.

There was more, and it was even more intriguing. Having recalled in such vivid detail her meeting with her father on the headland after Timmy had disappeared, Catherine described her frantic scramble down across the fields to Etta's place. How she could hardly see for her panic. How a cloud came over Joe's comical face when she broke the news; how he snatched up his torch and jacket and raced off to join the search. How they rang for the police and how Etta hugged her and hushed her and soothed her. How she fell asleep – a reaction, she supposed, for it was only midday – and how when she woke up, she and Etta were alone, and the police had been and gone.

'When did they ring for the police, Catherine?'

'The instant that Joe went out the door,' she said. She looked puzzled. 'There was no delay.'

I was equally puzzled. 'You said "they", Catherine. They rang for the police. I understood, once Joe had gone, that there was only you and Etta.'

When Catherine replied, there was a kind of wonder in her voice. 'And the other man,' she said.

She thought in silence for a moment, and then it all came out. He was a bulky man. He'd seemed fat to her, but then she was only a child. And old. Ditto.

He was visiting Etta, of that she was sure. Etta called him Tom. Catherine only saw him for the few minutes before she fell asleep. She had no idea who he was, but she may – just may – have seen him with Etta before.

'And did you mention this man to the police? Did Etta?'

'I don't know about Etta. I certainly didn't say anything. I hardly noticed him; in all the panic, he was just a shadow in the corner. When I woke up he was gone. And by the time Etta said I was strong enough again to speak to the police, I must have forgotten.' She kicked a few pebbles with the toe of her boot as we crossed the driveway of the compound. 'There were other, more important things to think about.'

We stepped inside the Cables' cottage. The building work was progressing quickly. Some of the timbers in the walls were exposed and the floors were strewn with wires and lengths of copper pipe. We speculated about what it might look like when it was finished. That distracted

Catherine and seemed to cheer her up. Seeing her in a brighter mood, I asked a question of a different sort.

'Shouldn't you be back at university, Catherine?'

I asked it gently. But apparently not gently enough.

'I hate it there!' she burst out. 'I detest it – all those meaningless papers and the worry about grades and the stupid parties. I never want to go back.' She spoke with a venom which seemed, for those seconds, to be directed at me.

Liam changed the subject. He did it deftly and lightly, as if he'd been trained to diplomacy. 'Let me see,' he said, taking her hands in his and spinning her once around. 'What will you do instead? Something really wicked?' he declared. 'Something really cool, I mean.'

The last comment was for me, I realised. Liam was mistaken in his assumption – I knew what *wicked* meant – but deft again.

He stopped spinning but continued the fantasy. 'Everyone should do something really special, don't you think, just once in their life. I've always wanted to do something really, really good. Something that would make other people happy. What would you like to do, Cathy?'

But Catherine waved sentimentality aside. 'You softie,' she said. She had more glamorous pursuits in mind. 'I'll be a dancer. Not a boring old ballet dancer, with no breasts to speak of and bleeding toes. I'll be a flamenco dancer, with a red dress and a lace mantilla and high-heeled shoes, and I'll strut and sway and all the men will be in love with me!'

And with that, she did it. She toed and heeled across the empty floor like a bailaora born and bred. We clapped and whooped. Ian Ostler and his mate stuck their heads around the stairs and clapped too. Catherine fell, laughing, in a heap on the floor.

Liam gave her a hand up. She stepped to the window and gulped in great breaths of fresh air.

'You're just like my sister,' Liam said.

I held my breath. This was the first time he had spoken of his relationship to the Cables in my presence. But I'd misunderstood.

'My sister Gemma,' he explained. 'She loves dancing. In her case it was stage stuff, amateur musicals, that kind of thing. She had a starring role in the local production of *West Side Story*. But her husband, Cliff – he doesn't like her dancing in public, so she had to stop. Now the closest she comes to performing arts is as an instructor at Tumble Tots.'

It was a long speech, for Liam. It seemed like he might continue – as if he, too, were opening up – but he was interrupted by an excited whisper from Catherine.

'Look,' she said. She made room at the window so we could see too. 'Look at Daddy and Uncle Max. Whatever can be the matter?'

I looked over Catherine and Liam's shoulders. It was easy to see why she was taken aback.

Jack Cable's Lexus – less clean now, less polished – was pulled up in the driveway nose to nose with Max's BMW. The men were nose to nose in conversation.

Jack stared at the ground in agitation; he waved his hands emphatically; he shook his head. Max kept one hand on Jack's shoulder throughout the conversation, as if to stop him rushing off. He looked as if he might be trying to soothe his brother-in-law.

Suddenly Jack Cable broke away and climbed back into his car. Without a backward glance, he started the engine. Catherine threw open the window.

'Daddy!' she cried.

She was too late. He didn't hear. Jack Cable drove off towards the coast road and Catherine was left, disconsolate, looking after her father again.

It didn't take me long to pick up my photos in Camden Town. I did it the lazy way – caught the train in King's Lynn, barrelled through to Finsbury Park and taxied to the office. The cab waited in the street while I ran up the stairs, with an energy that made me feel more confident, and down again. In the Aardvark office my luck held – Stevie wasn't around to ply me with questions. Vanessa, on the desk, did her best as Stevie's stand-in, tossing a raft of queries my way – 'I'm fine,' I replied – but despite her best efforts I was back on the train and bound for Basingstoke before she could say, 'Take it easy.'

As long as you can grab a seat, trains are first-rate places for work. They bounce too much to allow any but the mildly soused to sink into sleep. The loos are to be avoided and the food is unappealing. What's a girl to do but work? Providing you don't overshoot the stopping-off point, you'll arrive at your destination with two or three tasks ticked off and wonder where the time went.

That was precisely how I disembarked in Basingstoke.

I'd read the morning paper as we passed through Cambridgeshire on the way down to London, from the headlines to the weather report. Severe frosts on the way.

Crossing London, between King's Cross and Waterloo, I'd admired the photos I'd taken with the covert camera. Liam, looking determined after our confrontation over the camera; he smiled triumphantly from the

318

car window, with a forearm resting on the top of the door. It was the face I was interested in and I'd got that, close-up and clear-featured. As he turned his head towards me, I'd snapped and snapped and snapped again.

I held the sheaf of photos tightly along one edge and fanned them with my thumb. They formed a primitive moving picture – Liam turning, slowly, slowly, so that the photos showed his enviable cheekbones and his ear and his jawline from a variety of angles.

It wasn't art, but I liked it.

And I'd learned things I needed to know as the countryside swept by.

I learned about the builder, Ian Ostler. He had been interviewed by police officers twelve years ago; the list Nicole had left with me confirmed that. He'd been interviewed three times altogether. Once because he was among the crew working on the windmill; everyone in the immediate area, everyone who joined in the search, had been seen. The second time, after Olivia's flash of memory about a vehicle on Beach Lane, because Ian Ostler (like many other small builders, he insisted) owned a white van. Then there was a third and final interview after the police established that his alibi was valid. They checked a few more things and gave him, in effect, the all-clear.

I read the file in detail as the train raced

through a wooded area. I learned a great deal about the inhabitants of Cleybourne, perhaps more than I wanted to know, but one thing was conspicuous by its absence. There was no mention, none at all, of a fat man who'd been with Etta at the time of the disappearance. Joe appeared three or four times in the interview schedules; that was all.

So who was the mystery man? Someone who might have visited Etta before, Catherine thought. Someone whom Etta ushered out quickly; she didn't introduce him to Catherine. Maybe that was because Catherine was distressed; perhaps Etta considered, as many people did, that to be a child placed you outside the usual courtesies. Or maybe there was another explanation; maybe the visitor had something to do with the disappearance.

I had a hunch about all this. It was only a hunch, but it was enough to make me impatient for the results of Nicole's inquiries in Leicester.

I knew it was too soon, but I rang Nicole's mobile anyway. I couldn't resist. I got an irritating burst of 'Born Free'. For a clever woman, Nicole has appalling taste in music. Or maybe she thinks the laudable sentiment expressed in the title makes up for the limpness of the song.

When the strains of the music clicked off,

a robot invited me to leave a message, and I did.

'Nicole, it's me. Call,' I said, and disembarked in Basingstoke.

# Chapter 22

Barbara Dobson; that was the name Jack had given me. She was the forensic artist responsible for the terracotta head that had now been destroyed. She worked for a charity, he'd said – a helpline for the families of people who'd disappeared.

On the internet, it had been the work of a moment to track her down. I wasn't overly optimistic, I'd prepared myself for the possibility that the trek down to Basingstoke would turn out to be a waste of time. But mentally speaking, my fingers were crossed; maybe, just maybe, Barbara Dobson could help me establish once and for all whether Liam was the boy the Cables mourned.

The address I'd been given led to a dreary stretch of high street. There were hardware shops whose front windows were crammed with plastic storage containers and dish drainers and mops; software, I would have called it, if the computer industry hadn't already commandeered the word. There were wine merchants with trailers for cheap Rioja chalked across the windows. There were discount car accessories shops to help you turn your beat-up Ford Escort into your own little corner of heaven, and used-car dealers to help you flog it.

The cab slowed down and the driver began to scan for numbers. We passed a hairdresser's – Rollers, it was called, which said as much about its clientele as its technique; a pet shop with rabbit hutches stacked outside; and finally, wedged between two supermarkets, the door that I'd been looking for. The National Missing Persons Helpline.

Barbara Dobson didn't keep me waiting long. She buzzed me in, walked me through a low-ceilinged, dimly lit room with row after row of volunteers on phones and escorted me into a smaller, quieter office.

'My little kingdom,' she said.

The room was simply furnished. It was unadorned except for an African violet on a windowsill and dozens of faces pinned to the walls. Some faces were those of people missing and longed for, people whose absence had been reported by family or friends. Others, from bodies awaiting identification in the mortuary, were the unknown and unclaimed. Barbara Dobson took both the absent and the dead as her concern. She aimed to shift people, alive or dead, missing or unidentified, into the category of the known. She equipped herself to do so with techniques of forensic art.

'The police find them,' Barbara Dobson

said, giving credit where credit was due. 'I play a part. I provide the picture that allows the police to search more productively, or enables the family to identify the dead. I use post-mortem photos to search among the details of people reported missing for one who might match an unidentified body. To give a face to the name or a name to the face.'

I recalled fragments of a television report on the police investigation into the murders committed by Fred and Rosemary West. I asked Barbara if she'd been involved.

'One of our more celebrated cases,' she said. 'Without our help, two of the girls who were murdered by the Gloucestershire pair would never have been identified. But most of our work takes place without publicity. And the longer a person is missing, the more urgent my job becomes. After weeks and months – well, realistically, all the family can hope for is to identify a body. Just to confirm that they are dead; to have some idea of how and where. Then, you see, they can say goodbye.'

I remembered how Olivia had envied the mother whose daughters had died. To know what had happened to your baby, however dreadful that happening, seemed to her a kind of blessing.

I pushed Olivia firmly out of mind. I concentrated instead on Barbara Dobson, who was altogether an imposing presence. She was tall and stood with a solid dignity, a quiet assurance, that I felt intuitively had been hard-won. She had copper-coloured hair and strong, clear features and a large nose that imparted an impeccable air of authority.

She was utterly unique. Barbara Dobson was the only woman – that is, the only person – in Europe who was expert in computer-enhanced age progression. She'd come into this line of work as a volunteer counsellor, one of the people on the end of a phone. Slowly she'd begun to apply her background in design. Learned to examine the photos of the missing, and to alter them to reflect how they might appear after the passage of time: how they might look if their hairstyle altered, if they lost weight, if their jaw line sagged.

And then, while she was struggling to extend her technique – to show, for example, how the face of a corpse pulled out of the Thames might look if it were alive again – she was suddenly selected to train in the States. Her mentor, an ex-FBI agent named Horace Heffner, had developed a means of using computers to do age progression even better.

'Age progression?' Barbara said in reply to my query. 'The process of taking one set of photographs of someone who has disappeared and producing a plausible likeness of that person two years, four years, ten years down the line.'

Put like that, it sounded easy.

'Its most sophisticated application,' she continued, 'is with children, where the changes over time are most dramatic. Four years added to the life of a missing six-year-old could make her virtually unrecognisable, even to her nearest and dearest.'

Perhaps not so easy after all.

She scanned a photo into the computer and then showed me how the software made the image pliable. How she could then stretch the face along the vertical axis, and the horizontal axis, and along each of the diagonals.

The screen showed the big round eyes and chubby cheeks of a toddler from Wyoming. She'd been stolen from the family car while her father was inside a gas station using the toilet. Across the child's face was a fine-meshed grid of lines along which the image could be altered.

'So the software moves this girl forward in time? The computer makes her older?'

'No, my dear,' she said. 'The software doesn't age the image. I do.'

And then, as I stared over her shoulder at the screen, she demonstrated the three broad steps that comprised what was an infinitely detailed procedure.

'General growth patterns first,' she said 'You know, of course, that certain things don't change.'

I didn't, as it happened, but she told me. That by the age of two, the growth of a baby's eyeball and eye socket is almost complete; they remain similar in size and shape right through to adulthood. The eyes, therefore, are the starting point in any facial mapping. Moreover, eyes and nose and mouth stay in the same relationship to each other as the baby gets older. And generally speaking, fine and floppy hair maintains its texture; normal development won't transform it to thick or curly or kinky.

With children, she pointed out, all the major facial growth takes place below the eyes. The nose and the chin and the jawline lengthen; they move forward. And as they do, the button nose and the exaggerated eyes of the typical baby disappear.

Barbara Dobson altered the lower portion of the little girl's face, smoothing away her chubby cheeks.

'Next,' she said, 'come genetic characteristics. Family resemblances.' This part of the procedure required photos of older siblings – or at a pinch other members of the family – at the desired age. The computer software helped her to merge features that were peculiar to the family with those of the child under scrutiny. I watched intrigued as the girl from Wyoming took on a subtle resemblance to her older brother.

'Now comes the real guesswork,' Barbara said. 'Ethnic differences, cultural differences, fashion. The parts of a person's appearance that are there by choice rather than birth.'

The child on the computer screen was wearing a dress with a Peter Pan collar, the kind her parents might have dressed her in for a studio portrait; the forensic artist replaced this with a T-shirt. She gave the hairstyle more definition. She did all this swiftly and unreflectively. A proper age progression, she said, could take days.

But still, before too long I saw the face of a seven-year-old, cheerful and cheeky and sleek, emerge from the soft, round features of the baby. I admired the image. It was a most convincing seven-year-old.

Whether it resembled the girl from Wyoming remained, Barbara conceded, to be seen.

Barbara Dobson's demonstration was masterful, but I didn't catch on quickly. Three-dimensional stuff has never been my strong suit; Lego leaves me cold. But by the end I could grasp the mixture of technical prowess and informed speculation that made up the procedure. Could understand that the result was highly sophisticated; that it was, at the same time, far from precise.

Barbara summed it up succinctly: an age-reconstructed image is merely a collection of probabilities.

Any question from me was likely to seem – no, to be – naïve, but there was one thing I had to ask.

'How on earth do you know how children grow – in such detail, I mean? How do you know the size of a seven-year-old's jaw as opposed to that of a nine-year-old?'

'Good question,' she said. 'We have braces to thank for that.'

'Braces? As in super-white, super-straight smiles?'

'Precisely. Half a million British young-sters – and many more Americans – are receiving orthodontic treatment as we speak. And in the course of that work, the lower part of their face is analysed and X-rayed. Meticulous records are kept. Thanks to braces, for the first time in human history, we have detailed measurements – think of it, my dear, measurements! – of the alteration over time of the lower part of children's faces where most of the growth occurs.'

Awesome.

But however impressive the mechanics of age reconstruction, I quickly learned that it would be of little use to me. Age progression couldn't produce a telling image of Timmy as he'd look at age sixteen. I put the problem to Barbara in purely hypothetical terms, without naming names.

'Twelve years is a long time,' she said. 'You'd need plenty of good photographs of siblings at sixteen. How many brothers and sisters does this hypothetical child have?'

'Only one,' I admitted. 'An older sister.'

'Can't be done,' she said. 'I wouldn't raise the parents' hopes. I've done long-term age progressions in the Belgian paedophile investigations; but in that case, the family was exceptionally large and the family resemblance exceptionally strong. The circumstances you describe are very different.'

'And to make a head?' I asked. 'A terracotta head, say, from a photo? A three-dimensional figure?'

She gave a vehement shake of her own head. 'Not my field. Give me a skull and I can reconstruct the face and head. There are clues in the structure of the skull. But a three-dimensional head from a flat frontal image? From a photograph? It can't be done.'

'But you did it,' I protested. 'You made a head of Timmy Cable.'

Barbara Dobson stood up suddenly away from the computer. She was taller than me, and that's going some. She looked strong and solid. She looked – well, she was too genteel to display overt anger; she looked, shall we say, displeased.

'You said you wanted to consult me about a missing person, Miss Principal.'

'I do. Timmy Cable is missing. Has been for over twelve years. And I'm working for his parents now.'

She didn't seem mollified. If anything, she seemed more put out.

'I did my best,' she said. The tone was distinctly defensive. 'When he first went missing, we didn't have the software. I made some freehand images. It was Olivia Cable who demanded the terracotta head; I did it for her. She seemed desperate to have a more solid image of her son.'

'So you've never used these techniques on Timmy? But I'm sure I saw the pictures in the papers.'

'That was later, after I'd trained in the States. The police asked for my help.'

She took a few steps and tapped with a blunt manicured fingernail on the central image in a collection of children's faces. It was a good-looking boy with a short crop of fair hair and a lopsided smile. The smile reminded me, just at the edges, of Catherine.

'This took him up to age nine,' she said.

'You gave him a smile.'

'Of course,' Barbara said. 'This isn't a photo from real life, it's an image that I've created, but that never stops parents taking it to heart. It may be the first fresh view of their child's face they've had in years.'

'And if the child looked miserable or lonely, it would be a cause of great pain.'

'Unbearable. So I produced a smiling image for the Cables. But their beautiful boy remained missing. Timmy Cable is the police's only real failure, and he is mine too.'

I was puzzled by that.

Barbara explained.

'Young children who go missing in Britain are found. Virtually always, and usually quite quickly,' she said. 'Some are found dead, to be sure. Some have been taken abroad by a non-custodial parent; it may be difficult to get them back. Some are runaways and wish not to return. But all are found. The police are brilliant,' she said. She said it emphatically, as if I had just foulmouthed the Met. As if I'd slagged off Scotland Yard, and deserved to be corrected.

She was still cross with me.

I didn't let her irritation put me off my stride. 'Ben Needham?' I asked.

I knew before ever I met her – the internet again – that Barbara Dobson had worked with the police on the case of another English child who disappeared off a beach. That was in Greece in 1991. And, as the newspapers never let us forget, Ben Needham hasn't been found.

'That was abroad,' she said. 'It doesn't

count. Here in Britain there are only three outstanding cases of children who went missing under the age of fourteen, and are still missing. There is only one case of a child younger than twelve.'

'Timmy.'

'Just so. It was a great humiliation for the Norfolk police. They've never recovered their confidence, if you ask me.'

'Why does the mention of Timmy Cable upset you? Because he wasn't found?'

She agreed. She seemed relieved. 'Exactly. Because he wasn't found. The case almost broke my heart.'

I was quite convinced she meant that. The bit about her heart.

'What's this all about?' she said. 'What do you really want with me?'

'I'd like you to do some further work on Timmy Cable.'

She must have seen it coming, but she flinched nevertheless.

'You want me to go back there?' she said. From the tone of dread, this answer was as good as a *no*.

'Something's happened,' I said. 'A young man has turned up, aged sixteen or so. Name of Liam.'

I had her interest now. She sat down heavily and watched me closely as I spoke.

'He is blond and tall,' I explained. 'He has a toy that may or may not have been

Timmy's, and he knows very private things about Timmy's childhood.' I told her about the turkey farm in Norfolk.

'Does he claim he's a Cable?'

'He doesn't say one way or the other. But Olivia Cable is convinced. She's planning a party to introduce him to the world.'

Barbara Dobson chewed the tip of her forefinger for a moment. There was a crack as she bit off part of the nail. To my surprise, she pursed her lips and blew across the room. The fragment of nail landed with a click in the wastebin. What a shot.

'What do you want me to do?' she asked.

'I have photographs of this Liam, taken a few days ago. And I have photographs of Timmy, aged four. Will you give me your opinion – is the teenager an older version of the toddler? Are Timmy and Liam one and the same?'

'Facial mapping,' she said. 'I can do it, as long as you accept that it's inconclusive. A forensic artist can never prove someone's identity. Only dental records or DNA analysis can do that. Have you taken swabs?'

I shook my head. 'Olivia won't hear of it,' I said. 'She is afraid that any type of test will frighten Liam away. After twelve years of separation, she's not going to risk losing her son again.'

'I've seen that attitude before.'

There was a moment's silence while

Barbara Dobson considered my request. She swung her chair gently from side to side, her long legs bending first to the left and then to the right. She stood up, took a plastic watering jug and carefully administered water to the African violet that crouched on the windowsill. Finally, she sat down again and looked straight at me.

'Look, I spent a lot of time in Grantchester while I was doing the early images. I helped Olivia select the photos that I needed for my work. She was so agitated, she couldn't do it on her own. And I'll never forget what it was like for her. How everything – every tree, every sound, every beam of light – reminded her of Timmy. "These connections–" Olivia told me, "that Timmy sat on this chair and stood by that window – are all I have left of him."'

Barbara paused and smiled, a wan little smile of remembrance. 'I was there, you know, the first time Olivia forgot about Timmy.'

'Forgot?'

'He'd been gone – what? Five and a half months then,' Barbara said. 'The husband was in the Arctic. The housekeeper was in town. Olivia and I were in the kitchen, planning a new poster campaign, when an old chum of hers rang. She had brought relatives on a day trip to Cambridge; they had walked to Grantchester and stopped off at The Orchard. They were about to tuck into tea and scones. Would Olivia join them?'

'"You're coming too," Olivia said, sweeping her arm through mine, and just like that, we set off. To cut a long story short, it was a pleasant hour. The visitors avoided the subject of Timmy, which I believe was a relief for Olivia; the talk was mainly about school days and mutual friends from long ago. Then suddenly a child in a Fair Isle sweater raced between the tables. Olivia followed him with her eyes. Halfway through a sentence, she stopped speaking. The colour drained from her face. She stood up so abruptly that the teapot overturned. "Timmy!" she exclaimed. "Oh my God, how could I forget!"'

Olivia, it seemed, had never before left the house without making arrangements for someone to answer the telephone; someone to open the door. It had been unthinkable to her that Timmy might try to ring, or might be returned, and there'd be no one there to greet him.

'You must have felt immensely sad for her,' I said.

Barbara shrugged, as if that was the last thing that mattered. Then she leaned towards me and lowered her voice. I was being taken into her confidence.

'It was the daughter I felt most sorry for.

Catherine was only seven. She lost her brother – it was sudden and shocking – and then her father went away. Olivia knew that Catherine needed comfort, but what energy she had went into thinking about Timmy. She tried sometimes to be gay and hopeful for Catherine's sake, but she soon gave up the attempt.'

'Could the Cables have been kinder to Catherine?'

'What do I know?' asked Barbara impatiently. 'Who am I to judge? One thing's for sure, they're not the only parents to become obsessed with a missing child; we see it all the time.'

'And on the basis of what you've seen, have you any predictions about what will happen to the Cables? Now that they have their son back?'

'*If* they have him back, you mean?'

I nodded.

'I'm not a psychologist,' Barbara said, 'but I've counselled families through a few reunions. You can take it from me – it's a messy business. Not the way it looks on telly.'

'Television loves a reunion,' I said. And I should know; I just have to see two people running towards each other in slow motion, with outstretched arms, and I'm fighting back the tears.

'Absolutely, my dear. The teenager in care

is reunited with his "real" mother. The baby conceived by artificial insemination finally meets her father. The walkabout husband takes his place again at the family table. All happy endings. These are our contemporary fairy tales.'

'Or, in the case of the Cables … boy goes missing; family grieves; boy returns; all's well that ends well. It's not like that?'

'Of course not. Separation leaves its mark. Parents feel guilty for having let the child go; feel they have to make it up to him. Or the parents overwhelm the child with the pressure to compensate for lost love.'

'And in a case like this,' I said, 'with another family involved in the interim–'

Barbara Dobson interrupted. 'That's the problem in a nutshell. The Cables will see the other family as an interim family; but to Liam, they're his only family. He may not remember anything at all of a mother and father who came before. Suddenly to be told there's another family – that it's to them he really belongs – will be a shock. Liam is sixteen, you say?'

'Sixteen. More or less.'

'Sixteen-year-olds have to struggle anyway with their own identity. To work out how they are, and are not, like their parents. Throw this kind of upheaval into the mixture and you're likely to have one confused kid.' She shook her head. 'You have children?' she asked suddenly.

'No,' I said. This was a question I'd answered many times before, but it didn't feel quite so transparently true any more.

'I know. I have a son myself,' she said. 'It's not so long since he was sixteen. And then,' she added, 'there's the anger.'

'Whose anger?'

Barbara shrugged her sturdy shoulders. 'Everyone involved,' she said. 'I've seen it time and again. The parents blame one another, or perhaps themselves. They keep this anger under wraps while they're searching for the missing child, but once they have him back again, all hell breaks loose.'

She rose from her chair and pointed to a small black-and-white image. 'Here's another scenario,' she said. 'This boy ran away from home in Hartlepool. He's back now, two years later. But the parents are full of regrets and anger. They keep pressing the child for details. They can't seem to stop. The teenager doesn't want to share his time away; whether he is ashamed, or frightened, or whether he fears parental disapproval. I don't know, but he wants to keep the two worlds separate.' She shook her head. 'You just know, watching them, that it will end in tears.'

All this talk of anger made me think of the string of incidents in Grantchester. I thought of my stolen palm-top. Of the razor blade strapped to the gatehouse door. Of the monkey with the knife through its heart.

'What about the child himself? Do children who've been missing feel anger towards their family when they return?'

'It sometimes happens. There are rows at home and a child runs away; but what he really wants is proof of love. He wants to be fetched home again. Just imagine, my dear – if a child was abducted and he trusted that his parents would rescue him and he waited and waited but the parents never came. He might feel abandoned.'

'He might feel unworthy. As if he weren't worth rescuing.'

'Or,' she added, carefully, quietly, watching my face, 'he might feel angry. All the terror he felt as a small child could come flooding back when he's older in the form of rage.'

Could it be? Liam was a mild-mannered boy. That was what I thought. But he had certainly seemed put out when Olivia had seized upon Mickey Monkey. When she'd flung her arms around him and danced for joy, his coldness had been obvious to everyone but her. Maybe Liam had some dim childish memory of the Cables. Maybe he blamed them for whatever horrors had confronted him while he was away.

We'd been speaking hypothetically again.

Now I brought it back to the Cables. 'But at four years old,' I said, 'Liam was too young to run away. And if he had been kidnapped, surely he wouldn't harbour a grudge against his parents for that. It wouldn't be–'

Barbara broke in with that superior smile again. 'Rational?' she said. 'Relationships within families aren't rational, Laura. Any more than those between lovers are. Just be a fly on the wall at any family Christmas gathering.'

The familiar strains of buried grievance bubbling to the surface. The small slights festering beneath a veneer of warmth. The disappointments from the distant past becoming current again. *You always do this... You never do that...* The jealousy, the competition for approval and for love, the greed for little family treasures that often exists, side by side, with love. Sometimes, occasionally, the cruelty.

She pushed me one step further.

'So far we've assumed that wherever Liam grew up, he was loved and cared for and treated like a son. But what if that wasn't the case? What kind of sixteen-year-old would he be if he'd been mistreated? He could be more than simply sad,' she warned me. 'He could have emerged, as some people do from neglect and abuse, into a deep self-loathing. Into an inability to form relationships. Into a need to injure as he'd been

341

injured. Into a blind, buried anger.'

Liam could be sad, all right, I realised.

He could be bad.

He could even – let's face it – be dangerous to know.

# Chapter 23

On the train journey back to London, I mused over my conversation with Barbara Dobson. Not so much the technical information; more her observations about what the future might hold for Liam and the others. I thought of what she'd said: how the parents may put so much pressure on the child that their company becomes oppressive. How the child – however unconsciously – may resent the parents. How the siblings may be hidden from each other under a canopy of hurt.

The only thing I felt sure of was that the period of hurt hadn't come to an end. As Barbara Dobson had pointed out, Jack and Olivia had nothing but pain to show for the long period during which Timmy had been missing. They had no memories of family parties or birthdays or football matches, of exam nerves or laughter or adolescent rebellion. The moments that made up the pattern of a shared life were gone for ever.

I recalled how my friend Helen had reacted when KwikSnap misplaced a roll of film she'd brought back from holiday. 'All those shots of Ginny water-skiing,' she moaned. 'Gone.' But whether or not the photos were gone, Helen had the memories still. And without such memories, over not just one holiday but a period of twelve years, you might be left wondering: in what sense was your child your child?

Suddenly I realised that was the question that Olivia had been avoiding.

And soon I'd have an answer. Barbara Dobson had agreed to undertake a minute comparison of the photos of Timmy then and Liam now. A facial mapping.

'Hang in there. I'll have an opinion for you by the end of the week,' she'd said. 'Latest.'

I was tired but I didn't want to stop. So many questions – about Liam, about Timmy, about what happened on the beach – and so little time.

At King's Cross I passed up the fast train to King's Lynn in favour of another, slower train with a different destination. Call me crazy, but I was overwhelmed by the urge to visit Stevenage. I was on the trail of the woman Liam called his sister.

Whoever claimed that three's a crowd knew little about logic and less about investigation. With only two hard facts – a sister named Gemma and a town named Stevenage – finding Liam's family was like looking for a toenail clipping in a fleecy white carpet. But with three facts, I was flying. Once I knew that Gemma of Stevenage taught toddlers to twist and glide at Tumble Tots, then all it took for me to track her down was a couple of phone calls and a lie or two about my intentions.

I had a surname now. Gemma Tooley lived on an affluent tree-lined street in a large Edwardian home. A shrub-shrouded fence shielded the front lawn from public gaze. The semi-circular driveway must have been where Liam had perfected his three-point turns. The lucky Tooleys; as long as everyone went in the entrance and out the exit, they'd never have to turn their cars around.

I was impressed with Gemma Tooley too. I generally try to avoid stereotypes, but she reminded me at first sight of a footballer's wife. She was thirty and pretty and pert-looking, with heavy straight hair that rode on her shoulders like a veil. She wore tight designer jeans. Her fingernails were polished and her skin was polished, though quite how she got that burnished look in the dead of winter I'd never know, and her hair was a glimmery, shimmery golden brown. Behind her trailed a young girl of about five and a younger boy, with pudding on their faces.

Standing in the shadow of a pretentious porch, Gemma became instantly attentive at the sound of Liam's name. The children were quarrelling. She picked up the youngest and held him on her hip, away from the fray.

'How is he?' she said. 'Is he all right?'

'Any reason why he wouldn't be?'

'Who, Mummy, who?' asked the five-year-old. She clutched with puddingy hands at the designer jeans.

'Your Uncle Liam, darling.' She turned back to me. 'It's just that, the last time I saw him, he – he–'

The five-year-old began to chant. She clapped her hands together. 'Li-yam. Li-yam. Li-yam.'

'The blow to his head, you mean?' I said. 'It's healing now. Apart from the traces of a bruise, he seems fine. You wouldn't happen to know who hit him?'

'Li-yam. Li-yam.' The volume was growing steadily louder.

At that point a car pulled into the driveway. Gemma Tooley looked up uncertainly. A Honda Civic came to a halt in front of the porch.

The driver was a woman of about fifty, tired and drawn but also rather glamorous. The tanned hands that rested on the steering wheel were crusted with rings. In the passenger seat was a much older woman with a wasted face and sharp, anxious eyes.

'Mum. Nan.' Gemma Tooley stepped down off the porch with the baby on her hip. 'Guess what? This lady' – with her free hand she gestured towards me – 'knows where our Liam is. She's seen him. She says he's fine.'

The elderly woman didn't look up. She fidgeted with the clasp of her handbag, opening and closing it, opening and closing, in a steady rhythm.

The little girl came to stand next to the car. 'They're talking about Uncle Liam,' she said. 'Li-yam!'

The beringed woman, who I took to be Liam's mother, opened the door of the car. 'Hello, sweetie,' she cooed. 'Come to Granny.' She lifted the child on to her knee. 'Isn't she a picture?' she said, addressing me for the first time. 'Look at that smile, just like Gemma's. Gemma won her first beauty contest when she was a year old – loveliest baby, remember, Gem?'

Gemma smiled dutifully. 'It's a long time ago, Mum.'

'In her teens she made it all the way to the regional finals. Had a promising modelling career. And,' she said, with an expression as close to coy as you could find on a fifty-year-old woman, 'you might not believe it, but people used to take us for sisters. "Oh," they'd say to Gemma when we signed up for competitions, "I see you've brought your big sister along."'

The little girl began to wriggle. Her granny took a tissue out of her pocket, wiped the pudding off the girl's cheek and set her on the ground.

'Not any more,' the woman said.

'Sorry?'

'They don't take us for sisters now. Not since...' She paused, shaking her head. 'Bringing up a boy has taken it out of me. So you know where Liam is?'

'Yes, I do, Mrs–?'

'Rhodes. Sandra Rhodes.'

'Could I ask you a few questions, Mrs Rhodes? About your son?'

She didn't respond.

'Routine questions,' I reassured her. 'Won't take long – place and date of birth, where he went to nursery school, that sort of thing.'

She looked over my shoulder, towards the porch, at Gemma. I couldn't read the expression on her face.

'Mrs Rhodes, do you have some kind of reason for not wanting to talk about your son?'

The little girl began tugging at her mother's arm, trying to capture Gemma's attention. But she failed to do so; Gemma was clutching the baby and staring at her mother.

Four generations of Rhodes women – great-grandmother, grandmother, mother and daughter, and each with her own agenda.

The little girl returned to her chant. 'Li-yam! Li-yam!' Her voice was so compelling that the anxious old lady released her handbag. It fell, spilling its contents on to the floor below the passenger seat. She leaned over and grabbed Sandra Rhodes's sleeve.

'Is she talking about Gemma's boy?'

Gemma sighed and leaned forward so that she could lock eyes with the old woman. 'His name is Julian, Nan,' she said, giving the little boy on her hip a quick hug. 'You know that. Julian.'

Sandra Rhodes was less understanding. 'Shut up, Mother,' she said. And to herself, like an all-purpose complaint, 'Oh, hell.' With a wave to Gemma, and an exasperated sigh, she put the car into first gear and drove off.

Gemma took me into the house then. 'It's my husband,' she said nervously when we were seated in the breakfast alcove with cups of tea. 'He and Liam had a fight.' On the floor nearby, the little girl showed her brother how to bash coloured poles with a wooden hammer. Gemma's eyes flicked past them to the door.

I tried to keep her on topic. 'Your husband's name is–?'

'Clifford. Clifford Tooley,' she said, then gave an unexpected giggle. 'Doesn't have much of a ring to it, does it?' she whispered.

'I met him at one of his nightclubs. I was in a beauty contest there. He spoke to my mother that very night. "I'm going to marry your daughter, Mrs Rhodes," he said.'

Gemma swung her legs gracefully up on to the upholstered bench of the breakfast table; whatever position she was in standing, sitting, holding the baby on one hip – she seemed to fall naturally into graceful poses. She smiled to herself, recalling their courtship, and then gave a big sigh. 'The name Tooley was the only thing about him I didn't like,' she said. 'At the time.'

'Couldn't you keep your maiden name? Call yourself Gemma Rhodes?'

'Pull the other one. Cliff wouldn't stand for it.'

'So it was Cliff who gave Liam that whopper of a bruise?'

Gemma nodded, sadly. 'It's that Holly Swallow. She's older than Liam, and she's been in a lot of trouble, and Clifford called her a slag and said that Liam was throwing himself away on a girl like that, and Liam said he was leaving and I cried and that's when it happened. And then Liam left.'

There was a shriek. The little girl tried to wrest the hammer away from her baby brother, and he bashed her knee with it. Gemma told him off for hitting his sister, and ordered the little girl to let him keep the hammer. She kissed the girl's knee and dared her to build the world's tallest tower with brightly coloured bricks. The girl began construction with a fierce concentration. The boy continued to bash, bash, bash with the hammer.

Gemma sat down again and picked up her story as smoothly as pie. 'Don't think badly of Clifford, will you? He's a good man.' She thought for half a second, watching the children out of the corner of her eye and casting around for evidence. 'When we got married, he bought a house for Mum. So she and Liam could move to Stevenage to live near us. He's good to them. To all of us,' she amended.

'And you've been married – how long?' I asked.

'Eleven years,' Gemma said.

'Cliff wasn't around when Liam was born?'

Gemma stopped watching the children. She looked up at me, her eyes like saucers. The burnished skin had lost some of its glow.

I didn't wait for her to answer. 'And your mother. Sandra. Has she always been so – ambivalent – towards your brother? He has the idea, you know, that she doesn't care about him.'

When Gemma answered, her voice was little more than a whisper. I leaned closer to hear. 'It's not fair to blame Mum,' she said.

'She was quite depressed after Liam's birth. It took a long time to feel her old self again.'

'Post-natal depression?'

'You could call it that.' Suddenly, there was a sound from the other side of the kitchen. Gemma's head swerved. I turned too.

A man was coming towards us, moving swiftly, noiselessly, like a cat.

The children noticed him. 'Daddy, Daddy,' they shouted and dropped their bricks and rushed towards him, each one trying to move in closer than the other. He scooped one up in each arm and stood up again. He offered his cheek for each of them to kiss, and he laughed, and seemed to glory in their excitement.

But all the while his gaze was fixed on Gemma. And on me.

I looked back. Clifford Tooley wasn't a big man. He was slim and neatly built, with close-cropped hair and thin, almost elegant features. But somehow he gave an impression of power. Maybe it was his eyes; they seemed excessively alert, as if nothing could happen that he wouldn't know about. Sharp, I would have called him. In all the senses of the word.

'Who had post-natal depression?' he said.

Gemma stood up. 'Oh, sweetie,' she said, 'we were just talking about Sandra. Remember, I told you what she was like after Liam was born. You've heard about that.' She kissed Cliff carefully. He put the boy down, slipped his arm around her waist and pulled her close.

'And this is?' The question was for Gemma, but he was speaking of me.

'Laura Principal,' I said. I held up a business card. Set it on the edge of the table. He set the little girl down on the floor and, with a pat to her bottom, sent her on her way. He picked up the business card and read it carefully, glancing at me over the top as he did. Then he slid into the alcove opposite me. Gemma came, nervously, and stood near.

'A private investigator,' he said. 'And what would a private investigator want with my wife?'

I explained. I had turned Liam up in the course of another investigation, I said. I realised he'd run away. Just as a courtesy, I'd come to tell the family that he was all right.

'You believe in family, Mr Tooley?'

He didn't reply. He reached in the pocket of his tailored leather jacket and took out a wallet. He opened the wallet and pulled out a small piece of shiny paper. It was folded and folded and folded again. He began to open it.

'No, Clifford,' Gemma said, 'please don't.' She looked embarrassed.

He unfolded the paper and smoothed it

out with his palms, then passed it across to me. 'This is my family,' he said.

It was a page torn from a magazine. There were columns of small entries, and one larger entry, with an advertisement for hand-made lingerie and a photograph – small, and black-and-white, but still recognisable – of Gemma.

'Isn't she something?' He was proud. He was possessive. Here she is, this sexy thing; and she belongs to me.

But I could also sense a threat, and it was targeted at Gemma. Today you're a suburban mother, with two lovely children and a luxurious home. Not so long ago you teetered on the edge of respectability, posing for glamour photos with your breasts all but bare and your midriff exposed and the tops of your stockings on view. You're only here because of my money. You could always go back there.

That was the threat I read in his gesture.

And Gemma seemed to think so too. The instant Clifford had left, which he did suddenly, abruptly a moment later, she ushered me out. She wouldn't answer another question.

'Tell Liam I miss him,' she whispered. And that, in a word, was that.

The train was late leaving Stevenage. I congratulated myself on finding a quiet carriage. But I'd jumped the gun. Thirty seconds later, the platform rang to the sound of small feet. Just as we were about to leave the station, a class of children from an infant school, and their attendant adults, piled into the carriage. I was surrounded.

'Sorry,' one of the adults said, catching my eye. 'We're getting off in two stops.'

'No problem.' I said it with more confidence than I actually felt.

The children were excited. You could feel it in the air. Incessant movement. Sudden bursts of anxiety. Laughter and giggles and snatches of song. The noise they made was tremendous – a cacophony of sniffing and shrill voices and scraping shoes.

I had intended to work but the charged atmosphere made it impossible. I scrabbled through my briefcase, and pulled out Olivia's memoir instead. I chased forward to a chapter near the end, where Olivia described the weeks and months and years following Timmy's disappearance.

A little girl stood in the aisle, sharing out sweeties with her classmates. Someone tried to take the package from her. She drew her arm back, swiftly, and her elbow went into my side. She spun around. Her face was inches away from mine. At first she looked as if she thought I might tell her off, and then, as she realised I wasn't cross, she threw her head back and let out a childish giggle.

Her hair was tied in soft brown bunches on either side of her head. A small pink slide above each ear held the errant wisps in place. I stared at her for seconds longer than I'd intended to. Suddenly, as if she'd had enough of me, she spun away.

The children's noise and bustle crashed around me like rush hour.

I forced my eyes back to the memoir.

Olivia wrote:

*Sometimes I saw a child running along a path towards me, two or three or four years old, and I could almost imagine that his eyes sought mine out, that he was running to me. It was all I could do not to bend my knees and place myself into his path. All I could do not to scoop him up into my arms. I ached for the head on my shoulder, the snuffle close to my ear, the little hand around my neck.*

I read that line and re-read it... *I ached for the little hand around my neck.* And on every side, children's cheeks glowed and their fingers grasped and their lips made mouth-prints on the dirty windows of the train.

And I rested my own head against the window, so that I couldn't see them any more, or could see them only in reflection, and let the tears pour down my cheeks.

The children were too tactful to comment. If they noticed at all, they did me the kindness of letting me cry.

I probably would have wept all the way to King's Lynn, had I not been shaken out of my melancholy when the pocket of my jacket began to stir and wobble. I looked around as if the cause might be found in the carriage, and only then realised that it was my mobile phone.

Sonny was calling. He was in message mode. He didn't seem to notice my tear-husked voice.

'Get off at Cambridge. Jack Cable's been looking for you. Something's happened,' he said.

*Cambridge*

# Chapter 24

Sonny was waiting on the platform when I disembarked at Cambridge. He knew instantly that something was wrong. We went straight back to Clare Street, where I had a long and not entirely satisfactory telephone conversation with Jack Cable. He told me the news; things had got a lot more complicated. I filled him in on what I'd found in Basingstoke and Stevenage – just the facts; I wasn't ready to draw conclusions yet – and waited for instructions.

'Come to Grantchester Farm in the morning,' he said. 'Olivia wants you there. I want you there.'

'Why?' I asked. But I knew before I asked what his answer would be.

'In case something else happens,' he said.

Then Sonny and I sat cross-legged on the floor cushions in my sitting room in Clare Street, and for the first time I put words to some of the things I'd been feeling. Disoriented. Insecure.

'I thought, Sonny, that after all these years I knew my body. But now I'm not so sure. What else could it be hiding?'

Fourteen weeks I'd been pregnant, firmly

into the second trimester, and I'd known nothing about it. I'd noticed one or two changes, that was all. I hadn't been aware of quickening, hadn't suspected that the baby was moving inside me.

Sonny hesitated before asking: 'That new feeling, Laura, that you mentioned to me a couple of weeks ago – that feeling of happiness.' He looked away, embarrassed.

'Could that have been the pregnancy? Is that what you're wondering?' I smiled at him. 'Who knows, Sonny? Maybe that was the oestrogen coursing through my veins. Maybe that fluttery feeling was my womb pressing on other organs. And maybe–' I paused.

'Maybe what?'

'Who knows? Maybe I was just happy.' It all seemed a long time ago.

I picked up my wine glass and then, after a small, reluctant sip, set it down again. Couldn't help but think of all the alcohol I'd consumed during those fourteen weeks of pregnancy. Of all the times I'd stayed up too late and taken over-the-counter medicines and eaten not wisely but too well. Would the pregnancy have lasted if I'd done it differently? What if I had loved this foetus and cherished it – what if, above all, I had wanted it?

Had the baby sensed my ambivalence? Was it weakened by my doubt?

Sonny stretched out on the floor, facing towards the hearth, with some of his weight on his elbows. The light from the fire made his face look alive.

'Laura,' he said, 'you don't have to answer this question, but I do have to ask. Did you want the baby?'

I stood up and placed some more coals on the fire. Then I lay face down next to Sonny, so that our hips were almost touching. I rested my chin on my arms. I looked at the fire, rather than at him. It was easier that way.

'I wish it had gone on longer, Sonny. Sixteen weeks, maybe. Seventeen, eighteen, nineteen. Just so I could remember a swelling abdomen, a heartbeat – something real, Sonny. Not just this might-have-been.'

'You wanted it, then.'

'It's not as simple as that.'

I could feel the shudder in his shoulder as he tensed.

'Laura, there's something I want to tell you.' He took a deep breath. 'All this – it meant far more to me than I expected. That could have been our baby – a child for the two of us, together. Dominic and Daniel are growing up so fast; Dominic and his friends went into the West End by themselves on Thursday evening, did I tell you? It won't be long before the boys are out in the world and don't really need their dad. This might have been my last chance.'

There was nothing I could say that would help. I nuzzled up a little closer and touched my lips against his cheek. He submitted. But then he put his question again.

'And you, Laura. Why won't you answer me? Either you wanted a baby – this baby. Yes. Or you didn't want it. No.'

No or yes. Yes or no. Should be simple.

'All I can tell you, Sonny, is the truth. Yes, I wanted the baby. And no, I didn't.'

Impatiently, he began to get to his feet.

'No, wait, Sonny. Can't you understand? Pregnancy changes things. It's one thing to be a woman who hasn't decided to have a baby. And it's another thing to be a woman who had a child growing inside her and couldn't keep it alive.'

I'm not sure whether or not Sonny understood. I'm not sure *I* understood. It wasn't guilt – I didn't will the miscarriage, I didn't make it happen. It was about the loss of the conviction that I could bear a baby if I wanted. The loss of my own sense of fertility, I suppose.

But whether Sonny understood or not, he cared, and for now, that was enough. He dropped his questions. He eased me over on to my back. He took his finger and traced a long, slow, steady circle around my tummy, round and round and round, gradually circling to the centre. And when he reached

364

the centre, he smiled at me, and placed his head on my belly, and fell asleep.

The instant I woke up, even before I'd seen Sonny's face – even before I'd opened my eyes – I knew something was different. My bedroom was bright with light. This wasn't the grey, wintry light we'd stumbled around in for the past few weeks, but a light as sharp and clear as a laser. I opened the blinds.

Clare Street was transformed.

Instead of the grimy bricks of the terraced houses opposite, in place of the rain-slicked slates of their roofs, instead of the messy telephone wires that crossed diagonally from a neighbour's eaves to mine, providing a perch for strings of gloomy pigeons, there was a bright, clean counterpane of white. White sparkled on the roofs; it offered a pristine backdrop to the gentle smoke that wreathed upwards from the chimneys. White bunched softly along the windowsills. White piled on the porches and glimmered on the pavements and softened the twiggy hedges and leggy shrubs and the bleak browns of the borders. Nothing looked ill-kempt any more; even the broken pavements and the toys in the Tredgolds' front garden, even the jumble of bicycles belonging to the students at number 85, emerged this morning clean-lined and beautiful.

And on the way out to Grantchester – Jack

Cable had sent a car for me – the chestnut trees were soft and full with snow and the Mill Way gleamed like a tunnel of ice. I wore sunglasses. I smiled for the moment, in spite of the sober news that had led Jack Cable to summon me there.

Donald Good was dead.

The builders who'd been working on the Cables' cottage in Cleybourne, Ian Ostler and his mate, had climbed into the loft and found a body lying face down amongst the timbers. The man appeared to have been bludgeoned to death. In spite of the damage to his face, a local police officer recognised Cleybourne resident Donald Good. His wife, Mary, was brought in for formal identification. She collapsed when she saw the body of her husband.

I recalled meeting the Goods on the cliff edge. First the little boy, Brian, huddling in the pillbox with litter bobbing around his wellies. Then Mary Good, with wisps of ginger hair frizzing round her face in the fog, wary at my approach, but warming up; looking shyly at her husband as she described how he had managed to come up with the down payment on a house. And Good himself, friendly but inarticulate. Donald Good was not a man for conversation, I'd concluded.

Not now, that was for sure. Now he was dead.

I scrunched from the driveway to the front door of the Dower House accompanied by the hard-edged sound of barking. It was vigorous and sustained, and it was aimed at me. Having found a new home, Wonder was, apparently, determined to defend it against all corners. I extended a hand carefully, hoping that his bark was worse than his bite. He sniffed it with interest, and went back to barking again.

Jack Cable opened the front door. He looked more decrepit than the last time I'd seen him; he carried himself stiffly, like a much older man. He turned on Wonder and shouted at him with such ferocity that the dog jumped back and was momentarily silent; then the barking began again and continued until we had gone inside and closed the door.

I followed as Jack limped ahead of me, through the corridor and into the conservatory. Beyond the conservatory windows, the woods were white with snow. Inside, the temperature was tropical. I removed my jacket and scarf and greeted the Cables. They were all there.

Robin was in the pool, doggedly doing laps. Up and down. Up and down. He didn't acknowledge me. He was too busy counting.

Liam was treading water in the deep end.

As I watched, he suddenly lifted his knees and ducked his head and did a somersault. It was smooth and controlled. He came up laughing.

Catherine sat on the edge of the pool. As Liam emerged from his somersault, she used one foot as a paddle to splash his face. As far as I could tell, her hair and her bathing costume were dry.

Someone had made the conservatory more habitable now. Besides the pool, there was a cluster of parlour palms and a cast-iron table and chairs. Olivia sat by the table, with her feet propped up. Her dress was blue like her eyes. Like the winter sky. Like the water in the pool. Her hair was as white as the snow on the trees. She was scribbling with a pencil in a large hardbound note-book. She didn't look up until Jack spoke.

'Liam!' He barked it out.

Liam rose up from another somersault and shook his hair so that water flew on Catherine, who squealed. Then he hauled himself over to the side and looked at Jack.

'That bloody dog of yours – that unholy racket. Can't you do anything about it?' Jack glowered.

Robin pulled up alongside Liam and offered a glower that was more or less a twin to Jack's. 'Not a farm dog,' he pronounced.

'Well,' said Liam. He looked concerned, but didn't come up with a solution.

Catherine stood. Olivia stood. From different directions they converged on Jack. Each took one of his arms. 'I know,' they said. It came out absolutely in synch, as if they had been rehearsing for this all their lives.

Olivia smiled. 'You first, Catherine,' she said.

'Wonder thinks he's guarding the house. That's because he's out front. If we put him in the back, with the collies, he'll be fine.'

'Exactly,' Olivia said. She took Catherine's hand.

Liam nodded his appreciation.

Robin went back to doing laps.

Jack freed himself from his wife and daughter. He turned on his heel and went out.

'Come into the pool,' Liam said to Catherine. He was all smiles now. He looked like a kid again.

Catherine glanced at her mother.

'Go on,' Olivia said. 'I'm just finishing the menu for the party. Then I'll sort Wonder out.' She turned to me. 'Jack's in a state, Laura. The police have been asking about Donald Good. You've heard what's happened?'

I nodded.

'Only a couple of days ago, when Jack was at the cottage, and the renovation work was underway, everything seemed – well, optimistic. And now this–' She waved an arm vaguely in the direction that Jack had taken.

I had to agree. Optimism now looked a little premature.

'Did you know Donald Good?' I asked.

She shook her head. 'Not at all. Max tells us the Norfolk gossip, of course; he told us of the Goods' arrival, and of the birth of their son. But we haven't been back to Cleybourne since Timmy disappeared. Well, until now,' she amended.

Meaning, until Liam arrived, and everything changed.

There was a gentle splash, the sound of waters parting. We watched, Olivia and I, as Catherine dangled her legs in the water. As she pulled the band off her ponytail and shook her hair out. As slowly, gracefully, she slid herself down into the pool. She immersed herself, touching her toes on the bottom, and corkscrewed up again. She stayed submerged for another few seconds, her nut-brown hair floating on the surface of the water. Then her arms sliced up and with one smooth motion she rose and began to execute a graceful crawl.

'My water baby,' Olivia murmured.

I told Olivia to stay where she was, watching Catherine and Liam. 'I'll see to Wonder,' I said.

Wouldn't you know it? Now that I'd set

out to deal with Wonder, he'd gone all quiet. I looked for him in the obvious places; he wasn't any longer by the front door. He wasn't down by the barn; when I stuck my head through the arch, the workmen continued levering a beam into place as if there were no one else around. There was no sign or sound of him in the fields, and anyway, the gate was closed, so I doubted he'd gone that way.

I headed off down the driveway, towards the gatehouse, and at the last minute took a detour to the garage. There, tail swinging from side to side, tongue lolling out, was Wonder. He was savouring the attention of a child. She looked about twelve, her body delicate and immature, her features fragile, but her composure was that of a young woman. When she saw me, she swung a rucksack off her back. She extracted a map of Cambridge, pointed on the map to the Orchard Tea Room and asked me in strongly accented English, 'Which way to ze Orchard, please?'

'Just down there.' I pointed along the Mill Way, towards the back entrance of the tea garden. She trotted off clutching her map.

The garage door, I noticed, was slightly ajar. Apart from the E-type, it was full of rubbish – old newspapers and the like. I imagined that Joe was getting ready to recycle. I pressed the garage door until the lock clicked in place.

I wound my fingers around Wonder's collar to keep him with me – he was straining after the girl – and turned again to watch her out of sight. Looked at the padded jacket and the Alice band holding back her fine brown hair, and the thin little legs. Decided – I don't know why – that this little language student was definitely older than she looked.

Decided – it was the oddest feeling – that I'd seen her legs before.

The day passed slowly on Grantchester Farm. It was like living in a time warp, knowing that things were about to happen, but not knowing when. The telephone calls came in the late afternoon.

The first was from Barbara Dobson, who told me she'd reached a conclusion, for what it was worth.

I reckoned it was worth a lot.

The second was from my police pal. Nicole Pelletier told me that she'd found something in Leicester – something along the lines I'd expected – and she ordered me not to breathe a word. The person to break the news should be Detective Chief Inspector Raymond Gaines, from the Norfolk Constabulary. He and his colleagues were on their way to Grantchester Farm.

Times like this, I almost despise my job.

Here I was, possessor of knowledge that would mean the world to my clients, and unable to share.

When Raymond Gaines came in and introduced himself, first to Olivia and Jack, and then to me, I could see that it had been inappropriate to tease Nicole about having drinks with him. It wasn't the fact that he was wearing trainers with his suit that made it inappropriate; unusual as this footwear was in the CID, it could be taken as a sign of athleticism. It wasn't that he was unattractive; a bit stolid, maybe, but stolidity can be reassuring, and he had a warmth that might appeal. The trouble was this: he seemed so focused on his job, did DCI Gaines, that it was hard to imagine him stooping to a flirtation. You could believe he reserved such activities for his annual holiday, after which he cut off romance for another year and returned himself wholeheartedly to work.

Gaines took charge immediately. With the help of a detective constable, he herded everyone gently but surely into the sitting room. Jack Cable sat on his straight-backed chair. Olivia and Catherine curled up together on one of the sofas. Olivia asked me, quietly, to fetch Liam. When I brought him, she introduced him to the police officers.

'My son,' she said. 'Timmy Cable. We

know him now as Liam.'

I could see the shock on Gaines's face. And the irritation. And then I realised: he hadn't known.

Gaines had been working on this case for twelve years, full time for two years, part time for ten. Overtime, above and beyond what he was paid for, continually. He had had nightmares about the case – as many, maybe, as the Cables themselves; he had given himself headaches and had argued with his superiors and perhaps even lost promotion over it.

But the missing boy had been back for a fortnight – or so the Cables thought – and no one had had the courtesy to tell him.

He managed to swallow his annoyance and bite back his wounded pride. He managed to set it aside. 'For now,' he said, 'I think it's best if we just have the family.'

'I want Laura Principal here,' Olivia said. 'And Liam *is* family.' Her voice had the kind of stubbornness that means that someone absolutely won't give way.

Again Gaines let it go, though I had no doubt he'd deal with it – to his own satisfaction – later. There was clearly something else exceptionally pressing on the agenda.

'Something very important has happened in this case,' he said. 'The first real breakthrough in years.' He glanced at Liam, who was inspecting his knuckles, relaxed, as if all of this had nothing to do with him.

Olivia sighed. She kept her eyes fixed on the detective's face.

Catherine entwined her fingers through her mother's and squeezed.

Jack put his elbows on his knees and his head in his hands. He never once looked up.

Gaines was sharp and succinct. 'A colleague from the Cambridgeshire force,' he said, 'has been making some enquiries in Leicester.' He looked pointedly at me.

I nodded.

Gaines continued. 'Looking closely at the background of a man called Tom Humm. He is the brother, I believe, of your house-keeper.'

'Etta!' Olivia exclaimed.

Jack didn't move. He seemed sunk in despair.

'It turns out that Etta's brother Tom had a conviction many years ago, before your son went missing, for indecent assault. He worked in one of the Leicester municipal parks.'

'He's an odd-job man,' the detective constable broke in.

'He touched a young boy inappropriately. Witnesses came forward. He was convicted.'

'We didn't know anything about this,' Olivia said. Her eyes were as wide as saucers.

'Why would you? As I understand it, Etta

Humm left home after the incident; she was deeply ashamed and determined to go where no one would connect her with the scandal. If she never talked about it, how would you know?'

'But you're the police – surely you should have known.'

Gaines looked unhappy. 'And how would we know, Mrs Cable? We looked for sex offenders, of course, in the north Norfolk area – interviewed every single one. But Humm lived in Leicester. We had no way of knowing that he was your housekeeper's brother. And we've only just learned that he was actually in Cleybourne when Timmy disappeared. Neither Etta nor Joe ever mentioned it in interviews.'

I interrupted. 'I don't imagine Humm often visited, or otherwise the Cables would have noticed. But that week was a special week.'

'Because of Timmy, you mean?'

'Because Tom and Etta's father had been diagnosed with a terminal illness. Tom may have come to break the news to Etta in person.'

'An act of kindness,' Gaines said. He encased the statement in the kind of cynicism that only an experienced CID officer can command.

'There's more,' he added. He looked at Olivia and at Jack.

The room went quiet.

'When my sergeant got to Leicester, he noticed that Tom Humm has a rock garden. That the rocks resemble the ones you find on Cleybourne Hoop. He questioned Humm. Yes, Humm, admitted, he had brought these rocks all the way from Norfolk.' Gaines paused.

'In a white van?' I asked.

Gaines nodded. Then he was silent for a full minute. I reckoned he was allowing the Cables time to catch up with him. He knew perfectly well how stress could cloud the rational brain.

When he spoke again, the voice was gentle but the words were hard.

'We're taking his sister to Cambridge for questioning. And we're digging now,' he said. 'In Tom Humm's garden.'

Scarcely a word was exchanged during the next hour. Jack remained in his chair, leaning forward, head in hands. Olivia stayed rooted to the sofa. Only Catherine and Liam moved around.

Raymond Gaines went out from time to time to use the phone in the privacy of the corridor.

Sometimes, when the Detective Chief Inspector returned from one of these sorties, he just nodded and sat down again.

Sometimes he sat down again and

reported back. He let us see through someone else's eyes what was going on in Tom Humm's modest garden in Windsor Avenue in Leicester... The darkness; the neighbours drifting by; the floodlights; the makeshift tent to protect the site. The lifting of the larger rocks and then the digging, cautiously, slowly, spade by spade.

At the last, he came back into the room and remained standing. Everyone was acutely aware of his presence, of that I'm sure. But each took his or her time turning attention to the detective.

Olivia went over and stood by Jack; she placed her hand on his shoulder.

When Catherine, who'd been performing a simple dance in a corner of the room, noticed Raymond Gaines, her feet fell still and she pressed the off switch on the CD player. She edged closer to Liam.

Liam muttered something about going to the loo. He gave Catherine's hand a quick squeeze and then moved swiftly towards the door.

The room fell silent.

In the silence, I heard the quiet padding of Robin's feet as he went along the corridor on his way from the pool to another part of the house.

'We've found something,' Gaines announced.

There was a pause. Nobody and nothing

moved. Even the house seemed to be holding its breath.

'What have you found?' It was Olivia who asked. Her voice was as unsuspecting and clear as a bell. As if she didn't have any idea of the significance of his statement.

'We've found a skeleton. Of a child,' he said.

My mind went back to a case I'd worked on a year or so ago, to a tiny pile of bones in St Bartholomew's College. A baby's bones, fragile and poignant. But that was then, and this was now.

'A child?'

It was Olivia again.

'And something else,' Gaines said. 'Two tiny black discs. About' – he held his thumb and forefinger two centimetres apart – 'this big.'

No one else spoke. Even Olivia looked blank. It was left to me.

Forensics would of course confirm it. But I could make a pretty good guess.

'The eyes,' I said. 'Mickey Monkey's eyes.'

Information came in thick and fast after that. About the findings in the garden. About what Tom Humm said in the initial police interview. About what Etta said in the police station in Cambridge.

At times it seemed as if I were the only person listening. Jack scarcely moved from his position; he sat like a penitent, his back bent forward, his head bowed. Halfway through the long evening, he stood up and planted a kiss on Olivia's cheek. Then, without a word to anybody, he suddenly left the room.

Catherine came and went. She flicked through magazines to pass the time. She seemed subdued.

Olivia read and scribbled in her notebook. She fetched a bottle of wine on one occasion and offered drinks. She was the only person who took up the offer. To look at her calm blue eyes and her placid posture, you might think she was enjoying a quiet evening at home.

And Tom Humm spoke freely to the police.

He had buried the body, he claimed, but he hadn't killed the boy. He had been delivering news of their father's illness to his sister in Cleybourne, he said, when Catherine Cable ran in and announced that her brother was missing. Joe dashed out to help with the search. Etta rang the police. And Tom, urged on by Etta, left the Cable compound.

Etta hadn't wanted her employers to know of Tom's visit, so when he'd arrived that morning he'd parked his van at the end of Beach Lane. He had loaded up with rocks for his garden. When he'd finished, he'd walked to Etta's house, arriving shortly before ten. He'd stayed, talking to his sister and her husband, until the child arrived.

'And after Catherine rushed in?' I asked.

'After the police had been summoned, Humm says, he raced back to the car park. The back door of the van was ajar, so he locked it. He drove nonstop to Leicester.' Gaines relayed this in a deadpan voice. Whatever his feelings about the veracity or otherwise of Tom's story, he wasn't sharing them with us.

'He knew nothing of the body? That's what he says?'

'That's the story,' Gaines replied. Next morning, when Tom Humm rang his sister, and learned that Timmy Cable was still missing, he was deeply upset – not least for fear that questions might be asked about his presence. He decided to work on his garden. He opened the back door of the van and there he found the body of a little boy. The child was pale, Tom said, almost grey, and he was badly bruised. He was dead; most definitely dead.

At that, Humm panicked. Because of his conviction, he reckoned that people would jump to the conclusion that he'd killed the little lad. So he buried the boy in his garden and built the rockery over the grave. He never told anyone, not even Etta.

At Parkside police station, Etta confirmed much of the story. Yes, Tom had parked in the car park. Yes, he'd spent much of the morning with her and Joe, talking about their father. Yes, she'd quickly sent him away when Catherine came in. 'Somebody who's been convicted of a sex offence doesn't want to be Johnny on the spot when a child goes missing,' Etta said.

And yes, finally, Etta had done her best to keep the police away from Catherine. She'd suspected that if enough time passed before Catherine was interviewed, the child would forget Tom had ever been there. She was right.

When the police officer who was interviewing her pointed out that if Etta had been more honest, the Cables might have been spared twelve long years of agony – twelve years of not knowing the fate of their son – Etta's plain round face collapsed in tears.

# Chapter 25

Olivia just didn't get it. She had fresh pink skin and ivory hair and blue, blue eyes but she just didn't get it.

'What's with her?' Raymond Gaines asked. We stood near the French doors at the end of the sitting room, pretending to look outside. The moon was big and bright; the sky was black as mourning jet. And in the frost that had succeeded the snow, the lawn was hard and sharp and sparkling.

What's with her? I knew exactly what he meant by that. The police had reported that her housekeeper's brother was a paedophile; that he'd been nearby when her son had disappeared. They had dug in Tom Humm's garden, and there, underneath a pile of rocks, they'd found the skeleton of a young child.

All this, and no more reaction from Olivia than if she'd been told that a neighbour was down with the flu. She looked a little troubled, that was all.

And Jack? He'd left the room shortly after the police reported the results of the interview with Tom Humm. Before that, he'd been morose and withdrawn. According to Olivia, Jack had been in a state for days – at least since I'd seen him in Norfolk, in anxious conversation with Max. Maybe before.

'I think it's called denial,' I said. 'She's been sceptical for years; but now she wants to believe her son is back. And now you've turned her hope on its head. She can't face it, not yet. She doesn't want to hear that Liam isn't Timmy. That Timmy might be dead.'

I expected Detective Chief Inspector Gaines to pooh-pooh my suggestion. To make a comment about psychological clap-trap. But I had him all wrong.

'She'll have to face up to it soon,' he said. 'The police surgeon will be along shortly to take DNA samples from the family so we can make a formal identification of the skeleton. My ex-wife is a psychotherapist,' he added, by way of explanation. And then a final question. 'Shall we tell her to-gether?'

DCI Gaines sat down to break the news. He rearranged Jack's chair so that it faced the sofa where Olivia was still curled up. I settled myself at the other end of the sofa.

'Olivia,' I said.

She looked up at me, weary but relaxed. She twisted her lips in a small smile, and patted the seat next to her.

'I'm fine,' I said.

384

'You want some coffee?' She began to stand up.

Ray and I both demurred. No thanks. Not just now.

'It's late,' she said, as if noticing for the first time. The evening had ticked away. It was after eleven.

'Mrs Cable, we're waiting for the arrival of the police surgeon. He's going to take DNA samples from you and your family.'

Olivia frowned, and tiny lines appeared around her eyes.

'I don't understand, Chief Inspector. Why are you doing this?'

Raymond looked at me. I was silent. He continued. 'It's the only way to identify the skeleton that we found this evening in Tom Humm's garden. The only way,' he said, 'to be certain that it's Timmy.'

Olivia struggled to her feet. Her face was frantic. 'A skeleton? What are you talking about? Timmy's here.' She looked wildly around the room, searching for the others. Then she addressed herself to Gaines again. 'Liam's here,' she said, 'at Grantchester Farm.'

I couldn't hold off any longer. I felt like a psychopath plucking the wings off a bug, but it had to be done.

'Has Liam said that he's your son, Olivia?'

She drew a deep breath. Then she began, slowly and deliberately, as if she'd been brought in to speak to a primary school class. She didn't make eye contact.

'It's difficult for Liam, but he's beginning to open up. He tells me that the woman who raised him was cold. She didn't love him. She wasn't a real mother.'

'The woman who raised Liam is Sandra Rhodes,' I said. 'And I suspect he's right, poor lad. Liam's arrival marked her out as no longer young. She resented him every inch of the way.'

I could still hear the bitterness in Sandra Rhodes's voice. *They don't take Gemma and me for sisters now,* she'd said. That had ended with Liam's birth.

Gaines kept quiet through all this, but I could see that he was puzzled. The 'but' in his mind left a crease between his brows.

There was nothing for it but to plunge ahead.

'Liam's intuition is right,' I said. 'Sandra Rhodes is not his real mother, not as far as I can tell. But then, Olivia, neither are you.'

Olivia stared at me now without blinking. Her eyes darkened; they looked indigo rather than cornflower blue.

I couldn't shield her any more. All I could do was to tell the truth.

'Liam Rhodes – that's his full name – is Sandra's grandson. Her daughter Gemma would have been only fourteen or so when Liam was born. Why she kept the baby I don't know; maybe it was the one issue on which she stood up to her mother. But Sandra had Gemma lined up for beauty contests and a modelling career, and there was no place for an infant in this plan. Motherhood disqualifies a girl from most beauty pageants, did you know that, Chief Inspector?'

Step right up, ladies, take your choice. You can be beautiful, or a mother, but not both.

'It happened a lot in my parents' generation,' Gaines said. 'Lots of women raised an illegitimate grandchild as their own to avoid a scandal.' He shook his head.

I'm not sure what it was he disapproved of – the hypocrisy of a society that rejected the children of unmarried mothers, or illegitimacy itself.

He followed it up with a question. 'So Sandra Rhodes pretended, at least on the beauty circuit, that Liam was hers?'

'That's the way I figure it. And on one such occasion, in a nightclub in Stevenage, Clifford Tooley fell for Gemma. I doubt that he would have proposed if he'd known she had a baby. Clifford Tooley is a very jealous man. From Gemma's engagement onwards, the deception became permanent. Sandra took over as Liam's mum, in spite of her resentment. And Gemma became his elder sister.'

Gaines rolled it over in his mind. 'But why

would Sandra agree to raise a child she didn't want? What was in it for her?'

'Clifford Tooley gave his mother-in-law a new house for starters. It was a lucrative exchange.'

I looked again at Olivia. We both did. She was struggling to understand.

'Liam isn't Timmy, then?' she said. 'He's a different boy? With a family of his own?'

'That's exactly right. He's like Timmy, but not Timmy. And there's more,' I said. 'Barbara Dobson rang.'

I turned towards Gaines to explain – about the forensic artist; about the facial mapping – but not before I'd seen the blush that warmed Olivia's face and neck.

Olivia had mentioned her wobble, the one that had taken place while Jack was on his most celebrated expedition. Catherine had known the what but not the who of it. The who of it was Barbara Dobson. It was the only thing that fitted and Olivia's blush convinced me. But I'm not a person who tells for telling's sake.

'I know more about her,' I said, ostensibly to Gaines, but actually for Olivia's benefit, 'but some things are better left unsaid.'

Olivia looked at the oak floor and smiled.

Gaines raised an eyebrow.

I took refuge in facts.

'Facial mapping often leaves uncertainties,' I reported, 'but in this case Barbara

Dobson is adamant. Certain things don't change, she says, not even in twelve years. The eyebrow shape, the crown of the head, the way the lobe attaches to the ear. She can tell, from these–'

I heard a shuffle in the hallway. Someone else was on the way in, but I couldn't stop now.

'She can tell. Liam isn't Timmy.'

Olivia made one last effort. She stood up as tall as she could – which wasn't very tall – and she squared her shoulders and smoothed down her long skirt.

'That can't be right,' she said. 'It doesn't make sense.'

Checking whether things made sense was a step forward. Better than the things-will-be-what-I-want-them-to-be state Olivia had been in up to now.

I waited quietly.

Gaines waited quietly. Even his trainer stopped tapping for a moment.

And behind us, on the steps that separated the upper level of the sitting room from the lower, someone else waited quietly too.

Olivia managed to stammer out her objections. 'Liam can't be – an outsider. He has Mickey Monkey, and he knows too much. He knows about the turkeys. He knows about being stolen off the beach. How would he know any of those things unless he really is my son?'

389

Suddenly she turned towards the steps. Liam stood there. She smiled timidly and held out her hand.

Liam came and stood next to her. He looked as if he'd been waiting for this.

'I wanted to tell you,' he said. 'It was Holly.'

'Go on,' Olivia said. 'Who's Holly?'

'Holly Swallow. She's my girlfriend – well, she was, until last week. We met at a folk club in Stevenage, and she helped me, you see. When I had to leave home.'

I slid a question into the pause in his speech. 'After Cliff did that to you?'

There was only the faintest of marks visible on his forehead now. Liam ran his fingers over it, as if remembering.

'Cliff was trying to control me, like he always did. Holly had friends we could stay with, so she persuaded me to come to Cambridge. And I was busking, and you came along, Olivia, and Holly got all excited. Said she knew who you were. She'd seen your picture somewhere. And she went to the internet café–'

'CB1?' I said. 'On Mill Road?'

'That's the place. And she found more stuff on the web about Timmy's disappearance. I didn't want to do it, but Holly kept on at me that you were rich, and – well, she had this idea that you might give me a lot of money.'

Liam had the decency to redden when he said this, and lower his eyes.

'She said if I didn't go along with it she'd tell Cliff where I was. I let her push me into it, I guess. But you've got to believe me, it wasn't just because of her; that wasn't the only reason.'

'Liam, I know that.' They stood closely together. Liam towered over Olivia, taller and broader, and awkward in that moment, but beautiful. His eyes were lowered. Olivia watched his face, waiting for the moment when he'd look up. Finally, he did. His cheeks and his neck were still hot from shame.

'How do you know?'

'I might have been wrong about your birth, Liam–' Olivia's features creased with regret, but it was fleeting. 'But I know who you are. What kind of a person, I mean. I believe you had another motive for letting me think you were Timmy.'

Liam leapt at the opportunity to explain. 'I could see it all over your face, Olivia – you wanted it so badly to be true. It sounds crazy, but I – I–'

Liam had said to Catherine at Cleybourne, *I've always wanted to do something really, really good. Something that would make other people happy.* I had almost gagged at the *Sound of Music* sentimentality of it. But the fact was, the kid actually meant it.

'You didn't want to hurt me,' Olivia said.

Liam's good-looking features were washed with relief. Then something else crept in, something shamefaced. The words came in a rush, as if he'd forced them out, after a struggle. 'But I also wanted to drive the E-type.'

Olivia startled us all by bursting into laughter. 'Of course you did,' she said. 'You're a boy!'

As far as I know, no one has found a gene that makes men drool over cars, but that wasn't quite what she meant. *It's only human* might be closer to the mark. Olivia was saying that it wasn't a sin.

Gaines had sat quietly throughout this extraordinary exchange. Now he intervened.

'I don't think you've answered Olivia's question,' he said.

Olivia looked puzzled.

Liam looked blank.

'What's this about the beach?'

'Oh, you mean about the dream of being kidnapped – I'm really sorry, Laura. Holly was camping on Grantchester Meadows, down by the river. She was furious with me because I hadn't tried to convince you...' His voice trailed off. 'I made it up. The dream, I mean. And I lied about my age, too. I'm seventeen going on eighteen.'

'Surprise, surprise,' Olivia said, with a wry smile.

Gaines wasn't going to let this go. He tapped his trainer impatiently on the floor, twice, like a conductor tapping his baton as a signal to the orchestra. He waited until he had Liam's full attention.

'Look, I've lived with this case for twelve years. I know about Mickey Monkey. I know that Timmy was terrified of turkeys, and I know why. These things are on the file, and I reread that file every four months, without fail. But you, Liam – how did you get a monkey like Mickey? And how could you possibly know about the turkey farm?'

Liam shrugged. An I-don't-know sort of shrug, not a shrug of indifference. 'It was Holly. She found Mickey in a jumble sale. When I came out to the farm that day, she hid it in my rucksack.'

'But how did Holly know what kind of soft toy to get? That and the stuff about the turkey farm were never in the newspapers; we held them back. And I know for a fact they are not on the internet.'

'Holly told me,' Liam said. His face had the innocence of a newborn babe. 'I've no idea how she knew.'

Finally, I had a flash of luck. Like when you're struggling to assemble a piece of flat-pack furniture and the crucial component snaps into place.

'This Holly Swallow,' I said. 'What does she look like?'

'Well.' Liam screwed up his eyes in concentration. 'She's got fine brown hair and she's tiny – the name Swallow is perfect for her, she always says. She's almost nineteen, but she looks a lot younger, depending on what she's wearing.'

'And she speaks French?'

'Her mother was French,' Liam said. 'How did you know?'

Twice. I'd seen her twice.

'What's this about?' Gaines was impatient.

'Raymond,' I said, 'when all of this is over, you may want to plug a leak in your system. My guess is that it was the police who told Holly about the turkey farm and Mickey Monkey. I bet they were mentioned in your special information sheets.'

'But how in Christ's name would this Swallow girl get her hands on an information sheet? They're official use only. Restricted distribution.'

'The Cables have had lots of false alarms over the years. Right, Olivia? And the most recent one referred to a boy who'd been found by a French social worker. Did you receive a phone call from Paris, Chief Inspector, asking for information about Timmy?'

'Well I'll be damned!'

'Precisely. Check it out. I bet you'll find that the phone call didn't originate from a social work department. And that Holly travelled to France about that time.'

394

'She went to see her mother,' Liam said.

Olivia had been animated throughout this discussion, as if the urge to protect Liam had temporarily blinded her to Timmy's likely death. But suddenly she wilted.

'I'm so tired,' she said, and collapsed back on to the sofa. It was almost midnight.

Liam knelt down next to her. 'You want something, Olivia? A cup of tea?'

She smiled wanly. She shook her head. Something like despair began to creep into her eyes.

Liam looked down at his own hands, and then lifted them slowly and took hold of hers. She didn't resist. He was so gentle, so clear-headed, that I had to remind myself he was only in his teens.

He spoke to her, quietly, as if there was no one else in the room. 'Talk to me, Olivia. Tell me what it's like to lose a child.'

Shortly after midnight, Gaines and I stepped outside for a spot of fresh air.

We strolled towards the fields. We set our feet down firmly, taking care not to slip on the icy surface. We leaned on the gate with the woods to one side, and looked out at the line of tall poplars in the distance.

The moon was crisp and full, its silver edges sharply cut against the sky.

After a full minute of silence, Gaines spoke.

'Not easy for her,' he said.

I agreed. 'If it were Tom Humm – if he had kidnapped Timmy, and taken him to Leicester and murdered him there – at least it would be over.'

'You don't think it is?' Gaines asked. He didn't sound surprised. Mildly curious, merely.

I paused to collect my scattered thoughts. Went over what I knew of Timmy's disappearance once again. Of the sequence of events.

Jack Cable had taken his eyes off his child for the briefest of moments. It might happen to any parent – especially one who'd been chasing for the best part of an hour over the shingle with his son. When he focused again, the boy was gone. Jack searched frantically; he gazed up and down the shingle; he scanned the car park; he climbed the headland and looked down from the edge of the cliffs on to the beach below.

He saw nothing.

Well, not quite nothing. He saw Catherine walking with her cousin along the headland. Catherine and he had a frantic exchange, and he sent her tumbling down across the fields to Etta's.

'It couldn't be,' I said. 'Humm was in his sister's cottage when Timmy went missing. Catherine confirms he was there when she

396

arrived. When Tom Humm claims he knew nothing about the boy until he reached Leicester and found the body in the back, he's probably telling the truth.'

'It would be neat and tidy to have Humm as a murderer,' Ray agreed. 'There'd be howls of self-righteous outrage: another monster caught and condemned. But I suspect you're right. Tom Humm's not our man.'

We heard the sound of cars making their way up the Mill Way and began to walk back towards the house. We were just in time to see a police car from the Norfolk force turn into the driveway.

From the look on Gaines's face, it was expected.

Another car, a BMW, followed closely behind.

'What now?' I asked.

Gaines said nothing. We reached the front of the house as the passengers disembarked. Among the officers there were two civilians. A powerful-looking man in a suit, dishevelled now – Max Armstrong. He had been driving the BMW. And a woman with weather-roughened skin and dark ginger hair.

I recognised her almost immediately as the woman I'd talked to on the cliff top in Cleybourne – Mary Good, the wife of Donald Good.

No, I corrected myself, the widow; Donald Good had been murdered.

'What's Mrs Good doing here?'

Gaines looked at me with a smile of satisfaction. Who could blame him? I thought. Twelve years is a long time.

'Mary Good has something for the Cables,' he said.

We found Olivia and Liam in the kitchen. They were leaning towards one another, their heads almost touching, and leafing through a photo album.

'...his second birthday,' Olivia was saying as we entered the room.

It was twelve fifteen. The police officers looked weary. Olivia and Liam looked as if they could sleep for a week. I didn't kid myself that I appeared any fresher. But all of us were too dragged along by events to even think about sleep.

Olivia stood up and embraced Max. He held on to her for a moment or two, patting her back fondly and clumsily. Then he held her at arm's length and inspected her.

'How're you doing, old girl?' he said.

I thought of him, over the years, standing stiffly, alone in his study, listening to his nephew's voice: *Daddy! Daddy! I'm waiting for you.* Now, in a way, the wait had ended.

Olivia and Mary Good were introduced. With perfect ease on Olivia's part, and shyly on Mary's, they shook hands. 'I'm sorry to hear about your husband's death,' said the one. 'And I about your son's,' said the other.

The formality was somehow soothing.

Mary unzipped her shoulder bag. She took out an envelope and offered it to Olivia Cable.

There was a moment of hesitation. Olivia's eyes flicked to me and back to Mary Good. She examined the envelope.

'It's for me,' she said. There was wonder in her voice. 'Who is it from, do you know?'

'From my husband, Donald. The police found it when they searched our bungalow. It was inside a larger package, addressed to me. Donald left it to be opened in case of his death. I'm sorry,' she said, 'for all this–'

She waved a hand around the room – the hour of night, the police officers, the disturbance.

'–but the police insist it must be read immediately, in case it has anything to do with Donald's death. And I want to know too,' she said. 'Donald and I, you see, we never kept secrets from one another.'

Well, never before, I thought. Death has a way of turning things upside down.

Olivia looked once more at me, and at the detective chief inspector.

He nodded.

She opened it cautiously, extracting the paper from the envelope as if she expected a letter-bomb, and setting the envelope down. She skimmed through the letter once. Then she went through it again, more slowly.

As her eyes moved back towards the beginning, DCI Gaines stepped forward.

'Mrs Cable,' he said gently. He waited until she glanced up. He stretched out his hand.

She drew back and held the letter to her chest.

'Then read it aloud,' he said.

Olivia's voice was faltering and low, but as she went on, the meaning of the letter became perfectly clear. Donald Good began with an awkward apology.

*For doing what I did.*

*For not speaking out.*

*For prolonging your pain.*

*I love my son,* he wrote, *and I imagine you loved yours. I can guess how you must have suffered.*

The second paragraph brought the blur of tears to Olivia's eyes. I was standing close enough to see her dig the nail of her finger into the pad of her thumb, and the tears receded. She cleared her throat and read on.

*He was a lovely kid, anyone could see that. When we passed him that day, he was playing pig-and-wolf, racing along a line they'd made in the shingle. Your husband chased him and*

*growled, and your little lad was looking back-
wards over his shoulder and giggling. They
seemed so happy. I didn't have children yet, at
that time. I was almost jealous of them, not in
an awful way, just – well, I expect you know
what I mean.*

Olivia paused and glanced at Mary Good,
who was standing with her head bowed.

Gaines couldn't resist a question. 'Mrs
Good, you and your husband were the
couple on the beach that day? The
witnesses?'

She nodded. Yes, we were.

'Then why in God's name didn't you
come forward?'

She looked weatherworn, and deeply
unsure of herself, but her response was
dignified.

'You get used to secrecy,' Mary said.
'Sometimes it becomes like second nature. I
grew up in Cleybourne and I loved it there.
But my parents were hard people. And what
they called discipline was something no
child should have to face. I ran away.

'So you came back for a visit, is that right,
the day that Timothy Cable disappeared?'

'On our honeymoon. We didn't want my
parents to know. That's why we didn't come
forward as witnesses.'

'Your parents still live locally?'

'Lived,' Mary Good said. 'They died in a

fire. That's when we decided to move back to Norfolk.'

The statement burst out of me – and it was a statement, not a question.

'You are Mary Whitwell, then.'

Ray Gaines knew instantly what I meant. The name was as familiar to him as local superstition. No, more than that; it was the stuff of local superstition.

'You? You're the girl who disappeared from Cleybourne just before I joined the force? You weren't kidnapped, as some people thought? You ran away?'

'Only to Shropshire,' Mary said. 'I'd worked on farms before.'

'So that means there's no pattern of paedophile kidnappings in Cleybourne?' I asked.

Mary's voice was scornful. 'Donald told you that was nonsense.'

Gaines interrupted. 'We'll go back over this later.' He was obviously cross. An optimistic man might say that he'd just killed two birds with one stone. But to DCI Gaines, it felt more like chickens coming home to roost.

He turned to Olivia Cable. 'Finish reading the letter,' he said.

But Olivia had not been idle during the exchange with Mary Good. She had been fiddling with the letter, folding it. She had folded it in half so that it was back in the

402

shape she'd received it in. She had folded it in half again, and again. She continued, twice more, until it was little bigger than a postage stamp.

Gaines stepped towards her and extended his hand. 'I'll take the letter, Mrs Cable. And if you'll just—'

Olivia snatched her hand away. Her face was a hot pink. And when she spoke, she bellowed.

'You will not!' She surveyed the kitchen, taking in the police officers one by one. The uniformed officers in the corner took a step towards her. She fixed them with her glare.

Gaines spoke firmly, with the kind of authority that is built over decades of taking charge. 'Mrs Cable, I understand your distress, but may I remind you, this is a murder investigation—'

It was not, apparently, firm enough. Olivia turned both her gaze and her bellow on him.

'No, Chief Inspector, I'll remind you that this is my house. You are guests in my house. And this letter is my letter too.' She snatched up the envelope off the side table and hurled it at him. 'If there is one thing I've learned, at last, it is how to protect what is mine.'

Max had been an agitated presence in the background since Mary Good appeared. Now he came centre stage.

'Leave her alone,' he said forcefully. He pushed past the police officers and approached Olivia. She was hunched up and poised for action, like a puma on a ledge. Max put his arm around her shoulder, and I could see some of the tension drain out of her.

'Come on, Livi, old girl,' he said. 'It's time for bed.'

And without a word to anyone on either side, they made their way out of the room.

After a few seconds' stunned silence, all hell broke loose.

Gaines, in a fury, took two of the uniformed officers and chased off after Max and Olivia. I could guess what they'd be doing: Warning Olivia that the letter was an exhibit; that if it were to be damaged she'd be liable to prosecution. Gaines would leave at least one of the officers outside her door, and he'd begin the frustrating process of seeking a warrant to bring the letter into police possession.

But I wasn't thinking about any of that. No sooner had Max and Olivia swept out, with Gaines and his team close behind, than the back door opened. Liam had left the room minutes before; now he stepped back in, rubbing his hands together from the cold.

'What were you doing outside at this hour

of the morning?'

'Looking for Catherine,' Liam said. 'I checked her studio a few minutes ago; no one there. Laura, I'm worried about her.'

As far as I could remember, I hadn't seen Catherine for at least an hour. Jack had left the sitting room some time after the child's skeleton had been found, and Catherine had wandered out shortly after.

'What about the conservatory?'

'The lights are out. There's no one there.'

My impulse was to reassure. 'Perhaps she and her father have gone off somewhere together,' I said.

But even as I said it, it didn't feel right.

Then I looked at Liam more closely. He was back to being Mr Transparent again. There was no disguising the anxiety in his brown eyes.

'Any special reason for this concern?'

'It's Holly,' he said. 'She was angry when we split up. She made some dodgy threats. And now it's almost one o'clock and Catherine–'

'Threats like what?'

He was reluctant to say.

'Liam, if you care about Catherine–'

'Holly said she'd kill her. Tear her heart out – those were her precise words. I put it out of my mind. I didn't think anyone could be that crazy. But when we were talking about Holly a while ago, it all came back to me, and then I started to wonder–'

'Come on.'

Before we left the kitchen, I gazed around one more time. I looked at the dresser, bright with a new dinner service to replace the crockery that had been smashed. I looked at the door where Mickey Monkey had been impaled. I recalled how Joe had staggered into the office, blood spurting from his wrist.

And I felt, for the first time, a stab of alarm.

'Come with me,' I said. The old door to the kitchen rocked on its hinges behind us as we raced into the corridor and grabbed our jackets. One of the police officers called out a question, but we couldn't afford to stop.

Outside – in the small bordered area that adjoined the door, in the meadow that stretched down to the Mill Way, in the length of the driveway – all was dark. It was the kind of dark you only find in the countryside, where there's no softening glow from the city. Where it is deathly quiet, as if the night is holding its breath.

And then slowly, as we stood there, trying to decide which way to go, our eyes and ears adjusted, and the night came back to life. The moon rolled out from behind a cloud and shone its silver light along the icy driveway. A breeze sprang up from nowhere and ran its fingers through the branches of the yew tree. And a bat swooped down across the driveway and up into the eaves with a high-pitched squeal. I could feel the movement in the night air as it swept past.

The night was alive but there was nothing to indicate where Catherine might be.

In the fields, on the far side perhaps, near the poplars? In the woods near the church? In one of the outbuildings, where the scaffolding clung like a giant spider to the side?

Something small and voracious rustled in the border, but there was no sign of movement of the human kind. There was nothing to see except for the moonlight that reflected blankly off the windows in the renovated barn. I could hardly make out Liam's features, and he was standing right next to me.

I whispered my question to the place where his head should be.

'Has Holly ever seen you in Catherine's company?'

'It made her furious,' he whispered back. 'Jealous, I suppose. She was watching in the woods when Catherine showed me around; she saw us go into the gatehouse. We made ourselves a cup of tea, Etta didn't mind. And Holly – well, Holly was really cross about it. It's one of the things that made me determined to dump her.'

'Did you ever think that it might have

been Holly who left the razorblade on the gatehouse door? That it might have been her who trashed the Cables' kitchen?'

I didn't wait for him to ponder these questions. He wasn't the swiftest thinker and there might not be time.

'Liam, does Holly know about the E-type?'

As soon as I heard his *yes*, I set off. It was enough. Because in the distance, further along and off to the left, there was a sound. Not a night rustle this time. Not an owl or a hedgehog or a field mouse. It was a thump and a sharp click.

I jumped up off the slippery driveway on to the verge, where I could get up speed, and crunched through the rough grass. Liam was just behind me.

The sound echoed again in the night air, and this time I recognised it. I'd heard that very sound the other day, after I'd spoken to a girl with a French accent who'd asked directions to The Orchard. After Holly had left, I'd pushed the door of the garage firmly shut. Thump-click, it went, as the door closed and the lock slipped into place.

Now I heard another sound. A strange noise, like rainwater gurgling through the drainpipes. Except, of course, for once it wasn't raining.

We came to the edge of the line of garages. The woodpile was on the opposite side, within sniffing distance. I could smell the sap.

But I could smell something else, too. Something sharper and more familiar and more acrid. I put out a hand and stopped Liam.

He sniffed. He stiffened.

'Petrol,' he whispered.

The door to the garage where the E-type was housed was just around the corner. We heard the gurgling noise again.

I signalled that I intended to circle around the back of the line of garages.

'Whatever she's doing, stall her,' I said.

Liam didn't hesitate. He stepped out into the moonlight, where he could be seen.

'Holly?' I heard him say. His voice was none too steady.

I raced around the building. The ground was broken up and softened by sawdust. My footsteps could hardly be heard. As I approached the front of the garage, I heard Liam, on the other side, pleading.

Carefully, crouched as low as I could, I peered around the corner. Holly was holding a red petrol tin with a short spout. She shook it and sloshed petrol on the ground. Some of it splashed close to Liam's feet – he jumped back – and then trickled beneath the bottom of the door. With one hand Holly set the can down. She reached in her pocket.

Liam's voice went up a notch.

With a leap, I stepped on to the woodpile. I stretched for the beam that supported the eaves and caught it in both hands, then pulled myself up. The logs shifted under my weight.

For a moment I hung there. Then I touched my toe to the woodpile, just enough to recover my balance, and craned forward so that I had a view through the shallow window that ran along the wall below the caves. I had three seconds or so before the logs shifted again. But three seconds was enough.

I saw the inside of the garage, lit by the orange glow from the interior light of the Jaguar. The passenger door was ajar.

I saw the floor of the garage, covered in waddings of old newspaper, like a rat's nest. And the light reflected back off an oily-looking stream of liquid that trickled under the door of the garage.

But what I saw in the last second made my heart jump. There was a muffled movement from inside the car. The passenger door swung open, and Catherine Cable's body tumbled out.

Everything happened at once.

Catherine lifted her head, just a fraction. She was alive.

Liam's voice reached me, desperate now. 'Holly, don't do this. You'll only get in

410

trouble. Someone could get hurt.'

And then – as I swung my feet hard through the window, as I kicked ferociously at the glass that remained, as I clutched my jacket close around me and dropped on to the floor – I heard a vicious laugh. And the sound of a scuffle from outside.

I grabbed at Catherine and shoved her towards the window, shouting her name over and over through gritted teeth. She was conscious, but barely sensible.

I dragged the toolbox to the window and stood her on it and flung her upright, against the wall. I took off my jacket and tossed it over the window frame, where shards of glass protruded. I braced my shoulder against her bum and kept my hand on her back and lifted. Her arms moved as I hefted her weight. At the last minute, as she grabbed at the window ledge and went over sideways, breaking her fall, there was a roar at my back. A flash of light ripped through the garage.

I didn't stop to look. I hiked myself up and over the ledge and out the window. I bounced off the woodpile and landed hard on my shoulder on the ground. Catherine was standing next to me, supported by Liam. He grabbed my arm. We fled.

We reached the edge of the woods just before the explosion. We were still running, or trying to run, but we felt the heat of the

411

fireball and saw as the trees all around lit up in the glow. Pieces of metal and roof slates and glass sliced through the air. We took shelter behind the trunk of a fallen tree. We turned and watched.

We watched as Jack Cable's E-type Jaguar, his other baby, went up in flames.

# Chapter 26

## AT MIDNIGHT

*Years I've waited for this moment. Twelve long years, and four months, and, yes, seventeen days. For the return of Timmy. My Tim.*

*Since the moment that Olivia and I ran back along the dyke and found the car park empty.*

*Since the van disappeared down the lane with Timmy's body.*

*Since I woke up from my illness and found that days had passed, and his little corpse was still missing. Found Olivia firm in her belief that he had either been swept out to sea or stolen away.*

*I should have told her then – I would have told her then – but it seemed too late. How could I say 'Our son is dead' when there was no body? Our son has gone, Olivia, and there's nothing left of him. Nothing at all.*

*I couldn't do it. I didn't have the courage.*

*One day, I thought, when Timmy's body is found, I will be free to speak. To say, Olivia, here is your baby boy. You can bury him now. You can grieve.*

*When the police said they'd unearthed a skeleton, my heart leapt up: I thought the time*

413

*for truth had come at last.*

*But I hadn't counted on Max. Even though Timmy's body has been found, I am prevented from speaking out. To tell what I know about Timmy would be to reveal the truth about Max. I cannot do that. I cannot bring myself to betray him.*

*And yet, if they ask me – if the police ask me – my tongue won't let me lie any more.*

*So there's only one way out.*

*The water is cooler than I expected. Not as cold as the water around Lancaster Sound, where Moorhouse went missing; but cold enough to make me shiver. Was it like this for you, Timmy? Was the water cold, like this? Were you frightened?*

*Or did you feel as I feel now? Calm and clear, for the first time in years. And peaceful.*

*Not searching any more.*

# Chapter 27

Sonny's a conscientious sleeper, with a strong inclination towards seven hours in the sack, so I was surprised to find him up when a taxi dropped me back at Clare Street.

Up, but not awake. He was sprawled on the sofa, his sweater tangled around his torso, fast asleep. Blue light flickered from the television. I hunkered down and watched the black-and-white images on the film for a moment as a young man in a motorcycle jacket led a gang of bikers into a small American town.

Sonny stirred and blinked when I flicked off the television. Two other videos were stacked on top of the telly; part of a takeaway pizza and a half-empty bottle of Scotch lay on the floor.

'A wild one?' I asked.

'You got it,' he said, straightening his sweater. 'Marlon Brando.'

'I meant your evening.'

He didn't grace that with an answer. He ran his fingers through his flop of hair and peered at me more closely. 'My God, Laura, you look like hell. Something's happened?'

I looked better than I had done. Back at the farm I'd stripped out of my scorched and dirty clothes and accepted some of Jack Cable's cast-offs. The image in the mirror showed ill-fitting trousers and shirt, a jacket ripped and smudged with soot, a face that was scratched, hair that didn't bear thinking about. Flattery will get you nowhere, Sonny. Not a pretty sight.

'Everything,' I said.

I accepted a glass of whisky and downed it in one toss. The ember of warmth revived me. Made me anxious to be off.

'That was one for the road.'

Sonny protested, but when he realised that I was determined to drive to Norfolk again, immediately, he refused to be left behind. He sat in the passenger seat of the Saab, where a man as full of whisky as he was ought to sit, and snoozed. By the time he shook himself awake again, I'd listened to Aretha Franklin rock her way through two decades, and was ready for his questions.

I told him about most things that had happened in the course of the night. The child's skeleton. The facial mapping. Liam's parentage. Donald Good's posthumous letter. Holly Swallow's attack. But I hadn't been able to bring myself to tell him the worst yet. Sonny was already stunned by the speed of events.

'I leave you alone for only a few hours,' he

said, flexing his legs, 'and look what you get up to. Let's have some details. Is Catherine all right now, after the fire in the garage? And what's happened to that Swallow girl?'

'Catherine isn't seriously injured. Scrapes and bruises more than anything else; a bump on the head and a hell of a lot to think about. And Holly Swallow is in custody.'

DCI Raymond Gaines has a strong streak of suspicion in his soul, as any good cop should. He'd left a man to monitor comings and goings. Pacing up and down near the gatehouse in the cold, said constable heard the explosion and was ready and waiting when a bicycle ridden by a child – or what he thought was a child – shot out from the direction of the garage.

'Did she explain herself?'

'Not to me,' I said. 'Liam saw her before she was driven off to Cambridge. He tried to speak to her; she wasn't having any of it.'

After an initial interview, Gaines had summoned the Cambridge police, and turned Holly over to them. I remembered the scene vividly: the fire engines had been still stacked up in the driveway, their lights flashing and swirling in the dark. The garages were gutted by then, of course. The car was charred metal. The fire was out, to a layperson's eye, but the firefighters, last of the working-class heroes, continued to direct their arcs of water around the perimeter. A pretty blonde policewoman with as much bulk around the thigh as Holly had around the waist gripped her upper arm and walked her down the driveway past the fire crew. Another uniformed officer held open the door of the car for her. Liam had been standing with a protective arm around Catherine, watching the firefighting operation. He loped towards the police car. 'Holly,' he said, pleading again, 'the Cables – they're not like you imagine Holly, they're nice people. You've got to leave them alone.'

He didn't seem fully to have grasped that any threat Holly posed to the Cables would be strictly contained in future.

'She just stared straight ahead, Sonny, with her fierce eyes and her pale, set little face. She looked as if she'd been carved from ice.'

'Is she a nutter?'

'In legal terms? As in not responsible for her actions? I doubt it. If the Yorkshire Ripper is sane, if Myra Hindley is sane, then so is Holly Swallow. But morally speaking, in terms of what she felt justified in doing, she's stark raving mad.'

Sonny had twisted around, was reaching as best he could into the luggage compartment behind the seat. I braked into a bend, and watched him out of the corner of my eye.

'What about Liam?' he asked, facing forward again and running his hand under his seat. 'He's been exposed as an impostor as far as the Cables are concerned. His "mother", Sandra Rhodes, is not really his mother. His "sister", Gemma Tooley, is, but presumably she won't acknowledge that he's her son for fear of angering her husband. What will become of him?'

I rolled down my window a notch. The icy air shot in and sliced away my sleepiness.

'Impostor is stretching it, Sonny. Liam never claimed to be Timmy Cable. Apart from lies about his dreams and his age, he didn't try to deceive. He never put any energy into it. Olivia made all the running; Liam just hung around, enjoying the new sensation of being wanted. And about the rest, about what will happen now, are you interested in guesswork?'

'Try me,' Sonny said. He was scrabbling now through the glove compartment.

'Well, for a start, I have a hunch that Catherine and Liam have the makings of a real friendship. Both raised as only children, both on the receiving end of benign neglect.'

'Are we talking friendship here? Or are we talking sex?'

'Could be a brotherly-sisterly thing. Could be something else. Anyway, it's none of your business, Sonny. And none of mine. And why are you turning the glove compartment inside out?'

'Where's that CD you were playing the other day? That Muddy Waters?'

'Here.' I groped in the pocket of my door and tossed him the CD. 'What's more important, I get the impression that Olivia is genuinely fond of Liam. Not just of Liam-who-might-be-Timmy.'

'And Jack? I had formed the impression that Jack wasn't overly keen.'

He didn't know.

'Sonny, something else happened in Grantchester. Something that I haven't told you about yet. After the fire.' Immediately after, when Olivia was huddling with Catherine and Liam over hot chocolate in the kitchen, when Max had left for Norfolk.

Sonny dismissed Aretha Franklin and ushered in the King of the Electric Blues. A harmonica shuffled into action. Now, in the abuse-conscious twenty-first century, 'Good Morning Little Schoolgirl' sounded more sinister than it had when I was a schoolgirl myself.

Sonny danced his fingers on the dashboard in time to the rhythm. 'Such as?' he said.

'I went looking for Jack Cable. The Dower House was teeming with people, but no one seemed to know where he was. I set out to find him. I checked every room, including

some I hadn't seen before. Up a little staircase, above the master bedroom, I found a
room that looked like the sky on a summer's
day. The walls were pale blue, with fluffy
white clouds painted on, and blinds to
match. There was a small white armchair
with a blue cushion, near the window. It had
been Timmy's room.'

I paused for a moment, thinking of a story
I'd overheard. How Timmy had been playing quietly in his room one morning – far
too quietly – and Olivia had gone in and
found the toddler with a crayon clutched in
his fist. The lower portion of one wall was
covered in jagged streaks of purple. 'Oh,
Timmy,' she'd exclaimed, 'what have you
done?' And he had smiled back at her. 'A
car,' he'd said proudly. 'Vroom, vroom.'

'And was Jack Cable there?' Sonny asked.

'No,' I said. 'Not there.'

But it was there that I'd remembered an
earlier conversation, when Jack had told me
how Catherine loved the water as a baby,
and how she had trusted her father. How
she'd been willing to jump into deep water,
over her head, again and again, on his
instructions.

When he had told me this, Jack Cable had
been lying on the floor of the empty
swimming pool. In the conservatory. In the
dark.

'Jack wasn't in Timmy's room. But I

421

suddenly knew where to look. I went to the conservatory, even though the lights were out and it was dark inside.'

The first thing I noticed when I shut the door were the sounds. The rustle of the leaves of the parlour palms. The swoosh of air from the heating vent. The tick-tick-tick of something settling. The gurgle of the pump. They were noises that imitated life, as if the conservatory might be home to a huge animal, crouching there in the dark.

Sonny nudged me. 'What did you see?'

'At first my eye was drawn to the windows. To the moon. It shone above the trees like a giant opal. Moonlight cut a path towards me across the frosty lawn. It carved through the window panes. It lay across the surface of the pool like a ribbon of silver. But then I noticed that there was something at the bottom of the pool.'

I reached across and touched the back of Sonny's hand.

'It was Jack Cable,' I said.

The harsh glare of the spotlights when I switched them on left nothing to the imagination. Jack Cable lay on his back with his arms outflung. He was clothed from the waist down. His chest was bare. His wrists were wreathed in reddish-brown clouds; he must have sliced them with a knife. The blood had rippled outward and drifted lazily through the water, spreading in a widening circle like the fluid from an oil spill, until the turquoise pool was unsullied only at its farthest corners. Jack Cable's lifeblood had rendered the rest of the water a sour brown.

I'd hesitated only long enough to take off my boots. I dived into the murk, and tried to rouse Jack Cable; there was no response. I pushed rather than pulled the body to the side of the pool, and dragged it up on to the tiles. I shouted and shouted, a harsh, artificial sound, echoing madly off the walls of the conservatory, until I could hear urgent footsteps racing towards us. I listened for a heartbeat, and cleared his throat, and began artificial respiration. Still no response.

'He'd cut his wrists, Sonny. Twenty minutes we tried to revive him, me and two police officers in turn, before the paramedics arrived and the police surgeon declared him dead.'

Only then had I taken time to look at the message Jack Cable had left behind. Beside the pool near the steps, his shirt was neatly folded, his shoes and socks set out side by side. There was a felt-tip pen. There was a sheet of vellum, anchored to the tiles with a Swiss army knife. Scrawled on the paper in a bold but agitated script were the words: *Forgive me*.

Muddy Waters continued to plead his case – 'Baby Please Don't Go' – after I'd completed my account, but the silence from Sonny was deafening. Finally he clicked off the CD player and spoke into the hum of the engine.

'Jack Cable killed himself.' And then, under his breath, 'My God.'

I was sure, at that moment, that his thoughts echoed mine. *So the man who could confront the Arctic wilderness had found something he couldn't face.*

I edged the Saab down a narrow lane that ran alongside the Blakeney Hotel. We turned right at the T-junction and followed the coast road.

The tide was in. Small sailing boats bobbed to our left along the quay, so close you could almost reach out an arm and touch them. The sky behind them was bleaching slowly to a soft pearly white.

Sonny rolled down his window and took great gulps of the salty air.

'Was Jack Cable a murderer?' he asked. 'Did he kill Donald Good?'

'Why would you think that?'

'Those phrases you quoted from the letter,' he said. 'Donald Good was sorry for not speaking out. For prolonging Olivia's pain. And he was on the beach the day that Timmy disappeared. That suggests blackmail, and blackmail can be a powerful motive for murder, wouldn't you say?'

'I would,' I agreed. 'And blackmail fits in,

too, with the fact that, much to his wife's surprise, Donald Good was in a position to purchase a house in Cleybourne shortly afterwards. Someone had paid well for his silence.'

'Not Jack?'

'I doubt it.'

Sonny gave a tiny sigh of relief.

'Jack Cable was deeply disturbed by Donald's murder. But I don't believe he did it.'

'Then perhaps you'd care to tell me why he took his own life?'

I drove slowly as we slipped past Cleybourne. Except for one or two early risers, fishermen perhaps, whose yellow lights shone behind net curtains, it was as still and dark as an abandoned village. I fancied, in the distance, I could hear the whisper of the reeds on the marsh.

My mind was on a day twelve years ago rather than on the road.

'Why? Because he was responsible for Timmy's death. Because he'd known that Timmy was never coming back, but he'd kept it from his wife. He knew it was cruel to mislead her in that way; what probably counted for even more with Jack, he knew it was cowardly.'

A rabbit ran across the coast road in front of the car. I saw the flash, and slammed on my brakes, just in time.

'Do you want to know how I think it happened?' I said as we moved off again.

Sonny nodded. He reached over and pushed a strand of hair behind my ear, so that he could watch my face. Slowly, trying to piece it all together for the first time, I spoke.

'Jack Cable hadn't wanted to come to Cleybourne that day; he'd been on the verge of solving an important problem, and he wasn't in the mood for a holiday. But Olivia insisted; she was fed up with family holidays where she was the only parent present. Jack and his work, however, weren't easily parted; when he walked to the beach with Timmy, he carried his briefcase just in case an idea occurred. And an idea did. A new way of thinking about the Inuit oral histories of the Franklin expedition, an insight that enabled him to pinpoint the position of the wreck.'

Sonny was shaking his head.

'No, Sonny. I haven't just made this up.' I launched into an explanation. 'When Jack Cable left Cambridge, he'd yet to select a final destination for the expedition; he still had two quite different sites in mind. He didn't work that evening; nor did he get up in the night. I know that, because Max checked it out with Olivia a few days later; it's recorded in her memoir. Why did he check? Because when Max went through his briefcase during Jack's illness, and found the specification for the single site, he knew then, as well as I do now–'

Sonny interrupted, excited. 'That Jack Cable must have done the final work on the morning that Timmy disappeared. Jack told the police – told everyone – that he had rested for a minute, and when he looked up, Timmy was gone. You're suggesting it was more than a minute?'

'While Timmy was trying to catch a seal, Jack Cable was head down in his papers. It could have been five minutes, ten minutes, half an hour for all we know. But long enough, certainly, to allow for the drowning of a little boy.'

'And then?'

I slowed down at the corner and nosed the car into Beach Lane, heading for the sea.

'Jack glanced up and realised his son was gone. He panicked. He searched up and down the shingle; he ran in and out of the sea. He strode up to the top of the cliffs, to the pillbox where he and Timmy had so often stood, and scanned the beach, calling Timmy's name. That's where he met Catherine. And at some point in his desperate search, he found Timmy's body. He'd been drowned, and his body hurled back on to the beach. Jack would have known, better than most, that the boy was dead.'

We drove alongside a flint wall edged with

red brick. 'The Cables' compound,' I said, and pulled into their driveway.

I stopped in front of Jack and Olivia's cottage. The skip had been removed, and the front door was criss-crossed with blue-and-white police tape. This wasn't just a holiday cottage now; since Donald Good's death, it was a crime scene.

I switched off the engine and the cold air came rushing in. I rolled my window up.

'You can't stop now,' Sonny said. He wasn't referring to the car. 'What happened to the child's body?'

'Think about the view from the cliffs. From up there, Sonny, you can see – Jack saw – all the way along the raised path as far as Cleybourne. He saw Olivia coming towards him. He ran to meet her, got as far as the car park, but then he panicked. He couldn't bear to confront her right away with the body of their son. He'd tell her Timmy was missing first, he thought; he'd break it to her gently. And then, when she was braced for bad news, they'd find the body together. He looked wildly around for a place of concealment. He saw the van. When Tom Humm had finished collecting rocks, he'd neglected to lock the back door. It was ajar. Jack slipped Timmy's body in, laid it down gently and staggered off along the dyke to meet Olivia.'

I hadn't got the sequence completely

428

sussed, but if there were gaps in my account, Sonny didn't seem aware of them. He looked at me in horror. 'He would have been heading towards Olivia, with his back to the car park, when she looked over his shoulder and noticed the white van moving away along Beach Lane.'

'Precisely. Only when they'd returned to the car park together would Jack discover that the van had disappeared. Must have been a tremendous shock. Coming on top of Timmy's death, and the effect of running in and out of the icy waves, it might even have triggered his illness, who knows?'

'He was ill, seriously ill, for how long?'

'For the best part of a week. While the search went on.'

While lifeboats scoured the area, and the coastguard patrolled the coast, and RAF rescue helicopters circled overhead. While searchers walked the beaches. While Catherine huddled with Etta, terrified and bemused. While Tom Humm built his rock garden. While Olivia despaired.

'Jack was ill, feverish, sometimes hallucinating. After he came to his senses, he realised that days had elapsed, that Olivia had gone through the torment of not knowing, and gone through it alone. He couldn't bring himself to tell her the truth. That he'd let their son die and then he'd lost the body.'

'He was locked into the deception.'

'On and on for the rest of his life.'

There was silence for a moment, cut only by a gull's cry. Then a window in the other large cottage in the compound, Max and Robin Armstrong's, sprang into light. I began to open the car door. Sonny put a hand on my arm.

'Wait,' he said. 'Do you have any evidence for all this?'

I opened my door further so that the interior light clicked on. I reached down and slid my fingers inside the cuff of my cotton socks. Took out a tiny, intricately folded sheet of paper.

'Donald Good's letter,' I said. 'Olivia was asleep when I left the farm; Etta was watching over her. The police surgeon gave her a sedative after Jack's body had been taken away. I had only a moment to say goodbye. But in that moment she slipped this fragment of paper into my hand.'

'Goodbye, Laura,' Olivia had said, for the benefit of the police officers who were standing by. But when she'd kissed me, she'd whispered two words and I wish she hadn't. 'You decide,' she'd said.

I unfolded the letter and smoothed it out on the dashboard. I handed it to Sonny. I'd read it only once, in the taxi on the way to Clare Street, but I knew almost by heart what Donald Good had written. The crucial information was all in the last paragraph.

*I walked back along the shingle to look for my driving glove. As usual, I had my binoculars. I ran them over the cliff top in the distance and that's when I saw your husband, coming down the path from the pillbox. Your little boy lay flat in his arms. He lay with his head flopped backwards. Anyone could tell that he was dead.*

This was the passage that Olivia couldn't bring herself to read out loud in front of the police. But looking back on that moment, recalling Olivia's face as she scanned through the letter, I can see alarm in her expression, and denial, and dread, but nothing else. Olivia hadn't seemed surprised. Perhaps some corner of her mind had been fighting off suspicion all these years. But the habit of protectiveness dies hard; Olivia Cable had committed herself, after her husband returned from his expedition, to looking after him; it would be a while, if ever, before she was ready to announce to a news-hungry world the fact of his involvement in the death of her son.

'It's all settled then,' Sonny said. 'The body that was buried in Tom Humm's garden was Timmy's.'

I shrugged. 'You want settled, Sonny? I'm certain in my own mind, and the forensic tests will convince the police. But some-

431

times you have to accept probabilities. Not everything can be tied up with a red ribbon.' I stepped out of the car.

Sonny stood up too and leaned his elbows on the roof of the Saab.

'What do you mean by that?'

His voice sounded impossibly loud in the early morning silence. I kept mine low, almost a whisper. We leaned towards each other across the car roof so he could hear.

'Just this. We'll probably never know exactly how Timmy died. Not after all this time.' There would be no lungs to carry the evidence of drowning, no flesh to carry bruises. 'We'll have to live with uncertainty. Have to construct a particular death, as Olivia will, out of what we know about the characters of the father and the son.'

And out of what we want to believe.

Sonny nodded. He began to pull away. I reached across and touched his wrist. 'One thing more. I'm sticking to my story for the time being. It fits the facts as we know them as well as any I can imagine. But there's one thing about it that bothers me.'

Sonny shook his head, working on it. 'Something about timing,' he said.

'Yes. Something about timing. Catherine saw her father on the cliff top just before he ran to meet Olivia. He was alone, he was searching for Timmy. "Your brother's missing. Have you seen him?" he said. Then

432

Donald Good spotted him coming down from the cliff top with Timmy's body. Surely Jack wouldn't have had time to race down to the beach, discover Timmy's body and carry it up to the cliff top and down again to the car park before he met Olivia? It just doesn't work. I can't get any further.'

'And both the people with direct knowledge – Donald Good and Jack Cable – are dead,' Sonny said. 'I guess you'll have to let it go.'

I crunched across the pebbles towards the Armstrongs' front door. Sonny caught up with me just as I raised my hand to the anchor-shaped knocker.

'All right?' he asked. Meaning: would he be in the way?

I had time only to smile before Max Armstrong, looking smaller somehow, and more deflated, opened the door and beckoned us in.

We followed Max along a narrow corridor into the sitting room that looked out on the cluster of Christmas roses; they were faded now. The office side of the room was a mess. A drawer of the filing cabinet hung open and papers lay scattered around the fitted carpet.

'Apologies for the chaos,' Max said, courteous still. 'I've just come back to sort out a few things.' He looked hard at me. 'You know, don't you?'

I made a split-second decision. 'I know that your brother-in-law was responsible for Timmy's death. You knew from the beginning?'

Max carried on flicking through papers as he spoke. 'I guessed,' he said. 'When Jack was ill, I found his calculations about the expedition. It seemed horribly clear to me that if he had settled the site while he was at the beach, he hadn't been watching Timmy.' He fixed me with a fierce glance. 'That's all it was, forgetfulness. Inattention. Could happen to anyone.'

I said nothing. Max carried on.

'Then the letters demanding money from Jack confirmed it. I couldn't stand by and see him ruined. Couldn't see the project collapse, the family destroyed. I had to pay.'

'Jack never knew?'

Max shook his head. 'No.' There was a trace of pride in his expression. He'd paid blackmail money – over and over again; Olivia had said he wasn't good with money, thought he squandered it on his boat – in order to protect Jack Cable. And, possibly, to protect the Cable reputation, on which so much of their joint prosperity depended.

'At least, not until last week,' Max said. 'The relief postman delivered a letter to Jack's cottage by mistake, and Jack found it there. He confronted me. He was – well, he was horrified about the blackmail. He wanted to end it then and there. Wanted to tell the truth, he said, at last.'

'You persuaded him to wait?' From the window of the cottage, Catherine and Liam and I had seen the brothers-in-law locked in conversation. Jack had been agitated; Max had kept a restraining hand on his shoulder throughout. *Whatever can be the matter?* Catherine had asked.

Max straightened up, a folder clutched in his hand. 'I reassured Jack. Insisted it would be all right. And then I killed Donald Good. I laid in wait when he came to pick up the money, and I killed him in cold blood.' He looked at me in anguish. 'I did it for him,' he said. 'I did it for Jack.'

'Here,' Max said, taking up a leather document file from the desk and placing it in my hands. 'Will you give this to Olivia for me?' He saw what I was thinking. 'Oh no, don't worry. I'm not planning to follow Jack's example. I've made an appointment to speak to Detective Chief Inspector Gaines at midday tomorrow–' He glanced out of the window. The night was lifting. 'Correction,' he said. 'Today. And I don't approve of breaking appointments, so you can be sure, Miss Principal, that I will be there. Now, my dear, if you and your colleague will leave me alone, I have some final matters to sort out.'

Max stood still for a brief time, staring at

the folder in my hand, as if it held some answers. Then, as we left the room, he stepped over to a bulky old answering machine, flipped up the lid, snatched up the tape and placed it in his jacket pocket.

Sonny and I let ourselves out.

'Max must feel sick as a parrot,' Sonny said, as I eased the Saab back on to Beach Lane. 'He paid blackmail over and over. He covered up a death. He killed. All to save Jack Cable. And then Cable took the coward's way out.'

'I'm not so sure, Sonny. About the cowardice, I mean. Maybe Jack killed himself at least in part to protect Max.'

'How do you figure that?'

'You heard what Max said: as soon as he realised blackmail was involved, Jack wanted to come clean about Timmy's death, whatever the consequences. That's not the act of a coward. It was Max who prevented him; Max who assured him he'd find another way. Don't you see?'

'I see you'd better slow down. We're coming to the car park.'

I parked close up against the big bank of shingle, where the white van must have stood, all those years ago. Ours wasn't the only car there. There was a silver Renault Clio poised near the gap that led to the sea.

'So,' I continued, 'when Jack learned that Donald Good had been murdered, he must

436

have realised immediately that Max was involved. I expect he was appalled; but he wouldn't want to denounce the brother-in-law who had protected him so consistently, so misguidedly, for a decade or more.'

Sonny summed it up. 'Jack Cable was trapped. Suicide must have seemed the only way out.' He sighed, not for the first time. It's never easy to abandon your childhood heroes. To allow them to be flawed and fallible people.

'Don't sit there brooding,' I said. 'I recognise that Renault. Let's have a word with Catherine.'

We found Catherine balanced on the edge of a disc of driftwood, next to the sea. The air was still, for Cleybourne Hoop, and the waves were low. Everything – the shingle, the surface of the sea, the glisten where the tongue of the waves left an imprint on the shore – was a monotonous silver-grey, except for the breakers, which were white, and the sky. Where it met the sea on the distant horizon, the sky was a vibrant pink.

I stood near Catherine's shoulder. She spoke to me without turning around.

'Laura?'

'I'm here. I'm sorry about your father, Catherine.'

Her body swayed to the motion of the waves. She didn't say a word.

I glanced behind me, to the right, where

the path ran, swift and sure as a brushstroke, to the top of the cliffs. I couldn't
hold the question back.

'That day, Catherine, on the cliffs. When
you came across your father. He was still
searching for Timmy, isn't that what you
said? Timmy wasn't with him.'

Catherine didn't say anything at all for
minutes, until the first dazzling edge of the
sun had insinuated itself above the horizon.
It was too brilliant to watch. She turned
towards the cliffs. She linked arms with me,
and then, more shyly, with Sonny, and we
started off up the path.

'Left, right, left, right...' I whispered under
my breath.

She stopped inches from the pillbox. She
let go of our arms. Looking sideways, along
the length of the headland, she began to
speak. 'I told you the truth,' she said. 'Or
some of it. It happened just the way I said.
But there was something else.'

And she told us all over again, speaking as
if it were happening now. We didn't interrupt until she'd finished.

'Robin and I are on the headland, watching the storm as it shoulders its way towards
us. We've come in sight of the path that
leads down to the beach, and Robin lifts an
arm and points.

'"Isn't that your father?" he says.

'I shield my eyes with one hand so I can

438

see more clearly. My father should be easy to recognise, because of his straight back, and sure enough, there he is. He is standing alongside the pillbox, and he is staring down at the waves below.

'Robin gives me a signal and sets off across the fields to meet his chums. I'm not supposed to be on the headland by myself, so I hurry forward. "Daddy! Daddy!" I call. The sound carries above the wind.

'At last he hears me. He comes rushing towards me, stumbling, as if he were frightened, but I know that can't be. My father is never frightened.

'"Catherine!" He goes down on one knee, and peers at me closely. He looks so strange. He puts his hands on my shoulders, as if he might shake me, but he doesn't. "Catherine" he says, "your brother's missing. Timmy's gone. Have you seen him?"

'He's crying. Sobbing. I've never seen my father cry before. I didn't know he could. But his cheeks are all wet and his eyes are red and I am shocked at the sight.

'"Catherine! Did you see anything?"

'I can't take my eyes off him. I feel so very, very frightened. I shake my head. No.

'"Nothing?" he asks again. It is then that I see the relief in his eyes.

'"Nothing at all," I repeat. I catch a glimpse of the pillbox. A little blue sandal hangs loosely over the edge. It is just like

Timmy's Star Wars sandal.

'I steal another glance at the sandal and the fragile leg rising out of it, and then I look again at my father's face. And I look away.

'I can't bear to watch him any more. My heart is pounding. "Nothing."

'Nothing at all.

'And when the police ask me, eventually, I say it again. And again. And again.

'Until it is true.

'Maybe now my daddy will be pleased with me.'

# Epilogue

To the frustration of the BBC and ITV, Jack Cable's funeral was, by and large, a family affair. There were no cameras. There were two hymns and a reading from Job 28 about going to the ends of the earth. There was a low-key address by the vicar. He referred only obliquely to the tragedy that had overshadowed Jack's later life and, at Olivia's request, made no mention of Timmy's name.

The eagerness of the tabloid press to puncture reputations for probity is part and parcel of British daily life, but there are occasions – the death of a minor politician, for example – when the media pack may be called off, may eschew an account of failings in favour of fond reminiscence; the most bumbling and marginal Member of the House may emerge from such a treatment with the aura of a statesman. Something similar happened in the case of Jack Cable. Many column inches were devoted to Jack's qualities of leadership, his selflessness, his courage. Fellow explorers were trotted out to testify to his vision. The BBC pulled together a documentary in a matter of days,

441

in which someone from the Scott Polar Institute rehearsed the famous expedition and Moorhouse, the young geologist whose life Jack had saved – not so young now, with a paunch and a sour, dissatisfied look – dutifully recalled his debt.

Few questions were asked. The harsher facts that had to be confronted – the fact of suicide, for one – were treated as private tragedy rather than public scandal. The *Daily Mail*, purporting to quote a family friend, said that Jack had been depressed since the disappearance of his son. This was the account that circulated from paper to paper. Jack Cable's adventures seemed more heroic, not less so, when set alongside the misfortune that eventually overwhelmed him.

And in the case of Timmy's death, too, there was discretion. Tom Humm had concealed Timmy's body; he had obstructed a police investigation. But the police feared vigilante action if the name of a sex offender were linked to the discovery of the skeleton. Humm was persuaded to leave Leicester in the interests of public safety, and no charges were laid. The press release that was issued by the police said merely that a routine inquiry had turned up the remains of a child. This child had been identified as Timothy Cable, who had disappeared twelve years earlier from a Norfolk beach.

He was thought to have died from drowning.

The only persons who might have been in a position to elaborate on the bald declaration of death by drowning were those of us who knew that it was his father who had carried Timmy's lifeless body down from the cliffs. But none of us who had read the last paragraph of Donald Good's letter – Olivia and Sonny and I – were inclined to broadcast its contents. And even if we had, it would prove nothing, except that Jack had known about his son's fate and kept it a secret. Despicable, some might say; but not in itself evidence of murder.

Later, after interest in the Cables had trickled away, a small ceremony of remembrance was held for Timothy Andrew Cable in St Barnabas Church in Cambridge. Olivia, looking pale and still, was supported on one side by Catherine and by Liam on the other. Etta and Joe were across the aisle. Max and Robin sat behind them. Max, flanked by two policemen, looked shattered. Robin looked put out.

Afterwards, Sonny joined me and we tramped the rough path across the Meadows to Grantchester. It was a bright winter's day. A hoar frost had coated all the twiglets of the hawthorn hedge. Behind the glittering branches of the trees at the river's edge, the sky was impossibly blue. Even the narrow footpath that led from the Meadows into the Mill Way had disguised its desolate blacks and browns with a delicate scarf of silver.

When we stood behind the shoulder-high wall that circled Grantchester Farm, the Cables' home seemed like something out of a fairy tale. The woods behind the Dower House were silvered. The chimneys in the south wing gave off a soft grey smoke that curled upwards in the still air. Even the burned-out garage looked as if its charred edges had been dipped in molten silver.

I removed my glove. I reached in my pocket and picked up a handful of pebbles, cradling them in my palm. They were as cold as the grave, I thought. As smooth and untroubled as a baby's skin. As old as the sea. I placed them carefully, one by one, along the top of the wall. I shifted this one to the left, and that one to the right, searching for the arrangement that would suit me. Sonny watched with a mild curiosity.

'Are you all right, Laura? What are you doing?'

I looked at him. At his puzzled expression. At the way his anxious eyebrows almost met above the bridge of his nose.

'Isn't it obvious, Sonny?' I placed my bare hand in his pocket for warmth. My knuckles touched his. 'I'm saying my goodbyes.'

Goodbye to Donald Good's posthumous letter. Standing on the cliffs at Cleybourne,

I had ripped it into tiny shreds that caught in the breeze like banners. And I had let the wind catch them up and whip them around until finally, after a long, long time, I fancied some of the shreds fell and floated on the surface of the sea, out towards the faraway horizon.

Goodbye to Liam Rhodes. To the Cables: to Jack and Olivia and Catherine.

*Sometimes in my mind I see a terrible scenario,* Catherine had said to us, there at Cleybourne Hoop. Her voice had dropped to a whisper. *Timmy asking questions, over and over. Daddy trying to think, and demanding that Timmy be quiet, and then striking him when he isn't. Timmy falling and his head hitting a rock; dying instantly. It would be a sudden surge of anger, rather than a studied assault,* Catherine said. *But even so, it doesn't really fit with the daddy I knew.*

She didn't say it: the daddy she knew was a man who cared about his son more than anything else in the world.

Catherine had glanced up then, away from the sea. She'd fixed her dark blue eyes on me, and she'd looked, just for that moment, like her mother.

*And other times?* she'd said. *Other times I see Daddy excited about something, so he's concentrating really hard, and meanwhile Timmy is staring at a seal. The seal has huge dark eyes and its head bobs above the water only a metre from the shore where Timmy stands. And then, concentrating so hard himself – you see, he really is Daddy's boy – Timmy simply reaches out a slender arm and steps into the waves.*

'Goodbye,' I whispered.

Goodbye to Timmy.

Goodbye to someone else, who might have been.

This Large Print Book, for people
who cannot read normal print,
is published under the auspices of

## THE ULVERSCROFT FOUNDATION